July 17,

Shirley —

Many blessings
on your walk

M. E. Path

EAP

Winnie's Walk:

A Journey of Faith and Romance

By

M. E. Palmer

I thank my editor, Stephen D. Palmer, my two illustrators: Vivian Watson and Beth Ann Palmer, as well as my life partner, David Palmer, who was a great inspiration for me. Thanks, also, to many friends and family members who have previewed Winnie's Walk and provided me wise feedback. Without this team of helpers this book would be sadly lacking.

Winnie's Walk is dedicated to all who follow Jesus, past, present, and those yet to hear the call. Disciples truly do comprise the great cloud of witnesses that encourage us on our walk. I thank all Christ followers who have crossed paths with me — teachers, neighbors, family, church family — and helped me on my way. Blessings to all!

All Biblical quotes can be found in the NRSV, the NASB, or the NIV Bible.

TABLE OF CONTENTS

Prologue

The news came fast. *Bad news does, doesn't it?* They say that bad news travels fast, and so it was for Winnie. Mark was gone. That was the reality of the news — he wouldn't return. He would never again sweep Winnie into his arms to hug and kiss her. She had just lost her dearest friend, and a great chapter of Winnie's life has snapped shut.

Shock was the word for such an event, yet "shock" was far too limited an expression to satisfactorily describe the pain, grief, and emptiness Winnie now knew. She would forever wonder how it is that the English language seemed quite unable to express the depth of her grief.

The first days, as the news rippled through the community that Lieutenant Colonel Mark Taylor had died in a training accident in the gulf, found Winnie and her kids surrounded by kind neighbors, Air Force friends, and, of course, their church friends. Everyone wanted to express the pain and sadness they felt for Winnie's loss. It was a tragedy for the whole community.

Whenever Mark had been deployed before, Winnie had assumed the head-of-house role and accomplished those necessary functions, but things were different this time — more permanent — with no hope of Mark's eventual return. Winnie was now the sole parent of her little family.

Winnie and Mark had shared the responsibility of raising Claire and Paul, their two teenagers. Mark had been especially wonderful as the strong, father figure for them. He was very clear about what his children needed to do to grow up, yet he was funny and lighthearted too with his beloved son and daughter. Winnie knew they would miss their daddy immensely; she also believed Mark had set some well-placed standards for them to strive for and to grow into.

Winnie's loss, like so many others who have lost someone really close, followed through the various steps of grief—denial, anger, some bargaining, depression, and finally accepting things as they now stood. Eventually Winnie's grief became less watery and more like a constant, nagging, shadowy companion that refused to leave.

Winnie found comfort in a number of sources, including her close neighbors, the Air Force community, and her church. Her church friends prayed with her and helped out however they could to make her way a little easier, even just lending a friendly, listening ear. Claire and Paul were grieving, too, of course, and the three Taylors found some comfort just being together.

Initially Winnie felt as if the floor had fallen out from under her. She felt lost and alone, even when surrounded by others. She just wished someone would put a script in her hand, telling her what steps to take next. Without Mark to share confidences with, to discuss, or even argue with, everything seemed out of whack. Nothing about life seemed the same anymore. The world for Winnie had changed the day Mark died, yet gradually she began to grope her way into a new life.

Winnie's day to day routine helped her, as she got up to see the kids off for school. Her usual activities were still there, and she should engage them. She accepted her piano students back. They came after school several days a week, so she had to be there for them. She still had church choir and Sunday school to prepare for; in fact she had been the lead teacher in Sunday school for several years.

The greatest solace, Winnie realized, came from her faith. She read Scripture daily and prayed and gradually found there was a difference between being "alone" and experiencing "solitude." Being alone was a horrifying feeling of lostness and being uncared for. This feeling of being totally alone was the first feeling Winnie knew as the reality as Mark's death began to sink into her consciousness. She felt being alone to a degree even when in the company of others, but it was especially evident when no one else was around.

Solitude became for Winnie a time she intentionally spent apart from others. This time grew in importance. It was a time of finding herself, again—that she, herself, was a whole person even without Mark. She could enjoy time in devotion—reading Christian books, Bible, prayer, and meditation. She even began writing her thoughts in a journal.

Slowly, Winnie began to find her footing. She missed Mark, of course, and she missed being married to him. She didn't consider herself not married, even though, of course, she was. It was more like Mark was away somewhere, and eventually he'd be coming back. She felt she should remain his, exclusively, as she had been over their seventeen years together.

One day occurred to Winnie to go to seminary where she might seek a further degree that would lead to a position in the church, so she matriculated at seminary in Atlanta, not far from where they were living. Three weeks into the first semester, Winnie realized that seminary was more than she could have imagined — more enlightening, more interesting, more exciting, and much more demanding — and it was exactly what she could use to take her next step in her faith journey. She realized that she was being called into the pastoral ministry.

1. A New Appointment

Rev. Evangeline "Winnie" Taylor first heard the name "Muddy Creek United Methodist Church" from her District Superintendent. He called to tell her that the cabinet had just met and determined that her next appointment would be at the United Methodist Church in Misty Falls, Tennessee not far from Knoxville.

Winnie had been expecting to hear from her superintendent after the unfortunate incident that had happened shortly after she had arrived at New Oaks UMC. That incident, and the vote by the Pastor Parish Relations Committee several months later to remove Winnie from her post, would add up to her moving to another church in June following annual conference.

"I think this is going to be a very good appointment for you, Winnie. Muddy Creek was planted just after the turn of the nineteenth century by one of our early, Methodist circuit riders, so it's one of Tennessee's oldest churches. There are several families who have been members of the church since it was planted; they are great-great grandchildren of the church founders," the D.S. told her.

"You'll like the parsonage, too," he continued. "It's located down the street from the church, so it's not on church property, *per se*. It has all the required amenities for a parsonage— four bedrooms, a study with an outside entrance, a kitchen, a family room, and a generous-sized living room/dining room. The backyard is fenced in, the garage has an electric door, and there is handicapped access to the house," the D.S. went on. "The church members have told me that they will be repainting the parsonage before you move in, and they are planning to have the linoleum flooring in the kitchen and bathrooms replaced soon.

"Pastor Neely has decided to retire this year at conference, so that is why this position is vacant. Neely has had a fine tenure at Muddy Creek, and I'm sure the members will miss him, but, from what I've been hearing, they are looking forward to having a new pastor come," the superintendent shared.

Winnie was listening with rapt attention, all the while trying to jot down details about her new appointment on an envelope as her superintendent spoke. She asked, "Have they ever had a woman pastor before?"

"No, you will be their first, but I have confidence that you can help the Muddy Creekers see that you have been called to preach the gospel to them. This church is a good church. They have a reputation in the conference for being mission oriented and supportive of their pastors, and they are generally considered a healthy, small church. They see some sixty worshipers on a Sunday, including every age from tiny to very senior," the D.S. reassured Winnie.

Winnie had been preaching and serving United Methodist Churches in and around Chattanooga, since she graduated from seminary, which was more than fifteen years, now. Most of the churches she served were small, country churches, except for the three years she had been appointed on staff at a big church in Chattanooga. So it wasn't exactly Winnie's first rodeo when trouble came in the form of an "angry man" — a misogynist with an axe to grind.

Winnie had been the first female preacher in churches twice before. In both of those cases she weathered any initial discomfort from some of her constituents and found that within a few months, everyone seemed to be pleased with her as their new woman pastor.

But New Oaks United Methodist Church was different. Adam, the angry man, was a music volunteer at church. He worked with the children, teaching them contemporary, Christian songs and accompanying them on his guitar. Adam was a self-taught musician, and he worked well with the children, but working with a woman pastor turned out to be something he didn't want to do.

Adam was a very large man, who prided himself in being able to get his way in certain situations by sheer force of will, temper, voice, and physique. He told Winnie that he had been able to influence people in significant positions of authority to see things his way several times in the past.

Winnie recalled one of Adam's anecdotes vividly.

"Boy you should have seen me!" Adam told Winnie. "I was up at the Boy Scout camp Saturday, to pick up Norman after his week at camp. He took me around the compound to show me the facility, and I was shocked at the rundown conditions! The camp must be a hundred years old!"

Winnie was amused at Adam's passionate description of the scout camp, but she listened to hear his story.

Fortunately I had my camera with me, and I got some good pictures of the place." Adam pulled out his camera and began to scroll through his recent pictures of the camp. "Look at this one!" Adam showed Winnie a picture of the showers built of corrugated fiber glass, which were partially falling apart. Winnie agreed that the showers were sadly in need of repair. "And look at the dining room," Adam insisted, showing morel pictures of the room and the tables, which revealed heavy use.

Adam then related to Winnie how he had begun action against the Boy Scouts for allowing their camp to get into such a state. "How can they think our young boys should have to camp in such conditions?" Adam wanted to know. "I have already called Norman's scout master, and the man who is over him; sl will keep calling people until I get someone who can do something about that camp!"

Adam was infuriated and implacable. His ire had been engaged, and he vowed he would not rest until someone on the top paid for the mistake.

When he returned home that day Adam called other people, and he didn't stop haranguing his invective until he had called the governor's office in Nashville.

3

Winnie never learned if Adam got the response he was looking for after his many calls, but she did remember later how Adam bragged, "I just wanted you to see how far I will go to make my point. I won't leave a stone unturned, if I think it might help my cause."

One day, about two months after Winnie had arrived at New Oaks Church, she opened her email to find a note from Adam saying, "Enough is enough is enough! I won't work with you anymore. I'm outta here! I'm quittng all my jobs at the church. You can do it yourself — the children's choir, the new adult choir, the fish fry next month — all of it!"

Winnie immediately informed the chairperson of her PPRC about the email, and the chair responded by calling a committee meeting and inviting Adam to attend.

Everyone on the committee was eager to hear Adam's concern and to see how there could be some sort of resolution to it. After all, isn't that how Christians act ? They work to resolve differences. Unfortunately, Adam wasn't interested in any sort of resolution. He stormed out of the meeting in a great huff, telling everyone that he would not work with the woman pastor. Two of the committee members followed Adam out to the parking lot and pleaded with him to return and try to find a peaceful solution to his concerns, but his anger could not be assuaged.

So Adam was gone, but it was a very small town, and he was not really gone at all. After he marched away from the church, Adam began knocking on the doors of every home in the valley, telling them how angry he was at the new Methodist pastor. He told a long story about how Winnie had thwarted his work at the church, and he tried to gain sympathy for his cause. But Adam didn't leave the matter at that; he called the superintendent and the bishop, to complain to them about the woman pastor they had sent to New Oaks.

Regardless of Adam's tantrums, the year went along quite well at the church without him, Winnie thought privately. Adam was gone, she thought, and so she turned her interests to being the best pastor she could be. The church held a four-day revival and a fish fry in September; both events were much fun. The new adult choir was well attended and added good energy to the worship service. The children's programs didn't suffer in Adam's absence.

In fact, the kids worked on and presented two musical programs to the church that year under Winnie's direction.

The unfortunate incident with Adam inspired a second problem for Winnie, one which would leave her no tenure at New Oaks UMC.

Adam, who had left the church, was still very interested in seeing that Winnie lost her job there. He worked with a powerful family at church to see that she would not be around after conference. One of the family members, Patsy, happened to be a member of the PPRC, so it became her job to bring charges against their Pastor.

The trumped up charges that Patsy leveled against the pastor included forcing Adam to leave the church, indiscriminately switching two children's solos for the Christmas play, and not keeping regular office hours. At the meeting a number of committee members spoke in defense of Pastor Winnie, affirming that she excelled in preaching, teaching, and working with the community. She was a good pastor, and they were pleased to have her with them. Those voices seemed to be the saner, more thoughtful response, compared to the diatribe brought by Patsy against Pastor Taylor.

Two weeks later, before the next PPRC meeting came, Winnie was not concerned. She had complete confidence that this foolishness would be realized and that right would win out, so she was completely taken aback when the chair of the committee convened the meeting and announced that the PPR had only one purpose that evening — to determine Pastor Winnie's fate. Would she stay at New Oaks or be asked to leave? Only five people were in attendance the meeting, but their presence provided the necessary quorum. Winnie was in attendance, along with two of her strong advocates; the chair was also present, of course, as was Patsy.

Winnie's two friends voted that she remain at her post. Patsy voted for Winnie's removal, then the chair added, "I am abstaining, but I have the proxy votes of seven other committee members who are voting for Winnie's removal."

That was that. Winnie and Carolee, one of Pastor Winnie's strongest supporters, spoke in the parking lot after the meeting. "I can't believe what just happened in there!" Carolee admitted. "I had no idea this could happen!"

"I can't believe it either," Winnie agreed, "but maybe I had a foreshadowing of what was about to happen this morning when I was having devotions. I thought it was a bit coincidental when I read in 1 Corinthians. St. Paul wrote that he would be staying in Ephesus until Pentecost, because he was seeing effective ministry even in the face of difficult opposition."

Carolee, who was quite a Bible scholar herself, was intrigued with Winnie's reading that morning. "That is interesting, Pastor Winnie, because Pentecost comes right at annual conference this year, and that would be the time you will be leaving!"

Winnie nodded her head slowly and said, "Maybe that's a small prophesy from the Lord just for me today! I'll be here until Pentecost, and I'm doing effective ministry even in the face of serious opposition!"

Winnie sighed, "That was not a United Methodist action to vote on a pastor for dismissal. I've never heard of a UM pastor being 'let go' like that."

There it was; the vote had been cast; it was a *fait accompli*. Winnie would be moving in June to a new church.

While she remained incredulous at the events that would cause her to leave the church, Winnie didn't blame the general church community for what had happened, and she continued to serve them as their pastor until she moved in June.

It never occurred to Winnie that this strange turn of events was a sign for her to leave the ministry. Although some of her colleagues thought that she might leave, Winnie never entertained such a thought. As far as she was concerned, she was called to be Jesus' follower and to preach the good news of Jesus for all who would listen.

Winnie would put her finest efforts into her call, regardless of the circumstances, and she believed that when you set your course according to God's will, God will support you in that effort (cf, Ps. 37:4-6). So Winnie continued to serve her church to the best of her abilities, but she also looked forward to her new appointment and secretly believed it could be the best one yet; although the name seemed a bit wry. *Who really names a church "Muddy Creek"?*

2. Misty Falls

Misty Falls was not a thriving city or a sprawling metropolis. It was a small town — the sort of small town you wish you came from. Even if you don't come from the South and Southern is not your mother tongue, you'd like Misty Falls.

Misty Falls was a proud little town. At one point in her history she could claim to be one of the several key train stops in the entire south. Trains, coming from several directions, would pass through Misty Falls, leaving cargo and goods, picking up passengers on their way to the city and returning others to their homes. The business was good, and Misty Falls grew strong.

By the time the Gold Rush invited hopeful pioneers to make a bid for Pike's Peak or the gold fields of California, Misty Falls was realizing her own gold in the railroad. Rails were constructed through the whole valley, connecting the Shenandoah Valley in Virginia all the way south to Mobile in Alabama.

In Misty Falls, the train tracks hugged tight to Main Street, paralleling it through town. The rail business was responsible for nearly all the commerce in the town. It provided quick movement for cattle and other creatures destined for market and carried freight cars full of dry goods, mechanical products, mail, and produce coming from the great fruit basket of the South.

Many of the town residents found employment directly because of the railroad — traveling with and maintaining the trains back and forth along their routes. Many others made a living through the supporting businesses related to rails — craftsman who built the depot in 1850, workers and managers inside the depot once it was built, and employees of the hotel adjacent.

Passenger trains, too, joined the rail system. The day the first passenger train lumbered into Misty Falls and came to a lurching halt at the depot, it was welcomed by the entire, cheering community, including the mayor and an *ad hoc* town band. Parents dressed their children in their Sunday best and herded them to Main Street, as neighbors clamored for the best view through the gathering crowd to see the historic event of the first ever passenger train to arrive in Misty Falls.

In those days there was a general, almost palpable, feeling of electric optimism that buzzed around Misty Fallers as they seemed to be watching history unfold right before their very eyes. Already in their lifetime, they had seen the rise of steam powered boats and locomotives, the invention of the bicycle, the electric motor, photography, the refrigerator, the sewing machine, something called "rubber," the typewriter, and the safety match. There seemed to be a new contraption every time one opened the newspaper!

The passenger train was simply a spin-off from the other trains that the Misty Fallers had already come to count on to improve their lives, but passenger trains had something unique to offer as well: folks were now able to travel beyond their known, insular world and to venture into the unexplored realms of the world beyond — the infamous and enigmatic West!

Those were good times for Misty Falls, and it gained a longstanding, statewide reputation for being a good place to call home.

✳ ✳ ✳

Misty Falls' countryside was nothing short of beautiful and striking. It was graciously verdant and hilly, as you would expect the foothills of the Appalachians to be. It had been planted on the southeast side of McCurry Mountain, where the countryside was lush with life. The first white settlers arrived in the valley and identified plots of land at the base of the mountain, which was generously populated with live oak, evergreen, and a variety of deciduous trees. Every autumn the mountainside treated the townsfolk to a gorgeous display of color, as the trees turned gold, red, plum, and mauve, and the sight of McCurry's autumn hues inspired many an artist to strive to capture the autumn charm on canvas.

Main Street ran through the center of town, following the contour provided by McCurry Mountain — swooping along the mountain's southside, then curving sharply northwest at the center of town. The train tracks paralleled Main Street until the road turned west, but the tracks continued south, describing a distinctive "Y" at the town centre and creating an ideal space for the train depot and hotel to be erected.

One of the most beloved spots in town was the cemetery. The first settlers to the area, who arrived about the time Jefferson was taking office for his second term as president, chose a fine location — carved from the forest of trees that stood at the base of the mountain — where they could put their dearly departed family members to rest.

The result, which took several generations to develop, was a place of spiritual peace and natural beauty. The forest had been cleared, and a circular track was drawn, describing the twenty-some acres of land. Grass carpeted the area, spanning the entire park, providing a lush underground for the ubiquitous, flowering bushes. The cemetery held the final memories of Misty Falls' citizenry symboled by grey-white granite markers of varying sizes. Sprinkled throughout the cemetery were several quite, substantial gravestones demarcating the "whose-who" of Misty Falls from various years.

As beautiful as it was, the cemetery had one vestige of old-time thinking — it was for white folks only. Gradually the community began to realize that cemeteries shouldn't be segregated, but that new enlightenment couldn't change the past, nor could it influence the places where Misty Fallers had come to rest. The past was past, and in this case, it was literally carved in stone.

McCurry Mountain stood north of town, and "Peace of Heaven Cemetery" nestled just south of the mountain, guarding the town's former residents. West of the cemetery, before one arrived at Main Street and the train tracks, was a swath of land, populated by the town's gentry. This section of Misty Falls described the upper end of town, the "right side" of the tracks, and the homes of the town's elite.

This area was generally understood as Northside Misty Falls, or simply Northside. It was the privileged portion of town, boasting paved sidewalks and street lamps. The homes had been built individually by their owner's forebears, and they were considerable. Each home was a classic, southern plantation home, complete with two-stories and an encircling veranda. Northside was planned well, made up of cul-de-sacs on which no more than a half-dozen homes stood, and the resulting, smaller communities, developed into cozy neighborhoods of good friends.

Several churches also stood in Northside. St. Luke's Cumberland Presbyterian Church, All Saints Lutheran, and Faith Baptist Church had each been planted on Northside. Muddy Creek Methodist Episcopal Church, too, had originally been built on Northside, but it was moved across the tracks to the newer section of town early in the twentieth century. Muddy Creek Church had been named for a young river that scurried down McCurry Mountain and flowed just at the edge of the land where the church was built. In the spring when the river ran its fastest, the water would kick up the mud, lolling at the edges of the stream and fold it into the mix of tumbling rapids. The result, a muddy creek.

One of Muddy Creek's members, Mr. J. Herbert Reeves, owned all the land south of the tracks as far as the county road, several miles east. Reeves' grandparents were among the founding families in Misty Falls. They had farmed corn, beans, wheat, and hay for three generations. J. Herbert thought he would do business in a different manner, and he began to sell off his land to community developers.

J. Herbert's father, Jacob Alexander Reeves, had constructed his family's home close to the depot. It could have held its own among any of the homes on Northside, but Reeves had chosen to live on his land, so he built just south of the tracks. Around the turn of the twentieth century, as J. Herbert began selling his land to developers, he had his own house moved from the center of town to the center of his land.

Moving the two and a half-story, wooden mansion was a favorite legend in town. Everybody who could manage to get away from work, even for a short time, congregated around the workers to watch the slow process of transporting the mansion.

Many great trees had to be felled and moved to the house in order to roll the house inch by inch across the fields to its new location. Teams of horses had to be gathered and harnessed to be the engine that would move the house. After several days of hauling, the mansion came to rest at its current venue. It had made the journey intact, although it forever retained a slight list to the south.

It wasn't long after Reeves moved his mansion to its new location, that Muddy Creek Methodist Church also moved to Southside. No, the physical building was not transplanted, as Reeves' home had been, but when Reeves offered to donate five acres of land in the newly developing community to his church, the offer was considered too handsome to decline. Soon Muddy Creek Methodist Church had a new address in the town, but she retained the name of Muddy Creek as it would help carry her spirit with her as she now stood among the newly growing community on Southside. All the members worked together over several weeks before harvest one year to erect the new church building. This new edifice, made on an A-frame design and displaying a dozen stained-glass windows, quickly became one of the must-see sights when visiting town.

As time went on, the greater portion of the Misty Falls community occupied the southside of town. This new section of town was designed on a grid with numbered streets and avenues named after trees. Hundreds of homes — one story cottages and ranch style homes — were built as the development continued to grow.

When Winnie arrived, Misty Falls was still a good place to live and bring up a family. Its economy had managed to stay ahead of the troubles that plagued some communities. Surely the world of the railroad had morphed over the years, and the railway enterprise could no longer brag of having significant influence on the economy of Misty Falls; the hotel no longer existed, but still the depot functioned, albeit with a much smaller staff.

Several businesses provided good employment opportunities to many citizens — the paper mill, the rug mill, a uniform manufacturing shop, and a big utility company on the Tennessee

River. Infrastructure businesses — the schools, stores, churches, and community officials filled out much of the rest of the economy.

The greatest employer, initially, had been the farms, but small farms were on the wane. There were yet several good-sized farms surrounding Misty Falls, but they were perennially struggling with the competition of the larger companies that could do business more efficiently.

One farm family, the Randalls, who were also members of Muddy Creek Church, had enjoyed a good-sized land grant during the Jackson era and had been farming their land for five generations. Eventually, they took up horse racing on the side. At first the horses were just a diversion from the more serious business of farming, but several of the family members enjoyed working with harness horses.

The Randalls managed to acquire a pair of promising standard bred mares and a stallion from good stock, and soon they began breeding their own harness horses. Walter and Eunice Randall worked with the horses, and within a dozen years they began to see encouraging results at the track. They trained the horses to be trotters and entered their fastest horses in the Louisville races. Racing meant traveling several hours with their horses in tow and setting aside a week of farming every time a race was held. The family treated these trips as holidays for the whole family, giving everyone a break from the normal, heavy work of the farm.

The Reeves and Randall families were members of Muddy Creek Church, and their extended kin populated a lion's portion of the church's membership. It was their church. Muddy Creek was where they had been baptized, married, and buried. Muddy Creek Church was where they enjoyed youth fellowship, celebrated Christmas and Easter, worked together in the Women's Society and the Men's Missionary Outreach. Needless to say, Muddy Creek was near and dear to many people in the Misty Falls community.

The Reeves and Randall families were among the first to hear that their beloved Pastor Neely had decided to retire from preaching. After eight good years, he would be leaving his post in June, and the very next week the bishop would be sending them a new pastor — a woman. A woman! The news was met with silence when the chair of the PPRC made the announcement. No one spoke until, finally, Homer Randall spoke up.

He cleared his voice and said, "Y'all ain't sure about this woman comin' to be our preacher, but I think we all need to give her a chance. I suggest we fig're how we c'n make her welcome in our community and here at Muddy Creek Church. If she's got the word of God to bring to us, wouldn't we be foolish if we chose not to hear her because of our particul'r, funny way of seeing things?!"

Homer's words set the mood for the church.

✳ ✳ ✳

After hearing about her new appointment, Winnie planned to make a "drive by" later in the week. It was a blustery Saturday in March when Winnie made her trip to Misty Falls. *"Driving into town from the freeway is not as impressive as the superintendent suggested,"* Winnie thought. The route into the town was lined by several blocks of empty stores. The parking lots were messy, and the fronts of the stores were boarded up and needed paint. *Not the greatest first impression.*

Of course the first thing Winnie wanted to see was the church, and she made a beeline right for it. The church stood on the corner of a large lot near the center of town, and was surrounded by several acres of green grass with a copse of pine trees on one corner of the lot. *"The Sanctuary appears quite typical, a comfortable size,"* Winnie noted. *"I wonder what it looks like inside? I bet that large, extension building is the fellowship hall or Sunday school wing."*

In front of the church, standing a dozen feet back from the sidewalk, was an old, rugged, wood cross with the traditional symbol of Lent on it — a purple drape that snapped back and forth in the chilly wind. Winnie wondered what sort of folks had put up the cross. Already she was looking forward to meeting them.

Winnie ducked her head down slightly and tried to maneuver her small, lime-green VW through the town as inconspicuously as possible; *I don't want to attract undue attention before my official introduction in June.* She noticed the rows of houses, most of which sported large gardens. *These people may have come into town from the farm, but they have not forgotten how to put out vegetables and flowers.* Winnie had been the beneficiary of other country gardening communities and hoped privately that she would again be recipient of garden delights in this new place. *"One more reason to look forward to this new assignment,"* she thought.

Winnie continued into the center of town where she parked her car. The old depot stood on Main Street, and from the looks of it, it had been there for a long time. There were two sets of train tracks that ran along the back side of the depot. As Winnie stood gazing at the train station she could hear the advance of a train. The whistle was already sounding, but the sound was so loud that she couldn't tell if the train was coming from her left or her right; all she was certain about was that it was definitely on its way! Within a minute the train appeared, and Winnie stood riveted to her spot on the boardwalk as it swooshed past her and on down the line.

"Goodness," thought Winnie. *"I wonder if anyone ever gets used to having such a calamitous noise in their backyard?"* After the train had passed Winnie noticed the old hotel adjacent to the depot. Part of the hotel was now a museum for Misty Falls, and part of it was a diner. *History and lunch sounds like a great combination to me!*

Winnie spent the next few hours exploring the museum and enjoying lunch next door at the diner. She met a docent at the museum, who seemed to know everyone in town — at least she certainly gave that opinion to the visiting woman. Winnie thought she ought not drop her new appointment or her vocation on her helpful guide just now. After all, the appointment wasn't set in stone, and the bishop might change his mind about sending Winnie to pastor at Muddy Creek Church. No, Winnie would keep that bit of news to herself for the time being.

I think I'm going to like Misty Falls. Winnie could see the town and its community members would be like many other towns where she had pastored. The town's people would be similar: some good, some not so good, and all standing in the need of God's grace, just like we all are. She could feel herself beginning to grow hopeful about this new place to do ministry. *"Surely the Lord has some ministry for me to do here! Maybe there's something special that He has in mind for me in this place,"* Winnie told herself.

3. Fall Festival

Two years later — September 2008.

"*Saturday will be a full day,*" Winnie mused, as she prepared for Misty Falls' Fall Festival. There would be food, and games, and artisans displaying their wares; there would be a cake walk and a pie baking contest, and there would be prizes and opportunities for every age visitor. Winnie was expecting to see all that the festival had to offer, meeting friends she would no doubt see, and of course the pie. *I love pie!*

As she was about to leave her parsonage for the festival, Winnie's phone ran, snatching her from her reverie. The voice on the other end of the phone tickled her memory. Yes, there was something oddly familiar about the voice. It was deep and sonorous, obviously a man of maturity. It was a voice she didn't recognize immediately, but there was something pleasantly familiar about it. And then, Winnie remembered. Yes! She knew the owner of the voice. It had belonged to one, more youthful, but who had the same cadence of speech. It was John!

It seemed ages ago when Winnie and John were students at Mile High High School in Denver. They had shared a couple of the same classes, but they had not been close friends back then. Nonetheless, Winnie had had a great crush on him! Surely he had been an impossible *Objet d'amour*. It was a case of puppy love, of course, and at that time Winnie believed John to be completely "out of her league." He traveled in a different circle from hers, so she had to content herself with fascination of him from afar. She relished every detail about him — his blue-rimmed glasses, which matched the color of his eyes, his freckled face, his boyish grin, his intelligence.

"That first, impossible love is such a funny experience," Winnie thought, *"because while it is a deeply personal and isolating experience, it seems, when I think of it now, to be a universal plight of teenagers. I imagine everyone falls in love, desperately in love, with someone, who, for the most part, is out of reach when we're young."*

Winnie smiled as those silly thoughts rushed back — being so crazy for John, the young man. *Boy, was that a long time ago!* She grinned and shook her head, even as she tried to concentrate on what John was saying on the phone.

"Like I was saying", John continued, "I got your name and phone number from Roger Clemens. He's on the high school's Fortieth Reunion Committee and asked me to make a couple of calls, inviting former graduates to join us at the party in October."

"Goodness! Can it be forty years since we graduated, already?" Winnie asked rhetorically. "I guess it has been. We graduated in '68, and it's well into 2008 now."

John and Winnie had had a couple of classes together — an honors English class, called The Essential Ideas Class, and several years of Latin, which included Junior Classical League

"I do wonder, occasionally, what has happened to some of the people we knew back at Mile High High," Winnie responded. "Remember Mr. Guenther, our First Year Latin teacher?" "He was an odd fellow — probably pretty smart, although I don't think I thought he was back then. I actually had him again for chemistry class my junior year! It didn't occur to me as such a strange thing back then, but isn't it a bit unusual for someone to teach both letters and science?" Winnie wondered aloud.

"You'd be surprised at how often that can occur, Winnie," John answered. "I have a couple of colleagues who are fluent in disparate disciplines. One fellow teaches Russian and philosophy here at University of Chicago, and another professor, a woman, whom I've not met, teaches anatomy at UC, but she is also a concert pianist, who travels around the world concertizing.

"I don't know if I was aware of old Guenther being that sort of multi-disciplined person back when we were in school," John admitted. "Of course, I didn't have him for chemistry."

"It's interesting to hear about those talented folks. Are you up in Chicago, yourself, now? Is that how you happen to know about University of Chicago personalities?" Winnie asked.

"Ah, I should have told you. "I'm a lecturer at Chicago — have been for nearly thirty years," John explained to Winnie.

"I shouldn't be surprised, John. You were certainly one of the notable scholars in our class back in Denver. What do you teach? Are you a professor now?" she wondered.

John was amused with Winnie's sudden queries. "Yes, I'm a professor; I teach philosophy at UC."

Winnie gulped and caught her breath. "Philosophy! Of course, philosophy! That was my favorite class of all back in school. Our Essential Ideas Class with Mr. Holder when we were seniors was totally awesome! It caused me to really think, maybe for the first time. It was also the hardest class I ever took, but it was clearly the best!

"Do you ever give our Essential Ideas Class credit for the direction you pursued?" Winnie suggested.

John laughed and answered, "You could certainly be right about that. Before that class I was probably considering something in math or science for my future career, but that class was unique.I agree; it was hard, but it was the best!

"I remember you from those days. You sat over by the windows on the far side of the room, but I knew you were there!" John added.

"How do you like teaching today's young people?" Winnie asked. "Aren't they different from when we matriculated in college, especially with all the advantages of internet and computers and all?"

"The thinking is the same. Students still have to read and work with the material and develop their own understanding of the ideas, but they certainly do have a number of benefits from technology," John agreed.

Today's college students are much more technically savvy than we were in school, and it's odd for our older generation to have to look to the younger set to gain understanding in things technical. That's not supposed to happen. Young folks should learn from their elders, not the other way around! For today's young people the world is incredibly different from when we stepped onto our college campuses, or should I say "campi?" John teased.

"We'd have to admit there's been more than a generation change from the sixties to now. At least today's college kids aren't hippies! What a time that was!" Winnie added.

Their conversation continued on and on. No, John had not been caught up in the Viet Nam War himself. He had been in college when the draft lottery came up, but his number was 360! [Winnie remembered how the draft lottery worked, pulling birth dates out of a tumbling bin. The first birthdate selected was numbered "one;" the second date was numbered "two," etc. Apparently, John's birthdate was the 360th chosen.] He was never called to serve his country. "It would seem that I managed to skip that entire chapter in the American saga," John admitted.

John spoke about his work teaching philosophy to college students; or as he facetiously called it, "corrupting the youth" in reference to the indictment which killed Socrates.

Winnie was thinking it was about time to tell John that she was a United Methodist pastor herself, when something caused her to hold back.

John was talking about politics. He mentioned the upcoming elections and all the hype that was in the news regarding the state of the economy and how critical the elections were for the country.

"I heard some news reporters the other day, speculating about the influence that the church might actually hold on Evangelical Christians voters. Could the church sway their vote?" Winnie asked.

"I really don't see right wing voters coming from any particular denomination, so I don't think church has any real authority. Of course, I don't believe in church," John admitted.

A red flag flew up in Winnie's mind when she heard those words, but she wasn't exactly sure how best to respond. Somehow, a straight-on, theologically-based apologetic was bound to get too far into the academic trenches and ruin what was otherwise a rather engaging phone call. Agreeing with him was certainly not an option for her. Instead she contemplated her response carefully and decided on a flanking maneuver — humor.

"What do you mean you don't believe in church? I've seen it, in fact there are several in our town!"

They both laughed, and Winnie's tension abated.

John changed the subject, "Have you heard about our high school's reunion coming up? Perhaps you'd like to attend; it will be the last weekend of October — the 24th and 25th."

"I hadn't heard about an official reunion," Winnie admitted, pleased that the subject had changed. "Although, it did occur to me a few months ago that we graduated in '68 — forty years ago — and that someone would probably organize something."

"Yes, there's a committee in Denver, working on the details of the party. That's why Roger called and asked me to take a short list of names from our class to invite to the reunion."

"Hm. Let me guess," Winnie interjected, "Roger knew my whereabouts because of his sister Ivey. She and I have kept up with one another over the years, and she would know my current phone. Right?"

"See, it's not such a mystery, Winnie," John added. "I hope we will see you in Denver that weekend. Do you suppose you could make it?'

"You make it sound quite tempting," Winnie confessed. "I'll see what I can do about coming. Thanks for the invite!"

❋ ❋ ❋

Well, that was pleasantly unexpected! After the phone call Winnie plunked down in her kitchen chair, stunned. She had not given John a thought in years, yet his voice had been good to hear; it seemed to linger on in her head.

John's phone call had pulled Winnie back to a time before Mark. *"A thoroughly enjoyable call,"* she thought, *"save that one odd comment about church. If I see him at the reunion I'll have to find a better way to deal with the subject."*

It was very out of character for Winnie not to tell the truth, and she was feeling a bit uneasy about it. But her little white lie seemed justified in light that it did avoid a possibly unfriendly disagreement about religion. *"I'll tell him at a more opportune time,"* she assured herself.

With that most interesting conversation still spinning in her head, Winnie left her house for the festival.

Misty Falls had been putting on a fall festival every year on the second Saturday of September since 1953. Winnie hadn't lived in the town back then, of course — she had only arrived in town two years before — but she was calling Misty Falls her home now, although she knew that, as a "newcomer," she would always be an outsider, no matter how long she lived there.

One of the things that helped Winnie settle into new communities well was that she'd never met a stranger, as they say. Her mother had taught her that "people she didn't know were just friends she hadn't yet met." So, keeping that in mind, Winnie met new people easily. She also had a knack for remembering names, which definitely helped her when meeting new folks. *"It's always a compliment to others to be interested in them and to remember their names,"* Winnie would say to herself.

She walked past Jodi Lee Barrymore's garden. She was an expert in roses and grew wonderful varieties and colors of roses in her garden. Jodi Lee had grown up on a farm outside town, and she knew gardening — when to plant, when to weed, what to fertilize with, when the rains would come, and, most importantly, how to diagnose and eliminate the dreaded Japanese Beetle. Jodi Lee often came to church Sundays bearing a bouquet of roses right from her yard. What a great way to share the wonderful garden God had given her!

The Fall Festival was known throughout the surrounding area as an event not to miss. The day's activities had begun with a five kilometer run or jog around town, ending back on Main Street. Following the jog would be a community pancake breakfast. Winnie wasn't happy about missing the pancakes —she was very fond of pancakes. She had looked forward to sinking her teeth into a small stack of light, towering, fluffy goodness, but her unexpected phone call had delayed her too long. *"Oh well! Maybe I didn't really need those pancakes,"* she rationalized.

As she sauntered toward Main Street, it was obvious that something was happening in town — cars were parked along every street — and scores of people were making their way toward the center of town.

Nina Mattingly stepped out of her family's well-loved Lincoln Town Car as Winnie passed by; she reached gingerly back inside her car to take out a special parcel — her effort for this year's pie baking contest.

Nina called out to Winnie when she saw her, walking just ahead. "Winnie, wait up a minute!" she called out. Winnie turned around and walked over to see her friend. Nina set her pie carrier down, and the two women hugged. Then she picked up her pie in one hand and her bag in the other, and the two hooked arms as they strolled toward Main Street.

"Glad to see you this morning; actually I figured you'd be somewhere around today," Nina admitted.

"You can't live in Misty Falls and not attend the festival, can you? How long have you been coming to the festival? AND how many years have you won the grand prize for your pie?" Winnie asked pointing to the pie carrier.

"I haven't won first place <u>every</u> year! In fact I only took third place twice and runner-up another year, but I have been lucky to take the blue ribbon for my raspberry-apricot-walnut-crumb pie a number of times. Actually, I sometimes wonder if I shouldn't enter a different pie one year, just to see how I'd do."

"I don't know, Nina. Your raspberry-apricot-walnut-crumb pie is wonderful. Whoever said, 'If it's not broke, don't fix it?'" Winnie speculated.

Nina tilted her head, thought a moment, and then said, "That's good for a lot of things, but wouldn't it stifle creativity? Wouldn't we be boring if we never tried any new ways of doing things? I'll bet your God would say that, too. I'll bet your God would say He gave us a brain to use and be creative with." Nina winked at Winnie.

Winnie and Nina teased one another a lot. "That's one of the things I like about you, Nina. You keep me on my toes when it comes to things of faith," Winnie smiled back.

Actually, Winnie wasn't quite clear about where Nina stood when it came to matters of faith. Winnie had her suspicions about the source of Nina's resistance, but she was waiting for the right moment to explicitly address the issue. Nina always spoke, in this "left-handed" sort of way, as if she didn't believe, but then, she could surprise you by speaking about God when you didn't expect it. Winnie figured she should encourage Nina, however she could, about faith. The two women seemed to have an unspoken agreement that Nina could say whatever she wanted about things of faith, and Winnie would represent to the "party line."

The party line, of course, was the general understanding of "People Called Christian," which Winnie thoroughly espoused. She was known to share her convictions and her personal journey in faith, if anyone ever asked her, but that didn't seem to come up much outside of church.

The festival planners had invited dozens of vendors to come and share their crafts, hobbies, goodies, and treasures. A few blocks away, a very large, blue and white-striped tent had been erected just past Maple Street, for the community chicken and corn dinner, which would begin mid-day.

Nina was headed toward the pie-baking contest area to carry her (hoped-for) prize-winning pie; it would be judged later in the day. The two friends separated at the corner, and Winnie continued on her way up Main Street. Winnie stopped at FRIENDLY'S FOODS, the local grocery store. The store was open even during the festival. Tucker Joe (Tuck) Tennyson, the owner, looked up and greeted Winnie as she stepped inside. "Mornin' Miss Winnie," Tucker smiled. "Good morning," Winnie responded. "Do you suppose you'll get much business today? With all the folks at the festival, you'll probably not have many serious shoppers."

Tuck chuckled and said, "Well, you may be right about me not gettin' serious shoppers, but I do 'speckt some folks 'll stop by, 'n this store c'n use all the traffic it c'n git. See! You came on in yerself! Would you like some coffee?"

Tuck had been hoping to develop a coffee house in his store. He fancied putting in something like a local Starbucks at FRIENDLY'S FOODS— a place for folks to congregate, enjoy a flavorful coffee and, maybe, add a sweet to accompany it.

"Sounds great! What do you have?" Winnie asked.

Tuck turned to a pot of freshly brewed coffee, poured a small Styrofoam cupful, and handed it to Winnie. "I'm fix'in' to add a new section over here (he motioned with his left hand in the direction of the front left corner of the store). I'm going to call it FRIENDLY'S FOODS' 'Koffee Klatch.' I'm puttin' in some tables to sit at, and a big ol' flat screen, m'be I'll add Wi-Fi. I fig'r I'll make this store into 'The Place To Be' in Misty Falls."

Winnie took the cup of coffee and tasted it. "Mmmmm! Nice. Sounds like you've been thinking about your Koffee Klatch for a while. That might be just what Misty Falls could use." She took another taste and then dropped her empty cup into a basket and exited the store. "Have a nice day, Tuck. Thanks for the coffee."

Winnie stepped out onto Main Street again and continued her walk through the festival. Main Street was four and a half blocks long with stores standing side by each on both sides of the street; the red brick shops looked as though they had conspired to look alike. Their large, square windows — two across each shop — were topped with blue awnings, which protected shoppers during inclement weather and today shaded the visitors from the sun. The businesses, including FRIENDLY'S FOODS grocery store, Hanson's Drug Emporium, Misty Falls' Library, Post's Antiques, Smith's Antique Parlor, Richard's Tools, Nell's Specialties, as well as the depot, Misty Falls' Museum, and the Depot Diner, were open and enjoying the extra traffic today. The place looked very different from Main Street's usual appearance; the many kiosks and tables, displaying various wares and appealing merchandise, invited people to stop, look, enjoy, and "take something home."

Winnie saw the face-painting table and recognized the McBride family there. Janie McBride, the eleven year old, was proudly showing off the large red and yellow butterflies that had been painted on each of her cheeks. Her younger sister, Dawn, a petite six year old, was struggling hard to sit still while her face was being painted. She had asked for a clown face, and it would take patient work by the artist to get the ever-widening lips drawn on her face. Already Dawn's entire face had been covered in white makeup. Her brother Michael was waiting for his turn next. Mom and Dad McBride stood beside the table, watching their kids. They were glad to have a Saturday morning together that didn't involve the hassle of "house cleaning" — their usual family activity for Saturday.

The McBrides lived just across the street from Muddy Creek Church, and they occasionally attended worship there. Winnie exchanged pleasantries with the McBrides for several minutes before she continued on her way. As she walked down the road, she stopped and chatted to the vendors and took note of their enticing offerings.

A block further, taking up the whole width of the street, stood the chicken dinner tent. Winnie poked her head in and saw a busy crew of people moving around inside the tent, setting up for the meal. The sign outside the tent advertised that dinner would begin serving at Eleven. There were long rows of picnic benches and folding chairs for the festival goers to sit at. There was a makeshift kitchen at the end of the tent, where the chicken and corn were cooking, and the thick, aromatic cloud of roasted chicken spun Winnie back many years to the way her entire house smelled when her mother cooked a chicken all day in a pot. *Mother's chicken was always so well done, it fell completely off the bone, perfectly tender, saucy, and delicious.* Winnie savored that memory a few seconds before she let go the corner of the tent door and let it drop down. *Lunch will be worth the wait!*

As she stepped onto the street and looked back down Main Street, Winnie saw Kevin Thompson walking toward her. She knew Kevin from church. He and his family were also relatively new to Misty Falls, and had joined Muddy Creek Church shortly before Winnie arrived. Kevin and Sheryl Lynn had twins, Matthew and Marva Lynn, who were twelve years old and just now teetering on adolescence. Winnie was especially fond of the twins; they were

24

gifted children. Matthew was a star at mathematics and baseball, making him very popular with the guys and a natural heart throb of the girls, and Marva Lynn had a wonderful talent for art and dance.

Kevin smiled at Miss Winnie and approached her. "Mornin', Pastor Winnie. How about this festival?"

"Wonderful! Are you here with your family?" Winnie asked.

"I am, though you can't tell. The rest of the family will be meeting me here for dinner in a few minutes." Kevin dropped his voice, "Say, since you're here, I'd like to ask you somethin'. Do you s'pose you could stop by my work about lunchtime sometime next week? I have something I need to talk to you about."

Winnie straightened up a bit at Kevin's request and said, "Of course. No problem. Is there a particular day that would be better for you?"

Kevin smiled and said, "Just any day this week, 'round noon. I c'n get off then, and we c'n talk."

Winnie assured Kevin she'd put it on her calendar — probably Tuesday or Wednesday.

Just then, Sheryl Lynn and the twins arrived and the subject changed. They stood talking together as other folks began forming a line in front of the tent for dinner.

Winnie left the Thompsons in line; "See you in church to-morrow!" They agreed, "Tomorrow!"

Winnie left, wondering what Kevin might be up to. *Has something come up at home? I hope he and Sheryl Lynn are OK. Wonder what's on Kevin's mind? Hmmmm. Guess I'll just have to wait and see!"*

✳ ✳ ✳

By four o'clock Winnie realized it was time for her to leave the festival and turn back home. It had been a good day, but there was more for her to do before it was over, and she needed to put her feet up before getting to work on her sermon. Unlike most people, who relax on Saturday nights, Winnie's Saturday evening was always dedicated to work.

As she opened her kitchen door, she was glad to be home, but she also felt the empty lifelessness of the house. Pansy, Winnie's dog, wasn't there to greet her as she always used to with her overly exuberant greeting. Winnie paused in the doorway and Pansy's absence just hung in the air — a big blank!

Pansy, Winnie's dog of fourteen years, had died suddenly a few months before. She had been alerted to a drama in her backyard, as the neighbor's portly, twenty-five pound Siamese cat streaked across the backyard in hot pursuit of a local, lawn bunny. Pansy was immediately at the ready to join the chase, but the elder dog within her was not. *"The spirit was willing but the flesh was weak"*, Winnie smiled at her misuse of that quote. Pansy ran full out after the two fleeting creatures, but by the time she had reached the end of the yard her heart had simply given out. It was sudden, unexpected, and sad, of course, for Winnie, yet she tried to see the best side of what had just happened — *at least Pansy had left this earth doing something she loved!* Pansy was gone, and Winnie realized she probably should look for a new pooch for company.

An hour later, after she'd put her few dinner dishes back in their proper order and had sat her lap top on her lap, Winnie opened up the document she'd been working on all week and began typing. She'd be ready, or as ready as she could be, by tomorrow morning. That's what happened every week, miracle of miracles! The endless treadmill of preparing a weekly sermon was both a joy and a stress as each and every sermon to be researched, prayed over, thought through, and readied for Sunday morning. *I'll come together; It always does.*

※ ※ ※

It took Winnie several months to appreciate the fact that Muddy Creek Church was located "on the other side of the tracks." Yet it had been standing on that piece of land since the beginning of the twentieth century.

The church building was known for her exceptionally beautiful, stained glass windows of Christ. Twelve windows depicted the Lord from birth to ascension, including many, favorite scenes of miracles and wonders. Inside the sanctuary was covered in deep, rich, walnut-stained wood. The large, wooden beams shaped like the bottom of an upside down ship extended to a peak in the center of the ceiling.

Winnie had come to love the people of Muddy Creek. It had been a nervous moment when she led her first worship service at the church. Being Muddy Creek's first woman preacher, Winnie understood there were some folks who were not convinced that a woman could be called to be a pastor. To their credit, there were a couple of "misleading" passages in the Bible that seemed to justify such a position. Winnie was sympathetic to her congregants' hesitation but warmed them slowly to the idea of a woman pastor by teaching, preaching, and leading the church faithfully.

That first Sunday in worship at Muddy Creek two years previous, before her sermon, Pastor Winnie called the children to come forward for a Children's Moment. She wanted them to understand that God wants us all to grow up. She started by asking the children if they remembered how babies act, and one little boy immediately responded with a loud "Waaaaaaa" sound. His pretend bawling surprised the congregation, and many parishioners laughed out loud. The child, realizing that he had just captured the floor, continued with his wailing to more and more chuckles from the audience. This continued on and on for several minutes, and Winnie wondered which was worse — the howling child or the hysterical adults? Finally Winnie gave up on ever actually finishing her "children's sermon" and put a stop to the scene by saying the magic church words that instantly hush any crowd— "Let us pray."

Everyone had had a good laugh, and somehow those chuckles seemed to act as a release of nervousness or anxiety that some in the congregation had been holding. They relaxed a bit and found themselves pleasantly absorbed in their new pastor's sermon and her distinctive, feminine perspective on things.

4. Surprising Confessions

"Monday morning coffee — I love it!" Winnie declared audibly in the privacy of her own kitchen. *It's a very agreeable way to start the day.* Winnie recognized that she was among a small minority of people that actually *liked* Monday mornings, but, ever since she had been preaching, that's how it seemed to her.

Whereas most folks did not exactly rejoice on Monday mornings, Winnie relished them. After all, Monday morning was the farthest she could get from Sunday morning and her next sermon; she had a whole week to put together the new one. *Mondays are definitely good!*

The week ahead was filled with the things that regularly populated the pastor's days: some quick housekeeping, morning devotions, reading and studying, some administrative office work, making some calls, the Tuesday Bible Study, Wednesday morning prayer meeting, and choir that evening. Additionally, she had two special events on the calendar — Kevin Thompson's requested meeting about some mysterious subject and the area pastors' meeting on Thursday evening

This week will move right along. There's plenty to give it shape! Winnie smiled.

✳ ✳ ✳

Winnie made sure to put her visit to Kevin early in the week. He hadn't mentioned it again, even though she saw him at church Sunday, and Winnie was growing more and more curious to find out what he had in mind. She really couldn't imagine.

Might Kevin need to unload some burden he was carrying, some painful memory or some event he wasn't proud of? That certainly could be the case. Winnie had heard her share of such confessions over the years, and she recognized the position a pastor has to receive such disclosures and to help the owners realize the grace available through confession and acceptance of Christ's gift of forgiveness. When someone receives forgiveness for wrong actions or forgives others from hurting him or her, it is as if a fresh breeze has wafted into the room. Suddenly the burden is laid down, and there is a new, clean slate on which to write. Winnie had seen this many times, and she had also experienced it in her own life. She knew the value of confession and forgiveness had for Christians, making it possible to follow Christ anew.

Just before noon on Tuesday Winnie appeared at the shop where Kevin worked. He was an electrical technician, and he worked on small appliances. He used to have his own shop, repairing televisions, but with the new flat screen technology and the demise of the "tube television," he had to find a job where he could use his skill with electronics to make a living.

Kevin was already outside the shop waiting. They walked over to a bench on a side street and sat. After a couple of pleasantries, Kevin jumped into the issue. "Pastor Winnie, I need help, but I have to be sure that whatever I tell you will be held in the strictest of confidence. It's really important!"

"You can count on my discretion. If this is something you don't want talked about — and it's not about you harming yourself, someone else, or breaking the law — then you don't have to worry about me telling a soul," Winnie assured Kevin.

Kevin chuckled aloud. "No, no, it's nothing like that. You see, Sheryl Lynn needs to get a divorce from her first husband." Kevin stopped to let his words sink in.

"Excuse me!? Your wife needs a divorce? What?" Winnie was incredulous.

"It was more n' fifteen years ago; Sheryl Lynn was young. She met this guy, this loser, at some dance, and they got high on some stuff. Next thing she knew she was married to him. She lived with the guy for a while, but he couldn't keep a job. Her folks were very upset. Eventually the two drifted apart, and Sheryl Lynn moved back home. There had no children.

"Then, a couple years later she and I met at a dance, and we hit it off — right from the start. Sheryl Lynn told me, up front, that she was married but they were separated. That was fine with me. I really didn't think it was any big deal. That man wasn't part of her life, anymore.

"Pastor Winnie, you have to understand that back then I was not a Christian, and it didn't occur to me that what we were doing wasn't right. I didn't figure that out until I became a believer in Christ a few years ago. By then we had moved to Misty Falls and joined Muddy Creek Church, and now we're part of the community. Everything is going good for us, and I don't want to screw any of that up. I don't know what to do, but I know we need to make things right, somehow."

Winnie drank in every word, but she didn't add anything, yet. She wanted to let Kevin tell his whole story.

"We're not rich people, and we don't have money to pay a lawyer. What c'n we do? I'm hoping you could find a lawyer and find out what it would cost for Sheryl Lynn to get a divorce, 'cause we'd like to git married right," Kevin finished his thought.

Winnie smiled comfortingly. "Goodness! Who would have thought? I'll be glad to help. Being a pastor means I know lots of people!"

Winnie stood up and said, "Kevin, I'm glad you told me, you did the right thing."

Winnie was glad that Kevin had trusted this matter with her. No one at church had any idea that this family was anything but what they looked to be — a nice, intact family, complete with father, mother, and twins. There would be a terrible rumor loosed in the community if any of this matter leaked out — EVER!

❄ ❄ ❄

Winnie tried to spend time every day in study and sermon prep. She knew herself well enough to realize that she was not the sort of person who could possibly put such preparation off to the last moment. It wasn't like when she was in school — when she could cram the night before a test and come out pretty well. She did have a reasonably good memory for facts and numbers, but there was no way she could allow herself to wait until the eleventh hour to begin pulling a sermon together. She needed to have a considerable portion of her message well in mind BEFORE the weekend arrived. Then she could polish and practice delivering it to her private, captive audience — a collection of stuffed sheep which she affectionately called her "flock."

❋ ❋ ❋

Wednesday afternoon Winnie stopped by the library. As she approached the front door, she saw her friend Nina arriving from the opposite way.

"I'm guessing you took top honors for your pie, again," Winnie said.

Nina grinned and admitted that her pie had been a success, but that she really did need to think about a different entry for next year. "I shall do some experimenting this year and see what I can come up with. Might you be interested in helping me with occasional taste-testing?"

Winnie's face lit up with smiles. "You know I would! I love pie! Just let me know when you're ready, and I'll bring my taste buds over. That's one test I won't mind at all!"

The two agreed; gave each other a hug, and Nina disappeared through the library doors.

As Nina entered the library, Pearly Mae Moore was exiting the building, carrying a couple of volumes in her hand. Her appearance brought another big smile to Winnie.

"Afternoon, Miss Pearly Mae! Good to see you!"

"*Pearly Mae is one of the finest people in Misty Falls,*" Winnie thought. "*She has a way of making everyone she meets welcome in her presence, and I always feel a bit better inside after having spent time with her. She truly has the gift of hospitality.*"

"Pleased to see you, too, Miss Winnie. Are you here at the library to research something, or maybe you're looking for something on the lighter side to read?" Pearly Mae asked.

"I suppose we both enjoy our library for a number of reasons, don't we?" Winnie agreed, noting the volumes tucked under Pearly Mae's arm. "Looks like you might be doing some research yourself today."

"Indeed, I am, Miss Winnie. I like to keep up on a number of items, both past and present, and the library's a great place to do so." Pearly Mae nodded her head.

"When I was a younger woman, my Danny and I were very involved in civil rights activities, at least as much as we could from Misty Falls, and I still enjoy reading and learning about the personalities and the situations that populated our communities and made important changes for us black folks," Pearly Mae's eyes twinkled as she spoke. "Of course the story of civil rights hasn't seen the final chapter written yet, not by a long shot."

"Sounds like you and Danny were a part of history in the making! How remarkable!" Winnie answered. "Did you realize it at the time that you were actually walking into history? Did you ever meet anyone famous?"

"In most cases we did simple things around Misty Falls, but we did take the train up to D.C. late in August in 1963 and participated in that amazing gathering. The Southern Christian Leadership Conference was encouraging as many folks as possible attend the rally. They hoped it would be a peaceful means of promoting jobs and freedom. That sounded good to us, so we hopped on the train and joined the others up there.

"That Wednesday afternoon on the mall, downtown Washington D.C. we saw many people of note, and we were thrilled to see so many different people gathered, not just people of color, who were interested in equitable living for all. There were movie star, and politicians, and, of course, Dr. Martin Luther King, Jr," Pearly Mae remembered.

"I was personally touched by his speech that day, and I've tried to be a better person for it.

'You know, Miss Winnie, Dr. King inspired me to be known for the content of my character, more than the color of my skin. I loved his challenge to me; I think it's made me a better person." Pearly Mae smiled, remembering.

"Goodness, I think you've done that quite well," Winnie assured her friend. "Of course most people around here remember you for your work at school. I gather you taught fifth grade for quite a while. I'll bet you know a lot of folks here in this community for having been at the elementary school for so long." Winnie stated.

"I 'spect I do know a lot of Misty Fallers, maybe most of them. At least, I knew them as they came through the school. I also spent my last years at school as the vice principal at David Crocket Elementary. I think I had nearly forty years, all told, in education. Getting educated and helping others go as far as they can in education has been my life-long fascination," Pearly Mae admitted.

After a few more minutes talking, the two friends wished one another well, and Winnie proceeded through the big library door.

Winnie stopped at the desk where Jodi Lee was busy stacking books onto a cart. Jodi Lee Barrymore, the head librarian, was the sheriff's wife and a longtime member of Muddy Creek Church.

Winnie lowered her voice and said to her, "Jodi Lee! Nice to see you!."

Jodi Lee looked up at Winnie and smiled at her. She was enjoying her first woman pastor at Muddy Creek Church. Before Winnie arrived, Jodi Lee was not too sure what to think about a woman filling that position in the church. She had never met a woman who preached before. She'd heard there were such women, but she wasn't sure she liked the idea. "*Maybe women are not supposed to preach*," Jodi Lee thought.

It had turned out to be a non-issue for her. Pastor Winnie was doing just fine. She was serious about her faith in Christ — in following the LORD — and she was serious about carrying out her duty as pastor of Muddy Creek Church. For Jodi Lee, it was a "good match." Jodi Lee thought one of the reasons Pastor Winnie was doing so well was because she seemed genuinely interested in every person she met. She'd visited many of the church members, prayed with them, and she was slowly becoming part of the town "family."

"I ordered a book from the library system, and I wonder if it has arrived?" Winnie said. Winnie had good resources in her own library and online, but occasionally she found it helpful to read up on a subject that was coming up in her studies. The library was her resource for that.

Jodi Lee found the book had arrived and issued it to Winnie. "There you are; it will be due back here in two weeks."

Winnie thanked Jody Lee and exited the library. She drove around the corner and continued three blocks to the town center, which included the sheriff's office, the jail, the courthouse, and the volunteer fire department all housed together in a large, red brick building. Winnie stopped at the outer office where she found the sheriff's secretary working.

Janice Creighton was the wife of Ken Creighton, the pastor of First Baptist Church. Janice had been working for Sheriff Barrymore since James Roy, Creighton's youngest, had been in school full time — going on seven years now.

Winnie greeted Janice and asked if the sheriff was available to speak.

Janice pushed a button on her desk for the intercom and announced to the sheriff that Miss Winnie was in the front office.

"Have her come right in, Janice. The door is never closed to my pastor," the sheriff replied.

Winnie walked into the adjacent office and sat down in the chair opposite the sheriff's big desk. "I have a favor to ask of you." Winnie said.

"Sheriff Mickey Allen Bannister, at your service, Ma'am," he responded. "What might you need me to do?"

"Would that getting help is always so easy!" Winnie winked. "Actually I'm hoping you might be interested in helping out with games at the church, family picnic, end of next month. The ramada at the park has already been reserved for the church, and the food will come from the hospitality committee, but we need someone to honcho the games for the families. I know how well you work with our middle schoolers already, and I can't think of anyone who could better organize games for our picnic than you."

Mickey Allen, the tall, ruddy-complexioned sheriff, checked the date of the picnic on his calendar, and finding there was no conflict, said, "I think I can handle that, especially since I know I won't have to do it all by myself. I can get some of the other dads to lend a hand. I'll see which dads can bring what equipment — balls, horse shoes, that sort of stuff. Thanks for asking. Sounds like fun!"

Winnie knew that fellowship at Muddy Creek Church was an essential element of a faith community. *The family that plays together, stays together," she said to herself. "Well, that's not really the saying, is it? It's really 'the family who prays together, stays to-gether.' and that's, of course, true, but I think 'playing together' as a church family is important, just the same."*

✳ ✳ ✳

Winnie finished her dinner Thursday, did a quick clean up of the dishes, jumped in her car and drove to First Baptist Church. She was meeting with several other pastors in town that evening to prepare for the upcoming community Thanksgiving service.

Winnie walked into the fellowship hall with Dwight Gantry, the pastor at Ebenezer Missionary Baptist Church, and Matthew Brand, the pastor at Grace Pentecostal Church.

The meeting proceeded quickly with Pastor Gantry reading the minutes from the last meeting. Then Pastor Allen Remington (from St. Luke's Cumberland Presbyterian Church) passed out a spreadsheet detailing the activity of the community Traveler's Aid Account. This fund was kept for the explicit purpose of aiding travelers who might find themselves stranded in Misty Falls. It was generated by gifts given at the semi-annual community-wide worship services. All the pastors in Misty Falls each held vouchers that drew from this account, which were good for a tank of gas, a dinner, and/or an overnight stay at the local motel.

The main agenda item for this meeting was to set the date, time, location, and the preacher for the upcoming community-wide

Thanksgiving service. Minister Tinsley Booker, of Faith African Methodist Episcopal Church, offered to host the celebration at his church. "We just completed the renovation of our fellowship hall, and we'd be so pleased to serve as host for the Thanksgiving community gathering," Booker offered.

Everyone in the room agreed and thanked Minister Tinsley for offering his church.

"I'm sure my people will be happy to hear that we'll be hosting the event end of November. Of course the host church isn't the one to provide the preacher, so I'd like to nominate Pastor Winnie Taylor to be our speaker," Tinsley suggested.

As Tinsley sat down Pastor Matthew Brand seconded the motion.

"Yes, we should hear Pastor Winnie, after all, she's our newest clergyperson here in Misty Falls, and she hasn't spoken at one of our community gatherings. yet," Ken Creighton, the Baptist pastor, suggested.

It was decided by a unanimous agreement that Pastor Taylor from Muddy Creek UMC would be the one to bring the message on the Sunday evening just before Thanksgiving.

So, Winnie was signed up to preach. *"What an honor!"* She thought privately, and then a moment later, *"an extra sermon to prepare that week!"* Her initial elation abated just a bit with the second realization.

Tinsley agreed to design the service and to prepare the bulletin for it. The music would be in the hands of music people from the various churches, headed up by Joe Ed Rafferty, First Baptist's choir director.

A final prayer to close the meeting was in order when Pastor Allen Remington spoke up.

"I need to say something, but I'm not quite sure how to begin," he said. "I've been pondering this thing for a while. I made a mistake, and I need to tell y'all."

All eyes and ears were fixed on Brother Allen.

"Back in April our last community event was at St. Luke's, as you know. I had a good bit on my mind just then, and, you could say, I was distracted. Anyway, after the service everyone went over to Carter's Hall for fellowship. I remember talking to my trustee about the roof on our Sunday school building that was leaking. Another church member came over and the three of us talked in the corner for quite a while. By the time the ladies had cleaned up, and everyone else had taken off, I left for home.

"What I'm saying is that nobody picked up the offering that we took that night. It was still in the basket where it had been left in the sanctuary. The next morning I went to the sanctuary and looked for the basket with the collection, and the basket was there, but the money was gone. I thought, maybe, I'd put it somewhere different, but I couldn't remember if I had. I know I should have been more attentive about it, but obviously I wasn't."

Pastor Lorentzen asked, "So you think that someone else picked up the collection?"

"I thought something like that had happened. I know I would have been responsible for banking the collection the next day, but there wasn't anything to bank. I waited for a while, thinking something would show up, but nothing ever did. I waited and waited, and the money was just gone!"

"I know I should have said something about this before, but I didn't, and I owe y'all a great apology for that!"

A second later Tinsley chimed in, "I'm glad you shared this with us. It must have been a painful thing to have held it back for so long. I think we understand, and I, for one, accept your apology."

Everyone else in the room nodded or murmured a similar note of agreement to Pastor Remington. He smiled, weakly, and said, "Thank you Tinsley, for your kindness and the rest of you, too. I feel really foolish in all this, and the worst of it all is keeping it a secret for so long! How in the world did I ever think that was right? How in the world did I think I would be a good spiritual leader of my flock with that sort of thing hanging over my head?"

Dwight Gantry spoke up, "It sounds like someone helped themselves to the offering that night. An opportunity arose; the money was lifted; a crime took place. I suppose we should bring this to Sheriff Barrymore's attention."

Matthew Brand said, "Brother Allen, we're all sinners. We all fail, everyday, and we need the grace of God in Christ to pick us up, dust us off, and put us on the right path again. Thank you for sharing your pain with us, for trusting us with that. As far as I'm concerned, you are forgiven."

Again, nods were seen around the table. Allen Remington, who was still standing, smiled and said, "This calls for prayer. Brother Kenneth, would you lead us?" At this the whole group bowed their heads while Kenneth prayed, thanking God for the gift of forgiveness and the wonder of the Holy Spirit, Who was working among them and in their community.

Winnie was full of deep thoughts on her way home that evening, but she felt good inside. She had been moved by Brother Allen's admission of failure, and she was pleased to see how well his story was received and accepted, and forgiven, by his fellow pastors. *This is a good community to work and live in.*

✳ ✳ ✳

Sunday began before dawn for Winnie, as per usual, since she began preaching. There was always much to do before folks arrived at church, especially the final polishing of her sermon. Winnie liked to run through her message once in the sanctuary on Sunday morning, just to get a feel for the flow of her words, to secure within herself the direction she was going with it.

This morning she would be focusing on the times when people experience a "dark night of the soul" (as St. John of the Cross once put it) — a most painful time in life. Surely everyone has such an event at some time in their lives, and for some people, those dark times color much of what they live with every day.

It is Christ who brings healing and forgiveness, comfort and light, guidance and wisdom to us. When we look to Jesus, our Lord and Savior, for help we find Him there for us, ready to reach into our world and make all things new again.

Winnie planned to use an example from her own childhood to help listeners identify with their own dark times. Her example was laughable now, fifty some years after the fact, but when she was in first grade the lie she told to her teacher, and then to her mother, was not funny. Winnie saw the lie expand and grow into a bigger and bigger monster after each retelling. By the end of the week Winnie was in a frightful place in her spirit. She was very confused and in pain, until finally, with great, heaving sobs, she told her mother the truth. THEN! Suddenly, the heavens seemed to open and the sun came out and shown down on her, smiling. She was finally free of the lie, and all was once again well for her.

Winnie smiled and shook her head remembering that time, so very long ago, when she learned for the first time how painful sin can be and how wonderful the truth is, exposing the lie. It had been an important lesson to carry with her down the years, helping to remember the wisdom she learned at that tender age.

After church, as Pastor Winnie stood at the entry of Muddy Creek's sanctuary, shaking hands with her congregation, she heard several of her people whisper, "Thanks, I really needed to hear that." Winnie smiled and thanked her encouragers politely and sincerely. *"The truth is I need to hear your words, too,"* she admitted to herself. In fact the occasional kind remark from a constituent went a long way to help Winnie when she struggled with her studies to find the right message for Sunday. Knowing that she had been helpful to others as they sought to follow the Lord provided Winnie reason to work hard each week.

5. An Announcement

All the church had been abuzz with the news! Yesterday in Sunday School and at worship, Tim Owens made an announcement.

Tim and Mary Lou Owens had long been members at Muddy Creek Church — growing up in Misty Falls, going through school together, and being active in Muddy Creek's high school youth group. Tim continued on to state college, while Mary Lou joined her mother working at Misty Falls' Little Lambs Pre-School and Day Care. She married Tim when he returned to town and secured a position in management at a local factory. They had been married fifteen years and expected children. Goodness knows they were looking forward to having children. But none had come.

Winnie believed they had sought advice and help from several sources, but apparently to no avail. Winnie had met with the Owenses before, and she knew that having children had become a point of conflict for them. They had considered adoption, but that would be expensive, and they weren't sure it was right for them.

The announcement Tim made Sunday was about a cousin of his who lived down on the gulf. Tim's cousin and his wife had been in terrible automobile wreck the day before! The wife died instantly, and Tim's cousin wasn't expected to live. The whole church clutched as they absorbed the terrible news. Tim's announcement wasn't complete. It seems that Tim's cousin and his wife had four children, all under eight years old. The youngest was barely out of diapers. The children were with Tim's uncle and aunt, but they needed to be with their son who was lying in the Trauma ICU at the hospital.

Tim and Mary Lou would be driving to the gulf to pick up the kids and some of their belongings and carry them back to Misty Falls for the duration. They would be back in town in a couple of days, as soon as they could get things arranged.

While Winnie was shocked and surprised along with everyone else that morning, she instinctively led the community in special prayers for Tim's cousin and his entire family as they struggled with this great trial. She asked God to give the Owens family strength, wisdom, and love as they picked up the responsibility of caring for the four young children. She also asked God's help for Muddy Creek as they sought ways to help Tim and Mary Lou respond to this unexpected challenge.

Please God, let Your joy win out in this season of sorrow!

✻ ✻ ✻

A couple days later Winnie stopped at FRIENDLY'S FOODS to pick up a couple items and saw Tuck gazing out the window. Winnie couldn't resist asking him, "Is there something out there that we all should be looking at?"

Tuck seemed not to hear her.

"He's lost in thought," mused Winnie. She tried again. "Got something on your mind, Tucker Joe?"

Tuck turned around, saw Winnie standing there holding a small hand basket, and smiled. "I guess I was day dreaming," Tuck admitted.

"Sorry I woke you up" teased Winnie.

"No harm! I guess I was j'st thinkin'."s

"It must have been deep thought. I've been standing here a couple of minutes, and you didn't see me. Was it a good dream?"

"It j'st might be the greatest dream," Tuck admitted.

"I won't be nosey, but you can tell me, if you'd like," Winnie offered.

"Can't say nothin' yet. Too many 'ifs' and 'ors' to say anything, but maybe things are gonna change," Tuck speculated.

"Sounds a bit mysterious," Winnie answered.

Tucker answered, "I was thinking about something I saw on my computer this morning. It may mean nothing, but, well, I'll have to see."

Winnie saw that Tucker Joe was back to thinking to himself. *Wonder what's got him dreaming?*

She turned back to her shopping, moving over to the vegetable section and spotted Miss Jillian Post, the owner of one of the antique shops in town. Jillian was coming toward her.

Jillian, who was an attractively dressed woman (always fitted with the latest fashion and spiked heels), could be heard from across the apples saying, "Ms. Winnie, I see you over there pinching the tomatoes!"

"*I suppose she's jesting,*" Winnie thought, but just to be sure she said, "I'm not exactly pinching them, in fact I was just comparing this tomato (she held it up and turned it around) with a couple I was just given. I'm the thankful recipient of much produce — zucchinis, and beans, and, corn, and tomatoes — from my church members. That's definitely one of the bennies I get for being a country pastor."

Jillian had stepped over to where Winnie was standing and picked up a beefsteak tomato herself. "I envy you for that!" Jillian admitted. "Whenever I can get homegrown veggies, especially tomatoes, it's a whole different kind of taste experience than what we get from a store."

"I wonder what really makes the difference in the taste?" Winnie asked. "Sometimes really good-looking tomatoes have no taste at all! They're such a disappointment!"

"Miss Winnie, may I ask you a question?" Jillian ventured.

Winnie smiled, leaned a bit closer to Jillian, and said softly, "You can ask me anything you'd like."

"Well, I just wondered if you'd ever had an email pen-pal — an ePal?" Jillian asked.

"Hm. I probably have a couple dozen friends that I might call ePen Pals these days. But maybe you're talking about someone outside the usual bunch of folks we regularly email, right?" Winnie asked.

Jillian dropped her voice a bit and said, "I'm talking about someone I've never met in person."

Winnie had an idea where Jillian was headed with this thought. She said, "These days we have more ways of meeting people, what with all the fancy technology available, but I think you're asking me if I've ever 'met' someone online and begun a relationship there? Do you have someone specific in mind?" Winnie asked.

Jillian's smile was hard to squelch. She tried to hold in her news, but she realized that Winnie was intuiting her situation pretty well. "I don't think I'm at liberty to say much, just yet, but suffice it to say that, yes, I have met someone online, and I find myself spending more and more time thinking about him. I just wanted to know if you have ever known anyone like me, who has met a significant other that way?"

Winnie wanted to share Jillian's excitement, but she also thought she owed her a second opinion. "Sounds like you might be falling for this person!" (Jillian's eyes were opening widely, but she held her tongue.) "It might be pretty easy to fall for someone who sounds really interesting from afar, but how do you suppose you can really know such a person? We've both heard of situations when people have been duped by someone presenting him or herself to be something he or she is not. I suppose you just have to be careful!"

Jillian smiled a bit mysteriously and said, "You're right, I do have someone in mind, but there's nothing specific to say, yet. I met a man online, in a chat room, and he does sound like a genuinely nice person. I think he has good values, and we have enjoyed emailing back and forth. I've never met him, and I don't know how we might ever meet, because he lives quite a ways from here!"

43

Winnie lifted both her eyebrows and knitted them together. "Well, that does present several problems, beyond the usual boy meets girl sort of narrative. I do think, though, that you should . . . just be careful!"

Afterward, Winnie was thoughtful about her conversation with Jillian. She hadn't known her very well before this encounter at FRIENDLY'S FOODS. Their exchange had shed light on the owner of Post's Antiques. Winnie wondered if Jillian was lonely. She certainly could be.

As Winnie stepped out of the store, she saw another woman walking toward her. She was tall and tanned, possibly from a trip to the beach. She was a strikingly pretty woman, obviously new to Misty Falls. She smiled down at Winnie as they passed.

"She is definitely NOT from around here," Winnie thought.

＊ ＊ ＊

Two days later Winnie met Nina for lunch. They met at the diner next to the train depot. Nina was already waiting for Winnie, sitting in one of the side booths, sipping her iced, sweet tea.

"I see you've got a start on me, already," Winnie teased.

Ruby Anders, the diner owner, appeared and handed Winnie her menu. "Specials today are catfish fillets, meat loaf, and chicken fingers. Sides include fried okra, sliced tomatoes, smashed potatoes, collard greens, coleslaw, and pickled onions."

"Thanks, Miss Ruby. Sounds really good. I'll start with ice tea, unsweet, please," Winnie ordered.

Nina and Winnie met a couple years ago, just after Winnie arrived in town. She had decided to take a walking tour of the town, which, she had been told, could be accomplished in about ninety minutes. Winnie took her dog, Pansy, with her on the walk. They found Nina sitting on a stone bench in the town cemetery.

"It's a pretty day to sit here," observed Winnie. Nina looked up and smiled at the newcomer. "Yes, I come here about once a week to spend time. It's very peaceful." Nina agreed.

Winnie said, "I suppose you live here in Misty Falls."

"Yes, I've been here for nearly a quarter century. I came here as a young wife and mother when my husband, Dan, was transferred here. We came from New Orleans, via Jackson."

"Do you still have family there?" Winnie asked.

"Not since Katrina. I do have a cousin over in Slidell and another by Lake Charles, but no one in New Orleans," Nina told her.

"This is the first time I've seen this cemetery. It's really peaceful," Winnie noted, pointing to the many beautiful azaleas and honeysuckles that were blooming.

"Yes, it belongs to the citizens of Misty Falls. It's been here since President Jackson's time, nestled up against Mc Curry Mountain. I guess you can learn a lot of Misty Falls' history just reading the headstones," Nina suggested.

"I'll have to do that. I want to learn all I can about Misty Falls. I'm new here," Winnie explained.

"I figured as much. I haven't seen you before. What brings you here?" Nina asked curiously.

"I'm the new pastor at Muddy Creek United Methodist Church," explained Winnie. I was just appointed to preach there in June. Are you a church person?"

"No. I don't do church." Nina admitted.

Winnie smiled and nodded her head. She intuited Nina's reasons and didn't want to force her new acquaintance to defend her position. Instead she decided to voice them for her. "I understand some people have been hurt by church people. That's very sad. I'm sorry if you've had a bad experience!"

Nina smiled in relief and changed the subject. "How do you like Misty Falls?"

"I do. This is a good town, and everyone seems to be friendly and welcoming. I do know, though, that I shall always be a newbie as far as the Misty Fallers are concerned," Winnie commented.

"Yes, me too. Just because I've been here more 'n two decades makes no difference to the natives here. I'm still 'new'; I'm still from somewhere else," agreed Nina. "But Dan is here," Nina explained, waving her hand toward a gray stone marker. "I didn't want to leave him here, and the kids were only half grown and in school when we lost him. So I stayed and raised them here."

"What do you do here." Winnie wanted to know.

"I'm a nurse, an RN. I work for Dr. Sedgwick over on First Avenue; I also work some weekends at the clinic in town."

Winnie smiled as she learned about this new acquaintance. She was a talented woman who had raised her family alone. "Are any of your kids still in the area?" she asked.

"Not in Misty Falls, but my son, Todd, lives within a couple of hours drive. So I do see him pretty often. My daughter and her family are up in Illinois. I'd like to see them more often than I do. A grandmother needs to be able to see those grandchildren, don't you agree?"

"Yes! It's nice, if you can arrange it," Winnie said.

They talked on and on that afternoon. Nina joined Winnie and Pansy on their course around town and pointed out landmarks and spoke of interesting personalities that Winnie, no doubt, would meet as she came to know Misty Falls better. The day closed with the two having dinner together at The Depot Diner, next to the train station, and they had become fast friends.

They were back at the diner for lunch today and Winnie was pleased how their friendship had grown. She did wonder if there was a key to Nina's reluctance about things "spiritual," but she was determined to have patience and let Nina find her own way to tell her. "*Maybe she will share her thoughts on spiritual matters with me one day,*" Winnie hoped.

✳ ✳ ✳

Later at the office, Winnie found an attorney's website that looked promising, and she made a call. After explaining the situation to the lawyer, how she had a congregant who needed to find an inexpensive way to end a marriage, she heard the answer she was hoping to find. The lawyer would meet with the couple for half an hour for twenty-five dollars. They could explain the situation to him, and he would tell them what the cost would be to get the divorce. This would include the filing fees and whatever it took to get the agreement from the other spouse. This, of course, was all dependent on it being an uncontested divorce.

Winnie called Kevin with the news. He was pleased to hear about the attorney, and he promised his pastor that he and Sheryl Lynn would follow up on her work and see where it led them. They ended the conversation with much encouragement, hoping that there could be a wedding down the road after all had been said and done.

Church went well Sunday morning. Winnie seemed to rediscover each week that she really did like to preach! Despite being a normally gregarious person, Winnie had to consciously and physically fight her nervousness every Sunday prior to the moment she began to preach. After her first few sentences, however, she was completely engaged in the message, sharing with her community what she had been working on. She realized that when she found a message, and believed it was a good message, then it was a delight to share it with others. It was rather like a great story that she had come upon and now wanted to tell to everyone! It was fun, really; at least it was in hindsight.

6. Trip Into Town

Sunday was exciting! Tim and Mary Lou Owens arrived at church with their four new charges in tow. The kids were, for the most part, quiet and shy, especially the two younger ones who clung to their aunt and uncle. Little Carlie, who was not yet three, held tightly to her Aunt Mary Lou with both hands. Mary Lou, as a brand new mother, could hardly move with this terrified three-year-old gripping her with such determination. She couldn't quite decide if it was better to simply carry the child on her hip or set her on the ground and hold her hand. Carlie had been crying, you could tell from the streaks of redness on her face, but she had settled down once she heard Tim starting the motor of his car for their ride to church.

Mary Lou also held the hand of Katelyn, Carlie's sister. Five year old Katelyn was also struggling with this new experience, but she was trying to be a big sister for her younger siblings. Katelyn carried a large, well-loved chocolate-colored teddy bear in her arms. She had been clinging to her bear since the accident, and Tim and Mary Lou recognized the wisdom of having her good friend bear close by.

Tim was leading the two brothers — Thomas and Andy. He had taken each boy by hand, affording himself nothing with which to operate doors. The boys were silent, trudging after their uncle like little sleep walkers.

The kids were dressed reasonably well, considering how this young family was new to Tim and Mary Lou. They had not been able to bring much of a wardrobe of clothes for the children, as they were limited by space in their car. The Owenses had been up for several hours working with the kids, getting them all ready for their first trip out, which would be to Muddy Creek Church. Having absolutely no experience in getting children ready for church, they actually felt rather proud of their managing all the details of dressing and fixing breakfast for their charges before they left the house.

Letitia Washington saw the new family approaching the Sunday school building and opened the door, welcoming them in. Letitia, being the mother of a four year old herself, as well as a school teacher, responded immediately when she saw the need of settling these children into a Sunday school class and making them feel comfortable.

Letitia was one of the adult Sunday school teachers, so she sent word to her class to begin without her — that she would be coming before long. Then she led Mary Lou and the two younger kids — Andy and Carlie — to her son's class. Mary Lou stayed with them for the class.

Tim was able to find the primary class, which was the right group for Katelyn and Thomas. When they walked into their classroom and saw a dozen first and second grade children there they seemed happy to join them.

The whole morning went well. The new Owens family stayed after worship for the fellowship dinner, and the kids played on the playground with some of their new friends from church. They were beginning to feel a bit less strange and different in this new world of theirs. Tim and Mary Lou had just leapt the first hurdle in the game of parenting, and they were pleased with themselves to see that they had managed so far with their new project.

✳ ✳ ✳

Tuesday afternoon Winnie saw the same, pretty, tanned woman she had seen the week before outside FRIENDLY'S FOODS. She was exiting the post office and walking right toward her.

The two stopped and spoke to each other for a few minutes.

"Are you new in town?" Winnie asked.

"Not really. I've been away for a while, but I grew up here" Lucy Jane answered.

Winnie smiled. "I'll bet your family is pleased that you're home. What brings you back here, if I may ask?"

Lucy explained, "My husband, Chet, was diagnosed with an aggressive form of cancer back in May, and in less than six weeks he was gone! It was the second marriage for both of us. Neither of us had any children, but we were hoping to start a family, and then this." Her voice trailed off.

Winnie listened to the young woman and silently heaved a sigh. "I know how painful it is to lose your husband. It hasn't been very long for you, and your grief is still very fresh. I know it doesn't help to hear this now, but in time it will hurt a little less. It's good that you came back to be with family."

After a short moment, Winnie changed the subject. "Are you working somewhere?"

Lucy looked up and said, "Yes, I was able to transfer my job with the Red Cross to their office over in the city. I have a twenty-five minute drive in the mornings, but it's not too bad. I'm glad to have the job, and I'm also glad to be here. I tell myself, 'It's gonna' be all right, Lucy Jane. This is just a really weird time in your life. You just have to hang in there.'"

Winnie picked up Lucy Jane's hand and gave it a squeeze. "You are a wise young woman, Miss Lucy Jane. I've known some widows who can't seem to get their heads around their loss, and they get stuck permanently in pain."

"Oh, I have my moments, sometimes days and days, it seems, but I'm trying to see God's guiding me even in this time."

Winnie was pleased to hear these words of faith from Lucy. "You must be a woman of faith! Have you found a fellowship here in town?"

Lucy explained that she was attending church with her family — her father, her aunt, her brother and his family. They were long-time members of St. Luke's Cumberland Presbyterian Church.

The two new friends stood chatting for several minutes more before they went their separate ways.

"What an interesting woman! A new widow, but so young. Poor dear! She was smart to come home and start over," Winnie mused. She knew she would have good emotional support with her family and her church family close by.

✳ ✳ ✳

Winnie decided to stop by St. Luke's to check up on her friend Pastor Allen Remington. After his surprising admission at the meeting a couple weeks ago, she expected he would have met with Sheriff Barrymore to start an investigation. She hoped things would get ironed out or settled without much ado.

Winnie rang the bell and opened the door when the buzzer indicated it was unlocking. The pastor's office was just down the hall. Winnie saw the door was ajar, and she peeked in.

"Hi Allen!" Winnie called.

Allen, looked up, saw it was Winnie, smiled broadly, and said, "Well! Good to see you, too, Winnie. Come on in!"

Winnie advanced to a chair in the office opposite the pastor's chair and sat down.

"What can I do for you this fine day?"

"That's what I came to ask you, Allen," Winnie explained. "Your quandary has been on my mind, and I wanted to know how things are going for you now?"

"Oh! Yes. Actually, Ken and Tinsley went with me over to see Sheriff Barrymore the next day, and I put in a complaint about the missing funds. The sheriff agreed that the trail was pretty cold, but he logged the complaint and followed me back here. He looked all around the sanctuary to see how things are: where the collection plates were stored; where they had been placed after taking the offering that evening; where the side door to the chancel is located; if it had a lock on it; was there a separate door exiting the building that was not through the fellowship area, etc."

"He said he was afraid that the money might never be accounted for, especially given the tardiness of my reporting the crime. I think he's just going to let it go, and not pursue any legal claim against me," Pastor Allen explained.

Winnie's face showed relief, and she said, "I'm sure he's right about that. What good would that accomplish to indict you for forgetfulness? We know you didn't purposefully hide the money from yourself."

Winnie was pleased to learn that the matter had been noted officially with the sheriff. She said, "Sounds like y'all were able to set the record straight on the incident. Goodness knows if the thief can be caught, but at least you've done what you can for now."

Pastor Allen seemed much lighter of spirit today in contrast to his mood at the meeting. "Glad you stopped by, Winnie," he said as she turned to leave his office.

※ ※ ※

Winnie drove into the city later that week. She took Trudy, a young, African American mother-to-be, to the free clinic for an appointment. Winnie dropped her off at the office while she made several stops she needed to make in town.

The mall was one of those stops. Winnie was on the second floor of the mall when she spotted Tucker Joe Tennyson in front of her, just coming out of a store.

"Well! For goodness sakes! Tucker Joe! Are you here, too? I didn't know you took time off!"

Tuck grinned at Miss Winnie and said, "Yes! In fact I'm gettin' a regular day off nowadays. I can leave the store in Martha Reeves' care. She's been with Mother and me at the store for over twenty years. She knows the store inside and out. I've been taking Thursdays off, just for me, since. . ."

Winnie caught the drift of what Tucker was saying, "Since we lost Mother?"

"Yes, since we lost Mother. It's not that I couldn't take time off before, I could. But it was more often an afternoon, or a couple hours here or there. When you own a store, it's hard to git time off. Mother and I worked the store together ever since Pappy passed. He and Mother built the store and put their blood, sweat, and tears in it. I always owed it to Mother to lean into the job and make it good for both of them."

"And now you can find a whole day to take off. Sounds good to me. We all need time off from work occasionally. Even on a regular basis. What's that saying, "all work and no play makes Jack a dull boy?" Winnie teased.

"There's wisdom in that saying, I'm sure," Tuck agreed. "Anyway I'm here, and it feels good."

"That sounds like a fun change for you," Winnie observed. She was about to say, "since you lost your mother," but she thought better of it and didn't.

Winnie was aware that there are some men who don't marry until their mothers had passed on. She couldn't quite figure out why a man would wait so long, sometimes even into his fifties or so, but she had heard it happens, and she wondered if that might be the case here.

Winnie said, "Your family's from Misty Falls, isn't it? How many years have the Tennyson's been here?"

"On my father's side my family goes back five generations. My great-great grandfather was the first Tennyson to settle in this area. On Mother's side we go back four generations in this area. Mother's folks came from North Carolina. Back then they were all farmers, of course. They had a land grant from Jackson, like several families around here," Tucker explained.

"Your roots really run deep! You must know absolutely everyone in Misty Falls," Winnie said.

"I guess I do know a lot of folks, 'specially the ones I knew growing up. We go back a long way. But there are new folks these days I don't know much at all. Course, I know you! You're an easy one to get to know, Miss Winnie," Tucker assured her.

The wheels in Winnie's mind spun, and she figured that Tucker might know something about the woman she'd met earlier at the post office, and she wondered how to ask him, without sounding like she was insinuating herself where she didn't belong. "You would know a family named Smith, then. I just heard about them the other day," said Winnie.

"Smith! I'll bet there are a dozen Smith families in just this county, maybe more!" Tucker laughed.

"I met a really sweet woman the other day who told me she had just returned from somewhere out of state to live here. She said that she'd grown up here. Her maiden name was Smith," Winnie explained.

"You met Lucy Jane, did you! I heard she was back in Misty Falls. I haven't seen her in years. We knew each other in school. She was a year ahead of me, but we both played in the band in high school. I haven't heard much about her since she left, but she sure was a cutie when I knew her!" Tucker laughed.

Winnie could see all sorts of possibilities for the two of them down the road. She thought, *"Who knows what might come of this!"*

✳ ✳ ✳

On her way back to the clinic to pick up Trudy, Winnie noticed several of the cars ahead of her were swerving, as if to avoid something on the road. The car in front of Winnie moved aside, and suddenly Winnie saw a small, very furry dog running around in the middle of the street, not knowing which way to go. Winnie was nearly at the corner, so she maneuvered her car around the bend, slowed to a stop, and opened her car door.

As she opened the door the small, furry creature jumped into her lap!

"Goodness! Who are you?" Winnie asked the pup. she closed the door, so the pup wouldn't jump out again into further danger on the road.

"You are nothing more than a 'bit!'" 'Winnie told her. "What in the world am I supposed to do with you? You're not in the least like any dog I've ever seen before!" The puppy was sitting on Winnie's lap; she patted the pup's fly-away hair and noticed how very soft it was — like very fine, silky strands, thickly clumped together and sticking straight out from her body. The result of all this fine, thick mop of fur made the pup look about twice as big as she actually was.

"Goodness, Doggy, you've just begun in this life, and I'm sure there's a lot of work needed to properly care for you. Hmmmmm. I think maybe the LORD has answered my prayer about a companion in an unexpected way!"

Winnie talked to the pup all the way to the clinic, where she picked up Trudy. She told Trudy "I'll have to make some inquiries about this dog's ownership, but I have a feeling that my household has just increased by one!"

Trudy thanked Miss Winnie for driving her to the clinic and said something about coming to Muddy Creek for worship one of these days. Winnie always wondered what folks who say "I'll come [to church]" actually do when Sunday morning rolls around. "Do you suppose they are even aware that it's Sunday morning, and the thing to be doing is getting yourself to worship?" she asked the little pup.

7. An Unexpected Delivery

Life with the pup, who soon came to be known as Bitty, brought back memories of other dogs from other times for Winnie. She had not trained a puppy in years, but the pup's needs were pretty obvious. She needed to be fed, watered, exercised, and TRAINED for the house!

Bitty was a smart little pooch. She was friendly, as puppies are, and she very quickly became a great companion to Winnie. It wasn't long before Bitty was thoroughly familiar with her new home surroundings. She seemed to delight in racing full out through the parsonage, chasing after some unknown, illusive playmate. She would race in circles, round and round, in the open areas in the living room, and then she'd turn back to the bedrooms and zip around each room, as if she had a pre-planned par course she must accomplish in record time. Watching such activity in the new pup caused Winnie to shake her head and laugh, "Bitty you are a terrible scamp! Where do you get so much energy?"

Winnie realized that most of the dog paraphernalia she had on hand was too big for Bitty. Pansy hadn't been all that big a dog, but she was grown, and her accouterments were too big. Winnie made a quick stop at FRIENDLY'S FOODS' pet section and picked up a couple of items that would tide them over. "I don't know that I'm ready for you to be here. I didn't exactly choose you! But it seems, like it or not, I guess you're here to stay!" Winnie told to the little pooch.

Winnie mused that the good Lord surely loved all His creatures. "He helped you find a place where you'll be cared for," she told the pup.

Bitty was not a very large dog, but her fur stuck straight out all over her, and it was especially thick around her neck and tail. "Wonder what sort of pooch you are? You look like you got into an altercation with an electrical outlet and lost the battle! Your hair is an absolute mess! No matter, it's nice to have you around," she assured the dog.

※ ※ ※

Sunday had gone well, thankfully. The Owens family was back in church. Tim told his Sunday school class about the adventures he and Mary Lou were having being parents so unexpectedly. He said he'd heard from his uncle, the children's grandfather, who reported that the children's father wasn't expected to live; he was still in a coma from the accident— there was no indication of brain activity. Tim thought he'd be hearing more news soon from his uncle and the family would need to make another trip to the gulf soon when the news came.

Tim said that the kids were doing pretty well, considering the great change in their lives. The older two were settling into school, and the two pre-schoolers were with Mary Lou at the day care where she worked. Tim thanked everyone for their prayers and encouragement and mentioned the sizes of the kids, in case anyone had any hand-me-downs. The Owenses had brought clothes from their home on the gulf, but these children were growing, and new clothes would be needed soon.

※ ※ ※

Wednesday afternoon Winnie was just getting out of her car, having been away most of the afternoon, when she noticed something sitting next to the front door, something apparently left by a delivery person. *Wonder what it could be?*

Winnie jumped out of her car and went over to retrieve the package. It had her name on it: "Ms. Winnie Taylor."

The return address had only a street, city, and zip code, no name. *How curious!* She wasted no time in tearing open the brown paper wrapping and pulling out a book.

Who's sending me a book? The volume was small, soft cover, with a blue-toned picture of a lake with a dock and a large bird winging its way over the water. The title was *Finding Your Moorings* by Jonathan C. Daniel, Ph.D.

"That's John!" Winnie exclaimed to the air. "This must be one of his books! He did say that he did some writing, along with his teaching."

Winnie opened the book and saw an inscription on the inside cover:

"To find one true friend in a lifetime is good fortune; to keep him is a blessing." — Baltazar Gracian, 17 C Spanish philosopher. Here's to friendship! Yours, John."

Goodness! He just sent me a present — that's an intriguing move! She flipped through the book. It was filled with one page thoughts, almost like those in her morning devotional books, but, of course, these thoughts were not based on holy scripture. The book did have wisdom from various sources that were highlighted a day at a time. *"This is a sort of 'Devotional for the Armchair Philosopher,"* thought Winnie. "This should be fun!" She chuckled out loud.

Although John and Winnie had attended the same high school and even been in a couple classes together, they had not been friends — not back then. John, Winnie remembered, had been part of a small group of young men at her school who were exceptionally gifted. The seven or eight of them started a very exclusive club they called "The Oligarchy." It wasn't an official club on campus, but they <u>were</u> well known, nonetheless. They were the top students in the Class of 68, taking all the honors classes. and they would, no doubt, be among the leaders of tomorrow.

"I haven't thought about those guys forever!" Winnie smiled. *"Wonder what became of them? No doubt they have all gone their separate ways since graduation."*

Winnie had found the announcement of Mile High High School's Fortieth Year Reunion on Facebook, as John had told her. Winnie had attended the fifth and the tenth high school reunion. She missed the later ones — the twentieth and the thirtieth reunion, and she didn't realize it was time for the fortieth reunion until John called and mentioned it. *"It would be fun to attend."* Winnie thought. *"You never know who'll show up to those events, AND, of course, I could use the opportunity to check up on my folks."*

Attending a reunion could coincide with a trip to see Mom and Dad. They were still living in their home in Denver, and Winnie looked for reasons to visit them. *"Coupling such a visit with my high school reunion would make it a double blessing."* She decided to make arrangements to go. *"I'll have to find a substitute preacher for that Sunday!"* She realized.

※ ※ ※

Thursday afternoon Winnie stopped at the bank and was greeted by Bradley Washington, the bank manager and a member at Muddy Creek Church.

"Afternoon, Pastor Winnie," he said. "Are you coming to see me today?"

"Good to see you, Bradley," Winnie answered. "Actually, I'm here to make a deposit. I don't have any pressing bank business today. How's your family?"

Letitia, Bradley's wife, had a father who was a Baptist pastor in South Carolina. Letitia was a third grade teacher at the David Crockett Elementary School in town; she also taught the adult Sunday school class at church. Bradley and Letitia had a four year old son they called Little Brad.

"Little Brad comes home every day from his preschool with new questions. He's about to drive us crazy with his 'Why questions!' 'Why is the sky blue?' 'Why do I get thirsty?' 'Why do you go to work?' 'Why are there bugs in the garden?'" Bradley told Winnie.

Winnie laughed with Bradley at this long list of impossible questions Little Brad was plaguing his parents with. "Sounds like questions my own kids asked when they were about that age. The questions will change, of course, but the challenge continues: "How do I raise my child in the nurture and admonition of the LORD?"

Bradley winked at Winnie, nodded his head, and returned to his office.

As Winnie stepped in line to make her deposit, Vicky Jackson, who was standing two people in front of her, saw her pastor. She turned around and said, "Pastor Winnie. Wait for me a minute when we're through here, would you?"

A few minutes later the two women met in the vestibule of the bank and spoke.

Vicky spoke first. "Pastor Winnie, I just got some news!"

Winnie noticed that Vicky was looking serious. She asked, "What sort of news?"

Vicky nodded and explained. "We just heard that our shop is about to be bought by another business, and most of us will lose our jobs! Things don't look very good at the moment."

"How long have you known about this? Who else knows?" Winnie asked.

"I told Tom, of course, and the boys. It's just speculation, but we need to be prepared for whatever" Vicky confided.

Winnie asked Vicky, "What, exactly, does your shop do?"

"We make custom draperies for retail stores, mostly, although we can do custom work for designers, too. Our shop is being bought out by a bigger business."

"Maybe your news will turn out not to be news, after all," Winnie suggested. "I'd like to know what will happen. Please keep me informed, and let me know if there is anything I, or the church, can do."

Winnie was thoughtful after her bank visit. *"Sometimes it feels as if I'm living on the edge of life these days, like I'm watching everyone else living. The Washingtons and the Jacksons have their beautiful families to work with. Of course, I've already done all those parenting things, and Claire and Paul and their families are doing fine on their own now. I wouldn't have it any other way. They are both off doing what they should be doing in their respective worlds."*

"Winnie! Are you feeling sorry for yourself? Do you really think life is leaving you on the sidelines? You really do need to ask the Lord for forgiveness, if that's what you're carrying around with you! AND you also know that the He has great plans for you, even at your advanced age! You just need to be on the look out for them. Maybe that's what the Lord meant when he warned us to stay awake and watch!"

❋ ❋ ❋

The next day Winnie answered a phone call in her office from a woman in the city twenty minutes from Misty Falls.

The woman, who identified herself as Ms. Betty Hawkins from the mayor's office, asked to speak to the pastor in charge.

Winnie smiled to herself and told Ms. Hawkins that she, Pastor Winnie Taylor, was that person. "How can I help you?"

Ms. Hawkins explained that she was calling from the public relations department of the mayor's office. She was looking for a church that would be willing to accommodate a group of peace walkers making a trek across America. The walkers were on a mission of peace, carrying a flame from the city of Hiroshima, Japan all the way to Ground Level Zero in New York City. They had begun their American trek in Seattle about eight months ago. Their route took them down the west coast and then across the South before scooping back up the east coast to New York.

The twenty-two walkers, who were led by six Japanese, Buddhist monks, needed to be able to lay their sleeping bags down somewhere for the night. They had been averaging between fifteen and twenty miles each day on their long trek and had been staying each night at various churches. (A truck would bringing the walkers' provisions to their new overnight location each day.)

Ms. Hawkins explained that Muddy Creek was the first church she had contacted in Misty Falls to ask for help. "Would your church allow these travelers to use Muddy Creek United Methodist Church as a place to stop for the night?" she asked Winnie. "Oh! And they would appreciate having a nice breakfast made for them the next morning that would give them a good send off for their next day's walk." Ms. Hawkins added, "And they have a special request — they would really like to have grits on the menu; they've heard about grits and would like to experience the real thing, southern style!"

Winnie wondered, as she put down her phone, how her members would react to such a request. She had promised Ms. Hawkins that she would ask the people at Muddy Creek this coming Sunday if they thought this was something they could manage to do. She couldn't speak for them without asking first. She'd call Ms. Hawkins as soon as she knew how the Muddy Creekers would react to the request.

Winnie was intrigued with the idea of people from a very different faith coming to Muddy Creek and camping out in the church for a night. What should she think of that? What might she say to her folks about accepting or rejecting this proposal?

"This would be a great opportunity for Muddy Creek to show compassion and hospitality to strangers. That sounds like

something Jesus would approve of!" She smiled widely and thought, *"This is a fine opportunity for us to grow, maybe, in our understanding of folks who are different from us, but whom God has created in God's image, nonetheless. I hope my people will agree."* Winnie began looking forward to Sunday, just to learn how they would respond.

8. Sallie

Winnie was proud of her church members. She had spoken to the adult Sunday school class at church and explained to them about the peace walkers, telling them how the sojourners would be coming through Misty Falls at the end of October and were looking for a place to lay out their sleeping bags for the night. The walkers would prepare their own dinner, but they were hoping that the church members would make them a big, southern breakfast to gird them for their next day's trek. They would especially like to experience grits!

The request by the peace walkers was not met with open arms. Almost all of the fifteen Sunday school members had some objection. They speculated about what the walkers might do to their church property: "These people are not like us." "We don't know anything about them, except that their leaders are Japanese, Buddhist monks!" "What if they damage or steal something in the church." "We don't have any idea of what they might be bringing into our building; they might be carrying lice or fleas or worse!" "Who is going to be in charge of them while they are here?"

The concerns voiced by the Sunday school members gradually transitioned from worries about the physical logistics to what Winnie intuited was the deeper issue — that these travelers weren't Christians. They were Buddhists, and no one in the room really knew what that meant. "What do they believe? What does it mean to have non-Christians sleeping in our church?" "Might they influence our children in some way?"

Winnie understood that her people meant the best, but they were not thinking with very open minds about those who are a little different from themselves. She pointed out that the walkers hadn't received any bad press so far, and they had crossed a goodly portion of the country already, staying each night in places like Muddy Creek. "Bad news travels fast, doesn't it? We would have heard something about these folks if they had done anything newsworthy," Winnie pointed out.

"God tells us to be kind to the alien who is among us," Winnie added. "In Leviticus, Chapter Nineteen, we are told to treat aliens as if they were native-born. So if we need a scriptural reason for being kind to the walkers we have it right there."

Winnie further pointed out that there didn't seem to be too much required of Muddy Creek as far as accommodations were concerned. The travelers would be bringing their own sleeping gear, cook their own dinner, and clean up after themselves. The only real requirement seemed to be putting together a full-sized breakfast.

When Winnie reminded the class about the request for a big, southern breakfast, suddenly the mood of the group changed. Putting on a pot-luck meal was something this southern church knew it could do. Martha Reeves offered to make a couple of big pans of her famous, homemade biscuits. Her offer inspired Homer Randall to offer some sausage from his most recent load of pigs. He had just picked up the sausage from the meat packers. Bradley and Letitia Washington agreed to cook the scrambled eggs. Others chimed in with what they would like to include in the breakfast. In the end, not only did the idea of hosting the travelers pass, but everyone in class was excited about sharing their hospitality with these strangers.

Winnie chuckled to herself when she remembered how the class had navigated across a rather labored continuum, from being greatly averse to hosting the peace walkers, to making detailed plans for welcoming them! "Call Ms. Hawkins and tell her we'll do it!" There had been a couple of members who were still unsure about the project, but they agreed to not stand in the way of helping out the strangers.

✳ ✳ ✳

Monday morning, as Winnie walked over to the church, she saw a car parked in the church parking lot with a young woman sitting in the car.

Winnie approached the car, and the window came down.

"Good morning!'" Winnie said.

The driver of the car looked up at Winnie and smiled. Winnie noticed that the woman, who was not much more than eighteen or nineteen, was not alone in the car — there were a couple of car seats in the back of the car with two little children in them.

"Can I help you?" Winnie asked.

The young woman looked at Winnie and said, "I was hoping that y'all had food that I can git for my family."

Winnie nodded and told the young woman, "Yes, we have a food pantry here at the church. You're welcome to come in and get what you need."

The young woman opened her car door and got out. She waved at the back seat of her car and said, "My boys will be alright for a few minutes." She locked the car, leaving the window partly open and followed Winnie into the church.

Winnie introduced herself to the young woman and got her name, Linda Anderson.

Winnie learned that Linda was married to Josh. Their two little boys were a year apart, the older one being two and a half.

Winnie was pleased to meet this young woman — pleased that Muddy Creek could serve her in her family's need, and that, possibly, the church might help the family with more than just physical needs. Might it be that Muddy Creek could also help this young family to understand Christian faith? Might the church become a church home for them?

Winnie was always pleased to meet new people, being a very extroverted person herself. In the course of a few minutes conversation, it was apparent to Winnie that Linda and her family were poor.

Linda was barely twenty, yet she and Josh already had two babies. She had dropped out of high school in the middle of ninth grade and married Josh. *"Probably because child number one was on the way,"* Winnie hypothesized. Josh tried to stay in school to get his diploma, but taking care of the family and learning a trade came first. He worked as a carpenter's apprentice, which led the young family down to Florida in search of jobs and more training. Josh never completed his high school education, and after a couple years they decided to move back closer to home — to Misty Falls.

Winnie helped Linda fill a couple bags of groceries from the church pantry, took Linda's address and cell phone number, and saw her back to her car. Winnie was sure to invite Linda and her family to join her in worship at Muddy Creek next Sunday.

✳ ✳ ✳

Tuesday Winnie walked over to the post office after Bible study. The day was a windy one, and the temperature had cooled down several degrees, reminding everyone that fall was on its way. As Winnie arrived at the post office she saw Pearly Mae also arriving.

"Morning, Miss Winnie!" She smiled

Winnie smiled back at Pearly Mae. "Isn't it a gorgeous day, even with the wind?" she answered.

"I don't mind the wind; I am mighty pleased to just get around, even in this wind."

Winnie liked her friend's attitude and said, "Not everyone has your spunk! Wherever do you get it?"

"My Mama was a very strong woman! She could do the work of two men, I do believe. I think I git my strength from her."

Winnie wondered, "Is your mother still with us?"

"No, Ma'am. She was just short of a hundr'd years old when she passed back in '96." Pearly Mae answered.

"There's an age to aspire to!" Winnie winked at her friend.

"Sure it is!" agreed Pearly Mae, "But it's not so much the length of life that I deem important, as it is the kind of life I'm alivin'!"

"You're so right!" Winnie agreed.

"The kind of life we live is a great deal more important than the number of years we occupy this earth. When we follow Jesus we are called to be new creations, different from the people we were before," Pearly Mae declared.

"We are called to be the people that God wants us to be. I don't know that we really get a complete picture of what that means. We may have some surprises in the process," Winnie admitted.

"Most of the characters in the Bible were called to be something completely different than the world would have told them to be," Pearly Mae added.

Winnie enjoyed this little impromptu, theological exchange. She always enjoyed the quick conversations she had with Pearly Mae. Neither of them ever shied from speaking about their faith or the challenges they met along the way.

"That's one of the things I especially enjoy about you, Miss Pearly Mae! We don't just talk about the weather or things, we jump right into the good stuff, don't we?" Winnie teased her friend.

Pearly Mae smiled in assent. "Yes'M, We do. Since we're on the subject, I do have a request for a prayer from you," she continued, "My son, Dan, Jr., lives in Albuquerque, and he's coming out to see me."

Winnie's eyes sparkled. "How really special! You must be counting the days before he arrives!"

"I am, but I think there may be more to his agenda, and I'm not sure what to make of it," Pearly Mae confided.

"Hmm. Was it something he said?" Winnie asked.

"He did; and he didn't," Pearly Mae said. "He said something about hoping to 'close the loop' on something. He wasn't more specific than that. Maybe it was the way he said it, that made me uneasy."

Winnie nodded and said, "Maybe you're anxious about nothing. Anyway, it's not your business, you know. Your business is to support Dan Jr. and to be there for him. Trust the LORD to work the rest out in time."

Pearly Mae smiled. "I know you're right, Miss Winnie. I mustn't clutch or try to take over a problem that isn't mine. It's always good to remind ourselves that we must leave our trust where it belongs with the LORD and not run ahead of Him!"

Winnie said, "I'm here for you if you need someone to talk to. You know that!"

❊ ❊ ❊

Sometime back last summer Winnie met Sallie. She was an odd-looking woman who was standing under the eaves outside of FRIENDLY'S FOODS one afternoon, trying to avoid a typical summer downpour.

Sallie was not well dressed. She had worn down sandals on her feet and a sleeveless dress that almost covered her very, very, well endowed self. She was more than just a bit overweight; she was a very large woman.

Winnie couldn't quite remember how she and Sallie got into conversation, but the next thing she knew, Winnie had agreed to help the woman make a phone call to some little town in South Carolina. Sallie was most anxious to make the call, but she didn't have a phone. She seemed desperate to talk to her daughter.

Winnie thought it would be kind to help her make such a call, so she drove Sallie over to Winnie's office at church.

That was her introduction to Sallie, and eventually Winnie also became aware of Connie, Sallie's daughter. Connie lived in South Carolina, where Sallie had come from.

Apparently Connie was expecting a baby, and she and her husband had just learned that she was actually carrying twin girls! Sallie was very excited about the twins coming, as one might imagine, but there was more to the story, Winnie later discovered.

That was last summer. Sallie was living with her sister and brother-in-law in Misty Falls, but she didn't have a job. Winnie wondered what sort of work she might have ever done. Gradually, the story about Connie, her husband, George, and the soon-to-arrive twins came to light.

Thursday, about noon, Winnie received an animated phone call from Sallie. She was at the hospital in Knoxville and had called to say that the twin babies had arrived, safely, that morning — in a hospital in Knoxville, forty-five minutes from Misty Falls, not in South Carolina!

Sallie told Winnie that it was a long story, which she would explain to her very soon. Right now she needed Winnie to help her and Connie with some paperwork.

Winnie's ears naturally perked up when she heard that she might be able to help. Sallie agreed to meet Winnie at her office later that afternoon.

About four that afternoon, Sallie appeared at the church. Her sister had driven her to the hospital when word came that the twins girls had just arrived. Later that day, Sallie's sister dropped her off at Muddy Creek, so she could talk to Pastor Winnie.

According to Sallie, Connie and George had decided that their babies should be born outside of South Carolina. They were afraid that they might lose the babies to the DHR if they were born there. So the Oliver's (Connie and George) had taken a Greyhound bus to some place in Connecticut to stay with someone they knew who lived there. *"Could you make up a story so bizarre?"* Winnie wondered privately. The babies were nearly due when the couple began their trip to Connecticut, but upon arriving at the friend's house they realized that their plan wouldn't work. Their friend may have been horrified to learn that her visitors, and their soon-to-be-born twins, were planning on moving in with her and staying for an indefinite amount of time. That was much more than she had anticipated when she'd agreed to host them for a visit!

Where, then, could they go, Connie and George wondered? They would go to Sallie's!

Sallie, of course, was not living in a home of her own, rather she was staying with Sallie's sister and brother-in-law in Misty

Falls, TN. Nonetheless, the Olivers jumped on the next Greyhound bus and began the trip south to where Sallie was.

And, as it happened, Connie went into labor on the bus. By the time the bus was in Knoxville, Connie knew the babies would be coming pretty soon. Something needed to be done! The driver was informed of Connie's labor, so he drove to the nearest hospital and left the soon-to-be-parents at the hospital ER.

Shortly thereafter Sallie got a phone call from George saying that the babies were coming, causing Sallie and her sister to leave immediately for the hospital.

Winnie couldn't imagine that this was really happening, but there was Sallie sitting in front of her, completely swept up in the whole affair.

"How can I help?" Winnie asked, trying to figure out how she might weigh into this drama.

At this point Sallie related an even more bazaar tale.

"To begin with, Connie is my only child. I've raised her by myself, because her father has been in an insane asylum since she was small. It's not been easy; she's all I've got. Connie married George four years ago when she was still in school," Sallie told Winnie.

Winnie had her listening ears open, not wanting to interrupt Sallie's chain of thought; she simply nodded her head in understanding.

"They have had three babies before this, but they lost all three to the DHR." Sallie waited to see Winnie's reaction to that news.

Winnie's eyes opened wide and she asked, "The DHR, you mean the Department of Human Resources? They took the babies?"

"Yes, those guys. They took the children. They are now in foster homes in South Carolina," Sallie stated flatly.

"Hm. "I can certainly see how your daughter and her husband could be worried about their twins!" Winnie added.

"Exactly! They were immediately excited when they learned that their new baby was not one but two babies, and at the same time they were terrified that they might lose those babies!" Sallie remembered. "They feared that as soon as the DHR learned about the twins' coming they would be on their case and that their new babies might be taken, too!

"Excuse me!" Winnie interjected. "I'm missing something here. What in the world happened to cause the DHR to seize the children?"

Sallie explained that there had been an incident with the first baby. An allegation had been made that the child was not being treated properly — maybe it was a case of baby shaking. Maybe there was more than one incident. Sallie wasn't very clear about the events, but the final word was that the Oliver's new baby boy had been taken into protective services by the State of South Carolina.

The following year a second baby arrived. He had a slight case of cerebral palsy, and DHR was on the case quickly, due to the history Connie and George already had with them. The second child was taken from them for his own good.

The third child, a little girl, arrived the following year. Connie was nineteen by then. The baby didn't even come home with her parents from the hospital. She was put into DHR protection immediately.

When the Oliver's discovered that they were expecting again they had to do something to protect themselves from the DHR. Winnie could now at least understand why they fled. *"What does this woman want me to do?"* Winnie wondered.

Sallie explained that the DHR in Knoxville had already been notified by the hospital staff about the baby girls' arrival. (*Could it be the parents showing up in the last moments of labor, having been dropped off by the Greyhound bus driver, might have given the hospital employees a clue as to the unusual nature of these births!* Winnie mused.) DHR was on the case, and they were going to be sure the babies had these best chance to thrive in their new world.

Sallie explained that her sister and brother-in-law had a little cottage in Misty Falls, actually in the country just outside of town, and that this new, little family would move in with them. The DHR wanted assurance about anyone who would have contact with the babies — anyone living in the home. "I need you, as the pastor of Muddy Creek United Methodist Church here in Misty Falls, to speak to the DHR woman and say you know me, that I'm a very concerned grandparent, and I wouldn't let anything happen to the babies? Could you put something like that in writing?" Sallie implored.

Winnie took a deep breath and looked at Sallie. "I want what you want. I want your little granddaughters to have the best chance they can get in life. They should be with their parents, of course, and right now that's what the DHR is willing to allow. I'll be happy to talk to the DHR woman and tell her what I know about you."

Winnie was beginning to think that there was a lot in life about which she was pretty naïve. *"Maybe that's all right,"* she thought. *"I'm glad I don't know about those sorts of things and that they are not part of my history. Only God knows everyone's complete story, I just hope I can help these people find the right thing for them to do now."*

※ ※ ※

That evening Winnie called her friend Nina and invited her to the church picnic, which would be taking place Sunday afternoon coming up in the big park on the mountain.

Yes, Nina was free that afternoon, and, yes, she thought she would enjoy coming with Winnie. In fact, she promised to bring something to share for the picnic — her new creation, a sour cream. pumpkin, pound cake.

"Sounds like another winner!" Winnie exclaimed.

They agreed to meet at the church parking lot that afternoon to drive together up the mountain for the picnic.

"You never know," Winnie thought to herself later. *"There are many avenues into a faith community and fellowship is certainly a good one. Maybe Nina can grow a little more in faith as she gets to know more Muddy Creek members.*

9. A Short Week

The picnic had started out like any other Sunday afternoon getaway. Folks began arriving at the park on McCurry Mountain about two-ish and immediately began setting up for the events.

The women were at once focused on setting out all the many dishes as they arrived — casseroles, plates of veggies and salads, fruits, and more. A couple men put up folding tables for the goodies, while others built fires in the ramada's two, big fireplaces. The fires would need several hours to develop the smoldering required to cook really, tasty hotdogs. *Hotdogs are best when crisped over fire, burned down to glowing embers.* Even though the main course was simply hotdogs, the other dishes would provide gourmet flourishes to those humble wieners.

Mickey Allen Barrymore tapped Bradley Washington and Thom Jackson to help him set up the games. They set out a volleyball court, horse shoes, and the paraphernalia for a multi-generation relay game.

Meanwhile Matthew Jackson, Thom's oldest son, led the children in a game of Tag. The children's wild, joyous screaming could be heard across the entire area as they ran hither and yon trying to avoid being tagged.

Mary Lou and Tim Owens were especially pleased to see their new charges so happily engaged in playing with their new friends from church. Carly, who was barely three, wasn't ready to let go of her Aunt Mary Lou, yet, but her siblings were happily scrambling around the hill with the others.

The children were playing Hide-and-Seek, scurrying off in every direction to find themselves a nook or niche in which to hide. The mountain, with all its many rocks, caves, trees and bushes, afforded many a good hiding place.

Little Brad Washington and Andy Owens, both four years old, had become fast friends and had run off together to find a hiding place. They ducked behind a large, colorful bush to wait, but then Andy saw a large, deep blue butterfly, flitting around their bush. The butterfly moved past the boys around a high rock and onto some other bushes, enticing the two youngsters to follow. They scampered around the tall rock and down a hill, following the little, flying object. They didn't realize that they might wander too far away from the rest of the children — they were immersed in a new game of trying to catch the elusive butterfly. The little, flying beast stayed just ahead of the two boys, who continued to scamper after their objective.

It wasn't until the Hide-and-Seek game was over that anyone realized the two boys weren't among the group. They hadn't been found.

"Olly-olly-oxen-free" Matthew Thompson hollered at the top of his lungs to let everyone know that the game was over, and that anyone who had not yet been found was free to return without being caught. All the children gathered in the middle of the large, open meadow laughing and looking at one another. Who would be declared "IT" for the next turn? Who had been caught first?

Bubba Owens, whose real name was Thomas, first noticed that his little brother wasn't among the group. "Where's Andy? Didn't Andy get caught? Has anyone seen my little brother, Andy?"

Several of the parents heard Bubba's plea, and rushed over to the meadow where all the children were and noticed that not only was Andy missing, so was Little Brad. Tim and Mary Lou were immediately on the scene.

It didn't take any time for all the adults and the older children to start scouting for the lost boys, calling their names, imploring them to answer.

It might have seemed like longer, but actually the boys were not lost for long. Matt and his brother Bobby had taken off toward the tall rock and wandered down the hill on the far side. They were calling for Little Brad and Andy all the while. They found the boys further down the mountainside, watching their butterfly as it was sitting on a tree limb just beyond their reach.

The two older boys hoisted the four-year-olds on their shoulders and brought them back to the picnickers forthwith. As soon as they were close enough to be heard they called out that the boys had been found. All was well, again, and the rest of the picnic was all the merrier for that unexpected moment of panic.

The games had been set up, and everyone felt it wise to keep the generations mixed to stave off any further possibility of mishap. They would not lose anyone else! The picnic was a fine success, and the incident of the lost boys seemed to remind everyone how very tenuous life can be, and how very blessed they were. It was a good time to be thankful.

Before the afternoon was complete the families gathered around the fireplace and sang some old favorite songs. It was a moment right out the nineteenth century camp revival meetings, and it was wonderful. "Do Lord, oh, do Lord, oh do remember me!"

※ ※ ※

Monday morning was not a lazy time for Winnie. Most Mondays she could tarry over her morning coffee and paper, and not get to work too early, because Mondays were the furthest away from the next Sunday, and the "countdown" hadn't begun in earnest yet.

This week was different because Winnie wouldn't be preaching on Sunday. She would be in Denver at her high school reunion. Nonetheless, she had plenty to do before she could leave: prepare her Tuesday Bible study lesson; catch up on her reading for her class on church leadership on Wednesday; write a light-hearted, yet somehow inspiring and insightful, blurb for the bi-weekly newsletter; pick out the hymns and readings for the Sunday worship service; produce the Sunday bulletin; and finally visit several of the community's elderly on Thursday.

Winnie planned to fly Friday morning to Denver; she also had to pack and get ready to leave before then. Her folks would pick her up from the airport, so she would have several hours to spend with them before getting ready for the reunion.

The reunion was to be held at a resort in town on Friday and Saturday nights. Friday night's reunion agenda was simple — meet and greet old friends in the ballroom at the resort. Winnie expected there might be several friends that would show up. *"That's a funny thing about reunions, you don't have any control over who might attend. If I made a list of the people I would most like to see, it would probably be very different from the people who will actually come!"* Winnie mused. *"But, then, there's John. I have to admit I'm very curious to see him after all these years!"*

Their phone call over a month ago was still fresh in her memory, and she had enjoyed reading the book that he had sent her. *"To find a true friend!"* That's what John had inscribed in his book. *"I don't think I'm imagining anything,"* Winnie told herself. *"I think he's interested in me."*

She certainly had enjoyed talking to John, but his dismissive comment about church had left her feeling cautious. Maybe she misunderstood John's comment. Maybe it was really nothing at all. It was hard to tell exactly, but if John didn't even believe in God, then that was a problem.

Winnie's life was already very complete, she reminded herself, and she certainly had enough on her plate, what with all her responsibilities at church, not to mention trying to be a vital part of her children's lives. She really didn't need any personal entanglements now. *"I'm really just looking for a fun weekend — seeing old friends from long ago and spending some time with Mom and Dad,"* Winnie persuaded herself.

✳ ✳ ✳

Tuesday afternoon Winnie drove over to the address Sallie had given her. The Hardys (Sallie's sister and her husband) had a cottage in the country, so driving to their place was a matter of meticulously following the directions — *drive down country road 118 as far as the broken down old barn and take a right; drive a couple miles along that dirt road, (watch for the two flanking cow pastures), cross the small wooden bridge and turn left immediately.*

The cottage would be about a quarter mile further on the right side of the road. It stood alone among the trees, except for several weatherworn trailers along the dirt road.

Winnie was pleased to find the cottage without difficulty. She walked up the wooden stairs to the porch and knocked on the door. Sallie opened the door and showed the pastor to a chair in the front room. She explained to Winnie that everyone was in the back and that they would come out soon; she then disappeared behind another door.

Winnie had visited many people's homes over the years, while being pastor. She was aware that not everyone is comfortable with having relatively unknown visitors entering their private domain. In such cases Winnie always respected their wishes and didn't push for an invite.

On the other hand, Winnie had experienced many and sundry homes over the years — some being most inviting and comfortable and some missing even the least evidence of domestic pleasantry.

This little cottage didn't appear to be too grand or overly impoverished. It was a simple cottage built of wood with a stone fireplace at one end and a wood porch on the front.

While Winnie sat alone in the room waiting for someone else to appear she reviewed the room. *"Pretty modest living,"* she mused. There was a sofa, covered by a faded, blue chenille bedspread; Winnie thought it looked lumpy, but comfy. Two La-Z-Boy recliners looked to be favorite siesta spots and took up a significant portion of the available floor space. In the corner of the room stood a large, old television console. It was blaring into the room, even though no one was present, save Winnie.

Sallie appeared with Connie and introduced her. She was friendly, young, nice looking, casually dressed in jeans and a sweatshirt, and slimmer than Winnie had expected. *"Considering the great challenge she's given her waistline these past three or four years she looks great!"* Winnie thought. They spoke about the new babies — the big news for everyone. Connie produced pictures of the babies that someone had taken for her at the hospital.

George Oliver, Connie's husband, entered the room. He was also not what Winnie had expected, but then, she wasn't exactly sure what she expected the husband to be like. George was slight in stature and not a large person overall. He, too, was dressed in jeans and a sweatshirt, and he wore boots. He was somewhat reserved in his manner. Winnie understood George didn't know who she was or why she might be interested in this little family. He nodded to the visitor when she was introduced. George was older than Connie, in fact, George was possibly twice Connie's age! Winnie judged. "*There's more to this story than I've heard so far.*"

Winnie would have liked to see the babies, but they were napping in the back, so they couldn't be seen at this time. The women talked for several minutes about the babies — their size at birth, their eating schedule, their clothing needs, their sleeping schedule. So far both babies seemed to sleep and be hungry at the same time, which was fortunate. There were a number of helpful hands available to take care of any needs. George didn't add to the conversation; he let the women speak.

The Hardys came into the room and met their visitor. They seemed to be nice people who were somewhat surprised by this new influx of family and personality that had just descended on them. Considering these refugees, as it was, Winnie thought they were trying to do the right thing for everyone.

Winnie sighed to herself as she drove away, "*Lord! Help and guide that family! Help me know what is right for them and what I can do to help them.*"

✳ ✳ ✳

The week had really flown by, and Winnie had only one more day to get things together before her trip. She looked down to see Bitty at her feet and suddenly realized that she hadn't made plans for the dog, while she'd be in Denver. 'Bitty! I can't leave you alone for the weekend. What am I to do with you?"

Winnie mentally rifled through all the people she knew in town, trying to think who she might call for help with Bitty. The puppy really wasn't a great trouble, but she did need to be fed and walked a couple times a day. Finally Winnie decided to call Trudy, the young, expectant girl. Winnie thought it might be a good thing for Trudy to get in the mode of being responsible for another life.

She called Keisha Livingston, Trudy's mother, and asked if her daughter was home. Keisha handed the phone to Trudy, who answered, "Yes, Ma'am. This is Trudy." Winnie explained to Trudy, "I'm going to be out of town this weekend, and I need someone to watch my puppy,"

"I remember the puppy! How big is she now?" Trudy asked.

"Maybe a couple pounds bigger, but not much. She's so furry, though, she looks much bigger than she really is," Winnie supposed.

"Do you suppose you could 'puppy watch' for me this weekend over at the parsonage?" Winnie asked her.

"I'd love to!" Trudy assured Winnie. "I think it would be fun to play with the puppy. What did you name her?"

"I call her Bitty. How about we meet at my house later today, and I can show you what she needs. You'll need to walk Bitty a couple times a day, too," Winnie added.

"That sounds like fun," Trudy giggled. "I'll be able to play baby dolls with 'Itty Bitty'!"

"It really does sound like just the thing for you – practicing caring for another little being!" Winnie answered. "She's a sweet little pup; you'll enjoy her. Thanks so much. Please thank your mother for lending you to me this weekend. I'll see you around 4:30, OK?" Winnie asked.

They agreed to meet then, and Winnie was pleased that she remembered Trudy to help her out. "*She probably would like to have some time on her own, anyway, and this is a good place to play house*," Winnie thought.

✻ ✻ ✻

Winnie was hoping that everything was now in order for her to leave the community for the three days. She had a substitute preacher — a "supply" preacher — who would fill in with the message for Sunday morning. She had asked Gus Reeves, Muddy Creek's Lay Leader, to preach for her. He was the great grandson of the man who moved his plantation house across the town a century earlier.

Gus was a pharmacist, who owned the local drug store on Main Street; he was also a volunteer fireman and active in community affairs like the fall festival. His wife, Martha, worked at FRIENDLY'S FOODS, so they sometimes teased one another about "being in competition" with one another — Gus' pharmacy vs. the grocery store.

Winnie had discovered over the last year that Gus was someone who could be called on in a pinch. Moreover, he was willing to try new things — like preaching!

The Reeves family had experienced a very difficult time, as Winnie learned when she first arrived at Muddy Creek. Martha had invited Winnie over for dinner one Sunday afternoon shortly after she had arrived in town, and she and Gus told her about an event, actually two events, that occurred in their family, which they felt their new pastor needed to know.

The events took place fifteen years earlier when the three Reeves kids were still all at home. Tina, 18, was a senior in high school, Tommy was 16, and Julie was 14. That summer Tina graduated from high school and moved out of the house. The Reeves weren't even quite sure where she was living, but they had heard that she was staying with friends and had started working at a factory in the town nearby.

Several months later Martha heard that Tina was expecting a baby in the spring. Tina was very independent about her life and what she was choosing to do, and she wanted nothing to do with her parents. Gus and Martha would have loved to be part of Tina's life in any way she would allow, but she would not have any of it. Occasionally she would call them, and when she called they hung on her every word. All they could do was to pray for Tina's safety and the safety of their unborn first grandchild.

Later, that same summer, something else was happening even closer to home. It seems their son Tommy had a couple of boyfriends over to the house one afternoon while his folks were away at work. Julie, his younger sister, was also at home.

Somehow one of Tommy's friends found an opportunity to get alone with Julie. One thing led to another, and before she knew what was happening, the boy had his way with her! A month later Julie realized that she was expecting a child! She was mortified at the discovery, but, nevertheless, Julie came tearfully to her mother and father and told them what had happened. They loved Julie, of course, and they could see that she had hardly been a willing party in this situation. They would support her and see that this new child would have a loving home to grow up in.

That's exactly what happened. The baby came late the following spring, and she was brought into the Reeves's home and cared for as a member of their family. They managed to figure how to support Julie's high school education by working out a tag team plan for raising little Emma.

Gus and Martha never made a secret of this painful situation at church. The church family gathered around them, and prayed with them, and supported them emotionally. In every way they could, they helped to make sense out of this surprising turn of events.

Eventually, the older daughter, Tina, and her little daughter Sara Faye, began coming around. Ever so slowly at first, the Reeves were allowed to get to know their first granddaughter.

Both granddaughters, Sara Faye and Emma, were a delight. They were only two months apart in age, and they were devoted to one another, looking for opportunities to spend time together whenever they could.

Tina still lived away from town, but she was becoming more willing to share about her life to her parents. They could have hoped that things between them and their first child had not been so cool for so long, but they could see her hard work, providing for her little family. Tina continued to advance in the factory, and her income and position continued to increase. She was making a success of her life against all odds. Her life was not how her parents would have written it, but they were supportive and impressed nonetheless.

Julie, also, was a hard worker and an exceptional student even with the added duties of motherhood. She won scholarships to The University of Tennessee in Knoxville, so the Reeves found a way to see that she could go. They continued with the tag team effort, to see that Emma was cared for, and it worked out well.

Julie's story was remarkable. She managed to carry a stiff load of classes at UTK and graduate with honors. She studied pharmacology, following in her father's footsteps, and after graduation she began working with her dad at his pharmacy in town.

Winnie was touched as she heard this saga from Gus and Martha. They told her how they had not kept their troubles from the world, but had shared their crazy pain with their fellow church members. They had been open to God's healing in all their troubles. It couldn't have been an easy a road to walk, but Winnie could see how richly the Reeves had been rewarded through their faithfulness and willingness to see the trouble through.

Gus would bring a great message to the church on Sunday, because he had the respect of the congregation and an ocean of deep experience from which to draw. Winnie had no worries as she packed and prepared to leave for her reunion over the weekend.

10. The Reunion

The class reunion left Winnie with mixed thoughts, rather like her favorite author had phrased it: "It was the best of times, it was the worst of times. . ."

Winnie was aware of a feeling in the pit of her stomach — a certain emptiness, accompanied by several score of butterflies. She did not experience this pit-of-the-stomach queasiness regularly, but only when her world was somehow out of kilter, or when she was about to deliver a sermon.

Winnie had become particularly aware of this '*pit*' feeling when she began preaching on Sundays. The *pit* came upon Winnie just prior to her standing up to preach. "*It's funny,*" Winnie mused, "*how quickly the pit abates once I actually get into the sermon, but the time leading up to delivery is a mess!*"

The *pit* uneasiness was not just a prelude to sermon giving, it could come at other times, too, and it reminded Winnie that something was amiss, something was foreign or uncomfy for her. It usually indicated that she needed to find closure to some circumstance.

So it was with the reunion. Not all of the reunion was *pit*-making, but the initial hour, as Winnie stood outside the ballroom in a long line of what seemed to be hoards of unknown reunion attendees, was one of those times that invited the *pit's* arrival. Winnie noticed the *pit* emerging, yet it wasn't simply a large crowd of unknown people that was causing the *pit's* arrival, rather it was because she had to stand for the better part of an hour, waiting in line with total strangers. She was beginning to think she might be at the wrong reunion. *"Why did I bother coming here!"* she asked herself.

The last high school reunion Winnie had attended, Mark was with her. They stayed in the company of two other couples that Winnie had known from her high school days. The three couples stuck together, learning about their various families and business endeavors, enjoying their re-acquaintancing. But tonight Winnie was alone, and that made an enormous difference in the way she engaged the party.

It was not the fault of the reunion itself, which had all the expected decor, music, and taste-tempting finger foods that a reunion should boast.

After standing in line for over an hour, the attendees were finally admitted to the hall. They were given a name tag with their senior high school picture affixed to it, making it a valuable tool for memory-jogging. *"Goodness! Look at the changes we've had over the years. Our pictures are a far cry from what we look like today!"* Winnie sighed to herself.

Everyone had aged, of course, and the waistlines of most of the graduates had expanded, some to shocking measures! Many of the men were either bald or had facial hair, and Winnie had to work hard to recognize those sporting such facial additions. Nearly everyone had some gray hair, save those who had employed a rinse to masque what time would inevitably do to their locks.

Winnie noticed a distinguished-looking, silver-haired man walking toward her. He moved across the ballroom floor and right up to Winnie. *"Can that be John?"* Winnie asked herself. He looked something like she remembered him, but his hair was no longer reddish-brown. Silver was his new shade, and it favored him. He wore a maroon sports jacket with a gray cravat, reminding Winnie of pictures of old Hollywood stars.

"I see we both managed to make it to the reunion!" John observed.

Winnie smiled and said, 'Yes, I'm so glad you called and told me about it. This is turning out to be better than I had expected!" (And the *pit* vanished!)

"Did you like my book?" John asked Winnie.

"Yes, I did! I've never had a book, hot off the press, so to speak, and personally inscribed by the author, too!" Winnie admitted. "You write so well!"

Winnie commented on several of the daily selections in John's new book, which evoked a quick repartee between them that they thoroughly enjoyed. The two soon found that they shared a fondness for such thoughtful conversation.

"Reunions are an interesting mix of past and present, aren't they?" John commented.

"We've certainly had some good examples of that this evening," Winnie nodded in agreement. "Reunions surely are a mix of now and then. Or maybe you could say we reunion celebrators are a layering of past and present. I would think, though, that people are still the same, beneath our aged exterior. Maybe we look different —grayer, wider, and more wrinkly than when we were in high school, but aren't we the same persons, still?"

"I'm sure there are psychologists that would affirm your observation and cite a host of solid references for proof," John answered.

"I've heard that our personality is set by the time we are five years old, or that 90% of our personality is set by then. Would you agree?" Winnie asked.

"You're positing that one's personality is the basic structure of who a person is," John suggested.

"Either that or personality certainly is a major factor in how one lives one's life," Winnie returned. "Although, surely, there have to be other, similarly important elements that make up who someone is — dreams, economic advantage or disadvantage, natural talent, education, faith -- to mention a few," Winnie theorized.

So, you would say that the composite person, including the factors you've just mentioned, plus others, is what makes a person who he or she is today," John theorized.

Winnie was enjoying this tete-a'-tete with John and added, "I don't suppose the answer is that simple; people are complex entities, but are you suggesting that a person is basically the same person, no matter what he or she has experienced along the way?"

"Maybe. I suppose there could be some major incident that could alter a person's life forever — for good or for otherwise," John noted.

"I would agree with that, for sure, because I have to believe that no matter what a person starts with, there's plenty that can sway a person's thinking and doing. And, as a person of faith, I have to include the good things that God does for us, as a positive stimulus for choosing to do what is right," Winnie said.

"That's quite a mouthful. I see that you bring God into the mix," John observed.

Winnie held her breath a moment and then smiled and said, "Yes, I do. I have been a person of faith in Christ for almost as long as I can remember, so I guess I do bring God into the conversation, occasionally."

John raised an eyebrow and nodded his head. "You mentioned something about church when we talked before on the phone. Maybe you are pretty involved with your church?"

Winnie squelched a grin at this point. She was enjoying John's company too much to mess things up now. She wanted to know more of this intriguing man, before she threw her profession at him. A little time couldn't be a problem, could it? Instead, Winnie winked at John and said, "In fact I work at my church."

"So, you would have more than a passing acquaintance with church affairs," John concluded.

"Something like that. I do various things at different times. I do the bulletin each week and put together the newsletter and get it out to mail. I'm in charge of our prayer list, and I'm trying to learn how to put our church online. Come to think of it, I do a lot of things at church," Winnie smiled.

"Then I'd better watch my tongue, since I'm in the presence of a saint!" John teased.

"You're teasing me, but you're closer than you think about how we speak among ourselves at church," Winnie explained. "You see, everyone who follows Christ is a *saint in the making.* I certainly wouldn't go around calling myself a saint, but I do believe that, as we follow the Lord each day, we are growing closer to Him. We are 'saints' in the making," Winnie added.

John smiled and might have commented further when Jenny walked up to them and began to talk. She had been moving from one group to the next on the ballroom floor, talking with former classmates. She saw John, probably because he stood out a bit taller in the crowd, and she maneuvered over to where he was.

Winnie had known Jenny when they were coeds at Mile High High School. Jenny had been a tall, slender girl with long, jet black ringlets, flowing down her back. The one thing that distinguished Jenny in high school was that she ranked at the top of the class — even out of a thousand students she was on top. That was then.

"I go by Jennifer, now," she told Winnie. Winnie couldn't keep her eyes off the change in "Jennifer." Instead of being the slight, modestly dressed girl Winnie remembered, her hair was now very short, spiked, and hot pink. The new "Jennifer" sported a pink leotard and pullover, a green herringbone mini-skirt, and a matching bolero with a very low cut blouse.

"Jennifer" had apparently decided that the quiet life was not for her and had made a number of changes, not the least of which was a <u>very well endowed bosom</u>! She had an attitude to match her new look. She held an strong, edgy opinion on many subjects. She had traveled extensively, even experiencing life in some very primitive cultures, providing her some unusual insights into human behavior. She left her audience believing that she really had seen it all.

After some time Jenny moved on to another group. "I would never have recognized her, if she hadn't introduced herself to me," John confessed.

"How did the girl who missed the Hippies and the nuttiness of the Sixties become such a free spirit on her own?" Winnie laughed.

"Now there's an example of nature versus nurture, as we were saying before. I'd almost want to say that nurture has won out in Jennifer's case," Winnie concluded.

"You could make a good argument for that, I'm sure, but there's got to be something of the 'nature' side, too. What caused Jennifer to seek those changes? Was it something deep within her that was begging for expression?" John said.

John told Winnie about his life, following graduation. He had gone east to study — to Davidson in North Carolina — where he earned his B.A. in Philosophy and then on to graduate work at Boston University. He was awarded his PhD in 1979, and he moved to Chicago to teach in the early '80s.

John had been tenured at University of Chicago, teaching philosophy since then. He even served as an adjunct professor of philosophy at Garrett Theological Seminary, teaching Introduction to Philosophy.

"So, you've taught theologians!" Winnie interrupted him.

"Yes," John admitted. "Seminarians are usually good students, interested in understanding the rudiments of philosophy. I can always expect to hear good apologetics among my students, defending the influence of Greek thought into Christian orthodoxy. Discussions on how Platonic and Aristotelian thinking has continued to inform Christian doctrine are always vibrant. Those early Greek philosophers gave the church some sound tools for engaging theology. Western Philosophy is foundational to a seminarian's studies."

Winnie didn't offer the fact that she had been to seminary, even if theology school would have been something they would have had in common. *I think I'll just leave that subject to rest for now,* she thought.

As the evening went on they laughed and laughed, sometimes at things they were discovering at the reunion, like the dramatic change in Jenny, and other times they just seemed to laugh together at nothing at all.

John had never married. His early years were all about school and long hours of study. He spent a year abroad at Queens University in Belfast, Ireland. He was doing doctoral work there. He enjoyed being in the eastern hemisphere, where he could hop over to the continent and spend time poking through history and culture and practicing his French and German.

Winnie wondered about John's mother. *"Wonder if she played a role in his not marrying? Or maybe there's another reason. Hadn't thought of that!"*

Winnie told John about her world since high school — taking her baccalaureate at Colorado College in the Springs and marrying Mark Taylor, who had been a cadet at the Air Force Academy.

Their life with the Air Force moved them around the States to different bases, as well as to Germany for a couple of three year tours there. Winnie wondered if they might have been in Europe at the same time.

The two compared travel dates and times, and it turned out that they were both at the zoo in Dublin on Boxing Day in 1978. "How funny! What a small world we live in!" Winnie giggled. "Did you happen to notice the crocodile there?" she asked John.

"You mean the one who wasn't eating much on his preferred diet?" John asked.

Winnie laughed again. "Right! He was pretty sad, not having any teeth!" They both laughed. "What a small world we live in!" They said together as if they had rehearsed it.

"I discovered that Christmas is not much of a time to go visiting in Ireland. It's all about family time for the Irish then." John observed.

"We drove from Ramstein Air Force Base to Calais and took the hovercraft over to England; then we drove up the M6 to Dumfries and then over to Stranraer, where we took a ferry to Northern Ireland. We spent Christmas week in Armagh, with friends and drove all over Northern Ireland that week. Unfortunately, as you just said, much was closed, because of the Yule holiday. We did get a personal tour of the cathedral in Londonderry by the sexton there. We felt like V.I.P.'s the way we were treated then," Winnie recounted.

"I was at Queens University in Belfast that year, and Christmas break extended into the New Year, so I drove down to Dublin to look around, and then I ferried to Liverpool from there and then on to Paris and beyond. I actually got a good three weeks of traveling in then." John smiled at the memory.

On and on they talked. John wasn't always full of big words and ideas. He seemed very down to earth and most interested in Winnie as a person. She enjoyed his humor, too.

Saturday evening was more of the same. Winnie and John sat together at a small dining table in the resort's dining room. John was very attentive to Winnie all evening. He seemed satisfied to learn as much as she shared about her life. She told him about Mark, about the kids, where they kids were now, and about losing Mark. She explained how becoming a widow at thirty-seven with two half-grown kids had been very painful, of course, but things were better now. She had a full life what with her church work and her children.

Both John and Winnie had flown to Denver for the reunion, in order to get away for the weekend. John admitted that he really preferred to drive, when he could spare the time. Driving relaxed him and allowed him to think outside of his busy world.

He said, "I don't do much driving in Chicago. I suppose that's why my car has lasted me as long as it has. I have a '92 Honda Civic, which works quite well. I've hardly had to do anything to it 'cept give it gas."

"I drive a lot, especially since I live in the country. I have to figure on driving into Knoxville at least once a week, and sometimes more," Winnie commented.

"One good thing about not driving much is that I've never had a ticket!" John announced.

"I think I'm a pretty safe driver, too, and I haven't had any citations in years and years, but I have to admit that there was a time, when Mark and I were in Germany and the kids were little, that I managed to gather nine points on my license in about three months!"

John's mouth fell open, pretending to tease Winnie. "No! You had nine points on your license in three months! How did you manage that?"

"It wasn't very funny at the time, but I guess it sounds funny, now," Winnie began to explain.

"It started off with our car. We had a big Ford Econoline van, which was very long and had two little windows in the back; they didn't allow the driver to see below the back windows."

"Our car was parked in our apartment parking lot. There was a large dumpster sitting maybe fifteen feet from the back of our van. I was aware of the dumpster and planned to very carefully back out of the parking lot. Unfortunately, someone was visiting the apartments and had parked his car parallel to the dumpster. I hadn't noticed this small car when I got into the van. I maneuvered our car back, to avoid the dumpster, but the fender of the van managed to hit the little car! I heard the metal meet, and I tried to very carefully pull forward, back toward my parking space. It seems, however, that the fender had hooked onto the fender of the little car, and as I drove forward, the little car was dragged alongside the dumpster, leaving a nasty gash on the car!"

John had a very difficult time not bursting into laughter at this admission, but he could see that Winnie was not laughing, so he tried to contain his mirth.

"THAT was considered a MOVING violation, and I had three points on my license," Winnie said.

She waited a minute to see if John would comment, and when he did not, she continued. "A month later I was over at the air base at the chapel, where I was working with junior high kids on a Christmas play. I had parked in the chapel's parking lot. When I got into the van, this time, I noted that there was a car parked parallel to my car, and I had to be careful not to hit it when I opened the driver's door. I was completely successful in that effort, but later, as I was backing up, easing out of the parking space, I heard a S-C-R-A-T-C-H-I-N-G sound, and I stopped immediately to see what had happened."

John's eyes were bigger than before, "And?" he asked.

"AND! You remember how my car's bumper that had hooked onto the other car's fender the month before?" Winnie asked, rhetorically. John nodded his head, "yes"."Well, we hadn't fixed the bumper on our van, so it was still pulled out several inches, and it had scratched a terrible mark all the way across the side of the car door!"

"I suppose I could have left the parking lot and driven home, but I knew my car had been responsible for the scratch on the car, so I went to the chaplain's office and told him what had just happened."

"This is where the story gets funny," Winnie remembered. "I told the chaplain what had just happened, and the chaplain stood up, his face growing redder and redder. He slammed his fist on his desk and asked me about the color and make of the car. I told him it was a maroon color sedan, and the chaplain told me it was his brand new car; the one he had just bought his family for Christmas. After a moment the chaplain realized it was not his fault that his car was damaged, and he changed his mood. He wouldn't have to tell his wife that he had managed to scratch their new car. NO! It was not his fault, it was my fault!"

Winnie had been watching John's face as she was relating her story to him. She could see the wheels spinning in his eyes, but he never cracked a smile.

Winnie laughed. "As bad as this story is, I suppose it is funny in the retelling!"!

Her admission allowed John to relax and be himself. Then he laughed along with Winnie.

"Anyway, that was three more points on my license — in less than a month!" Winnie added.

"You said you had nine points, right?" John asked, a bit fearful to hear more.

"A month later, one early evening, I was driving out of the base on the access road. You have to creep along at 20 miles an hour on the base, and finally there I was on the road on the outside of the base, and I started to drive a bit faster. I was going, maybe, thirty-five miles an hour, when one of the SP's pulled me over for speeding! Turns out that the speed limit on that road was 30 m.p.h. I felt like a fish that had just been caught!"

"That added three more points — another 'moving violation! I never did hear anything about the nine points on my license, but you can be sure I was Über careful behind the wheel for a long time!" Winnie concluded.

The reunion was perfect for Winnie and John. They had discovered one another, and they were most pleased with what they found! They talked, and talked, and couldn't stop talking. They felt like they might be able to talk together, non-stop, for a month if it were possible! They each felt something fascinating about the other.

Of course, Winnie wondered how (or if) she might broach the topic of her bing a pastor. She got the impression that John had had some bad experience with the church and had been turned off of the whole subject. Therefore, she didn't suppose he'd be thrilled to learn that she was a preacher! In fact, she hoped to have more time to explore what John meant by his enigmatic inscription in the book he had sent her, before she addressed the conundrum of her work.

✳ ✳ ✳

Sunday at breakfast, Winnie's folks were full of questions about the reunion, especially about Dr. Jonathan Daniel, whom, they understood, had spent a good bit of his reunion time at their daughter's side.

"YES! He's very interesting and accomplished, and YES we had a really great time together at the reunion. But, I don't think he's a believer! I can't become interested in someone, if he doesn't follow Christ, I don't care how 'eligible' he seems to be." Winnie sighed.

11. The Peace Walkers

"No matter how much I try to get ahead of my work before I leave for a holiday, I still have much more to do when I return. It really makes 'getting away' a hard thing to do;. I have to pay for it afterwards — and before!" Winnie complained out loud. "It's almost not worth the going away, except I really did have a good time."

The trip was good for many reasons, but now, looking at the new week ahead with all its requirements, Winnie wondered how she could get everything done that begged her attention.

The walkers would be arriving at the church on Friday evening, and Winnie wanted to make a few calls, to be sure everyone was on line for the breakfast. She also thought there might be some interest among her people to come and meet these strangers, who were giving up so much of their life to walk for peace.

✳ ✳ ✳

Winnie decided to stop by Sallie's sister's home and see how they were all getting along.

Everything seemed much as Winnie had seen it before she left on her trip. The cottage looked just the same, although there were a few baby items strewn around the living room. There was a large box of Newborn Huggies by the kitchen and two infant carriers sitting side by each.

This time Winnie saw the little girls, and they were adorable — plump, blue eyed, with a few wisps of blond hair atop their pates. (Someone had pasted little pink bows on their heads, to announce, "I'm a girl!") They seemed to be good babies, and they were being passed around the room by various family members, holding them and cooing at them.

"*This seems to be working,*" Winnie thought to herself.

George was not present, and Winnie inquired as to his whereabouts. It seemed that George was already seeking employment in the community. He was a welder and had several leads on employment that he wanted to check out. He hoped he would be able to support his new family soon.

"*That's a good sign,*" Winnie thought. "*He's not a sluggard.*"

She wondered about Harry Hardy, Sallie's brother-in-law, and how he was accepting the invasion of this new family into his already-space-challenged, little cottage. He was silent, maybe hoarding his thoughts. Winnie wasn't surprised at his reticence to speak.

The baby girls were definitely the stars of the day. Their needs and their comfort seemed to be uppermost on everyone's mind. Winnie wondered how quickly everyone had accommodated themselves to this whole new situation.

Winnie left the family with various questions, wondering how long this amiable relationship would be able to continue. "*After all, the Hardys had just been dumped upon without any warning! And people are people,*" Winnie mused. "*I won't be surprised if arrangements don't eventually change.*"

* * *

Winnie discovered that she was getting email everyday from John!

His messages invited more 'conversation', as they had enjoyed such banter, and even some deeper thoughts, during the reunion.

He signed his email each day with "Appreciating our friendship more and more! John."

"Hmmmm! That's more food for thought," Winnie said to Bitty, who was sitting at her foot. "We're growing in friendship, according to John. I like that; it has a nice ring."

Winnie responded to John's emails, of course. She thought the banter fun — like playing tennis — you lob the ball back as soon as it hits your court.

Winnie signed her notes with "Your Friend, Winnie"

❄ ❄ ❄

Winnie had a date with Nina late Thursday afternoon. Nina had called earlier in the week to say that she was putting together a new dessert that needed a fresh palate to consider its merit. Winnie told Nina that her palate was a willing volunteer, thank you! She would come right away!

They sat at Nina's breakfast table in her kitchen. The object of the test sat in the center of the table, a tall, yummy-looking bundt cake with orange icing dripping down its sides. Nina had set the table with a table cloth, napkins, silverware, coffee cups, and bread plates. All was ready for a tasting verdict.

Winnie recognized that this special treat was about to throw her diet completely out of whack, but she decided that she would not disappoint her taste buds. [After all, didn't the Lord enjoy the occasional, lavish party with friends? Such a precedent must not be overlooked!]

The conversation at the table touched lightly on many subjects, the way it does among women. They spoke of the weather, of their children, last week's picnic on the mountain, and, speaking of church, Winnie mentioned the peace walkers who would arrive late Friday afternoon.

Nina was intrigued about their coming. She wanted to know all about these people: Who were they? Were they all Buddhists? Did they speak English? How did they decide on Muddy Creek Church to spend the night?

Winnie wondered, along with her friend, about the walkers. She thought it would be especially good for her church people to meet these outsiders and to help them along their journey.

This brought the conversation around to church in general. Apparently, Nina had been married in church, a big United Methodist Church in New Orleans. She and her husband had been students at Tulane, and they were involved in the Wesley Foundation, a campus ministry for young people. The school was just down St. Charles Ave. from the church. They were married in the church's chapel after graduation.

They didn't attend church during the early years of their marriage, but when the children came, the Mattinglys took them to church. It seemed like the right thing to do.

They were living in Jackson, MS by then, and they attended a community church. It was friendly, and most of their neighbors were members of the church.

Nina told Winnie, "One day news came out that our pastor had stolen a lot of money from the community! He had 'borrowed' money from various people around town and from the church itself. Then he defaulted on his 'loans'. Altogether, when the loss was added up, it was more than $35,000 that our preacher had absconded with!

"It was dreadful! Everyone at church felt as if we personally had been taken advantage of. We wondered, 'How could we have trusted the man! How can we believe anything he told us? How can we believe his preaching?' Many members left the church then — including us. We were deeply hurt. We didn't know what to tell our kids, Rachel and Perry. We were so disappointed in the pastor and in the way that many tongues wagged for months afterwards. We just left church altogether.

"Maybe there was a better way to respond to it, but that chapter in our lives had closed. We filled our lives with other things. We slept in on Sundays. The kids didn't seem to miss church; they never asked about it," Nina explained.

The Mattinglys moved from Jackson to Misty Falls a year later. By that time they were out of the church habit.

Winnie listened carefully and sympathetically to Nina's story.

"Oh!" Winnie sighed. "I'm so sorry you had to experience such a bad pastor!" Winnie wanted her friend to know she felt for her and her pain. "Too often people of the cloth do great damage to church, to members, and to one another. We should be a whole lot better people than our lay counterparts, but, the truth is, we're not. We stand in the need of God's grace just as much as anyone does!"

Nina was surprised to hear her friend speak so bluntly about the place and the people she was so involved with. "That surprises me," she admitted.

"Don't be surprised," Winnie told Nina. "Although we pastors should be on our best behavior as we live out our lives before the world, we also must lead the way as followers of Christ, and that means we must be first when it comes to being truthful and honest when we fail. Wouldn't our honesty in times of trouble show others how to act when failure comes along for them? There's plenty to ask forgiveness for, and, from what I understand, there's plenty of forgiveness available to those who ask."

Nina let Winnie's words sink in before she answered. "I can see what you mean. You're saying if a pastor is a genuine follower of Jesus, he or she has to be a leader in what he or she does. That means being honest about what you do and say. I like that, Winnie. That helps a little. Thanks."

Winnie was especially pleased to hear Nina's story and her apparent interest in Winnie's response. She seemed to understand how it was that the Mattinglys got separated from church and how painful it had been for them.

✳ ✳ ✳

Linda Anderson, who had visited the church's food pantry several weeks earlier, was sitting in her car in the church parking lot Wednesday morning, awaiting the pastor's arrival.

Winnie was happy to show her the church pantry and help her do a little shopping from the shelves. She filled two bags of canned goods, pasta, and paper goods. Winnie told Linda she would like to meet her family, so she hopped in her VW and followed Linda to an apartment a couple miles from the church.

The Andersons lived in a modestly furnished two bedroom apartment; the television was blaring loudly in the living room. Linda's two sons were home with their father, who lay stretched out on the couch.

The room was strewn with children's toys — trucks, blocks, crayons and paper, balls, and stuffed animals. The site took Winnie back to a time when her own kids were about that age. "*It's virtually impossible to keep up after them,*" she thought to herself.

Linda introduced her husband, Josh. Josh told Winnie that he was a construction worker. He had been learning the trade in Tampa, but he hadn't found a job in Misty Falls, yet. He was hoping to find something soon.

As they were talking, the front door opened and in walked an exceptionally pretty young woman carrying a baby on her hip. Her attitude indicated that she had more than a passing acquaintance with this apartment.

Linda brightened up immediately and introduced her sister to Winnie.

"Miss Winnie, This is my sister Laura Lee." She grinned.

Winnie told Laura Lee she was pleased to meet her. She peeked at the baby in her arms and inquired his name.

"This is Jasper," Laura Lee answered. A young boy opened the door. and came inside "And this is my son, Jason."

Laura Lee motioned to her sister, and the two young women stepped into the kitchen and pushed the door to.

Jason was a good-looking child with a mop of curry blond hair atop his head. Winnie judged him to be about three years old. He immediately walked over to the television, picked up the remote control, and began switching channels. He seemed completely at home in the apartment.

"*Do both of these families live together in this apartment?*" Winnie wondered to herself.

The door to the kitchen swung open, and Linda came out and announced to Josh. "Jerry's missing. Laura Lee hasn't seen him since yesterday."

"Who is Jerry?", Winnie wondered.

Linda looked at Winnie and explained, "Jerry is Laura Lee's boyfriend. They live in a trailer across the highway."

"I see." Winnie said. "Have you any idea where he went?"

Laura Lee spoke up then. "He's been looking for work, and he left yesterday to talk to somebody about a job. That's the last I saw him." She looked miffed.

"Will you be alright?" Winnie wanted to know.

Laura Lee seemed to think they were OK for now. "Jerry'll show up when he gets hungry."

"I'm glad you have family here," Winnie observed.

When she left the Anderson's, Winnie had the strong impression that she ought to drop by her friend Sheriff Barrymore. She couldn't give a good reason for it, but she felt it might be a good idea.

The sheriff's office wasn't far from Muddy Creek Church. Winnie walked into the office and saw Janice, sitting at her desk. "Hi, Janice! Seeing you reminds me that we're supposed to get together with Joe Ed tonight for the special choir rehearsal. Do you know what time practice will be?"

Janice smiled and said, "He's meeting at six o'clock at the church for 'The Massed Thanksgiving Choir rehearsal.' I'm glad to hear you'll be joining us. Is your choir coming, too?" Janice asked.

"When the folks at Muddy Creek heard that I was to be the preacher for the evening, they couldn't help but commit to showing up" she winked at Janice.

"You know, Miss Winnie, I've never heard a woman pastor preach before, but I've been married to Ken long enough to know that writing and giving sermons is serious business. How long have you been preaching?"

"Well, I didn't jump in with both feet right at the start; in fact I dragged my feet for quite some time. I wasn't aware that women were allowed to preach when I first looked into seminary" Winnie explained. "I had been working part time at a big United Methodist

Church in my town. Most of the time, I was working with the youth and Sunday school, but I became a lay speaker. That was when my own kids were early teens".

"Then after Mark died, when I got my bearings back, I decided to go to seminary to see about getting a degree that would allow me to work in the church. I had filled in and preached for our pastor a couple of times earlier when the pastor was sick, and that made me think about going to seminary to get a degree for church work, and in the process, I discovered that Methodist women have been ordained to preach since 1956!"

"My first sermons were very painful, probably for everybody, but eventually I came to realize that when I have worked on a message that has some value — something that others would do well to hear — then I got excited about sharing it. Suddenly it was a delight to preach! So, you could say I have come full circle, from not even thinking a woman ought to preach, to being convinced that I have a message I want to share with others at worship!"

Janice listened carefully to Winnie, nodding along with her as her story unfolded. "Yes! We were just studying the Epistle of First John last week, and he said the Apostles were sharing the gospel so that their joy could be complete. That's what you're saying, isn't it? When you have a message that is wonderful and exciting you can't be fully joyful about it until you have shared it with others!"

Winnie grinned. "That's exactly what I mean! You're not a bad theologian yourself, Janice!"

"Is the sheriff in?" Winnie asked.

"He's down there," Janice pointed down the hall toward the jail. "He'll be back pretty soon. He came in with a man in handcuffs late last night and took him back there."

Winnie didn't think that Misty Falls's jail hosted too many prisoners. She hadn't ever heard Mickey Allen mention having prisoners before. She asked, "Do you know who it is?"

Janice hadn't seen the man before. "No, he's not much more than a boy, though, maybe twenty years old."

Winnie was about to leave when the sheriff came into the room. His face lit up when he saw Winnie.

"Mornin,' Pastor Winnie!" he said.

"Looks like you've had some serious sheriffin' business to-day." Winnie said.

"Well, I came upon a fight late last night in the parking lot by the highway, and I broke it up. Two of the men took off runnin', before I could find out about them. I think they were Hispanics and didn't want any trouble with authority. The guy I picked up made the mistake of usin' some foul language at me, and I didn't appreciate it. I put him back there (he indicated the direction of the jail) to cool off."

"Is there something I can do for you this mornin'?" he asked Winnie.

"I'm not quite sure why I dropped by here, but I met a young woman about an hour ago, and she was upset because her boy-friend hadn't come home last night. Do you suppose that's just a coincidence?" Winnie asked.

The sheriff cocked his head, thoughtfully. "You may be on to something. M'be I'll mosey on over and see what's up. Where does she live?"

Winnie explained about Linda, Josh, and their kids, and how she had just met Linda's sister, Laura Lee, and her kids. It was her boyfriend who was missing.

The sheriff agreed to stop by the apartments and see what was up.

✳ ✳ ✳

Thursday evening the elementary school cafeteria was full to capacity, or so it seemed to Winnie, as she squeezed onto a bench beside Joyce Ellen Randall (the farmer's wife) and the Washingtons — Bradley, Letitia and Little Brad.

They had all come to hear about a playground building pro-gram for Misty Falls.

The mayor had contacted a design firm in Illinois that plans and designs playgrounds unique to a particular community's needs. The plan, from what Winnie had read, was for the playground to be built, "barn-raising" style, with everyone in the community coming together over a weekend to actually erect the playground.

Before that weekend, much work would be needed to raise the money and prepare for all the workers — skilled and unskilled — and all the needed supplies for the project.

Winnie had looked at several large posters hanging around the cafeteria which showed colorful examples of playgrounds that had already been built around the country, using this "barn-raising" method. Winnie could see how this would be a good project for Misty Falls to take on — *"a positive place for our young families to play in and grow."*

The evening was informative and interesting, and, by the end, everyone in the room was excited about having such a playground in Misty Falls. A steering committee was picked to oversee the project. Winnie wasn't surprised when both Joyce Ellen Randall and Bradley Washington were chosen to sit on the committee.

As folks stood up to leave the gathering, Winnie spotted Mickey Allen Barrymore, coming toward her.

"Evenin' Ma'am," he said to her. The sheriff leaned closer toward Winnie and spoke very low, "That was more 'n a coincidence yesterday."

Winnie straightened up as she realized he was referring to the young man who had "visited" the jail the day before.

She and the sheriff walked out of the cafeteria together toward the parking lot. The sheriff added, "Yep, he's the boyfriend alright. I drove over to the apartments after you and I spoke and met the family. I learned they're new in town, having just returned from Florida."

"Miss McKinsey asked me if I had heard anything about her boyfriend, Jerry Lane. I told her that was the name of the young man I'd put in jail last night.

"She was all smiles when I told her about him, and she asked if he would soon be free. She was obviously pleased to hear he was fine."

"I released him from jail when I returned from talking to her. He's probably back there by now," the sheriff said.

Winnie thanked her friend for sharing the information about that young family.

✳ ✳ ✳

Tim and Mary Lou Owens and their four charges left Friday morning, before the peace walkers arrived, to drive back down to the gulf. The news had come that the children's father had passed and that the service would be held Sunday afternoon. Before they left, Winnie stopped at the Owens' home to see them.

Mary Lou had called her pastor to advise her about their trip. This final word about the children's father re-opened their wounds, again, and the children were in various stages of unrest and grief.

Winnie quickly gathered up several items from the Sunday school supply closet that might serve to occupy the kids on their trip to the gulf. When she arrived at the Owens' home, she was greeted by the children who wanted her to know that their Daddy was gone. Their tears were real, and Winnie wanted to cry with them, but she decided it might be more comforting to approach them differently.

She was their pastor and the one who should bring the good news, the resurrection joy, to these small children, to let them know how God's love spreads even beyond life itself.

Winnie sat down on the floor with Andy and Carlie, the two youngest, on her lap and the older two seated Indian fashion before her.

She told them a story about Jesus. She began with the story of the disciples and the others, who were so very sad and in much pain because of losing their dear, good friend, Jesus. He had been with them for a while, traveling with them across many miles, talking with them, telling them wonderful parables and stories — about God's heavenly Kingdom. He was their teacher. He was even more than a teacher; he was a healer. He healed many, many people of sickness and disease. He did wonderful signs like calming the sea in a terrible storm and making a whole lot of wine out of ordinary water! He was so wonderful, and everyone who followed him and heard him speak loved him very much.

"But one day a terrible thing happened. He died. He didn't die because he was old or sick, he died a terrible and gruesome death because of some bad people! His disciples saw him dying, and they were in terrible grief, not knowing what to do. They couldn't help him, and they didn't want him to suffer or die. But he died."

"They felt so badly. Can you imagine how they felt?" Winnie asked the children. They nodded their heads and agreed. Yes, they could understand.

"Three days later, Jesus' friends were sitting together, still feeling sad, when suddenly Jesus was standing there among them! He was alive, completely alive, and he was standing there with them in the room! He smiled and spoke to them. He talked to them for a while. He was hungry, and they gave him some fish to eat."

"You can imagine the joy everyone felt when they saw Jesus was alive! They had no more reason to cry or be sad. They were filled with joy. They must have sung and danced together; they were so happy!"

"That is the greatest story in the world, isn't it?" Winnie asked the children. "Best of all, it's not a make believe story but an absolutely true story. And it is the reason why we can be glad, even when there is sadness in our lives."

"Your father is in heaven today with Jesus, and that's a good reason to be glad. And more than that, you can have Jesus here with you, too. He wants to be your friend and to go with you wherever you go."

The children had settled down and listened to Winnie's tale. They seemed to appreciate the distraction of her story, pulling them away from their sadness for a moment.

Winnie smiled at Mary Lou and Tim who had listened to her story, too. "You can give the kids the pictures to color on your trip. I also have some CD's of children's Christian music I found at church that you can use on your trip," she told them.

Winnie turned to the kids, again. "This isn't the easiest time for you kids, I know, but can you see how God is taking care of you, even in this very sad time? God has provided a wonderful home for you and a dear aunt and uncle to help you during this difficult time."

✳ ✳ ✳

The peace walkers came and went and everyone who met them was charmed by them! Winnie was pleased that it turned out so well.

She personally enjoyed meeting many of the walkers. Some of them were former Christians before they became Buddhists, and their apostasy caused Winnie to think about what might have happened to their faith in Christ.

One of the women Winnie met told her that she had grown up Christian, but there was Buddhist temple just five blocks from her house, where she would join them sometimes. The woman told Winnie that she was looking for more structure in her life, and she enjoyed the discipline that the Buddhists required.

Winnie noticed a significant amount of "discipline" among the walkers. They each seemed to have assigned tasks to accomplish — making and cleaning up their evening meal and organizing their equipment. They joined together in an evening gathering where they voiced their thoughts to one another. It was rather like a town hall meeting Winnie thought.

Their leader was a petite, Japanese, woman monk. She had decided to begin a five day fast; the only thing she would allow herself to take in was hot, lemon tea. Winnie noted the reverence that the entire group of walkers held for this minute woman. They were very impressed by her fasting, which she had apparently done on a previous occasion. The diminutive monk didn't speak English, so there was no communication between Winnie and the leader, but Winnie did note her irritation at those in the kitchen, having to do with not preparing her hot lemon tea in a timely enough manner.

"Discipline!" That's what Winnie heard from several of the walkers. They craved the discipline of the community, and they felt they were getting something from the Buddhists.

"Discipline doesn't belong solely to the Buddhists," Winnie mused. "Discipline's root word comes from the word 'disciple', and aren't we Christians disciples of Christ? *Aren't we to be disciplined about our walk with Jesus? How have we managed not to convey that message to our people? Being a member of a church has become far too easy! Salvation comes from Christ Jesus, but once we realize that it was Christ who has saved us by his sacrifice on the cross, THEN we come into a relationship with him and begin our disciplined life with Him!"* Winnie laughed at herself, adding, *"OK, I'm not even preaching to the choir, I'm preaching to myself!"*

Just before the walkers left, they gathered together, hand in hand, in a great circle. They included Muddy Creek's breakfast-makers, too — about fifteen of them. They stood in the circle, swaying slightly to the right and to the left and making a low, monotone sound that continued for some time, maybe five minutes. It was not a "note" *per se*, Winnie noticed, but rather a low, sustained vocal sound that anyone could make, musically inclined or not. *"Not exactly 'Amazing Grace'."*

The walkers departed by eight o'clock Saturday morning for the next leg of their journey. They left not a trace of their presence at Muddy Creek Church, save happy memories, touching the Muddy Creekers. They had been very efficient picking up for themselves. The church members were most pleased with themselves for having had the experience and for having stretched themselves beyond their natural comfort zone. They would remember the walkers for some

time to come.

12. An Invitation

Winnie opened up her email account Monday morning to a surprise.

John's email told her that he had an upcoming meeting to attend at Ole Miss with S.O.P.H.I.A., a group of philosophers in America. They would meet the first week after the New Year in Oxford, MS, and John wondered if Winnie might be able to meet him while he was in the South.

Winnie smiled at the thought. "That's an interesting invitation," she told Bitty. "He didn't say specifically where we might meet. Maybe meeting on neutral territory would be better than one of our own home turfs. There would be no avoiding the fact that I'm the pastor at Muddy Creek Church if he comes here," she commented aloud.

"Dear John," Winnie typed her answer. "Your trip south sounds like fun, and I would be happy to meet you somewhere for a day."

"Have you ever been to the Gaylord Hotel in Nashville? We could both drive a bit and meet there. It looks to be about halfway between Ole Miss and Misty Falls. I've heard the hotel there is a good place to spend time. Over the years I've heard a number of my friends tell me about going there and what fun they've had at the Gaylord. There's a wonderful garden inside the hotel that's several stories high. They have strolling paths all over the place with cute little shoppes here and there, as well as inviting cuisines from which to choose. There's also a Grand Ole' Opry museum nearby.

"What dates are you talking about?

"Hoping we can work something out, Winnie"

Winnie hit the "send" button and prayed a little prayer right then that whatever happened would be in God's will. *"Please, LORD, don't let this thing go where it should not go, if it is not in your will!"* She pleaded.

✳ ✳ ✳

Thom Jackson, the church trustee, told his pastor that the parsonage was due for some updating and that he was sending a man to the parsonage to take some measurements of the floors in the kitchen, laundry room, and the bathrooms. "That would be like an early Christmas gift. Nice!" She told Thom.

Jeff presented himself as the man whom Thom had sent to replace the linoleum floors. Winnie quickly learned that Jeff was new to Misty Falls; he had just moved down from Ontario, Canada. Turns out that he had met a woman on the internet who lived in Misty Falls, and they had become friends. Jeff had been a truck driver, and his route took him regularly between Ontario and Miami. He decided to stop one day and meet this ePen Pal of his. When they met they realized they had something worth keeping. They had each been alone for a long time, so they decided to marry. Jeff would move south, since Jillian didn't like the idea of the colder, Canadian winters.

As they were speaking, Winnie's eyes got wider and wider.

"Are you talking about Jillian Post?" she asked.

Jeff's face lit up. "Yes! Do you know her?"

"Yes, I know Jillian. In fact, we spoke not long ago. How fun to meet you! Obviously, you two are getting along well!"

"We think so!" Jeff said enthusiastically. "We're getting married over Thanksgiving!"

Winnie smiled and nodded. "You've both made some life-altering decisions pretty quickly, haven't you?"

"I'd say! Yes, but it seems so right for both of us. I am in a totally different environment from my Canadian roots, but I'm doing fine. My entire family lives in and around Toronto. Travis, my son, will probably join us down here after school gets out next summer. He's still got a couple years in high school to finish up. He's living with his mom right now."

Winnie showed Jeff the rooms he needed to measure. He said that he'd be back in a week with the new floor to begin laying it.

After Jeff left, Winnie began thinking about how his long-distance relationship had blossomed so nicely. Jeff and Jillian were apparently very happy with their new arrangement. *Wonder if these electronic connections that seem to be developing will continue to be blessed?* Of course Winnie was thinking of her own, personal, long-distance relationship that seemed to be humming right along.

* * *

Wednesday Winnie spotted Nina as she was stepping into The Depot Diner, so she followed her inside and sat down across from her. Nina lit up when she saw her friend.

"I didn't know I'd be seeing you today, Winnie," she admitted.

"Are you on your lunch break?" Winnie asked.

"Yes, I've got 'till One before I need to get back to the office," Nina answered.

"So, may I join you for lunch?" Winnie smiled.

"Oh, please!" Nina agreed.

"I don't eat out all the time, of course, but I was over at the post office and saw you going into the diner, so I decided to throw caution to the wind and follow you!" Winnie teased.

"Would the caution be for the food or the company?" Nina wanted to know.

"It would be for my waistline!" Winnie retorted.

They spent a few minutes deciding what to order, and then returned to their conversation.

Winnie opened with, "I've met a man."

Nina leaned forward, eyes wide, and said, "Tell me!" Nina exclaimed, "I'm all ears!"

"Actually, I knew John before I met Mark. We were in high school together back about the time of the dinosaurs!" Winnie laughed.

"AND! You saw him at your reunion?"

"Yes, we met at the reunion, and we stuck together like two Fig Newtons in a box!" Winnie grinned at her silly metaphor.

"I don't think I've heard that one! Is this a 'sticky' arrangement, already?" Nina teased back.

"No. I didn't mean that. It just popped out right then!" Winnie smiled.

"Actually, I knew John would be there, because he called me the morning of the fall festival, and we talked for quite a while. He had been asked to call a few former classmates and encourage them to attend our high school's fortieth reunion," Winnie continued.

"What's he like?" Nina begged.

"Well! He seems to be very eligible, from what I can tell. He's a professor of philosophy at The University of Chicago. He's been teaching there most of his professional life. He's traveled in Europe. He never married. "'

"Uh Oh!" Nina shook her head. "Wonder what that's about?"

"I really couldn't say, but I am intrigued," Winnie answered. "Maybe he sees himself like professors of long ago, when they never married. In fact they weren't allowed to marry.

"We both took the same Latin classes as well as an English class in high school, but we ran in different circles back then."

"Anyhow, we met at the reunion and spent both evenings together. We had so much fun! We laughed and laughed. We even discovered we had been at the zoo in Dublin on the same day back in 1978! How about that for a coincidence!"

Nina was charmed that her friend was finding such an interesting connection. "Where do you suppose this is going?" she asked.

"That's the thing. John knows I live here in Misty Falls. I told him I work in our church office and that I do a lot of things at the church — like the bulletins, teach Bible study, and such. But I haven't told him I'm the preacher at the church!" Winnie confessed. "Maybe I'm lucky that Muddy Creek United Methodist Church doesn't have a website, yet."

"I don't quite understand," Nina said. "Are you ashamed of being a pastor? Why wouldn't you tell him?"

"Of course I'm not ashamed of being a pastor!" Winnie assured Nina. "At first I thought he already knew about my profession, and so I didn't mention it," Winnie started to explain. "And then, when we talked back in September, John said something that made me think he had a problem with church, and somehow, it didn't seem to be wise to drop my vocation into the conversation at that point, so I didn't."

"I can see that," Nina agreed. "What did he say that made you think he wasn't too fond of the church?"

"He said he didn't believe in church.

"He caught me off guard, and I wasn't quite sure how to respond, so I made this lame joke, instead."

"So you actually don't know what he meant by his slur on the church, do you?" Nina said.

"Not really. Maybe it's nothing; maybe he was teasing me; but who knows!" Winnie said with exasperation.

"John sounds like he'd be a pretty terrific catch, though, don't you think?" Nina asked her friend.

Winnie smiled and nodded agreement. "On one level I do!" she said.

"This morning I got an email from John, and he said he'd like us to meet after the New Year. He's planning to attend a conference with other philosophers at Ole Miss on the first week of January, and he wrote to ask if we could get together afterwards." Winnie told her friend.

Nina's eyes opened wide, and a grin grew across her face."Now THAT'S got possibilities! Obviously, he's more than just a passing acquaintance!"

"I don't know, quite, what would be good. I can't disregard my feelings. John's fun to be with, and we seem to connect on a deep level somewhere. Maybe this is someone that is right for me. It could be part of God's plan for my life. I really want to be alert to what God wants for me at every step in my life!

"I don't know. Since we live so far apart, it's not so easy to figure things out. There's a lot I don't know about him — why he never married for one thing. What about his discomfort with the church? What about that? How can I be seriously interested with anyone who doesn't follow Christ?" Winnie asked, mostly to herself.

"You don't seem to limit your friends to just those who attend church," Nina winked at her friend.

Winnie smiled at Nina. "You're right. I have no problem with that. After all, Christians are supposed to be IN the world but not OF the world, if you know what I mean."

"IN it but not OF it? Excuse me?" Nina knit her brows.

"We're not supposed to run away from the world — like hermits — but we should be 'counter-cultural' in our approach to the world. We have something different than the world expects. We are not OF the world when we are following Christ. Christian thinking often flies in the face of worldly wisdom," Winnie explained.

"I see. But it's OK to live among the rest of us, right?" Nina asked.

"Sure. We're supposed to be good examples to everyone — and a blessing to everyone. Maybe people will see our way of doing things and want to follow Jesus, too. Maybe they will see something in our lives that they would like to have," Winnie said.

"Then how would that be different in a closer relationship, say marriage?" Nina asked.

"Actually, St. Paul wrote that if an unbeliever is married to a believer and has no qualms about it then it's fine for them to stay married. It is apparently up to the unbeliever to make the call. The Christian, who is married to an unbeliever, doesn't seem to have the same option to walk away from the marriage, simply because the spouse doesn't follow Christ," Winnie answered.

"There you go! You've answered your own question — sort of. If John has no problem with your being a believer. . ."

"You're going pretty fast there!" Winnie moaned. "We've just begun this — whatever it is."

"But now you're talking about a time together in the New Year," Nina reminded her friend.

Winnie nodded her head. "OK, I'm thinking about it, but I won't be other than who I am. If things work out right, I'll still be following Jesus. I'm not turning my back on my faith or on my promise to follow the Lord, no matter what."

They were well into their lunch when Winnie asked her friend, "How about you? Do you date?"

Nina thought for a moment before answering. "In a way I have, but not regularly."

"Uh huh!" Winnie grinned at her friend. "You're keeping something from me?"

"There's nothing, really, to keep from you. I've gone out with Tucker Joe a couple of times, but not recently" Nina explained.

"Tucker Joe!" Winnie grinned even broader this time. "He's a little younger than you, isn't he?"

Nina nodded ascent. "Yes, he is, but that isn't such a big factor in life, since we're both adults.

"Tucker Joe and I have known one another, actually, since Dan and I came here to Misty Falls, but I've been alone for more 'n fifteen years. He's never married. I suppose you knew that." Nina added.

"I always think it's a bit unusual for a man not to marry." Winnie answered.

"We used to call a woman who didn't marry an old maid, and it was a terrible pejorative. But for men there's no parallel nomenclature, like old gentleman. It doesn't have the same snap to it, does it?" Winnie grinned.

"No, it doesn't!" Nina laughed. "Tucker Joe and I went to the theater a couple of times. He's very wrapped up in FRIENDLY'S FOODS, of course. Getting him away from the store, he showed himself to be a whole different man. He really gets into acting — even at little theatre. He told me he was in his high school's production of Oklahoma, years ago. He still craves the stage, and the people, and the music, and that whole world. It was fun to see him in that different setting."

"Are you still seeing him?" Winnie asked.

"Well, Tuck's mother got sick, and he had to be totally focused on the store and working with her, and then she passed away, and he got even busier. So, no, I suppose we're not still seeing one another." Nina sighed.

Later Winnie reflected on this new information about Tuck, and thought, *"Looks like Tucker Joe may be a late bloomer, but I wonder if he's beginning to unfurl his wings to see if they'll support him. It will be interesting to see how things come out."*

❋ ❋ ❋

Winnie said to herself, *"I knew that wasn't going to work; I could have told everyone right at the start. But no one asked me, of course."*

Winnie had just put down the phone after speaking to Sallie. Things were getting touchy around the Hardy's little cottage, so she and Connie and George and the babies had moved to an apartment in town.

Winnie agreed to stop by and see them later in the day.

The place was easy to find, and, Winnie thought, it was surprising how quickly the new apartment had come together. Sallie and the little family had been in the apartment a couple days, already. It wasn't big, but there was room for Sallie in one bedroom and Connie and George and the babies in the other. Winnie noticed that the place was furnished rather nicely, and she wondered how in the world they would have been able to appropriate so much stuff so soon!

She asked about the furnishings, and Connie explained that she had met several of the neighbors in the other apartments. They were all very sympathetic about the new babies and this young family trying to get by on virtually nothing, and, before she knew it, items began showing up at their door. The neighbors had supplied a table, and chairs, and a rug, and various odds and ends. They even had a small, oak, roll top desk that had been given to them!

Winnie saw the baby girls, who now had names: Samantha Rose Oliver and Shelby Ann Oliver. They were adorable babies, and Winnie could see how much the family loved them.

Winnie agreed to call the case worker and tell her about her visit. Since she had written the letter saying she knew Sallie and was an interested party for the Olivers, Winnie knew it would be good to keep current with the DHR.

"*So far, so good,*" Winnie thought.

George had already found a job, so he was busy working. Connie told Winnie that she was anxious to get a job too. There was a small diner across the street from their apartment, which sat just off the highway. Connie would apply for a job in the next day or two. Winnie agreed to be a reference for Connie. Winnie understood that Sallie, who wasn't likely to get a job, would be the perfect sitter for the twins.

* * *

"Great! I'm really looking forward to seeing you! Love you bunches! Bye, Dear." Winnie put the phone down and smiled. She had been talking to her daughter, Claire, about visiting the O'Neill's over Thanksgiving. She would drive over Monday after her big day of preaching — two sermons in one day. It would be a five hour drive to her place in Kentucky, but Winnie had made the drive before. It was no problem; she was comfortable driving.

The O'Neill's lived nearly over to Missouri. They were a very typical family — a mom, dad, son, and daughter. The kids were still pretty small. Derry (Alexander) O'Neill was in kindergarten, and little Babsie had just turned three. Winnie didn't get to be Grannie as often as she would like, but she was determined to soak in as much family as she could in the short week they had together.

Fortunately, Winnie had already planned to have a substitute preacher for the Sunday after Thanksgiving, which was yet a couple of Sundays off. An old friend from seminary had agreed to preach at Muddy Creek. He wasn't filling a pulpit nowadays, as he was involved in an administrative job for the church, so he was pleased to be able to pitch in. Winnie would be present as the liturgist, but Bob would bring the message. *"How nice to have an actual week off!"* Winnie smiled to herself.

13. Trouble for Olivers

The fire was not life-threatening, at least that's what the fire chief's report stated, but nevertheless the kitchen was half-charred, leaving a big mess to clean up and rebuild at the Air Force Housing apartment complex in Sembach, Germany. The couple, whose residence had been burned, were provided a room in the *Gast Haus* on the air base where they would be able to stay while they awaited the rebuilding of their kitchen.

The McPhersons, the neighbors, who had just moved the day before into their new flat, directly above the burned apartment, didn't actually suffer any damage to their apartment, except for smoke. They opened all the windows in their apartment, allowing the breeze to blow through their third story flat, picked up a few overnight items, and left for the night, because the lingering smoky presence was too much to try to sleep there.

As they were coming down the stairwell they met Mindy Moore who lived in the four bedroom apartment on the first floor. Mindy had been watching the entire scene as the fire department responded to the fire across the hall and up one floor from her flat. She was greatly relieved that there was no more damage to the apartment other than the kitchen and that no one was hurt.

When Mindy saw her new neighbors coming down the stairwell, she introduced herself. The McPhersons were happy to meet this neighbor. They hadn't met too many folks, yet, in the community, so it was pleasant to get to know someone in their stairwell. Mindy realized that this new couple might be in need of a place to spend the night, owing to the excessive smoke in their apartment, and she had an idea. Mindy and Dan's apartment included maid's quarters in the attic on the fourth floor of the apartment, so she invited the McPhersons to spend the night up there. (That room had not been affected by the smoke.) She also invited them to have dinner with her family, an offer that Chet and Angela quickly accepted.

That was the beginning of a friendship that developed quite naturally. It turned out that Chet was a new tech sergeant in the same squadron where Dan was master sergeant, so they saw each other on and off the job. Over time, the families grew to be close friends.

Dan Moore, Jr., who was Pearly Mae's younger son, had enlisted in the U.S. Air Force after high school and made it a career. He had become a mechanic, working on just about every plane the Air Force flew. In his current job he was no longer hands-on working with the planes, but he continued to appreciate good work when he saw it. Dan was quick to observe the keenness that Chet approached his work on the planes, and a certain camaraderie developed between the two men.

Dan and Chet happened to learn about a real estate venture in New Mexico through a developer who was building new homes in Albuquerque and offering stock in his company. It seemed a good opportunity to invest, so they did. The two men pooled their money and bought stock in the development, which took off quickly in the early 90's.

Dan's next assignment took him to Kirkland Air Force Base in Albuquerque, which was, coincidentally, close to the development where they had been investing. The two friends kept in contact with one another, and Dan sent Chet updates about the growing development.

Last spring Dan decided to sell their interests in the development, and it turned out to be a fortunate decision to sell the stock when he did. Later in the year the market looked much less hopeful, in fact, as the days wore on, national news was showing serious trouble in nearly every aspect of the financial and business world.

"Boy, did I figure that right!" thought Dan. "I couldn't have made a better decision to pull out when I did, if I had been able to read the future!"

The stock had realized a tidy profit, and half of it belonged to Chet.

Dan had followed Chet's movements when they returned stateside. Chet's Christmas cards told the story. For a couple of years the cards had been signed by Chet and Angela, and then, after missing a few years, Chet sent a preprinted card explaining how he and Angela were no longer married. Five years later, he married a sweet, southern gal named Lucy Jane. They were newly wedded, looking forward to all that married life had to offer; they were residing in northern Kentucky.

That was last Christmas, but then Dan heard, through a third party, that Chet had contracted cancer and died, very suddenly, last May! He hadn't seen Chet for nearly fifteen years, and now, without any warning, he was gone!

Dan wished he could have been there at the end to see Chet one more time, but that was impossible now.

Dan wanted to do something to honor Chet's memory, maybe help his family somehow, and he remembered that Chet had left a widow — a woman named Lucy Jane. There was something about her name that sounded familiar, and then Dan remembered that he used to know a girl named Lucy Jane Smith back in Misty Falls. *She couldn't be the same Lucy Jane, could she? The world wasn't that small, was it?*

Dan typed her name in the Facebook search bar, and up came Lucy Jane (Smith) McPherson — newly married to Chet McPherson and living in Louisville.

"Man! How wild is that!" He exclaimed. "I know her family. Teddy Smith, would be her older brother. He and I went to high school together."

Dan felt for Chet's bride, and he decided he would figure a way to give Lucy Jane Chet's portion of the profit from the investment they had made.

A few clicks of research later Dan found that Lucy Jane had transferred from the Louisville Red Cross office to an office back home, near Misty Falls.

"She's living in Misty Falls again," Dan told Mindy. "I'm going to fly back to Misty Falls to see Mama, and on the visit I should be able to talk to Lucy Jane, Chet McPherson's new wife. I'll be home before Thanksgiving, and I'll bring Mama back with me. It will be good for her to see our family. Do you suppose we can host her through the holidays? Mama's not getting any younger, and it would be a really nice visit for us all."

Mindy, who was Pearly Mae's favorite daughter-in-law, was happy to see the holidays developing a theme. "We'll have four generations with us by Christmas. Won't that be merry?"

* * *

Winnie wasn't surprised to hear from Sallie, but her voice had a serious edge to it. She wanted to know if Winnie could come by today and see her. *I wonder what's come up?*

Winnie was out the door in no time and on her way to the apartment.

When Winnie arrived Connie and her mother were very subdued. The baby girls looked well enough, wearing cute little matching, pink outfits. *"At least the girls are fine,"* Winnie thought.

Winnie sat in the living room and Connie explained the problem straight forwardly: their secret was out. The DHR woman had made a visit to their neighbors and told them to watch out for any signs of trouble for the twin babies. She told them that the Olivers had already lost other babies to the DHR in South Carolina. The neighbors were instructed to contact the DHR if there was anything they saw that appeared to be the least bit amiss with the Olivers.

Connie was devastated, as was Sallie. They felt like their little family was now under a microscope, even being spied upon. All this DHR activity had re-opened the wounds of losing the other children, and the fear of possibly losing these two, precious, little girls was nearly more than either one of them could imagine.

This was a new idea to Winnie. She couldn't fathom the pain that Connie and George (and Sallie) had experienced having had their first three babies taken away from them.

Winnie spent some time with the women that morning. She didn't think she had any really good answers for them except to do the best they could for the twins. She prayed that this situation would resolve itself.

✳ ✳ ✳

Thursday morning Winnie turned on her computer, opened her email, and happily found a message from John.

He wrote most mornings, and Winnie was discovering how much she looked forward to these quick, first-thing-in-the-morning greetings from John. *"Our friendship is really taking shape,"* She thought.

The message was about the up-coming, Thanksgiving week. John would be going skiing. He was an avid skier and used holidays to get away from work and visit the slopes.

John would be flying to Aspen for the Thanksgiving weekend. He wondered if Winnie would join him there. He had reservations at a ski resort, same place he'd been using for years. He'd arrive there late Wednesday, since he couldn't travel until his classes were finished that day.

Winnie stopped reading. This offer seemed to involve a step that was probably very normal and expected for adult relationships, but for her, her convictions, and her vocation, it would need to be a different story. Of course, Winnie couldn't know exactly what John had in mind; his invitation was very open — come, enjoy — yet she couldn't assume there were no expectations either.

"He's really interested in me, obviously. I don't mind that," she smiled.

Winnie paused to dream. She had to be honest with herself. Here was an opportunity that had never presented itself before, and she realized at once that she was tempted to accept. Surely, she and John could enjoy one another's company in such a romantic and secluded setting.

Winnie's Walk: A Journey of Faith and Romance

Winnie had a very firm respect for the sanctity of marriage and the gift of marital intimacy. God had truly outdone Himself in that department — a great blessing — one she had surely missed for a long time. And, Winnie remembered, this gift ranked very high on most men's agendas. She wanted to respect that, too. She didn't want to toy with the issue.

The temptation for her was clearly there, but Winnie also realized it was just *that* — a temptation. Actually, John had not, in so many words, suggested that such a weekend might develop into this deeper relationship, but assuming otherwise would be a mistake.

Finally, Winnie faced the invitation squarely and decided, *"I can't take that step, not yet, besides, I could lose my credibility with my community and congregation simply by accepting such an invitation. A scandal in the church rarely needs anything more than the appearance of impropriety. But, pragmatics aside, the really important thing is, it simply wouldn't be right,"* she reminded herself.

Winnie had been married to Mark for nearly seventeen years. They had seen their marriage through various struggles, like most young marrieds, and they had watched their marriage mature and become solid and wonderful. It didn't happen overnight. No indeed. It took many trials, some difficult words and misunderstandings, and the advent of their wonderful children with all their added dynamics.

Winnie and Mark had grown confident in their marriage: It belonged just to the two of them. It was sacred, and they were faithful to one another. That was the way God had intended marriage to be. Despite much social and personal pressure they decided to not start their marriage until they were formally married.

They were aware that some couples chose to jump the gun before they married, and many of them never tied the knot. Perhaps this was because they had avoided the commitment piece to the relationship. They seemed to be committed to one another only as long as it felt good.

Marriage, on the other hand, was a commitment, a vow to God, that the two would bring their complete selves — all the gifts they could muster — to help build the marriage. It was not a pledge lightly given.

Those who didn't come before an altar or a judge and make those vows, didn't get that commitment. They didn't have the promise from the other to love, honor, trust, and respect from their partner. They missed knowing the other was committed to their venture.

Besides, giving things away too quickly didn't encourage commitment, rather the gift became cheap. Winnie remembered the old saw, *"Why buy the cow if the milk is free? Maybe that's a trite saying, but it's still a good question,"* she thought to herself.

With this in mind Winnie realized she didn't want to compromise a potentially good relationship (might marriage possibly be in their future?) by acting too quickly. Jumping too quickly into some physical arrangement was *not* the way to develop a strong relationship aimed at increasing commitment. It spoke of indiscretion, lack of self-control, and lack of respect for the other person. No, if this fledgling connection had any potential, she and John would need to feel their way carefully through the complicated vicissitudes of getting to know one another.

Now, how to explain this to John?

Winnie wrote,

Dear John, What a wonderful time you will have in Aspen skiing over the slopes! It sounds like a grand way to spend the holiday, and it's very kind of you to invite me to be your guest there in the snow and the fun, but I can't accept.

I've already made plans to spend the week with my daughter and her family in Kentucky, and I can't change my plans so close to the day. But, there is another reason why I wouldn't be able to come this time.

I am very aware that we are becoming special to one another, and I have a lot of respect for what our friendship might become. Because of this respect I would not want to do anything that might damage its potential. (Can you understand what I'm trying to say?)

I don't want to be too forward about this, but IF we find our friendship is growing into something greater, something that we would want to make more permanent — down the road — I want to give it the best foundation possible. That boils down to our being very circumspect in our deportment.

King Solomon wrote, "For everything there is a season, and a time for every matter under heaven." Surely that would include adult relationships, wouldn't it?

I can feel myself blushing as I even mention this (in an email, would you believe!), but I feel very strongly that this is right and proper.

I have known but one man in my life, and it is his name that I bear to this day. We had a loving marriage, which began the night we married. I would not want to settle for something less in the future. I pray you understand this.

Have a great weekend; DON'T break a leg!

Your Good Friend,

Winnie

***

Saturday afternoon Winnie saw Pearly Mae at The Depot Diner. She was with a man, who turned out to be her son, Dan, Jr. Introductions were made all around, and Pearly Mae explained to Winnie how her son had come to take her back with him to Albuquerque to be the family matriarch of four generations over Thanksgiving and Christmas.

They chatted together several minutes. Winnie was pleased for her friend Pearly Mae. What a nice way for her to enjoy the holidays, and what a fine surprise Dan had given his mother.

They would be coming to the community Thanksgiving service tomorrow evening. Winnie told them that she was preaching then, and she was happy they could come hear her.

***

Saturday evening had arrived, and Winnie was facing two sermons the next day. She hadn't preached two, different sermons on the same day before, but she had been working on both of them for several weeks. They were pretty much ready now.

127

It was a happy accident that she didn't have to preach the week after visiting with her family. Winnie remembered other times when she visited Claire's or Paul's family, but still had the responsibility of coming up with a sermon for the next Sunday. She had secluded herself in her room, laptop on her lap, working every morning to pull together her thoughts for the sermon, all the while being very aware of her family — those cute grandchildren — waiting her appearance. The one responsibility almost spoiled the holiday time she had come to enjoy.

"This time, maybe I've got it right. Bob will bring the message, and I can enjoy my time with the O'Neill's. After all, even God rested on the seventh day!"

14. The Best Laid Plans

Winnie watched as the road whizzed by under her car and with it the concerns in Misty Falls. Every mile carried her further and further from the town and with it the stresses and expectations she knew as pastor faded slowly. Those responsibilities were sometimes heavy and sometimes oppressive — like watching someone else's troubles and not being able to do more than impotently console those involved and pray with them and for them.

Everyone should get away from it all, occasionally, Winnie believed. *Whatever "it all" is — the office, studies, heavy work, the day-to-day grind — getting away is good for a person's interior, and exterior, self. No doubt, getting away from the usual grind can be therapeutic and cathartic. It can present a new perspective on one's everyday self, and bring new vigor to the humdrum and ordinary.*

Situations that belonged to others came and went, and Winnie could professionally distance herself from them, but the sermon requirement never abated — it came every week no matter what else was happening, no matter how well she felt or what else might be happening in the world. Giving sermons was, in the final analysis, much fun, but it was fun that came only after long hours of wrestling her message into a presentable form. Once Winnie found and understood the message, presenting it Sunday morning became a delight, but for some reason that was a lesson she had to relearn each week.

It was quite a paradox for Winnie, a real approach-avoidance thing. She dreaded it and loved it all at the same time.

"Goodness, My Dear," Winnie scolded herself, *"I don't suppose I should ever feel so put upon or heavily saddled with that responsibility! After all, I chose to do it. I could have gone into some other area of Christian vocation or even social work, but I chose this. And serving the Lord is a blessing, of course! O, Lord, help me put a better face on my sermon building. Help me to recognize the blessing it is — which I definitely feel when I'm actually preaching! Thank you, Lord,"* she prayed.

Winnie could feel herself relaxing as she passed through the new scenery. She was always reminded of God's marvelous creativity and faithfulness when she found herself close to nature, as these great forests and lakes brought to her mind. *"Isn't God great, and good, and incredible?"* she thought. *"How can anyone look into the immense beauty and grandeur of nature without being thankful?"*

Of course, Winnie had just preached about being thankful the evening before, and she was still filled with her message — being thankful in all circumstances. It was easy to be thankful for such a time as this, but Winnie's message was to remind her listeners (and herself) that even when troubled times come along, we need to stay focused on being thankful to God. An attitude of thanksgiving can push aside other, not so productive attitudes, like fear, or rage, or some other impropriety.

Winnie was relishing this Monday morning, as she did every Monday, because it was so far from Sunday, but this time, of course, she wouldn't have the countdown that she always had as Sundays drew closer. And that was another reason to be thankful!

The week with the O'Neills in Kentucky was especially good for Winnie, serving as a fresh wind blowing out the, almost, staleness of her workday environment.

The grandchildren stirred memories for Winnie of when Paul and Claire were young themselves. *Goodness, wasn't life different back then?* Winnie used to think that her life was mostly a big blur of activities when the kids were small, running from one event or chore to the next. This time it was possible to engage the children as much as she wanted and then sit back as an observer, watching the flurry of projects and frivolity.

Winnie's Walk: A Journey of Faith and Romance

Derry, who was five, was already reading. He went with his family to the library each week to hear stories read by the librarian and to pick out books to take home and read with Mommy or Daddy. He was riding a two wheeler, and he was navigating pretty well on his skates too. He was ALL boy! He was enthusiastic about getting outside at every possible moment, no matter the temperature. He climbed the trees in his backyard and others around their neighborhood.

Babsie was petite, tall for her age, and wiry. She wanted to do just as her big brother did, and followed closely whenever possible. not allowing her size or age to impede her from experiencing all that life offered a pre-schooler. She wasn't quite reading, but she would hold a book on her lap, absorb herself in the pictures, and then tell the story just as well, and, perhaps, more fluently, than if she was reading it. Babsie, like many girls, was all about PINK. She liked all things pink, and her room and her clothes reflected assorted variations on the color. Her favorite doll was a very-much-loved pink bunny called Mr. Flopsy which accompanied her wherever she went. (Winnie thought he was rather like Pooh, who had been dragged along by the leg behind Christopher Robin.)

Winnie's daughter, Claire, was completely focused on her family's well-being. She was a stay-at-home mom, which was a challenge for today's families, She and her husband, Alex, had agreed, before the kids came, that she would stay home with them at least until they were safely into school. Claire believed it was a great gift she could give her kids to be home for them while they were young; after all, her mother had been at home when she and her brother Paul were growing up, and she wanted the same for her kids.

Winnie and Claire talked nearly nonstop during the visit. Of course, Winnie told her about John, and they both speculated about what the future might bring — would he stay in the picture or not? Claire didn't seem unhappy with the concept of someday having a step-father. She certainly wanted the best for her mom.

Thanksgiving dinner could have been a scene from a Norman Rockwell painting. Everything seemed just perfect, the children, the dinner, the snowy weather outside, the crackling fire in the living room, everything was lovely. *"Didn't Rockwell always have a piece of humor in his depictions of life?"* Winnie smiled to herself as she watched a Rockwellian scenario unfold at the thanksgiving table.

The children had spent some time the day before making little place-cards for each family member. The cards were adorned with handmade, three dimensional turkeys. Derry and Babsie had worked hard to put their turkeys together, using pinecones, construction paper for feathers, and pipe cleaners for the turkeys' necks and heads. Each bird was colorful and unique, and the adults were full of praise at the efforts the two children had made.

Winnie asked Babsie if she had named her turkey. Babsie answered, "I shall call my turkey Fred."

"Why did you choose Fred for a name for a turkey, Honey?" her father asked.

"Fred is the name of the dog next door, and he is my friend," Babsie explained.

Everyone smiled at her logical naming of her turkey.

A minute later, however, Babsie came to a terrible realization. It hadn't quite occurred to the child that her place card turkey and the turkey that had been cooking all day for dinner were in some way related. It didn't occur to Babsie, until that moment, when she realized in horror that she was being asked to take a bite of turkey, which would be like taking a bite of Fred!

Suddenly the lovely holiday dinner table was the site of a very painful expression of unwillingness by Babsie. She dissolved into a different child in mere seconds — crying and wriggling and stretching herself board straight, causing her to slide off the chair onto the floor. The entire meal was stopped mid-bite, as everyone tried to assuage little Babsie's worries over her Thanksgiving meal.

Finally, Babsie agreed to eat the other, yummy foods on her plate and not to touch the turkey. Peace was restored; the dinner continued, and the evening, overall, was still enjoyable.

✳ ✳ ✳

Back in Misty Falls on Monday before Thanksgiving, Dan Moore, Jr. walked into Lucy Jane's Red Cross office, and asked if she could get away for coffee. It was only nine in the morning, but Lucy Jane wanted to give some time to this visitor, so she picked up her coat and handbag and followed Dan out.

They ordered coffee at the IHOP nearby. Lucy Jane's curiosity had been peeked when Dan called her earlier and explained that he was an old friend of Chet's and that he had some business that he needed to do for him. Lucy Jane, being Chet's widow, would be the logical person to receive this.

While they awaited their coffee's arrival, they began to figure how it was that Dan came to know about Lucy Jane.

Sure enough, Lucy Jane knew Dan's mother. Everyone in town knew Miss Pearly Mae Moore. After all Ms. Moore had been associated with the David Crockett Elementary School in Misty Falls for many years. Lucy Jane remembered her teaching fifth grade next door to her own class when she attended school.

They chatted back and forth identifying various personalities that they knew in Misty Falls.

Dan cleared his throat and said, "You must be wondering what my coming here is all about."

Lucy Jane agreed that her curiosity had been piqued after his call.

Dan began by telling Lucy Jane about his time in the Air Force in Germany. He and Chet were good friends then, and they had kept in contact since then. He explained how he and Chet had made an investment in a housing development in New Mexico back in the early 90's. (Chet had paid into it, but the account had been made in Dan's name.) Dan explained how he had been lucky to be stationed near the development when he was assigned back to CONUS (Continental U.S). He had watched the development for quite a while, and then he had decided that maybe it was a good time to cash out the investment, which he did, back in April. "We made a good profit, and half of it belongs to Chet!" Dan explained.

Lucy Jane was taking in every word Dan spoke. Her eyes widened and her smile expanded. "Really!" she exclaimed. "You're here to give me money?"

Dan reached into his inside coat pocket and took out an envelope. He handed the astonished woman the envelope and waited. Lucy Jane took the envelope and carefully, almost ceremoniously, opened it up. There was a cashier's check made out in her name for the sum of $15,846.27.

Lucy Jane's eyebrows knit together as she read and reread the number of dollars on the check. She hadn't expected this surprise; it was a really good surprise!

She put the check down on the table and looked at Dan. "Thank you. Thank you, so much! Obviously I didn't know about this investment or that it had been cashed out, but I'm very thankful that you remembered Chet's part and have acted so generously!"

Dan was amused to watch this young woman — her surprise and her obvious pleasure. "Can you think what you'll do with the money? It's not a great amount, but maybe there's something you'd like to do that the money might make possible."

Lucy Jane was thinking. "I can't say this minute. I didn't expect this, and it needs some thought to be done right. I do think, though, it needs to be something that Chet would have liked — some sort of project. I'll give it some careful consideration. Would you like to hear about it when I decide?" she asked Dan.

"I really would like to know, if you will tell me," Dan nodded his head.

The two finished their coffee, talking about Chet and his earlier life when Dan knew him. Lucy Jane was pleased to hear more about Chet's world when he was a younger man. It was like seeing old photos of times past. Lucy Jane thanked Dan again for the surprise and his thoughtfulness. They each felt a special goodness about the gift.

✳ ✳ ✳

Winnie's drive back home was uneventful. She had not thought of Misty Falls or her church work during her visit and she felt refreshed from the visit.

She arrived at home just before dinner time Saturday evening, unpacked, and made a light meal for herself. She thought, *"Tonight will be easy. This may be Saturday night, but all I have to do for tomorrow is get the bulletin duplicated, and that will be a breeze!"*

Winnie had just put the last of her dinner dishes away, when the phone rang. It was 6:30 p.m, and Bob was on the other end of the line. "Winnie," he said, "I absolutely hate to do this to you, but I'm sick! I've been as sick as a dog this entire past week! My whole family has been sick with the flu. I'm calling to tell you that I can't come to preach for you tomorrow. I really want to, but I'm sick, and I can't make it!"

Winnie listened to Bob's weak and tired voice. She realized this was NOT how she expected her Saturday night to be — figuring out what in the world to do for tomorrow! But, on the other hand, there was a certain amount of irony about it that was not wasted on her. After all, hadn't she wanted to get some rest, away from the constant requirement of building a new sermon? She had had that rest, and she did feel revived.

Winnie dismissed any idea of being angry over this turn of events. She might have nursed some thought of ire for having Sunday morning just dumped in her lap at the proverbial last moment, but she couldn't do it. *"Probably Bob had been hoping that he'd get better, or at least well enough to make the trip,"* she checked her anger.

Winnie said, "Goodness, Bob! I'm so sorry you've been sick! How completely un-fun!" Winnie paused for a moment, not quite sure what to do next. Such a situation had never come up before; she had always been so careful to prepare for her Sunday sermons. Before she had time to think, Winnie heard herself saying, "Bob, Don't worry about tomorrow. You remember Dr. Logan in seminary said that a good Methodist pastor should be ready to preach, pray, sing, or die at a moment's notice! Looks like it's my turn to rise to the occasion!

"I'm a United Methodist pastor, and it's Saturday night, so what else should I be doing but figuring out what I should say to my people in the morning. Actually, I've had a good rest this week, so I'll just look through my files and find something that's appropriate and use that. "Take care of yourself, and I'll try to get you to fill in another time!" Winnie assured Bob.

That was that. Suddenly Winnie's evening had a new agenda — one she knew very well: Saturday evening — dinner, a little TV, then pick up the sermon and get it ready for tomorrow.

Winnie was thankful that she'd been preaching for a while, and she had a good-sized library of sermons from which she could choose something appropriate. Somehow this thankful sensation seemed to her to have the ironic and typically cryptic timbre of an answered prayer. *"Fortunately, that's the only thing in front of me tonight!"* Winnie smiled.

There was no way she could have started from scratch and built a new sermon right then, so Winnie didn't even stress about creating something new. Tomorrow would be the first week of Advent (the church's season of looking forward to the coming of the Messiah), and Winnie had preached a number of times on that subject — Waiting. She would suggest that, as we wait for Christ to come again, we should do it with expectation, intention, and joy. Winnie would use examples of each to illustrate how we can proactively anticipate the return of the Lord. *Yes, this sermon should not be hard to give in the morning.* Preparing this sermon was even fun.

After worship Sunday morning Pastor Winnie stood at the back of the sanctuary shaking hands with parishioners when several folks inquired about their special speaker whom they had been expecting. Winnie quickly explained the situation — the flu, the last minute call, her efforts to pull everything together. She laughed with several of the members when she told the story of surprising evening. The whole service had come out just fine!

15. Signs of Christmas

The newly formed, icy dew created a satisfying "crunch" beneath Winnie's feet and announced that winter was coming as she and Bitty stepped out for their early Monday morning walk.

"Mondays are still the best," Winnie thought.

The late fall breeze was chilly and scooped up any unbagged leaves and whisked them in whimsical spirals along the streets. Winnie was watching this play of wind and leaves scuttling across the streets, when suddenly a dust devil appeared, coming right toward Winnie and her pooch. Winnie certainly didn't think the dust devil could be dangerous, but nevertheless she began to maneuver herself and Bitty away from the twister's path to avoid the blustery funnel.

Winnie watched the little dust devil, which couldn't have been more than fifteen or twenty feet high and, maybe, five feet in diameter, in disbelief as it appeared to be following her. Winnie began to trot— her top speed — across the grassy field in front of her, when the miniature twister caught her up, spun her several times 'round, and knocked her completely off her feet. Winnie let go the dog leash and closed her eyes tight. The zephyr vanished, but the evidence of the surprising event remained: her hat was no where to be found, her scarf was wrapped awkwardly around her neck and arms; she couldn't have been more blown about if she had walked through an automatic car dryer. As she sat on the ground, legs akimbo, she collected herself slowly and determined that she was totally unharmed, save for her sense of pride and fairness in the universe.

Before the odd pastor vs. nature moment Winnie had walked over to Main Street to see some of the newly set up Christmas lights, and, although she was now quite disheveled, owing to that brief encounter with the mini-twister, she decided to continue her walk and check out some of homes she had heard about. She picked up Bitty's lead and ran her fingers through her short, wavy hair to settle it a bit and continued her walk.

Some folks in the community had used the Thanksgiving weekend to string lights on their property. There were three houses in town, side by side, that were already especially well adorned. Winnie remembered hearing about their owners when she first arrived in Misty Falls. They were noted for their lavish Christmas decorations each year. Winnie wondered if the owners competed to make their Yule décor the best in the neighborhood.

The three houses, situated on Main Street and facing the railroad tracks, were owned by three, octogenarian sisters — two who had never married and a widow. All three were members of Muddy Creek Church. Winnie believed someone could write a book just about the three sisters, and it would be quite a page-turner! The sisters didn't attend worship these days, but Winnie had visited them numerous times, hoping to revive their interest in their faith community. The sisters were very good friends. They enjoyed their individual domains, keeping their homes up as they desired, but hardly a day went by without them visiting one another.

The three homes, stood adjacent one another — great, dignified, well-kept, antebellum edifices. Each sported a gracious veranda surrounding the house, which was, itself, surrounded by rolling lawns and tall conifers looming overhead, shading and protecting their homes.

Winnie was surprised the first time she met the sisters, surprised that they possessed such wealth, considering they were single women. They had once owned a dry goods store in town, started by their father, and had run the store for nearly fifty years before selling out to a chain store and retiring.

Winnie had tried to encourage the sisters to re-activate their interests in Muddy Creek Church. They had been faithful members in years past, but no longer. Winnie gathered that none of them had attended anything more than a Christmas Eve service, and/or maybe an Easter celebration, for some time. Winnie figured there was a story behind their absence from church, but she had not picked up any clues about why, yet. *"Maybe, one day, they will share with me what has interfered with their activity at Muddy Creek,"* Winnie told Bitty.

✳ ✳ ✳

Winnie opened an email from John on Monday morning. He had returned from his Thanksgiving trip to Aspen and had enjoyed the slopes and the refreshing change in scenery. His skiing holiday was pretty much like what he was used to — the travel, the resort, all the ski paraphernalia, the lifts, the actual time on the slopes — speeding down graceful passages amid magnificent mountainscapes and spotting the occasional wild deer amongst the trees. He wrote about the pristine beauty of the mountains and how he was sure he would never get over the thrill of coming down those slopes at breakneck velocity. "Exhilarating was the only word for it!"

Apparently John had skied in a number of venues downhill as well as cross country. He took opportunities to experience the slopes or a good cross country trek wherever he could,.even enjoying slopes in the Andes over a summer in Chili and Argentina. There the snow was in abundance in July and August!

But today John was thoughtful about his holiday. He came home realizing he was missing something. He admitted that he caught himself relishing the idea of seeing Winnie again. He toyed with various scenarios of how they might spend time together. He was finding his mind wandering to thoughts of her each day, and John wondered if Winnie might not be feeling similarly?

John spoke of watching several families at the lodge. These families brought their children — introducing them to skiing, letting them use the "bunny hills," before they ventured onto the steeper slopes. John saw them in the dining room and observed how the children always had so much energy! He wondered if he would have ever been able to work with small children. The children he saw were cute, although some were hyper, and he thought they were exhausting just to watch from across the room. John was thankful that he was not responsible for instructing and correcting children as they sat in the dining room.

That inspired John to ask Winnie how it had been for her and Mark when they had their own children at home? Had it been very trying to have children under foot all the time, or was it something you got used to? Since he'd missed out on being a father of small children, he really wondered how people could keep their sanity with so much commotion constantly going on about them?

John ended his email saying, "I think I'm beginning to realize that I'm missing something, and I've about concluded that what I'm really missing is you! John."

Winnie had come to look forward to John's frequent messages, and today she was warmed inside to read his comment about "missing something" and that the "something" was her. She felt a special closeness to John, and realized that she, too, as busy as her life was, was "missing something." *"And I think John may have named it for both of us,"* Winnie announced to Bitty, who was curled up on the rug next to her.

Winnie smiled as she thought to herself about the time when she had her own little children at home. It didn't seem that long ago in a way, yet, in another way, it was forever ago.

She wrote, "The deal with raising children is that God gives us a deep, deep love for them right from the start. They come to us as extensions of ourselves, so we learn to deal with their needs: the feeding, the changing, the comforting, the crazy hours and lack of sleep that are suddenly forced upon us. We grow along with the kids, re-experiencing life as they learn it for the first time. Yes! They are enormously requiring, especially in the early years, but all their care — all the long hours, changed agendas, new expenses, the loss of independence — all seems to be the right thing to do, even if it demands every fiber of strength we can muster.

"I discovered one weekend when the kids were tiny, and Mark was out of town, that being a parent can sometimes be *sweet-agony.* The kids had picked up a bug, maybe the flu, and they took turns throwing up all over their cribs the whole night long. I was awakened from sleep by the sound of little Paul retching in his crib. The next thing I knew I was cleaning up a crib, changing the sleeper for a clean one and comforting him; then a few minutes later, the baby Claire was sick and needing a cleaned up crib and fresh set of p.j.'s, etc.

"This same process continued again and again many times that night. I wondered, then, if I might ever look back on that night and think it was funny! First one child and then the other — then repeat! I was exhausted, but somehow I found the strength to carry on, to care for my dear little ones who were so sick. At one point in the middle of the night, having redone the cribs and the clothes and comforted the babies several times each, I sat on the floor between their two bedrooms and prayed — mostly for strength and for healing for the kids. Then I thought about singing. I don't re-member what song came to mind, maybe it was the *Tallis Canon.* (Do you know it?) Anyway, I sang the song again and again, and I came to realize that everything would be fine; I would survive, as well as the kids. Somehow the song, which praises God, helped me pull myself out of some healthy self-pity to a much better frame of mind. (I can see I'm digressing!)

"Parenthood is a wonderful blessing, even as it is a great challenge. It's certainly not one I would choose to miss. I would not want to trade a moment of my time at home with the kids for any other activity. It was just right for me. I wish I could impart some of my memories to you; would that there was a way so to do!

"You may have missed some of the best moments in life — realizing, for the first time that you're going to be a parent; holding your new child in your arms for the first time; watching the amazing growth in your child; seeing him stand free for the first moment — without anything to hold him up! Hearing her say "Mommy" for the first time. You get the picture!

"I could wish you had not missed those precious years; I believe you would have loved them. Surely there are many, many different routes to take in life, different experiences we can have. Surely we can't know them all. Some are mutually exclusive; at least they can't be experienced concurrently. I can't know, for instance, the wonder of being a stay-at-home mother and at the same time the excitement of being a single, professional woman. But! When time is added to the mix, then, surely, having numerous, challenging vocations can be had."

❋ ❋ ❋

Joe Ed Rafferty, the choir director at First Baptist Church, was working with children from several churches on a Christmas musical production. This year the children's Christmas musical was an actual play set to music. There were speaking parts, choral parts, and parts for children of all ages. The play would require a couple of sets and a variety of costumes — mostly angel garb: halos, wings, and long sleeved tunics.

Winnie stopped by to watch one of the rehearsals and saw what a great project it was, giving the children an opportunity to experience being part of a group that was doing something together and being responsible for remembering their parts. *"There are a number of really good reasons for children to get involved in little theatre. It evokes their best efforts, and that's a blessing!"* Winnie thought.

Winnie had spoken earlier to Joe Ed about the show and asked if there was anything that her church could do to help out. Joe Ed had told her that the angel chorus was coming from the four year olds in the pre-school this year, and that they would need eighteen, small angel costumes for the kids to wear.

Vickie Jackson's name came to Winnie's mind immediately, thinking she would be the perfect person to head up such a project. She told Joe Ed that she would check with Vickie and other ladies at Muddy Creek and let him know if they could manage such a project.

*** *** ***

Jeff Plummer called to say that the flooring materials had arrived and to ask if he could come Tuesday to begin work. When he arrived Winnie asked Jeff if he and Jillian had married over Thanksgiving.

Jeff grinned widely and said, "Indeed we did tie the knot last week. We took off to Gatlinburg for the weekend. Jillian has some connection there and made arrangements for us to get a one-room place right in the midst of all the tourist attractions. We got hitched first thing. We went to a little wedding chapel there and had the ceremony. It wasn't a big deal; it took less than an hour for the whole business, but I guess that short time is the open door to the whole world of marriage!"

Winnie shook her head in agreement and said, "I'd say that's an understatement! You've been married before, so I guess you know what you're talking about."

Jeff answered, "Well, hopefully I learned from before, and I'm a better man for it. Jessie and I were way too young to get married when we did. I was barely out of high school, and she still had a couple of years more to go, which she hasn't yet finished.

"Jillian and I have talked a lot about what we think marriage means — what it costs each partner, what can go wrong, and what should go right. We talked forever, it seemed, online about our past marriages before we actually set eyes on one another.

"We recognize how it takes two people, each working on the marriage, to make it work. It takes two people who are very interested in communicating — not just to be heard but to really HEAR what the other person is saying. We've set up a time at breakfast every Saturday morning to take five minutes and talk about what's going on — you know: what's on our minds, what's good for each of us, and what's good for both of us, what's working, and what's not. We call it our 'Target Time'. So far, which has been just one Saturday, it has worked very well!"

"Our trip to Gatlinburg was pure ambrosia. We took warm clothes for hiking, so we could take long walks each day. We saw the last good days of autumn; most of the colors were gone, but there were still some breathtaking sights up there."

"We had time to talk and share and learn more about one another. Remember, neither one of us is a spring chicken. We still have a lot to learn about one another. It's a little like unwrapping a package that's been bundled in many layers. It's fun and colorful, and Jillian and I think we each have found our 'soul mate'," Jeff blushed.

✳ ✳ ✳

Lucy Jane had enjoyed Thanksgiving with her family. The week had begun with a big surprise — Dan Moore bringing her the cashier's check, representing Chet's part of the investment the two men had made.

She hadn't told anyone else about it, yet. She deposited the money in a savings account so she would not accidentally spend it down. She wanted to do something with the money that might somehow speak to the spirit of Chet and what they had hoped and dreamed of doing together.

Lucy Jane and Chet had planned to have a family. It would be a late in life family, for sure, but they had wanted to include children in their life together. They wanted to experience parenting — how parents influence their children and help them to develop their personalities and values. They felt their marriage would be more complete with children growing in it.

They had only been married a short while when Chet got sick, and before they knew it, his time had come. Lucy Jane realized that she had a lot of healing to do before she could think about family or future. She knew she was emotionally fragile yet and needed more time to mend.

She decided that what she could do at this point was begin to think about what she might do when she felt stronger. There were any number of possible ways to use the money, many good places she was sure, but she wanted to remember Chet in some way in the process. She wanted their hope of family to be seen in whatever she decided to do.

Lucy Jane needed someone to talk to — someone she could trust, someone outside her family — and Tucker Joe's name came to mind. Lucy Jane had enjoyed the several conversations she had had with Tucker Joe, and she thought he might be a good sounding board for her.

Indeed, Tuck was pleased to hear Lucy Jane's voice on the other end of the line. Yes, he'd like to see her and could meet this week for a chat. They set up a meeting for dinner in the city, this Thursday evening. That would take them away from inquisitive eyes in town here. "It's a date!" Tuck announced. "See you Thursday at six."

✳ ✳ ✳

Saturday afternoon was the time set for the church to be decorated for Advent and Christmas. Of course, the Advent Wreath had already been set up in the chancel at Muddy Creek, and the first candle had been lit last Sunday on Advent One. The chrismon tree, wreaths, poinsettias, and the Advent/Christmas banners would be put out this afternoon by members of the church, followed by a Hanging of the Greens ceremony.

Thom Jackson, the church trustee, had already pulled the tree out of the storage unit and brought it into the sanctuary. The tree would be decorated entirely with chrismons — a crown, a lamb, a fish, an orb, various crosses, etc. Each chrismon was a different symbol of Christ, and had been made, painstakingly, by hand. The chrismons, along with hundreds of tiny white lights on the tree, provided an ethereal charm in the sanctuary.

Martha Reeves had brought homemade Christmas cookies to be enjoyed while everyone worked.

In the midst of decorating, Little Brad asked his daddy a question, and his dad referred him to Pastor Winnie. Little Brad walked over to the pastor and asked, "Daddy says I'm s'posed to ask you where the others are, who are part of Christmas?"

Winnie crinkled her eyebrows and knelt down to the four year old's height and asked, "What do you mean by the others, Little Brad?"

Little Brad thought he had asked the question as clearly as he could; he said, "You know, the others! There are lots of others that are in the stores. Haven't you seen them?"

Winnie nodded her head and said, "Yes, I do know what you mean. I'm so glad you noticed that our church doesn't have those different characters. Can you tell me what you see here at church?" Winnie looked around at the other children to see if they might have an answer.

Brenda Sue, the Barrymore's twelve year old, picked up a lamb chrismon and held it up. "Look, Little Brad, here is a lamb. Do you see lambs in the stores?"

Brad cocked his head and shook it. "I don't think so," he replied.

Matthew Thompson, Marva Lyn's twin brother, spoke up, "Little Brad, you're right; there is a difference between the decorations we see in the stores and the decorations we see here at church. The stores have more cartoon people, I think."

Marva Lyn added, "Maybe they didn't have cartoons back in Jesus' time."

Winnie was enjoying this repartee among the children. She said, "Marva Lyn, You hit the answer on the head! Do you know you did?"

Marva Lyn thought for a moment and said, "Well, Christmas is about the baby Jesus, isn't it? At home we have a cretzshe... Mom! What's that word?"

Sheryl Lynn said, "You mean the crèche. It's a French word for the place where Jesus was born. It looks like a barn with one side open so we can see into it."

Marva Lyn continued, "And the crèche also has shepherds and wise men and angels and animals in it."

Bobby Jackson asked, "Hey, don't we have a big set like that here? Don't we have one outside by the front of the church at Christmastime?"

Bobby's father, Thom Jackson, answered, "Yes, you and Matthew can help me get it out and set it up later this afternoon."

Winnie thought this might be a good opportunity for the children, and their parents, to understand more about the difference between Christmas, as the world celebrates it, and the celebration of the Incarnation.

She asked, "Who can tell me which came first, Christmas or Easter?"

Letitia Washington was enjoying this line of thinking along with her pastor. She asked, "Do you mean first according to the calendar, or which holiday was first celebrated, or which actually happened first, chronologically?"

Jodi Lee said, "Sounds like there could be three different answers."

Thom Jackson spoke up saying, "If I remember right, Easter was celebrated first. It was the first thing that happened in the church; I'm right, aren't I, Pastor Winnie?"

Winnie agreed, but she didn't want to interject her thoughts as long as there was such good interaction among the folks, so she answered briefly. "Indeed, Christ rose on the first day of the new week, which we call Easter Sunday, and people have been celebrating that event of resurrection every Sunday since then. Every Sunday is really a mini-Easter."

Letitia continued, "So Easter is the first holy day of the church. Of course, according to the calendar, Easter also comes first in the year, since Christmas falls at the end of the year. BUT! When we think of Christmas as being the birth of Jesus, then his birth certainly came before his death and resurrection!"

Winnie smiled at Letitia and said, "That's a good clarification. So, if Easter was first, when did Christmas come along?"

Jodi Lee spoke up, "I think that Christmas must have come a long time after the church began."

Winnie nodded to Letitia to answer. "Right. It was several centuries after the beginning of the church when Christians decided to celebrate Jesus' birth. They were having trouble with the pagans who held a great Feast of Bacchus, the Greek god of wine and drunkenness, during the darkest time of the year. The Christians couldn't join that drunken orgy, so they decided to celebrate the Light of the World coming into world during that darkest time of the year. Christmas was a counter-cultural way of stating who they were. Christmas for Christians is supposed to look different from the world's way of doing things."

"Can you see why we have different characters in our decorations, Little Brad?" Winnie asked.

Little Brad thought for a moment and said, "I can see why we have Jesus in our church, but why don't we see Him in the stores? And why don't we have the other pictures? They are fun to look at. I like them, too."

Winnie appreciated Little Brad's candor and pointed out to him, "Christmas is all about Jesus and his birth, 'He took on flesh and lived among us,' as St. John says. The others that we see in bright, colorful pictures in the stores have nothing to do with Jesus coming into the world. They have nothing to do with God loving the world so much that He gave His only Son, so that whosoever believes in Him will not perish but have eternal life.

"Mickey, Goofy, Donald, the Grinch, Scrooge, and Santa and have nothing to do with Christmas the way Christians believe," Pastor Winnie explained.

The group ended their decorating with a simple "Hanging of the Greens" ceremony, bringing in the wreathes, flowers and banners and turning the lights on the chrismon tree. The sanctuary was now prepared for Advent and Christmas.

16. A Busy Week

Winnie had barely opened her eyes Monday morning when the phone rang, and the sobbing voice on the other end of the line was one of her favorite parishioners, Evelyn Hobbs. She was calling from University of Tennessee Medical Center in Knoxville. Her son, Randy, who was just now home from his hitch in the Army, had been in a terrible collision the night before on a country road near their home. He was in the TICU — Trauma Intensive Care Unit. He had suffered a terrible blow to his head as well as a number of broken bones. The bones would heal, but his head injury was very, very severe. He was in a coma and was not expected to come out of it. Evelyn and her husband, Gerald, had driven to the hospital as soon as they heard the news. They would be there with their only son as long as he needed them.

Winnie dressed quickly, grabbed a banana and cup of coffee, and was on her way out the door to the hospital. It was a good forty-five minute drive into Knoxville, and the traffic on Monday morning was just what you'd expect — cars and trucks packing the lanes, everyone intent on getting to work on time. Winnie used her time in the car for a sort of *ad hoc* devotional time, since she was missing her usual time for that at home.

She prayed out loud, especially mentioning this most pressing concern — the young man, Randy, who had grown up at Muddy Creek and Misty Falls.

Randy had come home from his tour in Afghanistan un-
scathed. He had just completed his enlistment in the Army and was
about to begin work back home. Now this!

Winnie met Evelyn and Gerald at the visitors' lounge by the
Trauma ICU. She heard the story of the accident from the fright-
ened parents. Driving on country roads is too often hazardous, because one tends to drive down the middle of the narrow road. They
didn't know if Randy had been driving in the middle of the road, but
another car came from around a bend, and the two met, head on
just before midnight. Both drivers were badly injured.

It would be a long haul before this business was done,
whatever the outcome. Winnie was pleased to note the confidence
that Evelyn exuded in the face of this devastating situation. She
was doing exactly what she should be doing in the face of this very
difficult time — she was leaving Randy's healing up to the Lord.

✳ ✳ ✳

Later that morning after she had returned to the parsonage,
Winnie answered a call from Pastor Allen Remington. He was calling the various pastors who were part of the joint community services to update them about the Thanksgiving service.

"Winnie, I thought I'd call and tell you about the offering that
came in at the Thanksgiving service," Allen Remington said. "Tinsley Booker over at Faith AME just called to tell me that his treas-
urer had found an envelope and a note attached to it in the collection plate after that service. The envelope contained cash for the
amount of $496.35, and a note inside the envelope said, "I'm re-
turning this money to the community. I found it at the church after
the Easter service, and I want to return it to its rightful place. I hope
that by returning this money now, the missing funds can be 'found'
and our community chest will be 'right.' Thank you."

"Do we know who wrote the note?" Winnie asked.

"No name was included on the note; it was written in pencil
on a torn piece of notebook paper," Allen answered.

"Tinsley and I talked about it, and we think the matter is
closed now. Do you agree?

"Sounds like the thief has a conscience and decided to make amends.

"It's not really our job to determine if someone should be charged for the theft. That falls on the sheriff and the courts to decide, but, from what you tell me, I would consider the matter closed, especially since we don't know who it was that did the deed," Winnie answered.

Allen agreed with Winnie. "That's what I'm hearing from the other pastors, too. We seem to feel that whoever the culprit was, he or she seems to have worked it out, and the community gets the money back for our Traveler's Aide Account. No one was actually harmed or suffered from the theft. We hope that the person in question has grown in the process, which is what we all need to do as we follow Christ."

"I think that Tinsley will take the note to the sheriff along with our thoughts about what should happen. Sheriff Barrymore can use our input to inform his report and/or further investigation, if he needs it."

Winnie couldn't help smiling to herself as she remembered Pastor Allen's unexpected report about the missing funds. "There's a story in that, for sure!" Winnie told Bitty. "I don't suppose we'll ever know who it was that found the money and then returned it, but there's a story there. That's for sure,." Winnie wondered if it might be someone that she knew in town.

Winnie barely hung up from her conversation with Pastor Allen when the phone rang again. This time the voice was Connie Oliver's, and she sounded frantic!

"Goodness, Dear, calm down! Take a deep breath, and then tell me what's happening," Winnie assured her.

Connie tried to follow Winnie's suggestion, but it was hard for her to keep from crying. "The DHR woman just called me. . . just a minute ago. She says that she has received a phone call about noise coming from our apartment, and the caller thinks there might be some danger for my girls!" Connie stopped.

Winnie was alarmed, too, and she asked, "Did the DHR woman say anything more?"

"I don't know," Connie answered. "She didn't say we'd lose the girls, but she spoke very strongly about us being very careful with them!"

"So, she gave you a warning? Is that what she did?" Winnie asked.

"I suppose that's what she meant," Connie sniffed. "Now I'm all upset, and that doesn't make things any better."

"Well, it sounds like you've been called to give you a fair warning about the responsibility you have in taking care of the babies," Winnie said. "Was there anything factual about the report that the DHR woman heard?" Winnie asked a little anxiously.

"N-No, there wasn't really anything. Oh, I guess we were all talking real loud last night before dinner. George and Mother don't always see eye-to-eye, and I think he yelled something and walked out and slammed the door. I suppose that's what caused my neighbor to wonder if there was something dangerous for the babies, but, really, they were not in any danger!" Connie assured Winnie.

"Hm. It sounds like you're right about the noise in your apartment," Winnie agreed. "I think you've had a scare with the DHR woman's call, but she's not taking the babies, not yet, so you just have to be especially careful with them. AND watch out about any other loud voices that might attract the attention of your neighbors."

They spoke a few more minutes. Winnie wished, like everything, that this was not happening to Connie and her family, but she couldn't change the facts. All she could do was to be a friend to Connie and Sallie and hope they could follow through with their best intentions in caring for the babies.

✳ ✳ ✳

John had inquired about Winnie's plans for Christmas earlier. As a university professor the Christmas holidays didn't begin when the students left for vacation. Professors still had papers to read, tests to mark, and grades to be submitted before they could possibly get away.

John explained that his course load this quarter included two Introduction to Philosophy sections, which had several hundreds of students in each section. He had three other, upper division classes and a graduate seminar that were smaller, but which required research papers 20 — 25 pages per student. The finals for the Intro classes were objective in nature and would be graded by T.A.'s, but the research papers were solely his responsibility, and they took significant time to read, digest, evaluate, and grade.

John wondered what Winnie usually did over the holidays, and would she be free at any time. He offered to fly her up to Chicago, if she would like to come.

Of course, Christmastime was a major season for Winnie; she had Christmas Eve service to lead in the middle of the week and a sermon to preach three days later that she would have to prepare and give. Furthermore, Winnie's son, Paul, and his family were coming for Christmas. They would arrive late Christmas Day and stay for a week. This family time had been planned for some time, and Winnie, of course, was looking forward to seeing them.

Winnie wrote,

Dear John,

Sounds like being a college professor has some serious sides to it that we lay folks don't appreciate! And I thought the students were the ones with all the homework! It hadn't occurred to me about the reading and grading responsibilities that professors have following finals. How much time does it usually take you for that work? It sounds pretty detailed and thick. I haven't spent much time thinking about upper level philosophy subjects, but I can imagine any in-depth writings would take a careful eye and a thoughtful response by you, the professor. I'm sure you can't just rip through them!"

Winnie figured that Christmas wasn't the best time for the two of them to meet, simply because of the requirements of her job, and now she was aware of the demands of a college professor. Their getting together, especially around this big holiday, posed some challenges. Winnie tried to think more positively to herself, saying, *"but then there's our date in January for Nashville; I'm really looking forward to that time!"*

Winnie also explained to John about her son's family's visit, which was that week. Paul and his family were coming from Dallas. Everyone had been planning their visit for months, and their tickets had been purchased. Everything was set for them to come, and Winnie, as "Grannie," certainly wanted to see her sweet Taylor grandchildren!

✳ ✳ ✳

Winnie checked in on Evelyn Hobbs every day by phone. She had not left the hospital since the accident, but continued to sit in the visitors' waiting room, making visits every four hours, according to the schedule allowed for family visiting. Gerald had brought her a bag of toiletries, a few clothes, and a pillow and blanket. She was eating from the vending machines and sometimes at the cafeteria. No, there was no good news about Randy; he was in exactly the same state as the night of the accident: hooked up to many machines, not breathing on his own, and no signs of improvement.

Winnie asked Evelyn what she did when she visited her son. Evelyn told her, "I sit up close to Randy's head, hold his hand, and talk to him. I tell him that I'm there with him, and that he's going to be fine. He's going to get through this season of healing, and that he's going to come home and get a job and have a wonderful life. I tell him about how much Jesus loves him, and how Jesus healed so many people that we read about in the Bible, and, in fact, He heals anyone who is ever healed. I tell Randy that he's got angels surrounding him and watching over him. I sing him songs and hymns he knows."

Winnie was impressed with Evelyn's faith and her determined way of sharing her faith with her son, even as he lay in a deep coma. The doctors and nurses held out no encouraging words about Randy, but that wasn't going to sway Evelyn's faith. She planned to stay next to him, as long as they would allow.

Winnie was thoughtful about how this most difficult time might come out for Evelyn and Gerald. Randy was their only child, and his life hung in terrible jeopardy. There didn't seem to be much hope for him, but Winnie wanted to stay as positive as Evelyn and Gerald were about the future. *"It's one thing to preach about having faith and another thing to actually live it!"* Winnie reminded herself.

✳ ✳ ✳

Lucy Jane hadn't thought about getting involved with another man, not yet. Her pain was too close, having lost Chet just months ago. The move from Kentucky had been a good one for her, as it took her mind off her pain, just a bit, and brought her closer to her family.

Misty Falls hadn't changed much at all, not even in the nearly twenty years Lucy Jane had been gone. There were some changes, but the essence of Misty Falls — the people who made up the community — was the same.

Changes that had come to Misty Falls were mostly what Lucy Jane considered "cosmetic." The stop sign in town on Main Street, which had been one of the town's landmarks, had been usurped by the arrival of a traffic light on the highway. The advent of the traffic light had been a big deal for the town — a sure indication of progress!

Lucy Jane was not seeking romance now, but the thought of companionship, someone with a friendly face and an open ear, who could help fill up some of the empty hours, would be nice.

The few times that Lucy Jane and Tucker Joe had seen each other, she realized that she felt just a bit better.

Their dinner date was set at a nice restaurant in the city. They met at six at FRIENDLY'S FOODS, and Tucker Joe surprised Lucy Jane with a beautiful corsage — red and white rose buds surrounded by a netting of silver stars, very Christmasy. They hopped in Tuck's blue, '68 Mustang and drove off to the city for dinner.

It was an Italian place that they finally agreed upon. Soon they were seated at a table near the window, looking onto the bustling, Christmas shoppers outside.

The waiter left them with menus and filled their water glasses. He rattled off the specials being offered and suggested a wine to accompany their dinner.

"That's the big city for you," Lucy Jane observed after the waiter had departed. "They don't appreciate us hometown folks who don't drink, do they?"

Tucker Joe wanted to be amiable and perhaps follow Lucy Jane's lead, but he wasn't a teetotaler, and he needed to state that for himself.

"I know plenty of good folks who don't drink," he began, "and surely there are those who can't hold their alcohol, but I'm not one of them. I have a healthy regard for alcohol, but I have found that a nice, dry wine at a meal is an excellent addition. I wouldn't judge anyone for not drinking, but I think there can be a place for enjoying the fruit of the vine." Tuck completed his thought with a little smile, hoping he had a dinner companion who understood his position.

Lucy Jane nodded her head and admitted, "My husband, Chet, would have completely agreed with you."

"We had the same conversation on our first date. Chet enjoyed a nice wine with his dinner, and he was good about not bugging me to join him. We had a friendly agreement on the subject," Lucy shared.

The dinner was easy and casual. Tucker was a good listener, it turned out; he didn't press Lucy Jane for too much information, but he let her talk as much as she wanted.

She told Tuck about her first, dismal marriage, how it was a failure before it got started. She and Frank had met when she was on a trip one summer during college. He was working at a state park, and they had spent many hours wandering around the park. Frank was a mountain climber, and he spent all his money and time running off to far away mountains to conquer yet one more peak. It didn't take long for them to part ways. Their divorce was mutually agreed upon.

Chet, on the other hand, had been perfect. He had literally swept Lucy Jane off her feet, and she knew life had finally begun for her when they married. They had wonderful plans, especially ones that included children.

Chet's cancer diagnosis caught them completely off guard, and there was no time to respond. He came home from the doctor's office that first day, and they were aware that he needed to have some serious-sounding tests, to get a handle on his condition. The next week Chet went to the hospital for a whole battery of tests, and he never came home. There was surgery, and waiting, and then he was gone!

Lucy Jane hadn't eaten much of her dinner — she was too absorbed in her tale, sharing her pain with this kind man. She talked on and on, mostly about Chet, when suddenly she made a discovery.

Tucker Joe had been listening and saying little things like, "Yeah", and "OK," and "I understand." Finally he said, "I know what you mean about the funeral director; the same thing happened to me when Mama died."

Lucy Jane swallowed her Coke and looked straight at Tuck. She knitted her eyebrows, cocked her head, and said, "Did your mother pass, too?"

Tucker hadn't realized that Lucy Jane was unfamiliar with that piece of recent, community history, but he put two and two together and nodded his head.

"Mother died almost a year ago. I thought you knew."

Lucy Jane hadn't heard, but some things did make more sense to her now that she thought about it. She hadn't seen Miss Matilda Tennyson at FRIENDLY'S FOODS the times she had been there since she had returned to town.

"I'm so sorry to hear about her passing," she said. "You must miss her."

"Not anything like what you're describing. Sure, Mother passed, and we all miss her, but maybe it was her time to go. I miss her as a friend; and I sure do miss her as an associate at the store, but I don't feel the sort of grief you are experiencing."

Lucy Jane was relieved to hear that. She didn't want to think that she had been terribly insensitive to Tucker Joe's feelings, going on and on, as she had been doing about her own loss and not even acknowledging his. "Oh," she said, "I'm so sorry you lost her. I'm sure the whole town misses her."

Most of the dinner time was spent with such conversation, but that wasn't really what Lucy Jane had hoped to talk about.

Finally she changed the subject and told Tucker Joe about her unexpected gift and how she hoped to use it in some sort of memorial to Chet's fondness for children. That was a new idea, and the two of them agreed to meet again, maybe just after Christmas to consider it more.

"The evening went great! Tucker Joe assured himself as he drove home. *"Lucy Jane is quite a woman — a woman who has a deep passion for life — and she certainly is devoted to her husband's memory. I expect she'll come to love, again, one day."*

* * *

Saturday Winnie joined a half dozen other women from Muddy Creek over at the Barrymore's house. Vickie Jackson had assembled these ladies to put together the eighteen angel outfits for the community Christmas show. She had already found a pattern, a simple, wide-yoked gown with long sleeves. The outfit would reach down nearly to a four-year-old's knees. Vickie borrowed her next door neighbor's four year old, who, coincidentally, was singing in the angel choir, and used him for a model. She also picked up the necessary material and notions that she figured would be needed for the project.

By four o'clock their job was nearly complete. The ladies had become a team of efficient workers, and their results were obvious. Each of the ladies looked forward to coming to the Baptist church the following week to see their work on display in the show. They also realized that they had actually produced a good product in a reasonable time. Maybe they should consider using such a workforce for other needs that might arise. Maybe they could use this ability to help bring in funds for a mission program.

* * *

By Saturday afternoon Winnie's parsonage makeover had been completed: new floors in the kitchen, laundry room, and in both bathrooms. Most of the jobs were not complicated, but the main bathroom floor had to be rebuilt totally. Winnie had watched, off and on, as Jeff worked to tear out the old, rotted flooring and to install the new. The final result was a fine, linoleum-covered improvement.

The parsonage looked really fresh and clean with the new floors. It would be nice to have fresh floors in the parsonage when Paul and his family arrived.

✳ ✳ ✳

Winnie wasn't quite sure how to start her sermon on Sunday. She usually preached from the lectionary, choosing a Bible passage from that list to use as a springboard for finding her Sunday message, but this week's sermon was being stubborn, and she was suffering from a bit of writer's block. Winnie had chosen a passage from St. John's gospel about John the Baptist, and she wanted to highlight John's unusual character — he was not part of the pack in any way. John was his own man, God's man. He was the man who had a very special purpose, but she needed a clever segue into her main topic. After twenty minutes of unproductively staring at the blinking computer cursor and surfing the web, she decided that some fresh air would do her some good.

Winnie got all bundled up, as the weather called for layers, unwrapped her earphones for her MP3 player, and put the lead on Bitty.

They had been walking about fifteen minutes when Winnie saw Trudy. Winnie hadn't seen her since she had returned from her Thanksgiving trip, and three weeks makes a difference for an expectant, young lady.

The two women fell into step with one another and started toward the depot. Winnie thought she'd buy Trudy a cup of tea there.

Winnie didn't know Trudy too well. She lived with her mother, Keisha Livingston, in town. Trudy was eighteen years old and finishing her last year of high school. She was due to have her baby around the end of March. That's all Winnie knew about her, except that she had been helpful about caring for Bitty a couple of times.

Winnie didn't want to be too inquisitive about Trudy's situation, but she was willing to be a friendly ear, if Trudy wanted to talk.

Trudy was polite but not very talkative during the first part of their walk, but once they got inside the diner and tea had been ordered, she began to speak.

"It's just been me and Ma together always. Ma says that my father was from the city and that he moved somewhere up north. I never knew him. His name is Al Jackson."

"Ma and I get along pretty good, but she's not happy about my present condition. Oh, she's OK with my having this child, as opposed to not having it, but she thinks I'm too young to be a single mom."

"It's a big thing that's happening to you right now." Winnie observed. She wanted to be in Trudy's corner, if she would allow that.

"You're very right about that. I've seen how hard Ma has worked, so that we can have what we need; it's not been easy for her," Trudy added.

"Have you given thought to what you're going to do next?" Winnie asked.

"I'm almost finished with high school. We graduate at the end of May, and I've talked to my teachers and my counselor and they have agreed to help me do some work ahead of my delivery time, so that I can be finished with school by the time Little Mister Child arrives," Trudy explained.

"Is it a boy? Do you know already?" Winnie asked.

"Well, I should know by now, because the ultra sound could have told me, but I didn't want to know when I had the test. These days everyone knows ahead of time about the baby's sex, but I told the nurse not to tell me. Now I wish I had. Isn't that funny?" Trudy asked Winnie.

"Goodness! When I had my children there was no such thing as knowing the child's gender ahead of time. You had to be prepared with two names before the baby was born; then we'd know which name would fit as soon as it came."

"I suppose there are good reasons to learn about the child ahead of time. Do you want a boy or a girl?" Winnie asked her.

Trudy cocked her head to one side and thought. "I don't suppose I have a preference. Some would say, 'It's a man's world', and I can see how that could be, and that might have some advantage to a child — knowing he would have an automatic advantage."

"There's good to be said on both sides of that argument," Trudy theorized. "You could make a long list of reasons why girls have the advantage, and another long list of reasons why boys have the advantage. I suppose it's not so much about whether you are male or female, but how well you use what you've been given."

Winnie was pleased to hear Trudy thinking so deeply, and she added, "Goodness my Dear, I think you've come upon a very good thought! You are right. It's not whether a person is male or female that's important, but rather how you work with the stuff you have to make this world a little better. God has given us so many incredible gifts, and God expects us to grow up and use them. Men and women certainly do view their worlds wearing different lenses, so to speak, even when we tread the same streets and live in the same houses, we see things differently.

"I'm glad to hear that your teachers and school administration are willing to work with you, to help you through your final semester! I believe that getting the best education we can is important in today's world."

"What classes are you taking next semester?" Winnie wanted to know.

"We're on the block system at school now, so I'll be taking only two classes to finish my work. I'm taking senior English and world history. I could also take an elective, but it's not required."

Winnie lighted up, "That sounds like you'll have a lot of reading and writing in those classes, but working ahead certainly would be a good idea. Do you know that college courses usually work about double speed, compared to high school classes?"

Trudy looked surprised and said, "No! Really? That's hard, isn't it?"

Winnie explained, "It does require your attention and concerted effort."

"It's funny, though. You get your syllabus with the readings and tests and/or papers that will be due, and you plunge into the material, and eventually you see the work getting accomplished.

"The reason I mention it is because if you were to start classes in college next fall, which may be really difficult at this point in your life, you would be seeing that double-time-double-work there. If you are going to work ahead on your English and world history classes next semester, it will be very similar to doing the same requirement in college!" Winnie explained.

Trudy considered this idea and said, "That's really good, Miss Winnie. I hadn't thought about it before, but that does make sense."

Trudy and Winnie talked even after their tea had cooled. Trudy was planning to stay at home with her mother, same as now. Trudy's mother definitely had thoughts on this subject. She believed that her grandchild needed to have a father around. She had struggled hard to raise Trudy without one, and she felt it would have been better for Trudy to have had a father. She could only imagine how fine it might have been to have a father in the picture. She also wanted Trudy to complete her education, even go on to college, and get a place of her own.

"I really appreciate being able to talk to you, Miss Winnie," Trudy told her. "I don't have too many people that I can talk to these days. Most of my girlfriends sort of treat me like I've got some terrible disease. They don't know what to say to me. All they want to know is about the father of the baby. And that's not their business!"

Winnie understood Trudy. She needed to have friends she could trust — various friends — her own age as well as, maybe, an older woman in whom she could confide. Winnie said, "I can imagine your world has changed a lot since you found out about the baby coming.

"You're right, it isn't anybody's business who the father is, although, it may be the father's business. Have you given that some thought?" Winnie asked.

Trudy was silent. She sat across the table and stared. Finally, after some moments she spoke. "Maybe the father has the right to know. Maybe that's the law. I don't know. . . I'm very confused about it. I don't know what to do. I don't know if I want him in my baby's life."

Winnie could see this topic needed some time to develop, and so she changed the subject. "Trudy, maybe this is something you would like to think about. It's a subject that not only affects you, but also your child and the young man, your baby's father, too. It would have long-term implications. If you'd like, we could talk about it later. What do you think?"

Trudy was nodding her head slowly, agreeing with her new friend. She said, "Thanks. I will think about it. I'd like to know what my responsibilities are, legally."

Winnie agreed to email Trudy some information about paternity rights and whatever she might be able to find that would be helpful in figuring Trudy's decision. They parted, when they left the diner, going their separate ways. Winnie, who had tied Bitty to the post outside, untied her pup, and the two of them continued their walk back home.

✳ ✳ ✳

By the time she arrived home from her walk, Winnie had thought of a fun opening for her sermon on John the Baptist. "*I know exactly what I can say to open my sermon tomorrow. I'll explain about how I use my MP3 player when go on a walk to listen to music with a strong beat; it gets my feet to moving more quickly, and thereby, getting my heart to work harder. Then I'll say that John the Baptist was hearing a different drumbeat, a Heavenly Drumbeat, from the rest of the world. He wasn't listening to the drumbeat of the world; he was listening to God.*"

17. Paul Taylor's Visit

The pre-school, angel chorus for the children's Christmas musical nearly stole the show. They were adorable! Somehow the dozen and a half freckle-faced boys and rosy-cheeked girls, each sporting their newly fashioned, white, angel frocks and golden halos were especially endearing to the audience — they were so cute. These baby angels, being the youngest of the cast members, were seated along the entire expanse of the stage at First Baptist Church's fellowship hall.

They sat on the stage, legs dangling over, watching the audience of several hundred community members watching them. The proud parents, of course, had immediately identified their own youngsters among the chorus. Exchanges of recognition and waves passed back and forth between the stage and the onlookers. Some of the angels, having identified Mommy and Daddy, waved and smiled repeatedly, until Joe Ed, the director, gave several stern looks at the children, and the music started, The show had begun.

Of course, one cannot expect four year olds to have an attention span that could control them for the entire show, so the Joe Ed took a brief, unexpected intermission, after the fourth song, allowing time for the angelic-looking four year olds to find their parents and join them.

The show was a high moment of Misty Falls' Christmas season, and after the show, everyone — cast, audience, and all —

assembled in the fellowship hall for home-made Christmas cookies and punch. It was a good moment for folks from the different churches in town to mingle and congratulate the children. Even Santa made an appearance. It was beginning to really feel like Christmas, Winnie thought. The whole town was merry with the mood of the season.

* * *

Winnie kept in touch with the Olivers regularly, talking to Connie several times a week. Connie told Winnie that the woman from DHR had come out the day after Winnie had been there, and she talked to them for quite a while. She interviewed each of them — Connie, George, and Sallie, and she seemed to be satisfied for the moment that the babies were not in jeopardy. She did warn them, strongly, that another such incident, any other call from one of their neighbors, would result in official action.

"Oh, no!" Winnie exclaimed. "You mean she would come and take the girls?"

"That's exactly what she meant," Connie admitted.

Finally, after waiting a moment, in case Connie had more to say, Winnie added, "I can't imagine how you must be feeling right now, Connie."

Connie remained silent for a moment, and then she answered, "My neighbors are horrible! They're all watching us like hawks! We can't trust them. I don't even want to speak to them. I don't know what to do!"

Winnie felt for Connie. She thought it was almost easier to deal with a personal trauma than to watch on, helplessly, while someone else suffers. She really didn't know what to say or do for Connie. *"It's very hard to watch someone else's heart nearly break,"* she thought. All Winnie could do was to let Connie know that she would be there for her, in any case.

"How are the babies?" she asked.

"They are fine," Connie assured Winnie. "They are sweeter every day. You must come by and see them for yourself."

* * *

Rev. Paul Allen Taylor was Winnie's son, and he was also a United Methodist pastor. Paul had gone to Perkins School of Theology in Dallas right out of college, so he had been preaching for nearly ten years. Paul and his family would be arriving a bit late for their Christmas celebration with Winnie, due to his responsibilities to the church in Dallas. They would be attending Christmas Eve service at Paul's church and then leave on Christmas Day to fly up to Knoxville and drive to Misty Falls for their own holiday with Grannie Winnie.

Winnie loved the times she spent with her children. Sometimes she visited them; sometimes they came to her. Occasionally they'd all go camping or to the beach for a holiday together.

Paul had married Tricia after his second year of preaching. When he arrived at his first church it took no time at all before the ladies of the community recognized an obvious lack in their new pastor — he didn't have a wife. He was nice looking, well educated, and he definitely *needed* a wife!

Before Paul realized what the church folks were thinking, various young ladies were being introduced to him. Some were daughters or granddaughters of church members. Some lived in the community and heard the word as it spread about Pastor Taylor's "need."

Paul wasn't as convinced as the church was about his need for a wife. He was polite to the young ladies and a bit amused at all this extra attention he was getting. He certainly didn't mind being liked as a pastor, but he would prefer it to be for the right reasons! Paul wanted people to hear his message of Christ's love for all and His invitation to follow Him. Paul's personal life was his own, wasn't it?

Paul was aware of the blatant way he was being introduced to certain young ladies or invited to have dinner with particular families, and he began to realize that these invitations were inspired by his "need" for a wife.

Tricia came into the picture from a different source. She was the sister of a good friend of Paul's from college, so they had met during their college years. Tricia was dating someone else at the time, and then she took a couple of semesters to study abroad. Paul hadn't seen her after that.

Tricia was an accomplished singer, a mezzo soprano, and she had earned a position in a German opera company. She couldn't turn such an opportunity down, so she spent another year with the opera in Heidelberg.

Paul met Tricia again when he visited his friend's home. She had just returned from Europe and was living with her folks while she looked into teaching positions. It didn't take Paul and Tricia long to figure they were meant for one another, and their engagement was soon announced.

Paul's church was all abuzz with the news of his plans to marry, and not a few young ladies were disappointed that they were not the object of the honor.

Today the Taylors have two beautiful children: Susanna Marie, their lively eight-year old, whom they call Susie, and Paul Wesley, who would be five in the spring.

Winnie planned to celebrate Christmas when the Taylors arrived. They'd have their Christmas dinner and open presents on Boxing Day, the 26th.

Winnie was looking forward to having some "down time", just being Mom and Grannie to her family sounded very nice!

She did take time early in the week to work on next Sunday's sermon, as she wanted to be as free as possible for her family when they arrived. She realized that she was a bit resentful that her professional life interfered so much in her personal life, but then she would remind herself how very selfish that way of thinking was. She'd ask for forgiveness and move on. Winnie hoped that as she traveled this path of discipleship she was learning a thing or two!

✳ ✳ ✳

The Christmas Eve service was beautiful, and everyone said so. At the final carol, the sanctuary lights were lowered, save for the candles and the tree lights. The worshipers raised their individual candles high, as they lifted their voices together singing Silent Night. All were dressed in festive Christmas attire. The ambiance of love and anticipation stirred in each worshiper as they shared this sublime moment together, singing in the Yule.

167

M. E. PALMER

Winnie walked down the center aisle of the sanctuary during the last verse of the final carol, and as she walked, holding her lit candle high, she looked over her flock. She saw people, old and young, from many walks of life, standing, singing, smiling, welcoming in the moment — the day of Christ's incarnation had finally arrived! Venite Adoramus — *O! Come Let Us Adore Him!*

✳ ✳ ✳

Christmas morning dawned as an ordinary day for Winnie. Although it was Christmas morning, and at other times in her life she would have been totally engaged in the many responsibilities of the big day; this morning was unremarkable.

Winnie opened her email to find a note from John. He had been up early this morning, already working on his papers. He thought his reading and grading was coming along better than he had hoped, and he believed that he would be completely through with all the papers soon.

John was looking forward to his usual ski trip to Aspen, just after the New Year. This trip would come just prior to the philosophers' convention in Mississippi,

John had just noticed an advertisement about a ski resort in North Carolina, inviting skiers to try the slopes on the Appalachians. He hadn't skied there before, which would mean the challenge of new slopes to ski. This ski resort was offering a special wintertime package for the first week of the New Year, since that was a time when many skiers were already returning to work after the holidays.

It occurred to John that he might drive to North Carolina for his ski trip, and on the way, he could stop and see Winnie. He suggested that he drive to Misty Falls and take Winnie out on a New Year's Eve date. He realized that her son, Paul, and his family would be visiting then, and he hoped he would be able to meet that part of Winnie's family.

Winnie stopped reading and closed her eyes; she needed to think this through.

It was a fabulous idea! Winnie could feel little goose bumps growing on her arms as she read John's email. *"Goodness! Look at that!*" She touched her forearm, "*Wonder what it means? Am I sending myself a message?*" She recognized this potential visit had suddenly and completely captured her imagination. She was already relishing an evening with John — just the two of them, not surrounded by hundreds of classmates or anyone else that could project his or her agenda into their company. At the same time she realized that her little secret would finally be revealed — John would certainly discover her pastoral identity!

John was obviously interested in her, and she was thoroughly enjoying the chase. They would be going out together for New Year's Eve — somewhere in Knoxville, some place fancy. *How undeniably delicious!*

He would be coming to Misty Falls in less than a week if she said, "Yes."

Winnie hit the return button on her email and wrote:

John,

It's good to hear your work is progressing so well and you'll be able to take time off afterwards to get away for your own holiday before the new school term begins.

Yes, I'd love for you to come here. Imagine! We'll actually be in the same place at the same time. It's a grand idea! Yes, I'm sure Paul and Tricia and my grandkids will be happy to meet you.

If I understand you correctly, you'd like to arrive on the afternoon of the 31st, so you'll have time to meet Paul and Tricia and my grandchildren. Then we would drive into Knoxville to some nice place for dinner and await the New Year's arrival.

I could offer you accommodations here at my home; I have four bedrooms. Paul's family will be using only two of them, so I would have room for another guest. If you would prefer, though, there is a small motel on the highway here in Misty Falls. They would have room for you, I'm pretty sure.

Yours,

Winnie

Winnie hit the "send" button, and the plans were made.

"Goodness!" Winnie said aloud. "That really gives 'shape' to this holiday!"

"John is coming here!" She danced around the room with Bitty, who was surprised to see her owner so animated.

Winnie had a real struggle within herself trying to settle down and concentrate on her sermon for Sunday. Other ideas kept invading her thoughts, and she had quite a time quelling them in favor of focusing on the text she had chosen to use for Sunday. She had certainly preached on that famous passage of Mary's song of thanksgiving before, but she wanted to come at it from a slightly different angle this time. Turning her mind to her sermon after the news of the morning was a serious battle for Winnie.

Winnie hadn't yet told her son about John. She figured the subject of this very interesting man, who was rapidly becoming an important person to her, would certainly be a topic of conversation with Paul and Tricia. In fact Winnie was especially pleased to think that they would all have an opportunity to meet.

❊ ❊ ❊

Winnie spent the rest of the day doing this and that, readying herself and the house for her guests.

Finally the door bell rang at 8:30 that evening, and Winnie opened her door to the happy faces of Paul and his family! The kids crowded around Grannie Winnie, gave her a hug and then spotted Bitty. Quickly, they moved to the pup and showered their attentions on her.

Winnie welcomed the Taylors into her parsonage and showed them their bedrooms.

After all the luggage had been put away and the Christmas presents had been placed under the tree, everyone found themselves sitting in the living room enjoying the ambiance of the moment. Winnie brought in hot chocolate and iced, Christmas cookies for everyone to enjoy. P.W. asked his dad if they could open presents now, and Paul, spying a red, furry Santa hat atop a lamp, placed it on his five year old's head. "Guess you should be 'Santa' this year, Son", he told him.

Paul and Tricia had taken care not to encourage the myth of Santa Claus. They taught Susie and P.W., instead, about the real Saint Nicholas, who was a bishop in the church in what is now Turkey. He spent his life helping people and became known for his generosity to orphans, which was the basis for the story about Santa Claus. Rather than teaching their children a story they would later have to unlearn about Santa Claus, the Taylors taught their children to enjoy the spirit of giving, but they still enjoyed the fun of the Santa myth.

Paul now explained to P.W. how he should pull out gifts from under the tree and hand them to the person whose name was on the package. The family spent the better part of the next hour opening presents and "Ooooing" and "Awwwwing" over them. Soft Christmas music played in the room as a nice backdrop for their cozy gift opening time.

✳ ✳ ✳

The week spun by. The Taylor family completely filled all the available space in Winnie's parsonage with the sounds of children laughing and playing and enjoying their time at Grannie's home.

Winnie spent time with each of her grandchildren. Susie was very musical, just like her mother. She sang very sweetly for Winnie – she wasn't the least bit shy. She had a good set of lungs, and she loved to sing all the verses to whatever she was singing. She was already very comfortable playing the piano, even at her tender age of eight. Tricia had been working with Susie for years at the keyboard; Susie probably couldn't remember a time when she didn't play the piano.

Susie was gifted in many ways. She danced all around the house; she read "chapter books" and colored in the lines, too.

Paul Wesley, or P.W. as he was called, was already reading well at four and a half years, and he seemed to be a born builder. He was especially thrilled to get several sets of Lego's to construct. Very quickly, the front room had become a great maze of blocks, tracks, buildings, cars, and miniature characters.

Winnie looked on the newly decorated living room with pleasure and thought, *"How well I remember when Claire and Paul were small like these kids. That was a tender age."* She was convinced that her grandchildren, all of them, had wonderful parents! She felt herself very blessed.

* * *

Winnie brought up the subject of her unexpected guest when the Taylors and she were sitting in the living room after Christmas dinner. She told them some background — how John had called her out of the blue back in September to tell her about Mile High's reunion.

She recounted her trip to Denver and the reunion — how she and John had been inseparable there — how they had talked and talked non-stop — and they had been corresponding via email ever since.

Winnie admitted her interest in John — and her concern. She was hopeful that things would work out well between them, but there was an issue of John's lack of faith in God that was a major concern to Winnie.

"We haven't had a moment when we spoke seriously about faith. I dodged the question about my profession by telling John that I work in the office at church. I haven't told him I live in the church parsonage and am appointed to preach at Muddy Creek Church! He doesn't know that I'm a preacher."

This confession struck all three of them as pretty funny. Could John really not know about Winnie's work? Paul said, "Mom, if John comes here, he's going to figure it out pretty fast. Don't you think?"

Winnie had been turning this over in her mind ever since John's email Christmas morning. She said, "Yes, I know he'll find out. I'll be glad to have that silly confusion out in the open. It's beginning to feel like an 'elephant' in the room," she admitted.

"If my being a Christian (and a preacher) is a problem for John, then we have a problem, and there's nothing more to say. We'll not have wasted a lot of time or energy on a relationship that won't work," Winnie stated.

Winnie could tell that the Taylors were pleased to hear about John and that they would have an opportunity to meet him when he came — not that they would have any serious input to Winnie about John. It was her life and her decision, however she chose to go, but they were intrigued to be able to meet this man who was showing such interest in Mom. Their presence would help John to see something more about Winnie's world.

The Taylors had tickets to fly home on New Year's Day, which would be the day after Winnie and John had their date. They would drive to the Knoxville airport and fly back to Dallas; Paul needed to be back in his pulpit on Sunday. They would only have a short time to spend with John before leaving for their return trip. Winnie intended to invite John over to the house for breakfast New Year's Day.

18. First Date

John rang the doorbell at 2:30 New Year's Eve afternoon. The sound of the bell triggered a not-unexpected response from Bitty, who was at the door the next instant, barking loudly in her high soprano, doggy voice, announcing the presence of a newcomer.

Bitty's demanding announcement, paired with the tone of the bell, caused those sitting in the living room to cease whatever conversation they were engaged in and to shift their eyes, as if being directed by an unseen conductor, to the front door. Winnie picked up the TV remote, snapped off the program, gathered up Bitty, and answered the door.

There stood John, holding a large bunch of red roses and a Christmassy-wrapped gift; his eyes were twinkling. Winnie had transferred Bitty to her left arm in order to negotiate the door and the screen, allowing John admission to the room.

The next few moments involved general introductions. Winnie, who was not a little bit anxious, began the presentations, saying, "John, I want you to meet my son, The Reverend Tall Paylor —Winnie's face turned scarlet; she closed her eyes and wrinkled her nose and tried again — I _mean_, this is my son Paul Taylor, and his wife Tisha Traylor. No! I mean Trisha Taylor." At this point everyone was smiling and chuckling and shaking hands all around. Finally the children were introduced to Dr. Daniel. Susie came first; she said, "Hello, Dr. Daniel" in a very soft voice and sat down on the corner of her mother's chair. When it was little P.W.'s turn he surprised everyone by walking straight over to John and holding out his right hand to shake hands. John raised his eye brows and grinned at the child and held out his hand to shake. The small, child's hand was barely a quarter the size of the grown man's hand, but they solemnly shook nonetheless. After that the two children, recognizing that adult conversation was about to ensue, left the room. Bitty followed the two, perhaps figuring there would be more activity among the younger set.

Winnie and Tricia excused themselves to go into the kitchen for coffee and holiday cookies.

John and Paul fell into conversation. They both were athletes in their own right. John, of course, was a skier, and Paul competed in triathlons several times each year. After exploring the sports interests they shared, John remarked, "So, Reverend Taylor, I gather you are a preacher."

Paul nodded agreement and said he had been pastoring churches for ten years. He told John about his church in Dallas, St. Peter's United Methodist, where he'd been for four and a half years. In fact P.W. was just a babe in arms when they had arrived.

The church was an older church [meaning the congregation was "older"], but it was experiencing a revival of young families, like his own, coming now. They had two worship services, one of which was a modified 'contemporary' service.

"We've come a long way with our contemporary service," Paul explained. "The music was too loud at first, so we tempered it, and we've tried to listen to many voices in that community — what they find helpful in the way of connecting to the tastes of an unchurched generation.

"I think our new service is finally developing into a service most of us can appreciate. It seems to be well received. I can use the same style preaching in both of my services, although I wear my black, academic gown with the stole appropriate for the season at the traditional service and less formal attire at the other."

As John and Paul spoke about this contemporary service and how it differed from the traditional service, John reminisced about his own church experience. He remembered going with his mother to a Presbyterian church when he was in elementary school, but his father had teased him about going.

Winnie's ears perked up immediately when John mentioned his experience with church. "Why John," she declared, "I thought you didn't believe in church!"

John shook his head and said, "I guess we did mention church, when we were first spoke on the phone, but I'm sure I didn't explain myself very well then."

All eyes focused on John, and he took this to be an invitation to share his views on church.

John sat up a little straighter in his chair, cleared his throat, and said, "It's not a very interesting story, really, I just never saw a point in going to church, when I was growing up. Like I said, Mom and I attended church during my early years, but it didn't mean much to me. I thought the church services were boring and a terrible waste of a morning. Maybe that was because of my dad's negative comments. I suppose I liked the person of Jesus; he's obviously had an unparalleled influence on the world and could be easily ranked among the most influential moral teachers in the world, but I don't see the connection between respecting him and the thing that church has become."

"I suppose that sounds a lot stronger than I actually feel. I really don't mean to disparage your profession, Paul. I'm sure you're a fine man and a good pastor to your people. I'm just telling you how I see things."

Winnie was taking in John's every word. Finally John was speaking about his involvement (or un-involvement) with church. She was all ears.

John continued, "I guess what I meant is that I don't believe that you have to belong to a church to live a good life."

"That's quite a statement, John," Paul said. "As a Christian I would define 'the good life' as a life of faith and how one's faith is acted out in the world."

"What do you mean by faith?" John asked.

"Of course there are many definitions of faith, but one that might be helpful is 'living out what you believe each day.' Christians have faith in Christ, but just saying, 'I believe in Jesus Christ' is not faith. It may be an idea, but it's not real faith. Faith is about putting your belief into practice."

John knew well how such conversations had a way of developing into daylong events and realized that this topic needed to be tabled for the present. He had come to take Winnie out for New Year's Eve, and since they needed to be in Knoxville by six they would have to begin getting ready pretty soon.

John said, "I'd really love to continue to explore this subject with you, but I think Win and I must be leaving soon. We are going out on the town tonight, and we have reservations just after six in Knoxville."

Turning to Winnie he said, "Win, {did you notice I'm calling you "Win"?} I wanted to surprise you a little, so I made plans for us to take a cruise on the Volunteer Princess tonight for dinner on the Tennessee. We board the boat at 6:15, and if my GPS is right, we'll need forty-five minutes to get into town and a few minutes to park and get to the boat. We should leave here by four-fifteen. Can you be ready by then?"

Since the cruise returned at nine, John and Winnie would have time to walk around downtown and end up at Market Square to see the ball drop for the New Year. John suggested that Winnie bring along some comfortable shoes to wear for their walk.

"*This afternoon is turning out to be even better than I imagined,*" Winnie mused. She considered John's admission about his thoughts on faith, but she wondered if perhaps he had not really heard the gospel message, not really, not completely. John had not turned it down, he had just not yet heard it clearly. *There is still hope!*

John had reserved a room at the motel on the edge of town, so he zipped over to the motel, picked up his room key, showered, shaved, and put on his suit. He was back at Winnie's home at exactly four-fifteen.

The trip into Knoxville was filled with newness for John and Winnie. They found they were able to relax and enjoy one another's company; it was delightful to finally be together, at least as close a bucket seats allowed. They laughed and chatted on and on about current events — Paul and his family's visit, John's work at the University, his new appointment to the Mortimer J. Adler Chair in the department, and his plans for this coming week. John would have several days to ski, then he'd drive to Ole Miss for the philosophers' gathering, and, finally, he would make his way to Nashville to meet Winnie.

John mentioned Winnie's visitors, "I can't imagine having such a family — with grown children and even grandchildren! Your family is so warm and welcoming, even to me — a stranger. I don't have anything like that. I'm alone these days, since my folks passed, and my older brother, Scott, is gone, too. My life is much simpler than yours. I seem to have a lot fewer significant others in my life than you have in yours.

"Your home is so cosy! It's just what I might have envisioned for you," John told Winnie. "How long have you been there? I have to say I'm surprised you have such a big place for a single woman."

Winnie sensed where the conversation was going. She took a big breath and said, "I live in Muddy Creek's church parsonage. A parsonage's size and amenities are determined by a code that is found in the church's rule book, The Discipline, which dictates the number of rooms and other requirements for the pastor's home."

There is was.

John slowly nodded his head. "I was fast coming to that conclusion. You haven't exactly *said* that you are the pastor at the church, but I should have guessed.

"Did you mean to mislead me?" He turned and winked at Winnie.

"No, not really." Winnie shook her head. "I didn't want to mislead you about my profession, but when you said you didn't believe in church, I quickly squelched my panic and moved to a diversionary tactic. Do you remember?" Winnie admitted this referring to her silly comeback on the phone — "'You don't believe in church? Why there are several right here in my town!' Please forgive me for my deception!"

"You're forgiven. I think I can see how that happened. I haven't spent any time with pastors before, so I'm on virgin territory here; if you'll pardon the expression!" John laughed.

"How did you happen to get into pastoring? Or do you call it preaching?" John wanted to know.

"Goodness, that's a long story, I suppose." Winnie began. "I grew up in a Christian home, and we were active in our church in Denver. Back then we lived in the city and were members of Park Hill Methodist Church.

"I believe I was called to "full-time Christian service", when I was a youth; of course, being in full-time Christian service could be realized in many ways. When my kids were little I worked at our church doing Christian education, mostly Sunday school and Vacation Bible School. I became a lay speaker and spoke to women's groups. One time our pastor got sick and I was asked to fill in for him a couple of weeks. That was an experience! I was terrified, but everyone was so encouraging."

"After Mark died I decided to go to graduate school and get my degree in order to preach. The kids were in high school when I matriculated into seminary, but by the time they were both in college I was at my first church as pastor."

"I can see how that developed. Wasn't it expensive for you to be in school when you didn't have an income?" John asked.

Winnie explained that Mark, who had been an Air Force pilot, had taken out extra insurance for the family "in case." She decided after he was gone to use some of that money to pay for school, so she could be earning an income and not just living on what Mark left her.

✳ ✳ ✳

The Volunteer Princess was beautifully decorated for the New Year's Eve party. There were festive hats and streamers and silvery stars all around the hall. John and Winnie were seated at a table right in front of the stage.

After dinner the orchestra began playing Glenn Miller music, and John surprised Winnie by asking her to dance. The smooth, muted tones of the Moonlight Serenade filled the room, inviting dancers to step into the music. The next thing Winnie knew, she was swirling gracefully around the dance floor in John's arms.

Winnie had not danced, not one step, since Mark had passed. Suddenly, memories came flooding into her mind. The motion of their two bodies moving together to the lazy beat of the music, the lilting sound of the dance band, the smell of John's aftershave, the squeak of his shoes on the floor; everything seemed to come together, and Winnie thought perhaps she had arrived in heaven!

John held her tightly around the waist and guided her easily across the floor; he was a smooth dancer. Winnie had no idea that he danced, but his moves seemed completely natural. John led Winnie around the room like he was master of the dance. It was spellbinding.

When the music ended, they sat down at their table to catch their breath. Winnie admitted, "This is more fun than I even expected. Getting to know you is turning out to be quite an adventure, Dr. Jonathan Daniel!"

John couldn't have been more pleased. "Indeed it is fun! Win, I think it's too bad we've let so much time pass already."

They danced, and danced, and danced some more. By the time the boat had docked, and they were back on dry land, they both felt they had stepped into a new dimension together.

They returned to John's car, and Winnie changed her shoes for walking shoes. They strolled all around the area holding hands, stopping in a small cafe and ordering hot chocolate. They talked non-stop, completely fascinated with the other.

By the end of the evening, they had arrived at Market Square where a big, time ball was about to be dropped. People were swarming from every direction to watch the moment when 2009 would be welcomed in.

Finally, the moment came. An announcement from the loudspeaker counted down the last seconds, before the clock would proclaim the New Year's arrival. The crowd began counting in time with the speaker: "Ten, nine, eight, seven, six, five, four,

three, two, one!"

The great, flashing ball began its descent onto the square; the band struck the opening notes of the obligatory Auld Lang Syne, and John put his arms around Winnie, pulled her to him and kissed her tenderly.

On the way back to Misty Falls the two were thoughtful. Whereas, earlier in the evening they had been talking non-stop; now things were different — they didn't need to fill the air with constant conversation. There was a feeling of deep delight, fun, and adventure, and now something new — an added dynamic between them had made its debut.

John walked Winnie to the door of her parsonage and waited while she unlocked the door. He gave her another hug and kiss before he left for his motel room. They agreed to meet later that morning — about nine-thirty for breakfast.

✳ ✳ ✳

New Year's morning Winnie appeared in her kitchen humming a tune — something she'd danced to the night before; she was moving lightly around the room, as she began putting out breakfast goodies for the final meal before everyone left for their respective destinations. John arrived for breakfast just as the grandkids were sitting down to eat.

The morning was filled with the excitement of the day ahead, not to mention that of the previous evening! The Taylors would be leaving for the airport, and John would be driving to his ski weekend in North Carolina.

Tricia inquired about their date, and Winnie quickly produced a colorful brochure she had picked up at the Volunteer Princess the evening before. She passed it around for all to see. She pointed out the great ballroom on the boat where she and John had tarried over their dinner. "Dinner was wonderful. We had shrimp cocktail, a grilled seafood platter with scallops, mahi mahi, stuffed shrimp, and crab cakes; and then, to top it all off, we had shared a New York style cheese cake. I don't have to tell you how good it was!"

The best part of the evening, Winnie admitted, came when the band began to play and John had asked her to dance. She didn't offer more about the evening, but it was obvious that Winnie and John were happy to have become reacquainted, and that something special was at work between them.

The Taylors had already packed their rental car, so after breakfast they excused themselves to begin their journey. Winnie waved good-bye to them. *What a wonderful visit.*

John needed to leave, too, but he and Winnie found it difficult to say good-bye. Finally they parted, knowing that they would be back together in Nashville in eight more days. They could pick up right where they left off.

After John pulled his car away from the house, Winnie plunked down in her front room and sighed. *"I'll never forget this Christmas,"* she told Bitty, *"and I have a feeling this may be the beginning of something very special! Thank you, LORD!"*

19. The Week Between

Winnie was still glowing inside from her eventful holiday week. After preaching Sunday, she came home to revel in all her memories!

There wasn't anything about last week that was not good. Of course she was thrilled with the visit of Paul and his family. They were so dear, and she didn't get enough time to be with them. Their visit helped a little. Winnie realized that it's not possible to be bonded with grandchildren, when time and distance keep you apart.

Of course, the greatest part of last week was John's visit! Winnie didn't expect to hear from him for a while, as he was off skiing. He wouldn't even be close to a Wi-Fi hook up; he was literally out of touch. This period apart would give them some time to reflect, and that was probably a good thing.

Winnie had plenty to digest. She needed to put her emotions on hold for a bit and try to think clearly about what was developing between them.

They had touched on a few items that needed addressing. She was more than relieved that John now knew of her profession. She had been most uncomfortable keeping that from him, as if it were some dark, mysterious secret that she shouldn't divulge. That wasn't the case, of course, but the longer she had kept it from John, the odder it felt. She was relieved that the "elephant" was finally out of the bag. *"Now there's a mixed metaphor!"* She teased herself.

John had taken that news very well, and it didn't seem to change his attitude toward her; if anything, he seemed be pleased about the disclosure. Winnie hadn't expected that. She had feared that John's discovery of her vocation might totally ruin whatever could be developing between them. She was relieved that, in the end, they both laughed about her reticence to divulge her work to him. Maybe John thought he had found a new opponent for arguing philosophy — here was an interesting woman who had a certain perspective, and it might be fun to engage in debate with her on the finer aspects of law, and ethics, and God. Maybe, or maybe not. Whatever the case was, Winnie was most pleased about how the evening had turned out.

✳ ✳ ✳

Winnie gave Evelyn a call to catch up on her son Randy's progress. Evelyn explained that Randy was being kept in a medically-induced coma, to let his body heal without his thrashing around.

"Anytime the nurses or attendants see Randy's blood pressure going up or his heart beating rapidly, they call me to come sit with him," Evelyn told her. "You know, he's hooked up to all sorts of medical equipment, and he can't speak, so when he wakes, he gets very agitated and begins to move around. Of course the nursing staff in the TICU can't have Randy pulling on things or moving around in bed, so they come get me. They realize that I can comfort him.

"I go into his room and hold his hand and tell him I am right there. I tell him about all the people who are praying for him. I remind him about his dog, Rascal — how he is missing his master. I tell him whatever comes to mind. I want him to hear my voice and know I'm right there for him. I've told him again and again how God is the master healer, and how Jesus is healing him, from the inside out. I'm very positive that he's going to be healed," Evelyn told Winnie.

"I sing softly to him. I sing every song I can think of, especially songs he's heard in church, which I hope are comforting to him. I hold his hand and caress his arm and sing.

"Gerald comes here most evenings to bring me changes of clothes and other useful items. He's very worried about Randy,

184

wondering, if he survives, what sort of life he'll have. I tell Gerald that if the Lord brings Randy through this, it will be a miracle; and if God will do one miracle, God can do another and give Randy a life, too.

"I have really been blessed by folks from the church who have come here to see me. They don't get to see Randy, because of the TICU rules, but they have helped me so much in getting through this trial each day. They have prayed with me and for Randy, and they have given me so much to hope for. Their faith and encouragement help me more than I can tell. They keep me going. I don't know what or how to pray, but all the members who came by have given me hope."

Winnie could see how the whole church had been working together to hold Randy up in their prayers. They were a wonderful example of the Body of Christ.

* * *

Tuesday evening Winnie and Nina had dinner together. They chose a restaurant in the town nearby for their meal, and settled into a large booth. It was a cozy place with various sorts of American memorabilia hanging along the walls.

They chatted about their respective holidays. Nina had flown to Chicago to have Christmas with her daughter, Elise, and her family. "They have a house in Wheaton west of the city. It's a good community. I love what the kids have done to their house. They added an extra room in the back, which becomes a place to put me when I visit."

Winnie told Nina about her date with John. Nina remembered John from their earlier conversation. She could tell something more had been stirring and wanted to know all the details. Winnie's memory of the evening was great fun, Nina thought. She listened with trained ears as long as she could, but finally Nina had to know, "What's going to happen? When will you two see each other again?"

Winnie explained about John's ski trip, his meeting in Mississippi, and their date in Nashville — this coming Friday and Saturday!

"Really! You'll be back together Friday night in Nashville?" Nina asked.

"Right. We plan to meet for dinner at The Gaylord Hotel. You've been there, I suppose." Winnie asked.

Nina lit up, "Dan and I went there with the kids right after it opened, in 1977. It really is a grand place. We returned a couple of years later, just the two of us. It's a marvelous place for roaming around, taking in the gardens. The place will be perfect for you two.

"Will you be there for the whole weekend?" Nina asked.

Winnie shook her head, "no," and explained. "No, that's the life of a preacher, I'm afraid. I'll drive back here Saturday night. I can't get a replacement preacher every time I think it might be nice to get away."

Nina tried to understand her friend's decision about coming back so soon and having just one night with John. It wasn't Nina's decision, of course, but wouldn't Winnie rather take the whole weekend?

Winnie recognized Nina's apprehension and explained, "We both have to get back to our appointed duties. John's classes are beginning, and you know about Sundays for me. Neither one of us can get away longer."

Nina thought it was a fun change of pace to be having "girl talk" with Winnie. She couldn't see exactly where things were going with this relationship, but she was keen on finding out!

✳ ✳ ✳

The first week of January seemed to be just another regular week in the life of a busy pastor.

Winnie had agreed to take Connie and her twins for their doctor's appointment in the next town over. It would be a full morning's outing, so she picked up some study materials to fill up any waiting time that might come along.

Connie was ready with her two, darling babies and all their paraphernalia — two carriers for the girls to be strapped into the back seat, as well as Connie's big diaper bag with all the various items for "just in case."

It took the whole morning, and Winnie was a bit set on edge because of the long wait. After an hour waiting in the reception room, there was another couple hours waiting in a checkup room before the doctor finally arrived to look at the girls.

While they waited the nurse arrived. She placed both babies on their backs on the gurney and undressed them in order to check their vitals. Winnie was amused to see the way the two little girls reacted. They couldn't see one another, as they were lying on their backs, starring at the ceiling, but they somehow knew they were near one another. As Winnie watched the babies, they reached out with their arms and touched hands. They knew the other twin was near. Winnie thought, *"Their nearness to each other must give them some sort of comfort! What a beautiful sight!"* She also thought these two babies had just shown her a tiny glimmer of truth— *"would that we could know the 'nearness' of God who is just within reach, right there next to us, waiting to be grasped!"* Winnie made a mental note to remember this tender moment, since it could be a good sermon illustration one day: God is in our lives — there within a moment's reach, if only we'd call out.

The nurse left, and they sat a while longer in the room, waiting.

Winnie had spoken to Connie before about her other children, and Connie had not been in the least secretive about them. She had shown scrapbooks she was making for each child and showed them to Winnie. There were pictures of Connie's children in their new homes with their new parents. One of the mothers wrote often to keep Connie informed about how her son was doing. Connie realized that her children had good homes and were receiving loving care. She didn't ever expect to get the children back, but she wasn't totally removed from them. Connie knew they were having a good life.

Connie's acceptance of her first three children's new circumstances was not easy for Winnie to accept. Winnie knew within herself that, had she been in Connie's situation, she would have fought tooth and nail to keep her children with her. Surely Connie had had more time to think about the whole business of losing her children and knowing that other parents were raising them instead of her — that things were now the best for her children. Although Winnie realized how Connie felt inside, about a mother losing her children, she did understand that it was emotionally healthier for Connie to come to the resolve she did.

While they awaited the doctor's arrival, Connie told Winnie one of the strangest stories she'd ever heard.

It seems that when Connie was growing up, she and her mother lived next door to George *and his family*. George was then married to another woman, and they had five children. Missy, George's youngest child, was Connie's best friend. The two girls were in second grade when they met!

Connie didn't tell Winnie what transpired over the next several years, but by the time Connie was sixteen George had divorced his first wife and married Connie!

Winnie couldn't believe her ears, and it took a minute to process the whole picture. *"There is something horrifyingly creepy about that whole scene. Connie has been under the influence of George since she was a child; how does such a 'relationship' begin? What a grotesque, illegal, and immoral situation!"* Winnie could see how the DHR, if they had any idea of George's other family, would not be pleased with his presence in the lives of his children.

* * *

Over in North Carolina, John was thoroughly enjoying his holiday. The whirlwind evening he had just spent with Winnie had turned out to be well worth the effort of getting there.

Winnie brought back fine, old memories of John's high school years, swhen life was less complicated and going quite well for him. Those old, school times — the memories they shared from times gone by — served simply as a preface for this new saga beginning for them.

John was characteristically introspective and recognized that something was astir within him since last night — something new and fresh. This newness reminded him of another time long ago when he and Helen began to fall in love.

His life would have been so different if Helen hadn't died. Her death had brought John's own life screeching to a halt. When he learned of her death, something inside him died, too. He felt completely alone and deserted. He felt dead inside — devastated, hardly able to put two thoughts together in a sensible string. He had retreated into a painful world of wanting to strike out and fight back.

The pain had stayed with John for years, and John knew he had clutched that pain close to him. As painful as his grief was, somehow his grief helped him stay connected to Helen, and he grew fearful that, if he lost the pain, he would lose her, too.

John was only too aware of the long years of loneliness and darkness he had suffered. He felt as if his very reason for life had been completely centered on Helen and what life with her would be when they married. All his hopes for their future were sent careening into an abyss that terrible day he lost her.

His response to Helen's death had been to retreat into his academic world — the place he had always found success before. There in the halls of higher learning John delved into his discipline and found some small peace there.

Now, John found himself tantalized by a new feeling, a feeling that he was young again and that things could be different. The old, nagging feeling of grief had vanished. Hope was returning to him, and he was pleased and reflective of what it might bring.

The weekend raced by, as John sped downhill on the most challenging mountain slopes. He welcomed the strenuous workout of the ski runs. He could feel his mind clearing as the crisp temperatures stung his face while flying down the snow packed mountains.

❄ ❄ ❄

Monday morning John packed his car and drove to Oxford, Mississippi — to the campus of Ole Miss. John was a philosopher who enjoyed the peace of a long car ride. He arrived at the hotel near campus Monday, shortly after dinner.

John noted several S.O.P.H.I.A members sitting around the lobby, engaged in conversation, but he didn't see anyone he knew. The philosophers' crowd was a goodly mix of thinkers gathered from every corner of the country — young and old, conservative and liberal. John expected to see several old friends when the conference began in the morning.

✳ ✳ ✳

The breakfast items available to the hotel guests included a very taste-tempting array of goodies to energize hotel guests for their day ahead. John had been pleased to hear that the hotel included free breakfasts for their guests. He always liked to see his dollar stretch as far as possible.

John was *not* a cook, and most of his meals were either fast food or frozen meals he could zap in the microwave at home. His usual breakfast was oatmeal and brown sugar, which was reasonably inexpensive, especially as John was careful to use store brands and not advertised labels. The many, tasty-looking choices at the hotel invited John to indulge himself today, after all, breakfast came with the price of the room!

He had just chosen a couple of old fashioned donuts to dip in his coffee when he felt a tap on his shoulder. John glanced around and found an old acquaintance of his, Dr. Victor Borkowski, standing next to him.

"Well, I thought I might run into you here!" John smiled at his colleague. "I'm glad to see you were able to make it to the seminar."

John had known Victor when they both attended Davidson College in North Carolina. They weren't close friends back then, as they were separated by a couple of years in school. They did take one class together, share the same advisor, and had many of the same professors, since they both studied the same discipline. They actually became better acquainted at seminars, like S.O.P.H.I.A.

The two men found a small table in the corner of the dining room, overlooking the courtyard, and exchanged a couple of pleasantries — mostly concerning courses they were currently teaching. John told Victor about the new honor he had just received, being named to the "Mortimer J. Adler" chair at his school.

Victor was struck by a coincidence when he heard Adler's name, and he interrupted John, "I was just reading about Adler. Did you know him?"

"No, I didn't. He left UC in 1952, so I missed him by a generation, but a chair was named for him when he died in '01. The chair was given to the Philosophy Department by a family who had greatly admired Adler's work, especially his work at Chicago, helping to set up *The Great Books of the Western World* and making them available to the masses," John explained.

"What brought Adler to mind?" John inquired.

"I think you and I are good examples of most Western philosophers today — not avowing any particular faith. Really, since the Enlightenment we philosophers have not believed in God. We knew better, right?" Victor smiled at John.

John cocked his head slightly and nodded affirmation with Victor's statement.

"There was a time when I thought anyone who believed in God had to be some sort of nut case. Belief in God doesn't seem to bear up to empirical facts," John admitted.

Victor continued. "See, you and I come from a long line of non-believing thinkers. We have been above all that foolishness."

"You've got that right. That's the way it's been for us philosophers, and I admit to having long been among of them!" John agreed.

"Anyway, your mentioning Adler reminded me of some research I've been doing recently, which is how I came upon his biography. Do you know that Adler, who was born into a non-observant family of Jews, and who considered himself a pagan, actually came to faith in Christ and was baptized when he was in his 80s!" Victor smiled.

"No, I didn't know that," John shook his head. "I've heard more about Adler's work. He was passionate about common people being able to learn from the best thinkers of the ages — after all aren't all human beings endowed with the same basic tools for thinking? Why should anyone be deprived of the great ideas that have been handed down over the ages. Much of Adler's work was finding ways to make great thoughts available to young people.

"What sort of research have you been doing?" John asked.

"I'm not doing this as a philosopher so much as I am searching for my own interests," Victor admitted. "I've been reading about a number of scholars, who represent a host of disciplines, who started off as pagans, or agnostics, or atheists, and later in life have come to faith in God."

John raised an eyebrow and nodded. "Sounds like you're pleased with what you've found. One of stumbling blocks for me is the whole debate between science and religion. It would seem there's a great divide between those two worlds, and it doesn't make sense. As philosophers many of us are sitting in the midst of the two, angry positions, and, as you say, most philosophers would side with the logical, empirical world as science represents it. Yet, some of us have certainly taken a place among theologians. Philosophers had heavy influence on the church over the years."

"And you know, before the Enlightenment, philosophers did believe in God; they believed they could get to proof of God through nature. Philosophers used to say that God gives the world a purpose for existence, so humans have purpose because God gave it to us," Victor added.

"John, I have been in the atheist camp for a long time, figuring anyone who admitted to having faith in God as being seriously demented — even down right foolish, but very gradually I've come to respect men and women of faith. They seem to be deep thinkers and are genuinely happy in this world," Victor announced.

John listened with interest to Victor's thoughts. His world, too, seemed to be changing — mostly because of Winnie. It was not because he was falling in love with her, which, he had to admit, was the case, but because she, herself, was obviously, deeply involved in following Jesus.

They hadn't talked about her faith, not much at all, but John was aware of Winnie's commitment to Christ. Her faith informed every part of her life. Wasn't that what her son had said — "Faith is living out your belief every day."

⁂ ⁂ ⁂

In his room that night, John got on the internet and called up an article about Dr. Adler. Ken Meyers, who had interviewed Adler in 1980, just after he published his book *How to Think about*

God, asked Professor Adler why he had never accepted faith in Christ himself. At that time Adler acknowledged his respect for many Christians, but he hadn't himself made such a commitment.

Adler did eventually commit to faith in Christ and was baptized in the Episcopal Church several years following that interview. He later admitted in *Christianity* magazine: "My chief reason for choosing Christianity was because the mysteries were incomprehensible. What's the point of revelation if we could figure it out ourselves? If it were wholly comprehensible, then it would just be another philosophy."

John added these thoughts to his new, and growing, catalog of memoranda about faith in Christ.

20. Some Answers

Friday had come, and Winnie could feel herself getting giddy inside. *"You'd think I was a teenage girl!"* she chided herself.

She had spent time, on and off, preparing for Sunday through the week — especially her sermon. She hoped she was ready with her message, as there would be no time on Saturday night to work on it. She and John had agreed to meet at the Gaylord Hotel in Nashville Friday night and Saturday, but she would have to get back on the road to Misty Falls sometime that evening, in order to be up and ready for Sunday morning services. Winnie couldn't quite let go the image of Cinderella, who had to be sure to be home by midnight or her entire entourage would melt back into the creatures of their former lives.

Before leaving town, Winnie took Bitty over to the Livingston's; Trudy had agreed to watch the pup over the weekend until Winnie could retrieve her on Sunday.

Winnie had plenty to think about on her drive. The roads were packed with cars and trucks on the highway. *What should I expect? It's Friday afternoon!*

✳ ✳ ✳

John arrived at the hotel before Winnie. He had never been to Nashville before, much less to the Gaylord Hotel, so he was not prepared for the sumptuous mansion that spread before him. The hotel was designed in the manner of an old, southern plantation, complete with the tall, white porticos and spreading verandas out front.

John saw Winnie as she entered the hotel, pulling an overnight bag. She was wearing a green and black plaid, wool scarf on top of her charcoal grey overcoat and matching tam; she looked terrific, John thought. Their final moments together last week had been pretty friendly, but he didn't want to appear too anxious. Instead, he took her bag and the two proceeded to the registration desk.

A bright-eyed, hotel desk clerk was most accommodating to his new guest. "Yes, Ma'am. How may I help you?" he asked. Then, noticing John, who was standing next to Winnie, he added, "Oh, are you two together?"

Winnie smiled at the desk clerk and explained, "No, we're not together. We are friends, meeting here at your hotel today and tomorrow, but we have separate rooms."

"Of course, Ma'am," the clerk nodded his head. "And what name would your reservation be under?"

In another moment the hotel keys had been picked up, and Winnie and John proceeded to take their bags up to their respective rooms.

The Gaylord Hotel was particularly well known for its botanical wonderland. When Winnie saw it she remembered the several occasions when she, and Mark, and the kids had traveled to similar castles in Europe — Shönnnbrunn in Vienna, Versailles in Paris, and Linderhof in Germany — were each adorned with enchanting gardens often in front as well as in back of the mansion. The garden at the Gaylord was several stories high and was under a covered, glass dome, making the weather always perfect for visitors to enjoy.

The hotel itself served as the entryway to an upscale mall — complete with fountains, waterfalls, a river that winds for acres throughout the park, and wonderful shops and restaurants to explore.

John and Winnie stepped from the hotel lobby into the garden and found themselves immediately surrounded by lush greenery and beautifully presented flowers, each looking as if it was vying for a state fair honor; it seemed to the couple as though they had come upon a new world that beckoned them invitingly.

There were restaurants offering enticing cuisines, and as evening was fast approaching, they chose an outdoorsy setting for dinner. The host at The Water's Edge Marketplace Buffet led them to a table right on the river where they could watch the the occasional small boat, carrying merry passengers, slip past them. They were in no hurry tonight; this evening could stretch out as long as possible.

Although the two certainly were never at a loss to find a subject worthy of reflection, they found it unnecessary to fill every moment with constant chatter, rather they sat and were filled with the charm of the moment — the sounds and sights and even the smells were in their own ways delicious, inviting them to drink in this captivating moment.

John reached over, picked up Winnie's hand, and gave it a squeeze. He didn't say a word. Being together, looking at one another face to face stirred something indescribable in each of them, something that neither Winnie nor John had felt in too long. Loneliness, which had been the dull, aching constant for each of them, had melted away.

While they waited for their dinners to arrive they spoke of the news, which was more and more shocking each day — the market plunging further and further down with no end in sight, the unemployment panic, the housing bubble burst. They exchanged the highlights of the news and speculated on where America was headed in this most unusual time. Discussing the current headlines might have kept them fully engaged in wondering about the country's future or, perhaps, recalling the Great Depression, which their parents had all lived through, but as they spoke about these surface items, Winnie was trying to imagine how to bring up a subject that she felt they needed to address — she was unsure of how to approach.

Finally, just as they were reviewing the terrible housing situation — so many, many home owners being forced into foreclosure — Winnie interjected, "You don't own a home do you?"

"No, I don't," John assured Winnie. I live downtown Chicago near the school. In fact, I've been renting the same apartment for nearly thirty years."

Winnie was thoughtful, "So, you've been alone in your apartment for quite a while?"

"I have," John was noticing how the subject had segued into something much more personal.

"And. . . you've never married?" Winnie ventured.

John sat back in his chair and straightened up; he thought about what would come next. He realized that he and Winnie had reached the appropriate time to share this piece of himself.

John began, "I was engaged to be married, once. . ." He stopped and closed his eyes and let a moment pass, then he turned back to Winnie. "But it didn't happen; actually it couldn't happen," John dropped his voice, took a deep breath, and continued. "This subject has been difficult for me for a long time. You have to understand.

"During my sophomore year at Davidson, I met Helen. She was in my Psych 101 Class; it was one of those really large, introductory classes, but she and I were also in the same, small discussion group. We met there.

"Her full name was Helen Helga Erikson, and I was totally bewitched by her the moment I saw her. She was tall and blonde, a real knock out! She was from a little town in Wisconsin, and she looked like she must have had Viking blood in her.

"For weeks I didn't dare speak to her. Then, about the end of September, we ran into each other at the library, and one thing led to another, and we ended up going out for a Coke. Helen was easy to talk to, it turned out. In fact she and I had a lot in common — we were both what you might call geeks and had been very competitive in school. We got on splendidly; she agreed to meet me for dinner that Friday night.

"We began seeing one another regularly, taking every opportunity to be together. Since we both had a full load of classes and needed time to study, we worked together, then afterwards we would get a bite to eat or take a walk around campus.

"Helen was a sorority girl, and it was nearly time for the school homecoming when the Greeks were building floats for the big school pep rally and bonfire. I got roped into helping with the float along with her sorority sisters and their friends. After that Helen and I attended her sorority's Christmas formal at some fancy resort. Dancing was a great discovery for us that night. We had both attended cotillions when we were young teens, so we knew basics about dancing. We realized how much fun it was to dance. That evening was enchanting — great exercise, growing friendship, festive environment — we decided to take some dance lessons together. We spent every Friday night on the dance floor, mostly dancing swing and ballroom. It was the perfect way to work out the kinks after sitting so long all week.

"Our romance moved right along, and we dreamed of having a full life together. The night we graduated I gave Helen an engagement ring. Unfortunately, our story didn't have a good ending." John stopped. His voice was noticeably shaky, but he continued.

"Helen and I had a problem; we would be continuing our studies in different parts of the country. I planned to do graduate work in Boston, hoping to get into the PhD program there. Helen, on the other hand, was a scientist. She had taken top honors in her work at Davidson. She had even won a government grant for her chemistry studies while she was an undergraduate. She had been accepted to a special program in Berkley, so we would be separated for the next four years by thousands of miles.

"We looked at the programs we were about to undertake and realized that it might be better for us to be separated while we delved into our work. When it was all done, we'd each have more to bring to our world together, and it would be a great reunion.

Winnie was nodding her head, imagining this cute couple with so much in front of them.

John continued. "We each went off to our respective sides of the continent. We would talk on the phone and write, of course. That was long before internet or cell phones, so we just had to wait and save up our thoughts for a once a week phone call.

"Anyway, we probably would have tried to see each other during the summer break, but that summer after the first year of graduate school Helen got a job teaching tennis. She played and had nearly gone into professional tennis. I think the only reason she didn't pursue pro tennis was because she was dead set on finding a cure for cancer.

"That summer Helen found a job teaching tennis at a camp in Wisconsin, and she occasionally played in tennis tournaments on the weekends. We had just talked before she left for a tournament one weekend.

"I got a phone call a couple of days later from Helen's parents. Of course, we had met when Helen and I graduated, and they knew about our engagement. They considered me part of the family, so they called me as soon as the news came to them.

"Helen had fallen asleep in her car on the highway on her way back from the tournament, and her car had driven straight into an eighteen wheeler, parked on the side of the road; she was killed instantly."

John stopped. He gazed beyond the little restaurant out onto the canal, studying it. Finally he turned back and continued, "I couldn't believe that she was gone — that I had lost her! I wanted to scream, and fight, and kick, and gouge out someone's eyes! How do you fight what's not there? How do you fight death?" John whispered; his voice chocked.

Winnie's eyes were filled with tears. She felt John's pain, and she understood his anger. Having been a pastor for so long, she had come across such pain in others, but that didn't lessen the pain she felt for John now.

She reached across the table, and grasped his hand in both of hers.

"I'm so sorry! Helen sounds so perfect for you; you were just right for one another. I can only imagine how you felt when you lost her! It must have been devastating," Winnie said.

"When Mark died, it was also an accident. His plane was lost. It varied off its course over the gulf coast and was lost to the air traffic controllers. Later debris from the plane was found in the water near some of the small islands off Texas. That was weeks later, but we knew the first day, when we heard the news, that he and the other pilot were gone.

"It was incredibly painful to think I'd never see Mark again. I was so shocked and disbelieving at first — like you felt. I couldn't fathom the idea that I'd never see Mark again. How could that be?

Then, too, our kids had just lost their dad, and I couldn't do anything to help them.

"I guess what I'm trying to say is that I can understand some of your pain." Winnie ventured to say.

John was thoughtful again. "Yes, but I didn't come through it very well. You put your life back together and moved on. You've done well, going on to seminary, becoming a pastor, watching your kids grow up and move on."

Winnie looked John in the eyes and said, "Yes, but I wasn't alone. I had my faith, and my family, and my church family that included many, good friends. So many people reached out to me at that time. They didn't know what to say or do, but they listened to me, and they helped me through the rough spots.

"It was a very hard time when I lost Mark. I can't tell you how many times I cried myself to sleep, yet I felt God was there for me. I kept remembering many of the promises that God made to us — that God would be our God, and that we are God's people; that He forgives us no matter what we have done; that all things work together for good for those who love God, who are called according to His purpose; that nothing can separate us from God's love; that Jesus has called us to follow Him, to be his disciples. Somehow those promises kept coming to mind, and I was encouraged by them. Very gradually, as I began to pick up the pieces of my life, things began to take on a fuller picture. I still missed Mark terribly, but my life was moving on.

"And one more thing that maybe made a difference," Winnie suddenly remembered, "I had read St. Paul's words to the Thessalonians many times, and there were three, little commands that Paul left to the Thessalonians: to 'rejoice evermore, in all things give thanks, and pray without ceasing.' One day about six months after I lost Mark, I woke up remembering those three — 'rejoice, be thankful, pray.'

"I thought I could understand those three things, for most situations, and I agreed with them, but right then I realized that I had not been thankful in some time. In fact, I couldn't remember when I had truly felt thankful at all. And, goodness knows, I had many, many things to be thankful for.

"Anyway, I couldn't get the thought out of my head. Finally, I realized that those commands in the Bible were for me, and that I should pay attention to them.

"And I thought, you know, if I am unthankful in this time, I'm sort of putting my pain and unhappiness ahead of God. That's actually breaking the First Commandment, which, as I understand it, means nothing is to be more important than God, and feeling hurt or grieved, for an extended period, is doing just that.

"I realized at that moment I had been feeling sorry for myself. You know, 'poor me, I've just lost my best friend and my lover.' I realized that I was enjoying a certain amount of attention because of my loss, and I knew, then, that I needed to begin being thankful to God for all He has given me.

"That was an important day in my life. I think I took a great leap in discipleship that day. I sank to my knees and asked God to forgive me for being unthankful and to ask His forgiveness. That may have been the beginning of the rest of my life," Winnie pronounced. Then she added, "Oh, John, I'm sorry if I've carried on so much about me. I think I was also talking to me just then, as I was telling you about what had happened," Winnie said sincerely.

John was touched by Winnie's admission. It was a strange thing to hear about being thankful to God. It had never occurred to him that believing in God required being thankful to Him. But John respected Winnie's memory and that she would share it now with him, revealing such a personal story about herself. He felt he almost had some responsibility to Winnie, now that he had heard her confession.

John said, "My response when I lost Helen was to bury myself in my work, which first meant finishing up my doctoral work and then landing the position at Chicago. I was miserable inside; I could hardly be with others, because I felt so wretched inside. I didn't want anyone asking me about myself. I didn't want to have to explain what had happened or how I felt. I just turned away from others and dug into my studies."

"Your answer to loss had better traction. It sounds like it was more helpful than sheer work" John said.

Winnie could see now how it was that John had never married. He had withdrawn from society. Perhaps he was afraid of being hurt again. Winnie could only speculate his reasoning.

"I can see why you stayed single," Winnie admitted. "Come to think of it, I didn't remarry, did I?"

They both laughed at her revelation.

"Maybe this is a new day for both of us, Win. Do you think?" John smiled.

This question brought the two abruptly before new questions: What about now? What about the two of them? Is this a new day for them in this New Year? Might they be on a new journey now? Where might this odyssey lead? Were they finally ready to move on to something greater now?

The evening waxed into night, and John and Winnie strolled together through the walks, stopping frequently to breathe in the beauty of the gardens. It was an enchanting place, altogether.

They took a ride on a Delta flatboat and sat close to one another. John put his arm around Winnie "to be sure she wouldn't slip off the bench." They enjoyed their propinquity.

It wasn't easy to say good night, but by midnight Winnie teased John about the bewitching hour and suggested that they could meet for breakfast and the entire next day together.

John escorted Winnie to her room and waited for her to open her door.

Before he left John whisked Winnie into his arms and they kissed. This time the kiss was longer — the squeeze that accompanied it, more scrumptious.

"See you in the morning, Sweetheart," John said to Winnie. "Shall we say eight o'clock?"

"You've got a date!" Winnie smiled as she slid into her room and closed the door.

* * *

Winnie's Walk: A Journey of Faith and Romance

Saturday brought more of the same; it was all like a dream. John found himself thoroughly amused and enamored by this vibrant woman. She seemed to bring life to him that he had forgotten he had. He definitely felt younger, and he found himself imagining ways that they might be together.

Winnie was also amazed. John seemed to be (almost) too good to be true. He was brilliant, and accomplished, and had a solid position at the University. He was fun to be around. He made her heart sing. They really did seem to be in sync with one another, even anticipating what the other was about to say. They had become devoted friends, which Winnie knew was a key component to a serious relationship.

John seemed to be perfect, but for one thing — well, actually two.

The matter of faith in Christ was of no small significance to Winnie. She told herself over and over again that she must be careful not to fall for someone who wasn't following the Lord.

By noon the two needed to be packed out of their rooms, as they were not staying a second night. They brought down their bags, paid their bills, and took their bags to their respective cars. They would need to depart for their homes after dinner.

The day had been so perfect neither of them wanted it to stop. They lingered over their dinner menus, not deciding on an entrée for quite a while. Finally the waitress returned to refill their decaf cups and ask, again, if they were ready to order. So they did.

By the end of the meal John finally asked Winnie what she thought they ought to do? What sort of relationship might they work out?

"I suppose there are several possibilities to choose from, and I think we're getting to the place where we'd like to take things to another level. But! I have to be completely honest with you . . ." Winnie started to say.

John already knew where Winnie was headed, and he touched his fingers to her lips, to keep her from speaking the words he didn't want to hear.

"You're about to tell me how your faith in Jesus is more important to you than anything else. Right? And that you can't consider developing a relationship that might lead to a commitment with someone who doesn't believe. That's it, isn't it?" John asked.

Winnie nodded her head slowly. "I'm not trying to say that I've got the right way of thinking and you don't. It mustn't be *sine qua non*! I'm not so self-centered as to think I have to have my own way in this.

"My problem is that my life is not my own. I gave my life to Jesus a long time ago. It belongs to Him. I follow Him, at least the best way I can.

"It's actually not wrong for a Christian to marry an unbeliever. In fact, St. Paul said that it's up to the unbeliever to stay with a marriage or not. If the unbeliever desires to live with the believer, it's fine. The believer doesn't get the same choice, though. St. Paul said that the unbeliever might be sanctified by the believer — meaning the unbeliever could be influenced into following Jesus, too," Winnie explained.

Then she added, "This is very confusing — maybe for both of us! We're being very cerebral about this relationship, which has its merits, but at the end of the day, where does that put us?

"I'd like us to have a chance. Who knows where we might end up? Who knows what good things lay ahead? BUT I have serious concerns about the long-term outcome of my getting involved with someone who doesn't believe in Jesus!" Winnie closed her eyes and dropped her head.

John reached over and touched Winnie's hand and said, "We can't make big decisions about our future tonight; that's apparent, but I will make you a promise."

Winnie slowly lifted her head and gazed into John's blue eyes.

"I promise that I'll give it a go. I promise that I'll read your book and . . ," John thought for a moment, "and I'll do some outside investigation. I'll see what I can see. How's that?" John asked, hopefully.

Winnie was stunned. She hadn't expected any such offer from John. He had been very open about other things about himself, but as for his interest in things spiritual he had been silent. Was he now willing to consider faith? Was he saying this just to please her? What could he mean by this promise?

"John!" Winnie exclaimed. "That gives me hope. That's a great step to take! I couldn't have asked for more!

"I'll tell you what you can do," Winnie suggested. "Reading the Bible is an enormous project, and I know your time is limited. I would suggest that you start with the New Testament. It's about a quarter the size of the entire Bible, and, of course, it's all about Jesus and the early church."

"I'd also suggest that you pick up a copy of *Mere Christianity* by C.S. Lewis. He was a confirmed atheist in the early twentieth century, but he came to faith in Christ after careful examination of the evidence," Winnie said.

John could sense that his compromise had brought Winnie much pleasure, and that pleased him. As for reading the Bible, he found himself growing quite intrigued with the project. Reading was what he did, what he loved to do."*Reading that famous tome will be a piece of cake*," he thought. Already he could see benefits from such an effort — specifically, Winnie'a apparent delight at his offer. John nodded his head as Winnie was speaking. He had meant to open the door for them, maybe just a crack, and already he could feel the wind whistling in. It amused him; he smiled.

Winnie changed her tone a bit, saying, "I don't want to force you to be something you don't want to be, but, as I understand it, when we come into a relationship with Christ, we are set on a path to become the person we *were meant* to be — a better person, a person who has a fuller existence, one with real purpose."

They lingered for a while in the parking lot, as they prepared for their trips home, but their departures were inevitable, and they knew it. They would keep in touch, daily. Final good-byes were said. Hugs and kisses were lingered over, and they began their journeys homeward.

❊ ❊ ❊

"Time apart." Winnie thought. *"This is a new phase for John and me. But we'll be doing a lot of 'time apart' so I better get used to it."*

The two would talk on the phone each day and be thinking about each other — all the time — but they had their jobs to do in their own parts of the world.

John called every morning before class "just to chat" — a great way to start the day. He bought himself a Bible that had been recommended to him by a clerk at a bookstore, and he began reading Matthew's gospel. *"It's funny how much is familiar,"* John told himself. He had never read the Bible before, and he supposed it would be new material to him, but he found he recognized much of what he read.

Winnie was delighted to hear that John was being faithful to his promise to her. While she was most pleased to hear of this progress, Winnie didn't want to overwhelm him with her own enthusiasm. If he had decided to take a journey — to delve into faith — it was his journey, and she needed to leave him to it and not be meddling too much. Even as much as she would like to see him come to faith in God in Christ, it had to be his decision. *"Of course, if he asks my opinion on something or for some suggestions I'd be happy to speak up then!"*

❋ ❋ ❋

The next several weeks went by with the usual community activities. Winnie spent time with Trudy, helping her sort out her thinking and feelings about her baby's father.

Winnie told Trudy that, from what she could learn, it was up to the mother to notify the father. There didn't seem to be anything that the father could do until he knew he was in the picture.

Once a father has been notified about a child's immanence there are legal steps that could be taken for the father to gain some sort of entrance into the child's life. The father would be given the opportunity to help support the child, and he could be given some visiting rights or even a shared custody of the child.

Trudy listened with care to everything that Winnie was saying.

"I think you're right, Miss Winnie," she said. "I suppose I have several considerations to make.

"Do I want to bring the father into the picture? I'm not sure it would be good for a couple of reasons.

"I don't know him very well. I think my news would totally rearrange his life, and I don't know if I want to be responsible for that.

"As far as my baby is concerned, I don't know that I can make that decision for him or her. Is it fair to make such an important decision that could affect his or her entire life?

"I didn't have a dad growing up, and so I don't really know what I missed.

Winnie could see that Trudy had been thinking about this, and that she wanted to do the right thing.

"What is the right thing to do?" Trudy asked.

Winnie thought a moment and said, "Ask yourself, is this father one who might be prone to hurt your child? Would you consider the man a selfish sort, who would be bad for the child?"

Trudy looked shocked as she heard Winnie's question.

"No! He's a very good person. I think he's one of the greatest guys I've ever known," Trudy answered.

"That's good to hear. There are some men who have fathered children by attacking women. Those men started off with a bad deed, so they are suspect right to begin with. You're telling me this man is good." Winnie repeated Trudy's words.

"Yes'M, he is. I think he's wonderful," Trudy admitted.

"OK then, that tells me that this man doesn't have any strikes against him already," Winnie pointed out.

"How well do you know him?" Winnie asked.

Trudy was quiet for several minutes before she answered. "I don't know him well. I met him last summer at a party with some friends. We liked each other right off, and he asked me out on a date. We went out just once more. He didn't have any weird ways, not that I could tell; he was just the best," Trudy explained.

"So, from what you know about him, he hasn't any objectionable traits that might be dangerous. In fact, you're telling me that he's got many good qualities." Winnie said.

"That's the thing. He's got a fantastic scholarship to school. He's on his way to becoming someone important. I'm afraid that once he learns that there's a kid on the way, and it's his kid, his whole life will come apart, and it will be all my fault!" Trudy had dropped her voice to a near whisper, as she made this final admission.

"How about your life? Don't tell me this baby's advent isn't making a difference for you!" Winnie pointed out, "Don't you have any goals or hopes for a future?"

Trudy hadn't thought about it that way before. She was just like her mom. She was following in her footsteps. What more could she expect?

"I don't know if I have changed my mind about notifying the father, but you have given me some stuff to chew on, as they say," Trudy told Winnie.

Trudy agreed to continue to consider the father. It was her decision, but she had more to think about now.

✳ ✳ ✳

One day in late January Winnie got a call from Connie Oliver. She said that the DHR had just called her and told her there had been another complaint from a neighbor. The neighbor had accused the Olivers of fighting in their apartment. The neighbor apparently had heard loud voices and banging in the Oliver's apartment, and was fearful for the babies' safety.

That incident forced the DHR to react, to put the babies into foster care, while Connie and George would have to take anger management classes. The classes would last for at least eight weeks. If they completed the classes and passed them, then the Olivers could get the babies back. The DHR was coming by in the afternoon to pick the girls up.

The news was hard to take in. Winnie knew that there had been warnings by the DHR, but she had been hoping that this time things would be different for her. She had only known the Olivers for a few months, but they weren't bad people, and she had been expecting things to work out better for them this time. She had to have an answer for Connie, and the only thing she could think of was, "I'll be right over." She hung up the phone, grabbed her purse and keys, and headed over to their apartment.

When Winnie arrived, Connie was subdued and didn't want to talk. Winnie could understand her reaction, under such difficult circumstances. Winnie talked with Connie and Sallie for a short while; George wasn't present, and no one offered any information on his whereabouts. Winnie would have prayed with them to ask God's help for this new turn of events — to help them get through it — but they didn't seem receptive to such a suggestion. They did recognize that they were being given a way through this trouble by the DHR. George and Connie could attend the required anger management classes and prove to the DHR that they could handle their ire.

The DHR came later that afternoon and took Samantha Rose and Shelby Ann to a foster home. Connie could visit them at the DHR office every Friday for ninety minutes. *"What a painful place to be! What a horrible thing to go through!"* Winnie thought to herself.

✴ ✴ ✴

Winnie spoke with Evelyn via cell phone most days, and she learned how Randy's case was evolving. The doctors had decided to do surgery to see what they might be able to do to release the hematoma in Randy's brain. Since he had not died, yet, and seemed more stabilized at this point, surgery might give him a chance to heal.

Winnie drove over to the Medical Center in Knoxville to be with Randy's parents, as they waited through the surgery. Finally, good news came from the surgeon, who told them that they had been successful in their efforts to reduce the hematoma, and they expected Randy to come through the recovery and begin the long, healing process.

That was very good news, indeed! Winnie prayed with the Evelyn and Gerald right there in the hallway after the doctor had left, thanking God for the surgery, and the care and healing for Randy.

* * *

Dood-ley-doo! Dood-ley-doo! Winnie's cell phone was ringing. She had set the ring tone to this bright sound to tell her it was John calling.

"Morning, Win" John said. "You're up early."

"Yes, I've been up for a while, of course, I'm an hour ahead of you, too," Winnie laughed.

John wasn't calling just to chat this morning, though. "I was looking at my calendar last night, and I realized that the University will be having a mid-semester break the third week of February. It actually begins after class on Friday the 13th and runs to Tuesday the next week. Anyway, I was thinking I might drive down and see you then," John ventured.

Winnie's eyes flew open wide, and she said, "That's wonderful! But it's a long drive from Chicago to Misty Falls in a short span of time."

John laughed and said, "I don't mind the drive; I enjoy taking trips; it gives my mind some peace and quiet — a good time to think. That's what philosophers do!"

"Of course I'd like to see you then! I'm so glad you're considering the trip." Winnie assured him.

"I know you work on the weekends; will that be a problem for you? Will I be in the way, if I arrive on Saturday afternoon?" John asked.

"Yes, of course I work on Sundays in the morning — I'm preaching at eleven o'clock, and there's Sunday school before that, but that doesn't have to be an impossible burden for us. In fact, I'll make you a homemade dinner Saturday, if you can arrive about six; we can eat here at the parsonage," Winnie offered. "Of course, I can't stay up to all hours that night, because of Sunday, but I think we can manage."

"I'm planning on staying at the little motel where I stayed before, so I can just leave and go there when you need to focus your thoughts. I'll be out of your hair as you prepare for your sermon, and we can see one another after church," John suggested.

"You're very understanding, John," Winnie admitted. "I'll try to have things pretty much *ready* to go before you arrive, so I won't need the entire evening," Winnie said.

"This weekend visit will be different for us. It won't be decked with New Year's trimmings or the charming gardens, shops, and walks of the Gaylord. But this time we'll be have a chance for a nice, ordinary weekend. "I wonder if John might come for worship? He might, and wouldn't that be special for him to hear the gospel that morning?" she mused.

21. Valentine's Day

"Wish there was some way to reduce these butterflies!" Winnie sighed. *"Whoever suggested that falling in love was a feeling reserved just for young people? Whoever it was, didn't know anything about a mature romance and the erratic way it plays with one's heart! I should know better, yet I can't help how I feel!"* Winnie thought.

John was due to arrive in the evening, and Winnie figured that by now he was already on the road. She planned to cook for John tonight. She had never cooked for him before, and she was looking forward to showing him her domestic side.

Cooking, for Winnie, had become a favorite escape, a time apart from all those claims on a pastor's time. *"Preparing a meal for John feels so right, so natural. He says he eats out all the time, so this will be a nice change for him. How sad — how lonely —to always eat alone."*

Winnie stopped right then and corrected herself, *"Look who's throwing stones at someone else's castle! I eat alone, too! Ninety-five percent of the time, I'm eating all alone,"* Winnie admitted to herself.

"This 'date' is almost more fun than our first two dates. I have a feeling it will be even better in this domestic setting," she mused.

"Think I'll go with my favorite chicken and broccoli dish but jazz it up using a rotisserie chicken with shrimp. It's always a big hit at church fellowship dinners." Winnie suspected her church folks liked the chicken dish because she tweaked the white sauce with a pinch of ginger and curry and added a little white wine.

After the casserole was in the fridge, ready to be warmed before John arrived, Winnie took time to work out the details of her Sunday morning — both her sermon and Sunday school thoughts. *"I can hardly push him out of the house after we eat, when he's driven so far to get here,* I've really got to focus my thoughts now."

✳ ✳ ✳

"Oh what a beautiful morning," John sang aloud to himself, as his began driving his Honda down the interstate; *". . . everything's goin' my way."* John's eyes had snapped open very early that morning; this was the day he would drive down to Misty Falls to visit Win for the President's Day weekend. He would make the trip straight through, stopping only for gas along the way. He could be at the parsonage by six, even losing an hour with the time change.

John was relishing this very crisp, Saturday morning and the potential this long weekend held for him and Winnie. He didn't have any specific expectations for the trip, but he was keeping an open mind about whatever might come along.

On the trip south, John made a discovery — it was Valentine's Day! He had forgotten all about that popular holiday, but he was suddenly reminded of it, when he stepped into the shoppette to pay for his gas. There before him stood a large rack of red, heart-shaped, Valentine boxes, ranging from minute to oversize.

"By Jove! You've nearly made a fool of yourself," John spoke sternly to himself. *"I can see the egg you would have all over your face if you arrived at Win's house tonight without a Valentine's gift! You really are a cad! But see here, Old Fellow, you can make amends before it's too late, and no one will be the wiser,"* John continued, figuring he had just skirted past a dangerous precipice in this new relationship.

As John was about to make his selection from the sizable array of Valentines, the clerk walked up to him, "I don't know if you

213

noticed our sign over there, but all our Valentine's Day items have been marked 70% off."

"You have just made my decision easier. Thanks," John answered the clerk, picking out the largest Valentine's box and purchasing it. *"Timing is very good, and I don't mind saving a little coin in the process,"* John thought to himself.

Half an hour before he was expected, John drove up the parsonage driveway. He had arrived in town a hour earlier but had stopped at the motel, picked up the key to his room, and taken the time to freshen up before heading over to Winnie's parsonage. John took the big Valentine from the car, walked up the front steps, and rang the bell.

The chime of the bell immediately sent Bitty into peals of barking, as she raced to the front door, and all the commotion caused Winnie to jump up from her seat, forcing her to grab her laptop quickly before it plunged to the floor. She had been sitting on the couch in the family room with her laptop on her lap, concentrating so hard that the sound of the bell snapped her from her thoughts and back to the present: John had arrived; her work was finished; the evening was at hand!

Winnie unlatched the door, opened it, and found John holding a very large, red satin Valentine out to her. "I hope I'm not too early," he smiled.

"Come in, come in! No, you're not too early! I've been thinking about your arrival all day. I didn't expect you'd get here quite yet. You had a good drive?" Winnie welcomed her guest.

"This is for you; Happy Valentine's Day" John offered the big box of chocolates to Winnie, leaned over, and gave her a kiss. "I have to admit, I hadn't realized that today was Valentine's Day, but every time I stopped for gas the shops were full of boxes of candy and red and white teddy bears. Today all the sweethearts in the world are celebrating!" John winked at Winnie.

Winnie flushed bright red across her cheeks. "Goodness!" She replied. "Thank you, John. Did you get the biggest Valentine in the store? It looks like it! I don't think I've received a Valentine in years, and I'm pretty sure I've never had such a big one. We'll definitely share this!

"Is your school really giving you a day off for Valentine's Day?" Winnie asked.

"The University takes off the middle Monday in February because of President's Day, so we get a mid-term break every Winter term for that holiday. The weekend just happens to land on Valentine's Day this year," John explained. "it does make for a fun coincidence, though."

Winnie had set the table in the dining room with a linen table cloth, her good china, sterling silver, and candles, each item adding to the gracious ambiance of the evening.

Winnie's home cooking didn't go unnoticed. "Delicious, Win; this recipe is marvelous! Do you cook for yourself like this everyday?" John wondered aloud.

Of course, Winnie was entirely pleased at John's reaction and assured him, "No, I don't have too many reasons to cook for others these days. I really had fun cooking for you today!"

"Are second helpings allowed?" John picked up his plate and passed it to Winnie.

"Glad you like it. I was hoping that you could have a taste of home tonight. Do you ever cook for yourself?" Winnie asked as she scooped a healthy, second portion onto John's plate.

"Well, I usually have breakfast at home, but I only have cereal or toast. I don't like to mess up the kitchen, and cooking does that," John explained.

The evening was off to a great start; everything was fitting nicely into place — the setting, the meal, the mood, the attitude of lightness and enjoyment for both of them.

Winnie excused herself to step into the kitchen. She had pulled her homemade cheesecake out of the fridge and placed it on the table in the kitchen so it could accommodate to room temperature before she served it, but, as Winnie walked into the room, Bitty jumped off the table, raced through the family room, and down the hallway. Winnie looked again at the dessert, which had been awaiting her arrival, and saw immediately what Bitty had been doing to her creation! That naughty animal had taken a large bite out of the center of the pie!

"Oh No!" Winnie screamed at the dog, who was now far away from her mistress, hiding in the back bedroom.

"What's the matter, Win?" John followed the noise into the kitchen and saw what Winnie was starring at.

"Bitty took a bite out of the center of our dessert!" Winnie could hardly contain her shock. She wasn't quite sure whether she should cry or laugh. It was funny, or would be funny someday in the retelling of the story, but at the moment dinner was almost ruined by her naughty dog.

John could see the consternation in Winnie's eyes and voice. "Win! It's OK. Dinner was perfect even without dessert. Every part of dinner was just right for us, and we're having such fun here, enjoying your home! The cheesecake was one more addition to an already perfect meal." John gave Winnie a big hug.

The evening was filled with laughter and fast-paced conversation.They found much to talk about — history, psychology, music, political and economic news, the wars in Iraq and Afghanistan, and more. Both John and Winnie were well prepared to engage in depth on any number of topics, but, it turned out, they didn't always agree.

The subject of famous people came up, and Winnie remembered a TV show, which was aired just before the turn of the century, which counted down the one hundred most influential people in the last millennium.

Winnie and John had fun listing names of men who might have been included in that notable list.

"Einstein was number one, wasn't he?" John asserted. "He was brilliant in several disciplines that propelled so many of the changes we are seeing today. We can't even understand matter in the same way we did, before Einstein came along."

"Actually, it wasn't Einstein who took first place," Winnie replied.

"I'm pretty sure I'm right. It would be Einstein." John said with a confident nod of his head.

"It wasn't Einstein, although he certainly has much to commend him. You're right about that. I remember when the countdown took place on that New Year's eve; I was watching it on TV, and I actually guessed the right person," Winnie reminisced.

"Are you sure? We're talking about the most influential person in the whole millennium, right? I think it was Einstein." John smiled with confidence.

"I don't want to burst your balloon, but I know I'm right, not that it matters," Winnie didn't want to actually disagree with John, but he <u>was</u> wrong.

"Who do you think it was, then?" John wasn't convinced.

"The top honor for most influential person in the last millennium was Gutenberg — the fellow who invented the printing press back in the fifteenth century," Winnie said. "The reason I figured it out was because I remembered what Dr. Campbell, my Christian history professor, said about why Martin Luther's ideas caused the Protestant Reformation in Europe. Luther happened to live shortly after Gutenberg's press began working, so Luther was able to publish his ideas, allowing many people to read his work. He couldn't be hushed up by the Catholic Church, because of the printing press. When I remembered that, I figured that Gutenberg's invention might make him the most influential person, and I was right."

"I guess I'll have to concede, then," John admitted, pretending to pout. They both laughed at his silly expression.

After dinner John followed Winnie into the kitchen and helped her clean up the meal, before they retreated to the family room.

Winnie had set a fire in the fireplace in her den, so the two sat on the couch, nestling close to each other. They were immediately transported back to the first time they had been close — the time on the Volunteer Princess when they danced together. They had discovered then that their world was changing — the loneliness they each had known for so long had vanished, and in its stead hung a tantalizing hunger for the other. It was a fresh, new feeling, one that neither John nor Winnie had experienced in far too long, and they found they were almost unable to resist its mesmerizing charm.

Winnie might have simply enjoyed the moment; it was totally sublime, but her mind was swirling around on several levels. First she was completely happy and content with the way the evening was progressing. John was a dream, and sitting with him in her cozy den made everything seem so right. On the other hand, a great controversy was waging war within her, causing her to wonder if she might be heading for trouble. *"I'm dying to ask John what he's thinking about faith now. He says he's been reading the New Testament. He might even be through most of it by now. How can I gauge where he might be on this journey?"* Winnie thought. *"Could we have a chance to be a real couple? I can't see us having a long term relationship, when we are both in such opposing camps, spiritually."*

"Could this beautiful friendship become even more than it is now? Could this be coming from the Lord? Might He have brought us together for a purpose?

"O, Lord, I do hope so. Please, lead us through this amazing time!" Winnie prayed silently.

As these thoughts were busily vying for her attention within, Winnie casually announced, "I'm doing a lesson from John's gospel tomorrow."

"Hm," John nodded, "John's gospel; his gospel is the different one, isn't it?"

"Yes, it is. I especially like to work with St. John; the church uses much of the language from John's gospel to speak about who Jesus is," Winnie added. "So, how is your reading progressing?" she asked.

"I wondered if you would ask," John answered. "I've completed the New Testament, except for a bit at the end of Revelation. That's really an odd book, isn't it?"

Winnie shook her head in agreement and said, "Yes, most of Revelation is strange, it's a different sort of writing — apocalyptic writing. It is unique in the New Testament. If you haven't read the last couple of chapters, they are really beautiful, all about the end of times when a New Heaven and a New Earth appear. It has a very good ending."

"As I've been reading, I can see my mind working on a couple different tracks at the same time, almost like I'm having a conversation within myself. For one thing, I have heard a surprising amount of the material in the New Testament already. Maybe this is simply because we live in America, a primarily Christian society, and there are many occasions where ideas from the Bible are mentioned."

"There were several parables that I had heard — The Good Samaritan, for instance, and the Prodigal Son, and the Lost Sheep. And then there is the business of Jesus walking on water. And, of course, everyone has heard about Jesus' death and resurrection, but I had never considered that story to be actually true. I believed it was a myth, and like other myths, it was just an interesting tale — you know, like Robin Hood or King Arthur," John explained.

"My world is all about thinking — argument, logic, truth. It's the venue I love. I'm very aware that truth doesn't have to be empirically factual to be true. Like the parables that Jesus told; there's much truth in them, but they are stories. So, maybe I've been figuring this idea of Jesus' resurrection is a truth, like you find in the parables.

"On one level, I was reading the Bible as a piece of great literature — really old, well loved literature. But on another level, I realized that I couldn't just read it as a disinterested party. There is something about the person of Jesus of Nazareth that is calling me to take note of him. It's as if he can make a difference in my life," John explained. "There's something compelling to me about this person Jesus. I've read many, many thinkers and philosophers over the years, yet Jesus stands alone — he truly is one of a kind. His message is, also, compelling. I like the way he thinks. I like the challenge he presents to his disciples, and I can't seem to get rid of the thought that his challenge is also to me. It's something I need to think about."

Winnie smiled as she heard John's words, because she knew exactly what he meant about not being able to disregard that voice within that challenges and calls one. "John, I can completely appreciate your quandary about that challenge. I know it very well. I've been aware of it for many years.

"I'm glad to hear how well your reading has gone; I think you're on a journey, and it sounds like you are willing to follow it where your investigations take you."

"That's a good way to put it," John agreed. "I do plan to continue my research."

The subject changed. John's visit was short; they had only Sunday and part of Monday before he needed to get back on the road again.

The next several months would bring more separation. Winnie and John took out their cell phones, pulled up their calendars,and looked for common ground — a couple of days when they might get together again, but there was no good time before summer.

"Goodness, John, we're going to have to be creative about seeing one another" Winnie sighed.

"We don't seem to find any logical answer for getting together other than just an occasional weekend. That doesn't really cut it, does it?" John agreed.

John picked up both of Winnie's hands and held them in his. He pulled her fingers to his lips and gently kissed them each. Then he looked into her eyes and said, "Win, you must know that I'm in love with you! I want you to marry me, so we can live together for the rest of our lives — under one roof!"

Tears welled up in Winnie's eyes and began their way down her face. She looked deeply into John's face. "I think we should be together, too. I want to marry you, but there are some serious problems to work out . . ."

22. The Question

The next morning John showed up at Muddy Creek's doors. In such a small church, visitors were obvious. Several church members welcomed John, gave him a bulletin, and showed him a place to sit about halfway back in the sanctuary next to Gus and Martha Reeves.

John hadn't been in a church in many years, so he watched carefully what other people did and followed suit, studying the bulletin with doctoral scrutiny.

Winnie appeared in the chancel dressed in her black, academic gown with a green stole. She took a seat on a large chair and looked upon the congregation; she was delighted to see John sitting out there.

When it was time for the sermon, Winnie stepped down from her pulpit to the main floor of the sanctuary, as was her custom. Winnie was more nervous than usual, knowing that John had come and would be listening to her talk. *"Look for the blessing; Look for the blessing!"* Winnie told herself, trying to calm down. She knew that once she began preaching she would relax into the message, focusing on what she had to say, and she would really enjoy giving the sermon. It was always the time just before she began that caused her agitation. Today was definitely not any easier.

Winnie said a silent prayer, *"Lord, guide my words and everyone's thoughts",* and began to speak.

This morning Winnie had chosen to speak about two disciples of John the Baptist. They were with the Baptist when he saw

Jesus passing by them, and he declared to all, "Behold, the Lamb of God!" John's disciples ran off after Jesus. At first they followed at a distance, but when Jesus realized they were shadowing him he stopped and asked them a timeless question, "What are you looking for?"

Winnie used Jesus' words as a springboard to elicit ideas from her community about what they might be looking for today in their world: a new tractor, a new job, the pitcher's position on the little league team.

From those answers she moved on to what else people, these days, might be looking for — things they hope will bring them fulfillment and satisfaction: friends, significant others, spouses, college degrees, bigger cars, houses, even, sometimes, alcohol or drugs. "We spend a lot of time looking for things that won't really give us complete satisfaction. Maybe we're looking for the wrong things," Winnie suggested.

Winnie moved back to the Bible story. The disciples had answered Jesus' question with another question back to Jesus, "Where are you staying?"

"Then Jesus answered, 'Come and see'"

Pastor Winnie added: 'I wonder if Jesus might have meant:

"Come and see…

"Come, and get to know me.

"Get to know **me**.

"Get to know me and the One who sent me.

"Come, become my friend.

"I will be the best friend you will ever have.

"In me you can place your trust.

"In me you can lay down your burdens.

"Come hear what I have to say:

"Come hear about the Kingdom of God

"Come hear my command to love one another

M. E. PALMER

"Come hear my call to discipleship.

"Come witness my ministry:

"Come witness the next few years

"Come witness the miracles I will do.

"Come witness the healing I will bring

"Come learn:

"Come learn my ways and my thoughts

"Come learn about my Father in Heaven

"Come learn

"'Come unto me all ye who labor and are heavy laden, and I will give you rest.'

"'Let anyone who is thirsty come to me, and let the one who believes in me drink.'

"Come and see...

"What I am about to do

"See me heal the sick

"Feed the hungry

"Bring good news to the poor

"Proclaim release to the captives

"And freedom to the oppressed

"Hear me proclaim the year of the LORD's favor to all.

"Come see how I will turn the world upside down.

"Come be filled with the Holy Spirit.

"Come and see

"Come, see, discover for yourselves

"Discover who I am

"Discover that I am the Lamb of God

"Discover what I can do for you

"Discover that in me you will find eternal life

"Discover who you are in me.

"Discover how you are more fully you, when you are in me."

Winnie concluded her sermon with a final question: "Isn't Jesus what we're all looking for?"

John had been listening intently to Winnie's sermon, but not simply because he was interested in the preacher, and this was a new facet to her, but he found himself listening to the message itself. John had not heard Winnie preach before, and he appreciated her casual, friendly way of addressing her audience, but he was more intrigued with the substance of her sermon than the method of her delivery. Her final question stuck in his mind: "Isn't Jesus what you're looking for?" John wondered, *"Did Win expect me to be here in the audience this morning? It seemed like she was talking directly to me!"*

✳ ✳ ✳

Following the service, Martha Reeves invited John to join them in the Fellowship Hall for coffee.

"John, this is my husband, Gus Reeves," Martha introduced her husband to the visitor. "Are you moving here to this area, or are you just passing through?" Martha asked John.

John wasn't exactly sure what sort of information Winnie might have dropped related to his coming, so he evaded, "I'm from Chicago, but I had a couple days free and thought it might be good to get away, so I drove down here."

Before the Reeves could press the question, Winnie came out of her office, dressed in civilian clothes, and appeared in the Fellowship Hall. "I'm so glad y'all have met. John did you tell these people who you are?"

Martha answered Winnie's question, "John was just telling us how he's here from Chicago on a short trip."

Winnie smiled and said, "John is actually here as my guest. (Martha and Gus exchanged knowing glances at one another.)

John and I are both from Denver; in fact we went to high school together."

Winnie turned to John and said, "It was good to see you here in worship this morning, John. I hope you enjoyed our service."

"This is a beautiful church," John answered sincerely. "I especially enjoyed studying the picture windows, and I think I could identify most of the Bible stories that they depict."

Martha spoke up, "Our picture windows are pretty new to us. We had them put in six years ago; before that, the windows were stained glass, but they weren't the wonderful scenes of the Lord we have now.

✳ ✳ ✳

Later, over lunch at the parsonage, Winnie and John had a good laugh. "I really didn't quite know what to say when Mrs. Reeves asked me how I came to be here," John told her. "I should have thought up something ahead of time."

"There's no need for making up something; you're here as my guest." Winnie grinned.

"Win, were you serious when you said you want to marry me?" John asked.

Winnie looked into his eyes and said, "John, I feel like we've put ourselves into a real predicament. I was afraid something like this might happen, but you'll notice I didn't do anything to discourage it," Winnie grimaced a bit.

"So, what have I gotten myself into?" she said, half to herself.

"Tell me what you're thinking Win," John encouraged Winnie, sensing her discomfort.

"You must know my conundrum," Winnie said, pouting slightly.

John put his arm around Winnie and gave her a squeeze and a kiss on the head. "I hope you know that when you're confused or hurting, I am too," he assured her.

Winnie smiled weakly and answered, "Yes, I love that about you. I think you really are trying to understand me."

"My problem is I feel like I'm being torn between two really wonderful things. How can that be a problem?" she asked. "You've asked me to be your wife, and I don't know how I can say, 'No.' I believe I have fallen in love with you, and I can imagine all sorts of marvelous ways we can have a life together," Winnie smiled at John.

"But?" John encouraged her to continue.

"That's the problem; it's the same thing I've been dancing around since we met at the reunion. By now you must know that my job in life is to follow the Lord. I've been doing that, the best I could, here at Muddy Creek and the other churches I've served. I've spent nearly twenty years being pastor in one community or another, and I know I can't give it up. I hope I'm making a difference to people I'm working with. I can't just turn my back on my call to ministry. Can you understand that, John?"

John didn't answer. He sat quietly and let Winnie's words hang in the air for a full minute. Then he asked, "I don't know anything about how the church works with pastors, but I wonder if the system in church is similar to how the university works when it comes to finding lecturers to fill positions?"

John's question led to a detailed discussion of how the politics work and differ in the church and the university.

Winnie explained about the different sorts of polity that churches use, some of which were probably similar to how universities function — searching for prospective candidates and calling them to particular positions. "The United Methodist system of pastoral appointments is different. We UM pastors are <u>sent</u>, that is, we are appointed to preach at a specific church, but we are moved to new appointments according to the needs of the churches. There's no guarantee that any of us will be in one spot for very long," Winnie explained.

Their discussion segued into conversation about their own tenures teaching and preaching.

"Which reminds me, Win, I hadn't heard you preach before, but I thought your sermon this morning was very good. Are you sure you didn't expect me at your church this morning?" John winked at Winnie.

Winnie nearly laughed at John's question, but instead she chuckled a bit. "Last night nothing was said about you attending Muddy Creek's worship service, and, although I was hopeful that you might show up, I didn't plan on it. I know worship service is not part of your normal Sunday morning activity.

"I was thrilled to see you sitting out there next to the Gus and Martha, although your presence didn't do anything to alleviate the '*pit*', which is what I call my preaching anxiety," Winnie explained. "I'm always nervous before I start my sermon, but this morning I had an advanced case of the "*pit*.'"

"I think you're are a good preacher, Win, although I haven't heard many others. I have to admit I always change the channel quickly, when I'm scanning for something to listen to, if I hear someone preaching. This morning I felt as if you were speaking directly to me. You were, weren't you?" John asked half-teasingly.

"I was preaching to anyone who would listen; I have never targeted anyone specifically," Winnie assured John.

"I think I've learned a lot over the years about preaching, and I feel much more confident, nowadays, that I am able to share a message once I've found it. That's the trick right there — figuring out what the message is and then figuring a way to impart it to my audience.That's two different problems, and there's no guarantee that I'll find those answers in the time allotted. After I've found the message, I still have to learn the message well enough to know where it is leading. I gave up reading from a script years ago, so I have to know pretty well the main points and in what order they should come when I preach."

"Sounds like you've got an approach/avoidance issue with sermons. Am I right?" John asked.

"Indeed! Being a preacher requires quite a balancing act, trying to do all the right things for your community as well as finding adequate time to study and prepare the new sermon, but I suppose that's what I signed on to do, when I agreed to preach," Winnie said thoughtfully.

"I don't think I know a pastor who doesn't have some degree of concern about preaching. Surely we learn a lot about the process of preaching, but it doesn't really get easier. Maybe we just get better at working on the sermons. I keep telling myself to 'look for the blessing' when I'm about to talk, because after I'm finished I do feel a certain glow inside.

"The deal is that United Methodists have a pretty good system of helping people do ministry, and I know I could get into ministry in some way up in Chicago. I am a member in good standing in my conference, so it's quite possible to transfer my membership from here to the Chicago area. I don't suppose I would be appointed to preach immediately, but something would work out, down the road."

John's eyes widened and a smile began to grow on his face. "What are you saying, Win?"

"I'm saying that between the two of us I'm in the more mobile position. I can see that. You have your tenured position and your new chair at the university, and when I think about it, I have no guarantee that they'll leave me here in Misty Falls; I don't know when my superintendent will call and tell me I'm moving; I'm not married to my place here at Muddy Creek."

"Then you're saying there's a way for us to be together! A way for us to get married! That's what you're saying!" John was beaming.

"Yes, I think we've got a reasonable solution figured out for that part, but my first concern hasn't changed — our difference on the subject of faith. I have a nagging thought in the back of my head reminding me that a believer shouldn't be married to an unbeliever. That's actually another point of wisdom from St. Paul," Winnie said.

"Win, I'm not nearly as worried as you seem to be about that. That's because I'm not worried about me. I know me," John grinned. "I can tell you, though, that in the midst of all that's going on between us, I believe I'm not the same person I was a few months ago."

✻ ✻ ✻

When John finally got to his motel room that night, he sat down on the edge of the bed and began to think. There was much to ponder. This weekend visit had loosed a myriad of thoughts that made John anxious for a few moments of peace to sort things out.

"This whole trip is like a dream. What more could I ask? Win says she wants to marry me!"

"It's almost like I'm back thirty years ago, and I have my whole life in front of me again — with a wonderful woman who will be at my side. I love Win's inner happiness — her joie de vivre — her humor — her interest in learning, thirsting to learn more and more — her funny way of springing into a song at the least mention of words from the same.

"And! She says she loves me; she feels about me as I do for her." John closed his eyes and smiled.

"There's something else, though. Something . . . something haunting me — begging my attention," John continued his silent soliloquy.

"I feel almost satiated with wonderful feelings — feelings that have been building inside me, since I came down here the first time. I don't understand it," John cross-examined himself.

"I have such a deep sense of joy. I'm sure part of it is be-cause of falling in love. The world knows well of the goofiness of falling in love, but somehow I feel there is more to it. This is not some terrific boon I've been given, like when I was awarded the Adler Chair last fall. I was pleased as punch that day, but this is different — it's consuming me.

"Win said that when she lost Mark she was grief stricken, and angry, and lost, and hurt. I know exactly those feelings, but she came out of her depression. She told me that she had forgotten to be thankful to God. Her grief had prevented her from being thankful or feeling thankful. She admitted that her grief took away her song; she couldn't even sing for a while, and for Win, that must have been serious!" John announced out loud.

"I can totally understand how she felt in her grief, but Win is so full of life and happiness these days. It makes me wonder if

she hasn't got a point about being thankful? Maybe it does play into how one deals with grief.

"Could that be what's happening inside me? Maybe this whatever-it-is, is what being thankful feels like," John said.

"You just said a mouthful! Need I remind you, Old Boy, that you usually stand somewhere between fence sitter and atheist. In fact, you usually champion the atheist. You know you have, and you've been rather proud of yourself for taking that stance," John chided himself.

"So who would you be thankful to? Giving thanks does call for an object of thanks," John prodded. *"I feel like I've just stepped into a new world, a place that is calling me — even expects me — to be thankful.*

"What an odd thought," John cocked his head. *"Could something expect me to be thankful? How does that happen? Is it a new idea? It's almost as if I'm in conversation with someone else — from within. This is not the same as me proposing two sides of some argument and throwing the thought back and forth. This . . . could I call it another voice? . . . is different.*

"Everywhere I look I have something to be grateful for," John continued. *"I've done well in life. I've got an education and a position, which I enjoy. I am well taken care of; I've always had all my needs met — food, shelter, all of it.*

"And this world is incredible — gazillions of creatures with complex, even exotic, life styles — lands and seas, beauty that takes my breath away; marvelous systems that allow this world to work. Mystery and wonder abound. When I look at this world I can only gasp in awe at its magnificence. I'm sure I haven't seen all there is to see, but what I know is profoundly impressive, and I am thankful that I have eyes to see and ears to hear and senses to perceive it.

"I haven't really had reason to object to anything, yet I lived for years on the other side of that equation. I felt robbed and denied of my future when I lost Helen. I was hurt, and I just couldn't seem to pull myself out of the muck and mire of pain. Too long, I allowed grief to consume my spirit," John shook his head.

"But, John, maybe you're getting smarter. Maybe you're thinking more clearly. All this Bible reading, and the outside reading you've done, has given you new food for thought.

"That Oursler fellow, who thought he could debunk Christianity, traveled all the way to the Holy Lands to follow the steps of Jesus of Nazareth. He had begun writing a book — *An Elevator Boy's View of Jesus* — but in the middle of his work Oursler discovered that he had been bitten by the faith bug himself! His novel that was supposed to prove Jesus was a fraud, ended up becoming *The Greatest Story Ever Told!* Now there's a real change of heart!" John laughed.

"And C.S. Lewis bragged about his atheism for years while teaching at Oxford. He loved to debate in the pubs and would argue his point with anyone who cared to take him up on the subject of God. Yet Lewis later admitted that as an atheist he had to argue that no religion in the world had any merit at all. That's a mentally exhausting position to hold; I'm well aware of that! After coming to faith, Lewis realized that the men he most admired in those debates were men of faith, but the men who lacked faith were intellectual lightweights. Atheists didn't have well thought-out reasons for not believing; they just liked to argue," John winced a bit remembering Lewis' words.

"It doesn't make sense to be thankful to nothing, and I'm surely not responsible for all this grandeur. I may have worked my tail off to accomplish the few things I've done, but I didn't give myself the resources for thinking or writing or teaching. Somehow those gifts were given to me, and it's not my fault that I have them. There must be a greater being than I am or than is in this world — something, or someone, that has the well-being of this world as its objective, who has given this world, and me, so many good gifts," John announced aloud.

"Win is so very clear about us. She can see God's hand working with us, bringing us together, giving us to one another as some sort of blessing," John reminded himself.

"She tells me our relationship is like an answer to her prayer, ending our loneliness and opening a new future for us. She's leaning on her faith in Christ to guide us through this whole time. She's even willing to leave her position as pastor to be with me. She's that willing to work things out for us," John mused.

"But what about me? What am I bringing to the table? What about my commitment? What am I willing to do to secure our relationship, to be the best partner I can be?" John asked himself.

John had heard a different question in worship this morning, and it had been pursuing him, off and on, all afternoon, even while he and Winnie spoke of their future together.

In her sermon, Winnie had asked her congregation, "Isn't Jesus what we're looking for?

"That's a very good question," John said to himself. "Maybe the answer is what I'm coming around to.

"I agree with Lewis, when he admitted the thing that really held him back from coming to faith was the great pain and suffering in this world. Pain, evil, and suffering are huge problems in the world. How can anyone believe in a God who allows such terrible trouble to exist?

John laughed at himself, saying, "Here we go again, John. You're about to have an entire, full-blown argument with yourself!"

John stopped, knowing how well he enjoyed an argument — lobbing questions and answers back and forth to an opponent — the mental competition, the jousting for position. Even without a physical opponent he could have good argument within himself. Arguing in his head was always a good way to hone and sharpen an argument for later when he met a real, flesh and blood adversary.

But this time something else was present, something calling him. "I have to be true to myself, and when I know I'm seeing things differently than before, I have to call it what it is. I feel as if I've just made a great paradigm shift, and it's a very persuasive position. It feels good to consider this new scene — being thankful, even living thankfully!

"There's the many places in the Bible — verses, that jumped out at me as I was reading them, which I underlined because they were worth remembering. There was wisdom and challenge in Jesus' words; he would not be an easy person to follow; he asks a lot!

"*Isn't Jesus what we're looking for?*" The words returned again. John closed his eyes and said. "*God, I think you know my name. I think You've known me all my life. I think You've been waiting for me to say, 'Hello'; to say 'thank You'; to say 'I love You.'*

"*I'm pretty new at this, but I've got to start somewhere, so here goes:*

"*I'm not a good man. I've been completely focused on myself for a long time. I've tended to my every need, without much thinking of anyone else. I think You know how angry I was, when I lost Helen. Her death turned my life upside down, and I was a bundle of nerves and pain. I guess You could say I was lost. The only place I could turn was to my books and studies. At least with them I could find some success. I didn't know You, and, if I had, I would probably have blamed You for Helen's death.*

"*That would have been wrong; I know that now. I think You are the giver of all good things in this world, and I think I'm just now realizing it. And I'm thankful.*

"*Somehow, things have changed for me, and I feel differently now. Maybe enough time has passed, and the cloud of grief has drifted away. My world seems to have changed, and I feel deliciously happy. I don't ever want this feeling of being thankful to stop. It feels so right — so very right.*

"*I'm happy to have discovered You, to know that there's a new relationship that has come into my life, and I am honored and grateful. God, forgive me for waiting so long to come to You.*"

"*Thank you for forgiving me and for the love You have given me and Win. I know I don't deserve her. Right now I'm feeling wonderfully new and different. If You are the author of love, You really are something! Your gifts are far greater than any others!*"

John opened his eyes. Tears were streaming down his face, but he felt clean inside, not weighed down with the stuff of old memories and pain. He felt peaceful and content. He slept deeply that night.

* * *

Monday morning John arrived at the parsonage at eight o'clock for breakfast. Winnie had been up for a while and had already prepared a nice breakfast table, complete with coffee and a newspaper at John's place.

John was beaming when he walked into the kitchen. He swept Winnie into his arms and they kissed.

Winnie wondered the source of John's jubilance; she didn't have long to find out.

"What a marvelous day it is, don't you think, Win?" John grinned.

"Absolutely! It's a wonderful day. We're still together, at least for a few more hours," Winnie answered, "but I sense you've got something else in mind. Hm?"

"I slept like a babe last night," John began. "I went to the motel last night with a lot on my mind, a lot to think about, and something happened."

Winnie was beginning to catch John's excitement herself. "And?" She encouraged him.

"I was thinking, and I was reviewing ideas we've been tossing around and some other things that I've been reading, and, I guess, it all came together," John raised his eyebrows and pursed his lips, adding a grin.

"H- Hm!" Winnie was trying to follow what John meant." And what would you say came together?" she asked.

"Did I mention how happy I was last night?" John's eyes twinkled. "Of course I did. How could I keep that from you!"

Winnie nodded her head and smiled. "We're both happy. Of course we're happy!"

"Well it occurred to me that I'm beyond happy, Win, I think I've fallen into thankfulness!"

Winnie's excitement grew; her eyes opened wide.

"And it occurred to me that being thankful is a two-way street. One is thankful for all sorts of good things, so one gives thanks for it. But the *thanks giver* has to have a *thanks receiver.* Right? And with that thought, I began a long series of questions and answers about the object of my thankfulness," John explained.

"I was about to jump into a long discussion with myself about the pros and cons of having faith in God, when another thought came to me," John paused as he watched Winnie watching him.

"And?" Winnie asked.

"And that thought was that I am a different man today, a new man. I have been feeling nearly overcome with thankfulness, and I want to give thanks. I told myself that I seem to be operating within a new paradigm in life, and I'd better recognize it," John admitted.

Winnie smiled and continued to listen.

"Anyway, I know how much I enjoy a good argument, and there's a place for it, but last night I wanted to stretch in a different direction. I felt called to speak not to myself, but to the the One who has given me, given us, this exciting new chance for life," John explained.

Winnie could hardly keep from interjecting her pleasure at hearing what John was saying, but more than that she wanted to hear him out.

"Win, I'm here to tell you that I actually prayed to God last night! It wasn't a very long prayer, but it was. . . it was good. It felt right, and I felt clean, and fresh, and at peace afterwards," John said.

Winnie moved back over to where John was standing and gave him a great hug and a kiss. "Praise the Good Lord!" She whispered in his ear.

After breakfast they drove into Knoxville and found a jeweler. John bought Winnie a brilliant engagement ring for her to show all her friends — a clear invitation for her to tell them that she would soon be marrying and moving to Chicago.

23. Nina's Update

Winnie poured Nina a cup of coffee and passed it to her across the table then pulled a chair out from the table for herself and sat down. She grinned at her friend and said, "I'm sure you must think this is all happening too fast, but I can promise you we are NOT having a shotgun wedding!"

Nina was still trying to comprehend the news that Winnie had just told her. She didn't want to appear judgmental, but really, *"What in the world was her friend thinking? She couldn't know the man very well. They'd only spent a little bit of time together — two or three dates,"* Nina figured. *"What could be the big hurry to get married?"*

Things had been pretty busy since Christmas for Nina. She had extra nursing work to do, and had only spoken to Winnie the one time after her first date with John in early January. There must have been some important details about what happened next that Nina hadn't heard.

Nina worked full time for Dr. Sedgwick as his nurse, and she had also been filling in at the clinic while a fellow nurse was on maternity leave. Unfortunately, when the baby arrived, he was extremely colicky, requiring the mother's attention longer than originally expected, so Nina had been holding down two full time jobs since January. Due to the extra work, Nina realized she was out of the loop when it came to the latest Misty Falls' scuttlebutt.

This afternoon Winnie and Nina had run into one another at FRIENDLY'S FOODS, and, seeing her friend, Winnie immediately held out her left hand and wriggled it before Nina, showing off her engagement ring.

Nina had been too surprised to make a coherent response. Her eyes flew open and her mouth the same. Winnie watched her friend, amused at her consternation, but she didn't say a thing.

Finally, Nina stammered, "You're engaged? When did all this happen? It's John, right?"

Winnie gave Nina a hug, right there in the middle of the cereal aisle, and said, "Yes, of course it's John. He drove down here over mid-term break last month and asked me to marry him!"

The two women decided this news was too big to talk about it among the Post Toasties, so they agreed to meet at Winnie's house in an hour. Nina would bring "a little something" to go along with coffee.

Back in her own kitchen Nina put her groceries away. She couldn't get her mind off Winnie's news. She had many questions about this new engagement, but chief in her mind was, *"Did Winnie know this man well enough to make such a life-changing decision! How could she really trust him?"*

Half an hour later Nina was seated in Winnie's kitchen, opposite her friend, as she proceeded to explain.

"I think I told you, before, that John and I both went to Mile High High School in Denver. We were in a few classes together then, but we didn't know each other well."

Nina nodded her head to indicate she remembered. She sliced a piece of her new French Apple Cake, slid it onto the Wedgwood dessert plate Winnie had provided, and passed it to her friend.

Winnie's eyes widened at the scrumptious-looking treat; "Thanks!"

Winnie spent the better part of an hour recounting, step by step, the progress that led up to her engagement. She thoroughly enjoyed remembering the entire story to Nina — the reunion, the book, the invitation to join John in Aspen over Thanksgiving.

"John invited me to join him in Aspen for the Thanksgiving weekend. He'd sponsor my skiing, if I would like to try it," Winnie told Nina.

"Of course, my trip to visit the O'Neill's was already planned, and I didn't want to suddenly cancel time with my family, but the bigger problem was the 'adult thing', if you follow me," Winnie blushed

Nina knit her brows together and leaned forward. She sat silent for a moment and then asked, "Are you saying that you told John that you wouldn't sleep with him? Just like that? Wasn't that a bit awkward?"

Winnie explained her belief on marriage — that fidelity in marriage, which should mirror our faithfulness to God, began with the marriage contract, the commitment the two parties would make to one another. "These days things seem to be so cavalier for people. 'Adult activity' seems to be completely expected," Winnie explained.

"So, the two of you haven't. . . you haven't. . .'" Nina stammered.

"No, we haven't," Winnie assured her friend.

"I emailed back to John and thanked him for the offer to go to Aspen, but I explained about my prior plans to visit Claire and her family. I also told him that such a holiday for us two in Aspen might lead to complications we didn't need to add to our palate just now. I wrote about my understanding of the sanctity of marriage and hoped he would understand.

Nina nodded her head trying to understand.

Winnie continued he story — their first two dates, admitting that she was a pastor, learning why John had not married, John's promise to her to read the Bible.

Nina gasped when Winnie mentioned John's promise. "That's an enormous book, isn't it? I'll bet not very many people have actually read it — cover to cover — except professionals, right?"

"Well, The Bible is the complete basis for the Christian story. I suggested that John begin with the New Testament, which is all about Jesus' ministry, his death and resurrection, and the beginning of the church. The New Testament is not very long. It has the four gospels, of course, and then there's the Book of Acts, and the letters from the Apostles to the churches. The entire New Testament is less than four hundred pages. That's not so big. I suggested that John be sure to read Genesis and Exodus, to get a flavor of the history of the Israelites," Winnie answered.

Nina seemed satisfied with that, and she nodded, ready to hear more.

"We continued to call on the phone and email daily, and then John drove down here on his mid-term break, which happened to be Valentine's Day. I made dinner for him, and the next day he surprised me by coming to church! I was so pleased that he came.

"That afternoon John and I talked about marriage. I felt like I was facing a great dilemma — falling in love with him, yet thinking I shouldn't get serious with an unbeliever. But finally I told John that I believe God has brought us together, and that if I marry him I would step down from my position here at Muddy Creek and move to Chicago."

Nina was listening carefully to Winnie sharing her romance. She shifted her weight in her chair, but she didn't say anything.

"The next morning, when John showed up here for breakfast, he seemed like a different man — he was jubilant, like a kid at Christmas. It didn't take long to learn that he'd had a change of heart, and he felt that he somehow he had stepped into a new dimension — what he called a personal paradigm shift. He told me that he had been almost overcome with thankfulness — for our love, and our plans, and his life, and much, much more. He felt called to give thanks the One who had given him such a wonderful life. He told me he prayed that night, probably for the first time in his life," Winnie let that thought sink in.

"We didn't have much time left, because John had to get back to Chicago, but we drove over to Knoxville to a jeweler, and he bought me this ring," Winnie wriggled her hand again. "We went to a coffee shop next to the jeweler to have lunch, and while we were waiting for our food, John said, "Win, I can hardly believe how much has transpired this weekend. I know I'm on a new trajectory now, and you must be part of it. Do say you'll marry me!"

"Of course, I agreed," Winnie told Nina. "We think we'll marry early this summer," Winnie caught her breath.

Nina waited to see if Winnie would add any more to her reflections — something that would make a more compelling case for such an abrupt marriage. When she was sure Winnie had said her piece, Nina spoke.

"That's so beautiful, Winnie! I can tell you are in love, and John sounds like dream – quite a catch, in fact. But I have a problem. I say this, but I hope I'm completely wrong.

"As your friend, maybe it's my duty to be the Devil's Advocate. I think I need to ask you, 'How do you **really** know that John is who he says he is?" Nina had other questions, but this one was good for starters.

Winnie was thoughtful, but she didn't speak. She would have liked to have the perfect response that would immediately and completely exonerate John — something that would prove John's identity beyond a shadow of a doubt. But when she thought about it, she couldn't. She had just spent the last hour enumerating all the delicious times she and John had shared. She felt very sound about John's promise to her, his apparent change of heart about God, and, especially, the deep love she felt in her own heart for him.

"When you ask, 'How do I know if John is who he says he is, all I can say is I **believe** he is who he says he is. I believe him with all my being," Winnie heaved a sigh, bit her lip, and looked at her friend with imploring eyes.

Nina had an idea, "How about we Google him? Let's use some of the new technology that's supposed to be at our fingertips to help us. We could check out the university's web page and see if John's name is on their list of faculty members. How about that?"

Winnie jumped up from her chair and signaled to Nina to follow her to her office. Their query in the University of Chicago's website was initially frustrating, but finally they searched for faculty in the Department of Philosophy, and they found him. There was John's name and next to it a description of what he taught: Logic, Philosophy of Language, Early Analytic Philosophy, and Introduction to Philosophy.

The two women were elated to find John's name on the school website. It gave him credence — he <u>was</u> a professor of philosophy at UC. They felt the university's assurance was a good step in unpacking John's identity.

"That one piece of information doesn't completely remove all doubt. Just because someone is a college professor doesn't mean he is without fault. I know you want to believe John, and so do I, but I'm just a bit leery of unknowns. It's a dangerous world out there, and you just never know. After all, you're planning to turn your entire life over to this man. He'd better be who he says he is," Nina cautioned.

Winnie realized that Nina was trying to be fair-handed about this, but Nina cared for her friend and didn't want anything untoward to happen.

"I think I'm fortunate to have such a caring friend as you, Nina," Winnie said. "You've given me something to think about, and, of course, I want to be on guard."

Nina smiled at Winnie and said, "I have no reason to doubt anything John has said or done, but there are so many stories out there that you just need to be cautious."

Winnie asked, "What in the world can I do to get a better picture of John?"

"Well, if it was I, I wouldn't jump into marriage until I was a bit more familiar with the facts. Surely there are people who know John, people who could vouch for his character," Nina suggested.

"I think, maybe, I should get a closer look at John's world. Maybe I should make a trip to the Windy City, just to see for myself," Winnie said half to herself.

Nina lit up when she heard Winnie's idea. "Ooooo! I love it! That could be a great way to allay any fears. Besides, if you're about to move up there, it wouldn't hurt to have a look-see at the place," she said. "Now that I'm in on all that's happened, you just have to keep me posted on future events!"

After Nina left, Winnie plopped herself down in her over-stuffed armchair and sighed a deep, satisfied sigh. She loved telling the story about John and all the S'wonderful/S'marvelous things they had discovered as they were falling in love. It had quickly become her favorite story. She was glad she told Nina about her adventure. She also realized that, in a way, she was on stage, and Nina was watching. She could see that Nina herself was toying with the idea of trusting Jesus and that she was watching Winnie to see how a practicing Christian makes serious decisions. So Winnie's decisions, be they wise or foolish, could influence Nina's own decisions about following Christ. "*That's another reason for doing the right thing,*" Winnie thought.

✳ ✳ ✳

As evening approached, however, Winnie recognized a certain tense, restlessness inside herself, knowing that John would be calling her soon. Her reticence came from her need to be forthright with John about what had just transpired that afternoon. Her conviction that John was exactly who she believed him to be was still intact, yet she knew Nina had voiced concerns that she, too, had entertained. How well, indeed, did she really know John? She found herself in that approach/avoidance place that psychologists mention – wanting to be truthful with John, but at the same time dreading the possible conflict. *"Oh dear!"* Winnie sighed.

✳ ✳ ✳

The phone rang, and Winnie snapped it up on the first ring; she jumped right into a confession. "I ran into my friend Nina Mattingly at FRIENDLY'S FOODS this afternoon and showed her my new ring."

John was surprised how quickly Winnie jumped into the middle of her though without even a "Hello" or a "How are you?" He briefly interjected, "You showed Nina your new ring?"

"Yes! Nina was surprised to hear about us, so we met back here in my kitchen, and I told her how we came to be engaged! She was excited for me, but she tried to bring me down out of the stratosphere to consider more logically what I'm about to do. She made me realize that I don't know you very well, and she cautioned me to make an effort to learn more," Winnie related.

John's warning antennae had been immediately raised as Winnie launched into her report of the afternoon. He continued listening.

"Then we spent the better part of an hour trying to find something on the Internet that might identify you," Winnie continued, "and we finally succeeded. It's all about doing the right query, you know. Anyway, we were very pleased to discover your name on the UC website! It was very informative! I didn't realize there were so many different areas of philosophy," Winnie caught her breath.

"Glad you found me there. I think my picture is about ten years old," John said.

"Even so, your being on staff at UC is only one indicator of who you are, and maybe I need to know more. Nina isn't trying to hurt us, but she's right about my need to be cautious. There are men in this world who prey on unsuspecting women," Winnie stopped.

"I wouldn't laugh at your concern, because there are too many examples of evil in this world — times when women have been seriously hurt — so there is a point here. But, Win, I have to say I'm totally not dangerous. For sure, I want you to have no questions about marrying me, but I know myself, and I know there's nothing to fear about me. I don't suppose that I'm particularly exciting, but I am who I say I am: a professor of philosophy at UC and a man who's deeply in love with you!" John assured her.

Winnie was not sure, and she wanted to be sure. John had not given her the least reason to question who he was or his motives, but still, marrying him was a major change for Winnie — giving up her pulpit and job, moving to a different state, starting her world all over again. She would be trying to fit into John's world — whatever that included — and trying to discover a new way to answer Jesus' call on her life.

Finally, Winnie blurted, "John, I think I should come to Chicago and see your world for myself."

John, who had been straining to understand Winnie's fears, was thinking hard how to bring calm to this moment, when suddenly, as if the clouds parted and the sun came out, there was the answer, right before them. The idea that Winnie fly to Chicago to spend a few days with John in his world was just the plan for them.

The conversation made a ninety degree shift right then as they began to consider Winnie making a trip to Chicago. She could get away for several days the weekend after Easter. As they talked about her coming for a visit, they were nearly transported into a fantasy of what three or four days together could bring them — what they would like to do, and see, and experience. They would stroll along Lake Michigan, walk the campus where John taught, and meet some of his colleagues from school.

The call, which Winnie had so dreaded, quickly filled with fun, and laughter, and excitement, as they were already dreaming of the next time they would be together.

Afterwards, Winnie took Bitty out for a stroll, even as late as it was. She couldn't just go to bed with so many plans bouncing around in her head.

24. The Windy City

"The Bible tells us not to be anxious," Winnie told Bitty. *"There are only so many hours in a day, and there's a lot on my plate just now. I just need to concentrate on what's important, and the rest will have to fall into place,"* she encouraged herself.

Of course, Winnie was thinking about her personal life and the immanent changes that were about to occur, not to mention the Holy Week events, which would culminate with a much-planned Easter morning celebration of the resurrection at Muddy Creek Church.

Winnie would fly to Chicago the Friday following Easter for a long weekend. She and John would have the weekend together, but, since John was lecturing and having class during the week, Winnie figured on poking around the city Monday and Tuesday, seeing John when she could around campus and in the evenings.

When she returned from her trip, Winnie would have only a few weeks left to preach at Muddy Creek before stepping down from her pulpit. There were many logistical and relational things to set straight between now and then, but all that would have to wait until after Easter.

"Seek ye first the Kingdom of God and its Righteousness, and all these things will be added unto you, Allelu Alleluia," Winnie started singing. She loved to sing; it always helped soften the bite of anxiety, and so she often sang lustily around the house to herself.

✳ ✳ ✳

Winnie's plane landed at Chicago's Midway Airport, and twenty minutes later she appeared through the double glass doors by the baggage claim area, pulling her suitcase and carrying a smaller bag and an umbrella.

John spotted Winnie immediately. He couldn't miss her; she was wearing the same, charcoal grey overcoat, black and green plaid wool scarf, and tam she had worn in Nashville. Her short, brown curls, peeking out from below her hat, looked as though they were trying to trade their detention for a romp in the open air. Altogether, she presented a slightly disheveled look, while exuding subtle confidence.

Their initial meeting was just a smidgeon nervous. When Winnie and John had said their last good-byes at her parsonage in February, they had shared several scrumptious moments of passion. Hugs and kisses were lingered over; sweet murmurs of love were exchanged. They were clearly in love, and completely immersed in one another!

Now, in the chill of the early evening and the rush and scrunch of so many strangers all about them, neither John nor Winnie was quite sure how to greet the other.

They compromised, there on the curb, by sharing a quick hug, putting Winnie's suitcase in the trunk of John's car, and getting seat-belted into the bucket seats of John's Honda.

"How was your flight?" John asked.

"I'm happy to say the flight was uneventful! That's the best sort of flight, you know," Winnie assured John.

"I suppose that's because anything that is worth mentioning about a plane flight might have an element of terror in it!" John laughed and raised an eyebrow.

"You've got it. You don't want anything worth mentioning happening at thirty-five thousand feet up," Winnie grinned.

They were immediately in heavy traffic, of course; it was Friday evening in downtown Chicago. Winnie hadn't been in a really big city in some time, and she had never before seen Chicago. *"This city is completely awesome!"* she thought. She had to arch her back and stretch her neck in order to look up at the ubiquitous sky scrappers. Winnie had been in other big cities, Atlanta, for instance, but Chicago seemed to outdo the others in sheer size and density. *"Can little old me really fit into such a strange and busy world?"* she wondered.

John's plan for the evening was to begin to introduce Winnie to his world — the University of Chicago. They would start with dinner at the exclusive Quadrangle Club. It was a members only club for university faculty and staff, which John had just recently joined.

Before long, they were seated across an elegantly-dressed table in the dining room of the club. Winnie felt welcomed as an honored guest by the well-mannered staff and the beautifully-designed décor of the room. The ambiance of the club suggested the management knew exactly how to cater to its membership of university professors and their guests with gracious attention.

The next few minutes were spent reviewing their menus and making choices for dinner. After the waiter retreated they each felt, finally, that they were free to launch into this most-looked-forward-to time together.

"Win, I made arrangements for you to stay at a hotel in town, but this morning I woke up with a better idea!" John gleamed.

Winnie's eyes opened very wide as she heard John's announcement; her brows knitted together in a curious way. "You've got my complete attention!" she exclaimed.

"What I remembered is that there are accommodations right here at the Quadrangle Club for visiting dignitaries! I don't know why I hadn't thought of it before. A room here will be perfect for you. I called today to see if there was a room available, and when I heard there was a spot, I made reservations for a single room for The Rev. Evangeline Taylor. It will be yours as long as you're here. Does that meet with your approval?" John smiled widely.

"I think you've hit on the exact, right solution for us! It couldn't be better. For a moment there, I thought you had something else in mind," Winnie teased.

John knotted his eyebrows and began to laugh, "You know I wouldn't do that without your approval, My Dear!"

Winnie nodded her head, partially from relief and asked, "Goodness, how much will staying here, downtown, cost? I have to be careful with my resources."

John shook his head, his eyes twinkled, "No, My Dear Win, you will have no worry about expenses while you're here! That's my treat. I'm so pleased that you have come here to see my world. The least I can do is pay your way while you're here."

"As I was making your reservation this morning, it occurred to me that everyone calls you 'Winnie.' You were Winnie back in high school, so you've been Winnie for a long time. Tell me how you came by that name?" John asked.

"It's simple," Winnie began to explain. "Surely you're familiar with Christopher Robin and his teddy bear friend 'Winnie Ther Pooh!' When I was a child, I loved those sweet stories. Pooh was my favorite character. He was a humble bear — 'a bear of very little brain' — yet he was loving, and faithful, and a great friend of all the dwellers in the Hundred Acre Wood. Somehow I just adopted the name Winnie from him," she admitted.

"*And*! I should tell you that my very worst curse word — my only curse word — although I don't employ it too often, is POOH FACE!" Winnie shared.

"Pooh face?" John asked.

"**POOH** FACE!" Winnie corrected John, with heavier emphasis on the POOH.

"I see," John said. "I'll be sure to take note."

The two sat for a moment in the peaceful silence, awaiting their dinners to arrive.

Then John spoke, "Win, I know you have a lot of questions about me, and I think you absolutely must try to satisfy every concern you have."

"I do find myself in a rather odd situation," Winnie confessed. "I want so much for us to get past this business of questioning you and get on with more interesting matters!" Winnie pouted a bit, wrinkled her nose, and screwed up her face to show her discomfiture.

John reached into his suit jacket pocket and produced several envelopes with pages in them. He handed them over to Winnie.

She slowly opened the papers and realized they were John's most recent bank statement and statements from a several investment accounts that belonged to him. She reviewed the pages one by one with careful scrutiny, noting the balances in the accounts.

John watched Winnie's countenance carefully, as she poured over his personal finances.

Finally she looked up quizzically and asked, "John! These statements indicate that you are very, very well off! Can that be right?"

"Wealth is such a relative matter," John assured her. "Certainly I'm not hurting, and I am thankful for that. In fact, I have to admit that one of my flaws is that I've been something of a Hoardisaurus — I'm sure I've hoarded my money too much."

"A Hoardisaurus? Goodness, I haven't heard about that funny character since I read that little book to Claire and Paul when they were small. You know the Hoardisaurus?" Winnie asked.

"My brother, Stewart, had a great library of children's books when his kids were small. I remember reading some of the Serendipity books he had back then. I loved the cartoon picture of the dinosaur with the great bone he carried around in his arm; it tickled me. I don't think I had connected that selfish cartoon character to me and my personality until recently," John confessed.

"One of the things I believe I need to do better, is to be more generous. I've been a bachelor for a long time, but I have not lived like a bachelor — I haven't indulged myself in stuff. Oh, I've kept up with technology — computer, cell phone, car — and I have allowed myself skiing trips. But other than those expenses, I've lived frugally. I've not been quite the Scrooge of Dickens, but I have held on to much of what I've made from my teaching and writing."

"You can see my apartment tomorrow, and you'll understand how I have not indulged in frivolous stuff. You could say I've been a mixture of medieval ascetic and Buddhist, being ultra conservative with my resources," John explained.

Winnie sat absorbing every word John spoke. She was relieved by his openness and candor and intrigued that he was willing to show her his accounts. Winnie had never had much money; she had been happy to get by with what she had been making, and she was not in debt. John's bank accounts and investments added up to much more than a tidy sum; it was so unexpected.

"Goodness, John, it never occurred to me that you might have money! You don't show it off. Money is an important tool, but it takes great care to use it well. Do you remember reading in First Timothy, *the love of money is the root of all kinds of evil?* That is, no doubt, very true. Certainly, when we begin to make any plans, cost is immediately a major consideration in the decision process. In fact, that will certainly be an item in our own future plans."

"I'm sure you're right about that. We'll have to set down some careful plans for a budget for us and work on how we use whatever income we bring in," John agreed.

"Money is a subject that no one can avoid, even if you wanted to. I can imagine you've even preached on it before. Right?" he asked.

Winnie was about to answer when the waiter arrived with their dinner, delaying her answer while they prepared to eat. Winnie and John had both ordered a cedar planked salmon dish with veggies and a salad. The next several minutes were dedicated to savoring their delectable meals and offering thanks for them.

Winnie swallowed a bite, looked up at John and said, "Yes, I have spoken on money — the use of money — a number of times. I like to point to John Wesley's view of money: *Make as much [money] as you can; save as much as you can; give as much as you can.*"

John brightened up as he heard those words of wisdom. "Isn't Wesley the founder of your denomination? I should add his writings to others I want to explore in my studies.'M*ake as much as you can.*' That's good. He's not suggesting that having a lot of money is wrong or sinful. *Save as much as you can.* I've done that — in spades! So far I'm doing right well in that department, wouldn't you say? And what was the last injunction? *Give as much as you can?*"

Winnie smiled and nodded her head.

"*Give as much as I can.* Hmmm. Well, I haven't done that. Not at all. I've just been trying to hang on to what I've earned. Your man Wesley has an entirely different take on things. Sounds like I need to look into it," John said thoughtfully.

Winnie softened her voice and said, "When we ask Christ into our lives, the Holy Spirit takes that invitation to begin working in our lives, giving us guidance, strength and encouragement for our walk with Christ — we begin to hear God's voice speaking to us. Many things that are revealed to us are things that help us clean up our lives. From what you've told me, you have been overly careful with your money. That's fine; wasting God's gifts is a different sort of problem. I suppose there is much to learn about using money well."

"When I say that to you, John, I'm talking to myself, too. None of us has arrived at perfection, not yet. We all have a lot to learn in that department," Winnie said.

John was amused at Winnie's mini lecture. He chuckled, "You flip with ease into teacher mode, yourself, don't you! And, yes, you're right. It hadn't occurred to me that this realization might come from the Holy Spirit, but I can see how that works — the little voice within that nudges one to do good. Maybe that's how God's Spirit communicates. I'm sure I need to figure better how to use the gifts I have," John agreed.

"The way you and I have used money is different. We've approached that subject from diverse positions. Perhaps the good thing, though, is that neither of us has become indebted to some credit card or scheme," Winnie added.

"I have tried to be careful with my money, but I haven't made much. I believe in tithing — giving ten percent to God — giving God of my *first fruits*. Whatever I make as income, the first ten percent belongs to God. I have tried to be faithful to that by writing a check for my tithe as soon as it's in my account. Of course, there are other, very good places besides the church to put our gifts, and I do that, too; I don't keep track of that, though. I find it's a great joy to give. Maybe my challenge is to 'save as much as I can', so then I have more to give," she said thoughtfully.

"I suppose money is always an important factor in life. I hoped that you could see from my banking and investment statements something more about who I am. You can see from those accounts that I am solvent — I pay my bills —1 and I don't owe anyone anything. I have depth in savings. Even in this crazy, financially painful time in our country, my very cautious investing hasn't lost as much as those who speculated more heavily. I lost quite a bit when the crash came, but I've been able to invest in the stocks, now, at a lower price. It will pay off," John added with satisfaction.

They talked for some time about money. It was the first time that subject had been mentioned between them. Winnie was about to step down from her position as the pastor, meaning she was about to leave her source of income.

She told John about meeting with her superintendent. "He was most jolly when he heard my good news!" Winnie recalled.

She had asked for a leave of absence from being appointed to a church in the next year. She and her superintendent both realized that Winnie would probably not be returning to the Holston Conference to preach. Her life seemed to be taking her into a new realm — and something of an adventure. She would be able to connect with the United Methodists in the Chicago area and would be able to seek an appointment there, when she decided she was ready for that. The superintendent would write a letter for her bishop to send to the Chicago episcopal office recommending Winnie for an appointment.

John wanted to help Winnie with her moving expenses. She explained that she didn't need to move all the furniture in the parsonage, because she only owned some of it — her bedroom set, her piano, her kitchen equipment and dishes, her china cabinet and related items, and, of course, her library.

As they talked, a couple from across the room walked over to meet them. John immediately stood up to shake their hands and to introduce them to his fiancé, The Rev. Winnie Taylor.

"Well, you old dog!" the man chuckled when he heard that John had an intended. "I didn't think anyone would ever catch you!"

John was smiling from ear to ear; he quickly completed his introductions, "Win, I would like you to meet Dr. Chester Twingate, a colleague of mine in the Philosophy Department. He teaches ethics, metaphysics, and epistemology to undergraduates and graduates, and this is Dr. Marian Quincy-Twingate who is professor of Christian History in our School of Divinity."

Winnie was very pleased to meet this couple who knew John. She stood up to shake hands with them.

Chester Twingate looked at Winnie and said, "Reverend! How good it is to meet you. Are you sure you know what you're getting yourself into by marrying this old codger?" He winked at Winnie as he spoke. She figured Dr. Twingate was teasing.

Winnie smiled at the couple and answered, "Actually, I believe that John is a well-hidden secret, and I count myself as a very fortunate woman to be in his life."

Marian picked up on Winnie's forthright answer to her husband's teasing and said, "Winnie, may I call you Winnie? I think you are quite right in your assessment of John. Chet and I have known John for nearly a quarter century, since before we were married, and we think most highly of him. He is a man of many fine talents and abilities. He may not have told you, but John is <u>the</u> most popular lecturer in the Philosophy Department. Some students will wait to take the Intro to Philosophy course, until they can be sure of having a seat in his class. And now it looks as if he's found himself a lovely companion." She turned to John. "John! You really are lucky!"

The two couples spoke for several minutes, and then the Twingates said good-night and hoped Winnie would enjoy her time in Chicago. If there was anything they could do to make her visit better — just call. They would be pleased to help her in any way they could.

When the two sat down again, Winnie grinned and asked, "I suppose you planted the Twingates here? They certainly are in your court! And! I just learned that you're a popular lecturer! Why hadn't that occurred to me before! Of course you're popular among the students! I love listening to you! You're articulate, and passionate about your discipline, and wonderfully able to communicate your thoughts. John, might I sit in on some of your lectures, while I'm here?"

John was pleased to see Winnie's enthusiasm about his work, and he agreed that she could slip into one of his lectures, or several, if she cared to, while she was on campus.

John had not planted the Twingates at the club tonight. He didn't frequent the club, as it was pricier than his thrifty, budget-minded self would allow, but he was most pleased that his friends happened to be present tonight. "They are a top-notch couple. Glad they were here for you to meet them!"

"John, I owe you a great apology! I am so sorry to have questioned you, or anything about you. I can see I was completely wrong to ever consider questioning who you are or your interest in me. Please forgive me," Winnie asked earnestly.

John looked at Winnie's countenance — so earnest, so imploring — and said, "Of course I forgive you, Dear. I have heard the same things you have about women who have been led astray or worse by men. Some have lost money; some have lost much more than that. You do have to be careful in this world. But you don't have to worry about my intentions; I'm glad you believe me. I really am trying to do the right thing for you and for us.

"In fact, we didn't finish our talk on money," John continued. "It's probably an on-going theme for us. It seems the character of money to be that way — always in the picture — somewhere.

"I realize I'm asking you to give up a great deal for me — leaving your position as pastor; losing your income; moving all your household up here. It's an enormous step for both of us, but especially for you.

"I want to make it as feasible and facile as possible, so I want to set you up with an account for your needs. Once we're actually Mr. and Mrs. (or should we be Dr. and Rev.?) we can get our names on all our accounts together.

"Illinois is not a community property state, I just discovered, but I plan to make you the beneficiary of my estate, so you will have access to my accounts now and always," John assured her.

Winnie took a big breath and tried to understand what John had just said. "Goodness! I didn't expect that, either! I don't want to be completely dependent on you, though, even if it takes me a little time to get my feet on the ground, I do expect to be productive in my new world."

John nodded understandingly, "I can't imagine you not getting involved in some Christian project, which, I suspect, which you'll throw your whole self into. Although I do hope that you'll spare some of you just for me!"

Winnie winked at John and said, "You will definitely be Number One in my book, always!"

"One thing we can do this week while you're here is visit an attorney, and have him draw up a pre-nuptial agreement putting this arrangement in legal form for you," John continued.

Winnie's eyes grew wider, hardly believing this generous offer from John. "You really are amazing, John. I can see I'll need some help, initially, as we figure how to move in together, and I be-

---

gin to find my way around, but what you're proposing is a fine way of cementing our marriage in a very tangible way. I want to bring whatever I can to our marriage, and, obviously, you do too."

"I expect to take this summer off from teaching," John said. "We lecturers can choose to teach the summer quarter or not, and this summer I've opted out of teaching. I'm going to be on my honeymoon!"

"I found something in Ephesians when I was reading," John recalled. "It sort of jumped out at me, having to do with marriage,"

"I'd love to hear it. There's a lot of good material in Ephesians about marriage, especially in the second half of the letter," Winnie agreed.

"Ephesians makes an interesting injunction — that married people should be 'subject to one another.' Have you ever preached about that?" John asked.

"'Subject to one another!' Of course, I remember that bit in Chapter Five, and, no, I haven't preached on that. I do think the idea that man and wife are subject to one another is a beautiful picture of love."

"St. Paul doesn't always encourage marriage, but that was because the early believers in Christ expected the end times would be upon them very soon. Paul was probably widowed early in life. The Jews had a very high regard for marriage, considering a man to be only half a man without a wife. Paul was a Pharisee — he followed the law to the letter. He must have been married, but he may have lost his wife very early."

"I really like the idea of married people being subject to one another, because it doesn't make one person always the leader and the other always the follower. It's pretty obvious that people come with various gifts. No one has all the gifts or all the best gifts needed in marriage. Couples need to share from their abilities and gifts with one another. When it comes to being 'subject to one another', I think that means we are responsible for the other person's well being."

"Which brings us to the Sixty-Four Thousand Dollar Question. When <u>are</u> we getting married?" John looked rather like a woeful puppy.

They took out their cell phones and scrolled through their calendars.

"When does your quarter finish up this spring?" Winnie asked.

"We're out the second weekend in June, although I will still have the reading and grading to do. Looks like I should be available by the third weekend in June, " John figured.

"I know I'm doing a wedding for a couple at Muddy Creek on the sixth of June, and my last Sunday to preach is the next day. I'll be packing out of the parsonage that week. I have to be out by mid-week so that the new pastor can move in then," Winnie said.

"You're marrying someone else? Tell me about it!" John teased.

"Well, I can't give you names, because this is really a 'hush-hush' sort of thing, but Bert and Naomi are a family at my church. They have two kids — twin thirteen year olds. They are very active at church. Bert met with me last fall and told me that they have a problem — they are not really married! Naomi married another man when she was very young, but they never got divorced! Bert didn't understand there was a problem initially, but, after he became a Christian, he realized that he was living with a married woman, and that was wrong."

"The two of them wanted to make things right. So he asked me to find him an inexpensive lawyer, someone who could do the divorce for them. I was able to put them in touch with a lawyer last fall. Bert called me in February to say that the divorce was almost final and that they had to wait ninety days, before they could legally tie the knot. They want me to officiate at the wedding for them, so we've targeted the sixth of June for the service. This all has to remain completely quiet. No one at Muddy Creek or Misty Falls must know about it," Winnie concluded.

John was amused by this narrative. He could appreciate the trouble that would accompany any sort of leakage of information in the community. "Well, well, My Dear, you're going to help make them very happy, I am sure!"

Just then the pianist, who had been playing soft, dinner music as a background for the guests, increased his volume, inviting the room's diners to become dancers.

The first piece was "It Had to be You". John looked at Winnie and sang softy with the music, "It had to be you. . ." While singing he held out his hand and grasped Winnie's in his. Standing up he beckoned her onto the dance floor.

Holding each other close and moving to the music was sheerly delightful to the two love birds. They swayed and moved together exactly as one body. They seemed to be completely in tune with one another's movements. Words did not need to be spoken; they simply moved together with the mood and the music.

". . . wonderful you. It had to be you—!" John finished the song as the pianist completed his coda. "That's how I feel, Win. My life has changed because of you. How lucky I am. How lucky we are!"

The music changed to a medley of Gershwin songs.

The two melted into one another's arms as they continued to move gracefully around the floor. They even tried an occasional deep bend or twirl that caused others in the room to notice the new pair in the room. They danced cheek to cheek, as the music invited them, and sometimes they picked up their feet to the rhythm and bounced to the more active beat.

Finally, Winnie begged John to let her catch her breath. They returned to their seats and rested, watching the others still on the dance floor.

"We haven't lost it, have we?" John whispered. "I know something new and wonderful was beginning to blossom between us that night on the Volunteer Princess. We both felt it; I know. I can almost count that dance floor as the real dawning of our love."

Winnie's face was still flushed from dancing, but she entirely agreed with John — they hadn't lost anything.

M. E. PALMER

They decided to call it a night and to pick up in the morning with a full day together. John stopped at the front desk to obtain the key for Winnie's room, which, the attendant explained, was on the third floor, overlooking the tennis courts. John went out to his car to pick up Winnie's bag and bring it up to her room. They said good night in the hallway outside Winnie's room, promising to meet for breakfast. John would be by to pick Winnie up around nine.

After he left, Winnie plunked herself on the settee and heaved a great sigh. *"I'm so glad I came here! There's no need to worry about John; He's shown me some very compelling reasons to trust him. I don't think we'll have any insurmountable troubles facing us."* Winnie sighed happily.

260

25. The Next Right Thing

John knocked on Winnie's door at nine the next morning, and the two went out for breakfast. They could hardly believe they had the entire weekend with no obligations to anyone but to themselves. How delightful!

John took Winnie over to a small cafe for breakfast, before they went to see his apartment in the neighborhood nearby. It was conveniently close to campus, right in the midst of the city. John and Winnie hadn't determined what their needs might be in the way of housing once they married. The big decision had been made — they WOULD be together. That was the important thing; everything else was much less significant, but these logistical considerations needed attention too. Perhaps, to begin with, they would start out in John's apartment. It had some good qualities — nearness to the university and reasonable rent, and, of course, they would only have to deal with moving Winnie's furnishings.

Winnie wondered if her mental picture of John, sitting by a crackling fire, in a nice, cozy, overstuffed chair, in a comfortable robe and slippers with a lamp over his left shoulder as he read his papers, was anything like reality. She hoped her picture of his home was close to the fact; she was about to find out.

John tried to prepare Winnie for what she was about to see. "I have to admit that I'm not much of a housekeeper. I get along pretty well for what I need, but compared to your place — your home — my apartment is rather basic."

John's admission alerted Winnie that it might be wise to be a little cautious in her response when she first saw his place. She had certainly visited many homes over the years — homes of parishioners, constituents, and others — and she was well aware that there were many styles and ways of putting a home together. After all, every family has its own way of living, their own way of building a nest and caring for it. Homes were lived in differently by different folks. That was just fine. It didn't matter to Winnie about someone else's housekeeping style.

Housekeeping was not an important detail when visiting someone. Winnie was much more interested in the condition of peoples' spiritual selves — clues indicating a person's inner self — worries, hopes, fears, concerns, faith, etc. than their tidiness or lack thereof. Winnie believed she was quite open-minded about a person's homemaking gifts, and, surely, John's housekeeping would not be an issue for them.

John's apartment was on the third floor of the building, so they took the stairs for a little exercise and because the elevator was often out of commission. John's place was one of four apartments on that floor. The stairwells and landings were a basic tan color — the walls, the tile, the doors to the apartments were all similarly colored tan. John walked to his apartment, unlocked and opened his front door, and then motioned for Winnie to step in. "Win, this is where I live. Welcome," he announced.

Winnie took a couple of steps into the front room and stopped; she gazed around the room and froze. The room, which was good-sized—maybe 18' x 20' — was not what she had hoped. It was the den of a collector! There were tall, library-style bookshelves stretched completely across two of the walls in the front room and a portion of a third wall. The shelves were filled with heavy books, looking much like the stacks Winnie had frequented in college. The shelves stood nearly to the ceiling, providing no visual space for a picture or piece of art to give some color or relief to the scene.

Looking about the room Winnie saw a huge, oak wood, roll top desk stacked high with books and papers. The desk, being a type of secretary, included many, small cubby holes. Winnie noted all of the cubbies were filled with papers and envelopes scrolled up and tucked into a hole. *"I'll be there's a good portion of John's history there,"* Winnie surmised.

A computer and a printer took up a goodly portion of the horizontal space on the desk top. Winnie mused a moment, thinking how modern technology didn't quite fit into the scheme of the roll top desk. The electronic additions vied for space on the desk top; many wires and small, blinking boxes of a technical nature were also tucked into space on the desk. Winnie could see a nest of wires tangled among themselves at the back of the desk, connecting the electronics to an outlet in back.

Looking around, Winnie saw a large, worn, La-Z-Boy recliner in one corner of the room; it sat in front of a wall of books. A floor lamp stood behind it, capable of shining light over the left side of a reader. Winnie was amused when she saw this chair, because it was exactly what she had imagined the setting would be like where John read his school papers. No, he didn't have a nice, warm fireplace to toast himself by, but the chair and the lamp were there!

Directly across the room from the recliner sat an old TV. It was hooked up to a DVD/VCR player. John hadn't bought a flat screen yet; his was an old, fifteen inch TV, which sat atop a small folding table. Winnie noticed some of the books on the shelves behind the TV were videos and DVD's. *"So! John does watch recreational TV,"* she noted.

There was a window on one wall, which had a heavy drape covering it. The drape was pulled back, exposing the light from outside. Winnie walked over to the window to see the view. There wasn't a view; there was another building, standing five feet from the window. The view from John's living room was the red brick wall of the building next door. Winnie wondered why a window would be put in such a place. Weren't windows for seeing things — into the world beyond. There wasn't much world to be found in red brick!

Winnie realized it would be appropriate for her to say something about the apartment, but, as she began to imagine moving into this place, she experienced a strange, dizzy feeling accompanied by an, almost, overwhelming sense of nausea. She started to sway unnaturally, and John quickly grabbed her arm and led her to the recliner.

Winnie plunked down on the chair and looked up at John. "Goodness! I don't know what just came over me! I was fine one minute, and the next I was lightheaded and woozy, and. . . I almost lost it! I'm sorry," Winnie tried to explain.

John left the room and came back a half minute later with a glass of water for Winnie. After a sip and a few breaths, she put on a brave face. "Thanks, I think I'm OK now."

John wondered what might be the impetus behind this sudden attack. "Win, are you sick? Is there something you need? I don't qualify for much in the way of doctoring, but I can call someone."

Winnie was feeling more herself by now. "No, I'm fine. I have no idea what just happened."

John asked, "What were you thinking before you got dizzy?"

Winnie knew she wasn't sick. She assured John, "I'm fine now, really. Maybe it was all the excitement of our being together here, but something happened when I walked into this room. I was looking at your apartment and trying to think how I might be part of this (Winnie gestured around the room with her hand), realizing this is going to be our home for a while. I must have been wondering where in this place would there be room for me and my stuff? That's what I was thinking when suddenly I got this crazy, queasy feeling in my head and in my stomach," Winnie explained.

John leaned over and put his arm around Winnie. It made her feel better, just having him close.

"Win, I wonder if this little episode could be your body's way of saying that this really isn't the best place for us, not even for a short while," John suggested.

Winnie perked up a bit at John's words, and raised an eyebrow.

"How about we take this a different direction?" John stated trying to salvage the situation.

"What have you got in mind?" Winnie wanted to know.

"I've been in this apartment since I moved to Chicago back in 1980. I couldn't afford much rent then; I was only an assistant professor, and I had my school loans to pay back. I was happy to get this place. I could afford the rent, and the location was close enough to the school. I've been here in this one bedroom apartment all these years.

"Since I was alone, and didn't need a lot of space, I got along just fine here. Surely, I haven't spent much on the place, and, as you've noted, it's in serious need of a housekeeper. I have been thrifty, remember? I didn't want to spend money on a cleaning woman, and it's easy to tell."

"What I'm trying to say is, we don't have to move into this apartment when we're married, not even initially," John said.

Winnie cocked her head as she heard John's words. "But it will be expensive to do anything else, and I know you are very careful with your resources."

John's eyes crinkled and a smile began to grow on his face. He was touched that Winnie was concerned about his frugal ways. "There's no good reason we have to start here. We've been talking about WHEN we get together — when we get married — we'll finally be in the same place. Our place needs to be just that — OUR PLACE, our very own, personal place. I don't know why we need to wait for some time later to start looking."

"Oh John! That's a really big step for us to take so soon, but I love the idea! Are you sure you want to do that? Can we afford it?" Winnie asked.

John was sure. He hadn't thought it through before, but as he spoke the words into the air, the idea sounded very right to him. It would be an adventure for both of them. Finding a place to begin life together in — fresh and new — would be exactly the right thing to do.

Suddenly the agenda for their day, which had been open, was now spoken for. They spent the next half hour in front of John's computer, looking for a realtor who might be available that afternoon to show them places in the general area of Hyde Park.

Fortunately, they were able to locate one quite easily. She would meet them after lunch to show them several places.

It was exciting to think about finding a house they could call their own. Over lunch Winnie recounted to John the many times she had moved with her family — to various Air Force Bases in the States as well as three of bases in Germany. Then, after she had been appointed to preach, she had moved several more times. She considered herself a veteran mover.

"One of the good things about moving is that you lighten your load. We tend to hang onto stuff for too long, but when you move every few years, you toss out items you haven't used. It makes one more streamlined," Winnie explained.

John had only moved a few times, and the last move was thirty years ago, when he moved to Chicago. He agreed that Winnie was probably right about his hanging onto things too long, but he didn't know how to go about reducing his inventory.

Winnie assured him that she was an expert at moving. She didn't have a great amount of furniture to move. "We'll have stuff coming from both our homes, and we'll be able to blend them into our new place." Winnie was getting excited about this new challenge, but before any of that could be decided, they would have to see what was available to them.

After lunch they met their agent, who was most pleased to find someone in the market to buy! The world of real estate had hit the skids since last fall, and nobody was buying. To find someone who was actually interested in purchasing a house was the best news the agent had heard in some time. It was actually a very good time to buy a house; housing prices were better than they had been in a long time!

＊＊＊

Five o'clock that afternoon found Winnie and John sitting on the floor of a living room in an empty row house in Hyde Park. They had been looking at places in the area most of the afternoon — a duplex, a single family dwelling, and a couple of condominiums. Each had good qualities as well as some serious problems.

John and Winnie found nothing of interest in any of those houses. Each time they arrived at a new place, walked through it with their realtor, and realized it was not what they wanted, their hopes sank a bit. They wanted so much to love their new place, but each house they saw was missing that certain rightness they instinctively knew they wanted. None of the properties they saw said, "Take me; buy me!," so they were glad there were still more places yet to consider.

And then, at last, they arrived at this row house. It was the second house of six houses on a small, side street. Winnie and John followed their realtor from room to room and up and down the stairs, growing more and more enthusiastic about it with each room. The house had much promise and great charm; already they could feel their imaginations sparking all sorts of plans for various rooms.

As they returned to the living room, the realtor excused herself for a few minutes in order to answer a cell phone call from her daughter. She left her new clients alone to look around themselves..

The house was completely empty of furniture, so they sat on the newly refinished, hardwood living room floor. It was fun to view the house from this unusual angle.

They had each arrived at the same conclusion about the house — it was wonderful! It wasn't anything like what either of them had ever lived in before. It was not at all what they thought they were looking for, but it felt right— as if it was calling to them.

The house was narrow (maybe eighteen feet wide) and very deep; it had four floors and four bedrooms, which they realized they could use, if they were going to blend their two households together. They would need at least one whole room for their library, as well as room for guests.

The first floor included the kitchen, dining room, and living room, complete with stone covered fireplace next to the balcony door. Winnie was particularly pleased to see the fireplace. *"There's a perfect place for John to read his papers by the fire!"*

Upstairs on the second floor were three bedrooms and a bathroom, then on the top floor, incorporating the entire floor, was one great, open room, which had been the master bedroom. *"We could dance right here; there's plenty of space,"* Winnie dreamed.

The basement had a laundry room, a family room, and a windowed-in porch, including a walk out to the patio and garden in back.

It was a novel feeling, this fantasy of sharing a future location together in this house. John and Winnie were still just imagining what it would be like to be married to one another, and here was a physical structure that could help shape their future.

The place was perfect; they both agreed. The big question was, could they afford it? They didn't want to fantasize about getting the house, if it was beyond their reach.

The realtor had already told them that the owners of the house needed to move because of business, and, considering the situation with the economy — especially the housing market — the house might not sell for quite a while, so the realtor was told to lease the house.

It seemed as if they had been sitting on the living room floor for some time when their realtor reemerged. She smiled at the two on the floor and said, "I don't very often find my clients making themselves at home so quickly! I hope your 'sit in' here translates to something positive!"

John jumped up and helped Winnie get to her feet. They admitted that they were very pleased with the house. They spoke for about the availability of the house and were surprised to learn that the owners had provided for a "rent-to-own" possibility. John pulled out his checkbook and wrote a check to the realtor to secure their interest in the place. They would meet back at the realtor's office Monday late in the afternoon to draw up the necessary papers.

✳ ✳ ✳

An hour later John and Winnie were sitting in a Greek restaurant, waiting to order dinner. What a day it had been! And what a surprise they had found — even putting money down on a house!

The house had added another dimension to their plans, and they were feeling much excitement over it. They were almost giddy with delight, and found themselves laughing together at almost anything — the large cowboy hat worn by that small boy; the very high heels the waitress was wearing; the two, identically dressed, little girls in the company of their grandparents.

Conversation between Winnie and John was focused on the house. They were trying to remember every detail they had just seen. Did the house include a garage? How high might the ceilings be? Did you notice if the appliances in the kitchen matched? Was there wallpaper in all of the bedrooms?

John pulled a pen from his pocket and began sketching the floor plans of the first three floors of the house on a large, paper, dinner napkin. Winnie hadn't seen this artistic side of John before, and she exclaimed, "John! I have so much to learn about you and your many gifts! I didn't know you could draw!"

"That's not exactly talent. It's mechanical drawing, which, I suppose, does require a certain amount of ingenuity. I took the class as an elective one year in school," John told her.

Just then their meals arrived and were placed before them. The waiter brought moussaka for Winnie and lamb chops for John. They spent several minutes savoring their dinners and sharing a bite of each other's meal.

Winnie asked, "Did you notice the size of the bedrooms on the second floor? Are they are three different sizes?"

"The two bedrooms on the backside are almost the same size — rectangles — and they are connected by a balcony that runs across the back of the house above the first balcony. The front bedroom, above the kitchen, is a bit smaller than the other two, and it's square," John answered. "What are you thinking about?"

"Well, I was wondering which room would be the best choice for us to make our master bedroom." Winnie smiled slyly at John. "Should it be on the second floor, or should we choose the top floor, the way the previous owners did?"

John smiled at the mention of the master bedroom, because he was quite pleased to note that eventually — maybe even
sooner than later — they would have need for a master bedroom.
He said, "Well, it might be a good thing to have our bedroom on the
top floor; all those extra steps would, no doubt, add to our health,
climbing up and down them several times a day."

"I suppose you're right about that; I should look for ways to
encourage good health, and those stairs could do the trick for us,"
Winnie agreed. "Hm, that does bring up a question, though,"
Winnie stopped abruptly, not knowing how to phrase her thought.

"I like questions. Fire away," John encouraged her.

"Well. . .," Winnie stammered, "It occurs to me that one of
us has been married before — for a number of years — and one of
us has not. . ."

John was following Winnie's words, and then she stopped.
"I don't think I heard your question, Win. Yes, One of us HAS been
married before, and one of us — meaning ME — has not," John
continued."That doesn't mean that we have a case of The Graduate and Mrs. Robinson, if that's what's worrying you!" John teased.

Winnie flushed, and nodded her head, indicating that John
understood her consternation, so she changed the subject. "I know
this is Saturday night, but it definitely doesn't feel like Saturday
night to me."

John wondered, "What usually happens on Saturday night
for you? Is there something we could do to help you feel more like
it's Saturday?"

Winnie shook her head and laughed. "No, I'm completely
content to be here with you. It's nice to have a week off from
preaching. It's just that I have been preaching every Sunday morning for so many years that my whole system seems to know I
should be focusing on my message for tomorrow. Even though I
know in my mind that I'm not preaching tomorrow, something inside me won't let me forget what I usually do. That's weird, isn't it?"

"No, I can appreciate that. Being a teacher, myself, I've certainly had the same sort of getting-ready-to-teach syndrome. It's
partly nerves and partly adrenalin surging through the body about

the new class — or, in your case the new sermon. We all have habit patterns that we get into, and when those are interrupted for some reason, our mind reminds us about them," John reflected.

"That does bring up a subject we haven't mentioned yet. Tomorrow is Sunday; would you like to go to church with me tomorrow?" Winnie asked.

John opened his eyes wider, "Sure, we can do that. I enjoyed the service at your church. Have you got some place in mind?"

Winnie knit her brows together and answered, "No, I don't know any particular church around here."

"You don't have to go to a United Methodist Church, then?" John asked.

Winnie tried not to laugh. She said, "No. We can go wherever we'd like to, but since we'll be making our home here in this area, I suppose it would be good to look around here to find a church where we can plug in."

After dinner they made their way back to the Quadrangle Club and up to Winnie's room.

Winnie had brought her laptop with her, so they were able to access the internet and find a church in the area for tomorrow. They would meet for breakfast first and then attend the eleven o'clock service.

They sat in the small, sitting area of the room on the settee by the window. Since it was mid-April, the weather was quite pleasant with a soft breeze in the air. Winnie opened the window of her room and the breeze caused the sheers to waft gently inwards. The half moon illuminated the tennis courts across the street. The two sat by the window in the dimmed light of the lamp charmed by the peacefulness of the evening.

Winnie broke the silence, saying, "I've been almost afraid to ask you outright about this, but I must admit, I've very curious. You haven't said anything about what's happening for you regarding faith. Will you tell me?"

John nodded his head. "I don't mind your questions," John said turning to look at his fiancé. "This has been the most remarkable season in my life. Not only have I found you, and you have agreed to become my wife, but I believe I have also found faith in God. When you put those two incredible events together it adds up to a totally changed life. It's amazing!

"This didn't come about instantly, of course. I think I must have been entertaining some thoughts about faith all along, but the thoughts were scattered and not demanding an immediate conclusion," John recounted.

"What sort of thoughts?" Winnie interrupted.

"Many, diverse thoughts — beauty for instance. There is beauty in this world in many places, every day. When I considered the beauty I've witnessed and enjoyed, I mused about how it all came to be. What caused me to recognize beauty? Why do most people agree that something is beautiful?

"Close to that idea is the way my heart feels when I see little animals or small children. There is something inside me that attracts me to them; they are beautiful in a different way. You'd probably call them cute. I'm thoughtful about them.

"Then, following that vein, when you consider the biology of creatures — the many, vastly complicated and intricate systems that operate in living bodies, which are absolutely vital for life to exist, yet it does — remarkably, wonderfully well."

"When I think of all the infinite details in this world, I am impressed, even overwhelmed. This world, this universe, must have had some great mind behind it. It couldn't have just happened!"

"I thought about my own world. I've been lucky, when I look back. Yes, I was hurt when Helen died, but I continued on. I was able to finish my studies. I've always had a good job. I've never missed a meal. I've been downright well taken care of" John took a breath.

Winnie interjected, "John Wesley would say that all those things you mention were various ways God has been calling you, evoking you, to look to God. Wesley said that God's Grace could be seen in four ways, and those thoughts you've just mentioned are a good picture of 'Prevenient Grace' — God's Grace reaching out to people, inviting them, attracting them to God.

"It sounds like your reflections follow the actions of Prevenient Grace in your life rather well," Winnie suggested.

"I think faith has been taking root in me for a long time — from an initial recognition of God as a Great Creator; but, as I consider the person of Jesus more and more, I see that God truly acted through Him," John said genuinely.

Winnie spoke up, "I can't remember a time when I didn't have faith. I have known about Jesus since I was a little girl, so I don't have the experience of how faith in Christ changes a person's life. In a way you're in an envious position, because you can see how faith is making a difference in your life.

"Of course, coming to faith isn't like graduation at school. It is not a one-time event, rather it begins, and it grows, and dwells in you as long as you welcome it. It's like a relationship with another person. When we first meet someone, we learn a couple of things about the person, maybe we learn a lot of facts in our initial association. There's more to know, of course, and if we want to really know the person, it takes time and effort. A relationship with Christ, like any relationship, needs to be nurtured, so it will grow. Our own relationship has blossomed in wonderful ways through these past several months, and each meeting is better and more delightful. And it's giving us so much to look forward to. I think that's not a bad picture of our life in faith with God; it grows with time, too," Winnie said.

"The turning point in my life, I believe, was that night in Nashville, when I agreed to read the Bible." John answered. "I hadn't given it a thought until that very moment, when suddenly I opened my mouth, and out came those words, 'OK, I'll read your book.' Suddenly, those words I had just spoken into the air, caused me to realize I had never taken Christian scripture seriously, nor had I actually delved into it beyond a verse or two. I had made you a promise that was important for me to keep. Before I knew it, I was beginning to walk a different path than one I had been on previously.

"When I got home I was excited to start my reading. I stopped at the bookstore and bought a Bible for my own. I began with the New Testament, and, as I read the gospels, I began to sense that the words on the page were speaking directly to me. It was as if they were written explicitly for me. Jesus' words to the disciples were words for me, too. Jesus called them to follow him, and he was calling me, too.

"It seemed a bit funny, because when I read about Jesus calling the disciples to follow him, I thought His invitation was also meant for me and that I must follow. I also remember thinking, 'There is no choice in this! I <u>must</u> follow Him; it is the right thing to do! I don't have a choice!' Then I remember thinking, "Maybe I can just stay where I am and ponder it — slowly — but somehow I couldn't let it go. It was there, staring me in the face, calling me to act. Finally, I gave in and accepted Jesus' invitation to follow him and recognize him as the Son of God! Since that moment, when I made that decision, I have had this tremendous feeling of joy, and peace, and wonder, and excitement. It's really like I'm living on a different plane than I had been before. It's remarkable!"

Winnie smiled broadly. John's words were so good to hear. His admission of coming to faith in Christ and being willing to share it with her was one more reason to believe in him. "John, I'm so glad you are telling me this. I feel very privileged to be part of it somehow. I think you've had a real conversion experience, and I'm excited for you and with you!"

John winked at Winnie and said, "I'm sure I have 'miles to go before I sleep', as Frost so eloquently wrote. I am just beginning this way of life, and there's a lot to learn. You know better than I do about the steps I need to take. All my life I've been in the world of academia, and that suits me well. I'm thinking that this new facet of my life will include growing in understanding of Jesus and His call on my life."

"That does make sense — to use your gifts as you begin your journey, following the Lord," Winnie agreed. "There are plenty of academics for you to enjoy. I've learned from a number of them, myself, and I'd be pleased to hear who or what interests you as you study. I think Augustine, Martin Luther, and John Wesley and were all great admirers of St. Paul. They might be a place to start.

"I like your metaphor of taking steps when we follow Christ, because a step isn't a very large measure; it's a comfortable, doable, sort of distance. We can take one small step at a time when we follow Jesus, and we can make simple corrections, when, or if, we see that the angle we took wasn't the best one. We might not be able to see too far ahead of where we want to go, but we can pretty well see one step ahead," Winnie offered.

"And the step I'd like to take right now . . ." John didn't finish his sentence, rather he pulled Winnie to him and gave her a lingering kiss.

Finally, John took a deep breath and said, "Win, I'm more than convinced we're on the right track," John observed. "You are exactly what I need!"

Winnie agreed. "Let's get married!"

John was tempted to do something rash in the fever of the moment, but instead he sat back and said, "Now I'll use your word, Win, 'Goodness!' Do you think I can't wait?"

This tickled Winnie, and she began to giggle and then to laugh. Then they were both laughing, real, solid guffaws with tears in their eyes. It took them some time get control of their laughter. It was a good catharsis and a clearing of the air.

Finally John caught his breath and asked, "Win, have you thought what you might like to do once we're married and all moved in?"

Winnie thought for a moment and then said, "I think I'd like to write a book —maybe something about a woman pastor, who is serving a small church in the south. She meets interesting people and gets involved in their lives, but, mostly, her life is shaped by the task of writing a new sermon week after week to help her community grow in their walk with the Lord. I think that might be a good way for me to share some of the stories and the people I've come across, and interject some thoughts on Christian living."

"Might you include this woman's personal journey of finding love in an unexpected place?" John winked at Winnie.

"Now there's an idea!" Winnie laughed. "Of course! That is certainly part of her journey! Romance was not where I expected it, and what fun love can be when faith in God is part of the picture. My heroine's story would be much more compelling when the miracle of love is introduced! The two sat by the window, cozily delighting in the closeness of the moment . . . and very slowly . . . fell asleep!

THE END

Not an Option (a sermon)

Luke 17:1-4

Jesus said to his disciples, '*Occasions for stumbling are bound to come, but woe to anyone by whom they come! It would be better for you if a millstone were hung around your neck and you were thrown into the sea than for you to cause one of these little ones to stumble. Be on your guard! If another disciple sins, you must rebuke the offender, and if there is repentance, you must forgive. And if the same person sins against you seven times a day, and turns back to you seven times and says, 'I repent,' you must forgive.*'

Have you ever heard how a monkey is caught in the jungle? It seems that a trap is set for the monkey. To make the trap you must first hollow out a gourd, leaving an opening just large enough for the monkey to reach into the gourd. Place a sweet treat inside the gourd; then attach a vine to the gourd and stake the other end of the vine in the ground somewhere out of sight.

An unsuspecting monkey will smell the treat inside the gourd and reach inside to collect the sweet morsel. However, the opening, which is just large enough for the monkey's paw to pass through, is too small for the clinched fist to pass back through. The monkey cannot escape as long as he still holds the treat. It's a simple thing, then, for the poacher to take the monkey!

That's the picture I want us to remember this morning. When we clutch onto something and refuse to let it go, we may find ourselves in a very, spiritually dangerous place!

That's what's happening to us when we don't forgive someone who has done us wrong. When we are unforgiving, we, like the monkey with his hand stuck in the gourd, are not free of the thing we are grasping, and we are in a dangerous place for our souls.

Our scripture today is about forgiveness.

Jesus tells us several times in the gospels that we are to forgive others.

In Matthew's gospel we hear Peter asking Jesus about forgiving others. Peter began by pointing to the Jewish law, which dictated if someone sins against you, you must forgive up to three times, but Peter, thinking that he was catching on to Jesus' new way of thinking, asked the LORD if disciples should need to forgive as many as seven times.

Jesus surprised Peter by saying, *'It is not seven times to forgive another, but seventy-seven times!"* [You may remember this number to be seventy times seven, which is how the number was translated in the KJV.] Jesus' point is that it is a very big number of times we need to forgive.

Then Jesus told a parable to more clearly express what he meant:

The Kingdom of heaven can be compared to a king who was planning to settle his accounts with his slaves. There was one slave who owed the king a great deal of money, something like fifteen year's worth of wages. The slave was brought before the king who demanded the money. The slave could not repay the king. The king ordered that the slave be sold with his wife in payment. But the slave fell on his knees and begged, 'Have patience with me, and I will repay you everything.' The king, out of pity for the slave, released the man and completely forgave his debt.'

'But!' Jesus continued, 'that same slave went out from the king and came upon a fellow slave who owed him money—one hundred denarii, which would have been worth 100 day's wages. The man seized his fellow slave by the throat and demanded that he be paid in full right then. The fellow slave fell on his knees and pleaded with the man, 'Have patience with me, and I will pay you.' But the first slave refused. He had the man thrown into prison until his debt was paid. When the fellow slaves saw what had transpired, they saw the injustice of what had just happened, so they went to the king

and told him. The king summoned the slave and said, 'You wicked slave!'

I forgave you all that debt because you pleaded with me. Should you not have had mercy on your fellow slave, as I have had mercy on you? Then the king had the man handed over to be tortured until he would pay his debt.'

Jesus added, *'So my heavenly Father will also do to anyone of you, if you do not forgive your brother or sister from your heart.'*

That story seems to say that our being forgiven is tied to our forgiving others.

Can that be right?

Does the forgiveness that Jesus offers me hinge on my forgiving others?

Remember when Jesus taught the disciples to pray he included, *'forgive us our trespasses as we forgive those who trespass against us.'*

Then, after teaching the prayer Jesus added, *'For as you forgive others their trespasses, your heavenly Father will also forgive you; but if you do not forgive others, neither will your Father forgive your trespasses.'*

Jesus calls us to forgive those who have offended us, or hurt us, or betrayed us, or built up some debt to us. If we were not forgiven ourselves, we would not have a mandate to be forgiving, but we HAVE been forgiven. The two forgivenesses are bound together. FORGIVENESS IS NOT AN OPTION!

Forgiving others seems to be one of those 'yeses' we say as Christians. That is to say, when we started following Jesus we said, 'Yes, LORD, I will follow you; I will go where you tell me to go; I will do what you want me to do.' That initial 'yes' implied other, yet unknown 'yeses' that will come upon us down the road as we walk with Jesus. Those 'yeses' may not be easy; and those 'yeses' WILL include forgiving others.

Before we get into how to forgive, I think it would be helpful to think about what forgiveness is not. Dr. Robert D. Enright suggests five things that forgiveness is not:

Forgiveness is not forgetting: Our memories are too good to be able to forget things that were bad enough to need forgiveness. Deep hurt can rarely be wiped out of our awareness. Time can fade the pain of some abuse, but the memory of it won't be forgotten completely.

When we are called to forgive, we are not expected to completely forget the event.

Forgiveness is not reconciling: Reconciliation takes two parties, both the abuser and the offended must agree to be reconciled. When we forgive another we are not expecting or requiring the offending party to be reconciled. [I'm sure it would be good if both parties would agree, but that is not the dynamic of forgiveness.

A good example is what Jesus did for us. He came to reconcile us to the Father through his sacrifice. God is willing to reconcile with us, but we have to be willing to be reconciled, or it doesn't work. Both sides have to agree for reconciliation.

Forgiveness is not condoning: We are not asked to excuse someone's bad or hurtful behavior when we forgive. The abuse still occurred, and we don't have to ignore it. We can forgive without excusing the person who hurt us.

Forgiveness is not dismissing: The evil deed still hurt and caused pain. It would be wrong to pretend it was inconsequential or insignificant. If we have been wronged, the offense should be taken seriously. The deed did take place.

Forgiveness is not pardoning: A pardon is a legal transaction that releases the offender from the consequences of an action such as a penalty. Forgiveness is a personal transaction that releases the one offended from the event. Let me reiterate: Forgiveness is a personal transaction that releases the one offended from the event.

Bishop Willimon, in North Alabama, once wrote: "The human animal is not supposed to be good at forgiveness. Forgiveness is not some innate, natural, human emotion. Vengeance, retribution, violence, these are natural, human qualities. It is natural for the human animal to defend itself, to snarl and crouch into a defensive position when attacked, to howl when wronged, to bite back when bitten. Forgiveness is not natural. It is not a universal human virtue."

What does it mean to forgive?

The dictionary tells us forgiveness means

> To give up resentment or a claim to requital for

> To grant relief from payment of

> To cease to feel resentment against [the offender]

Forgiveness is very much part of the Christian life, and maybe it is a part of our lives every day.

I remember the time I gave my life to Jesus, many years ago. There was a period of about three weeks afterwards that I found various memories of mine that began popping up in my mind—things like anger over something; irritation at someone, grudges, all sorts of unsavory things. And I felt the nudging of the Holy Spirit to forgive the people who had hurt me, and to 'come clean,' if you would. I was carrying around a lot of stuff that needed to be let go. So I spent those few weeks ridding myself of those old, unforgiven pains.

I believe it's very important that we do that to have a healthy, Christian life. We must not let painful stuff build up that needs to be let go and forgiven.

Recently I learned something more, something you might call 'the rest of the story' about forgiveness.

This is not the first time I preached about forgiveness. I spoke this sermon to a church I was serving a couple of years ago. I was using the Matthew text, which had Jesus and Peter's conversation and the parable about the wicked slave.

But when I began working on today's sermon, I wanted to use a Lucan text, if possible, so I thought I'd see if Luke had a similar passage to Matthew's.

And there is, but there were a couple of differences. The Luke passage says that if a fellow disciple sins against you, you must rebuke him or her and if he or she repents you must forgive. Even if this happens seven times in a day!

Rebuking and repenting were added to the formula about forgiving. In other words, if/when you have been harmed you have the responsibility to the offender to inform him or her that something wrong has occurred, and you have been hurt.

I hadn't really thought about that before, and I imagine that's a place where we Christians don't go. How often have we gone to someone who has hurt us and rebuked him or her?

There was a situation that occurred to me a while ago. A woman I knew hurt me, and when the event took place I knew I would need to forgive her. And I have tried to do just that, but the thought of her words continued to plague me.

Then I read this verse, and I realized I needed to confront this woman and tell her how she had hurt me. So I wrote an email to her saying that, [rebuking her] and then I hit the 'send' button.

The next day I got an amazing response from the woman! She admitted how badly she had acted and wrote a lengthy note telling me how she had been wrong and begged my forgiveness. She even included a prayer in her writing.

There was something about that email response that cleared the entire situation clean and finished. It's really done!

Learning to forgive is something that applies to every one of us here. There is not one person in this room who has not been hurt by someone at some time.

This scripture is a reminder to us to forgive our offenders, just as Christ has forgiven us.

There is a picture I'd like us to take away from this sermon. It is the picture of our hand…opened, not closed into a fist. When we have a problem with someone

> Some bad experience

> A blowout with a colleague

Abuse

Betrayal

Whatever it is

And we keep hold on it, we are continuing to be harmed by the thing. We are not allowing God to heal us from the event, and we are carrying it with us into future relationships. [I can imagine that some of us have kept such events alive by telling others of those memories and, in some way, even enjoying the attention and the sympathy we get from the telling.]

Just remember your hand gripping the thing and not letting go. You have then fallen into a trap, like the monkey who can't escape being caught, because his hand is stuck in the gourd. He's trapped. He's going to be somebody's dinner tonight.

Now imagine what we should be like, letting go of the things we're hanging on to that we need to let go of. When I mentioned this subject earlier I believe everyone here thought to him/herself about some situation, some person, with whom we're not too happy, whom we are still nursing a grudge or some kind of anger. Keep the picture in mind of opening your hand and letting go. You have no more reason to claim it, and you have no more interest in it. You have let it go! What freedom is ours! That's forgiveness!

Made in the USA
Charleston, SC
11 June 2015